AMERICAN PLAYGROUND

AMERICAN PLAYGROUND

Michael Isaac Shokrian

the
THIEVING
MAGPIE

American Playground

Library of Congress Control Number: 2025932613

Trade Paperback ISBN: 979-8-9925417-0-0
eBook ISBN: 979-8-9925417-1-7
AudioBook: 979-8-9925417-2-4

Cover design: Glen Edelstein, Hudson Valley Book Design
Book design: Glen Edelstein, Hudson Valley Book Design

Printed in the United States of America
17 18 19 20 10 9 8 7 6 5 4 3 2 1

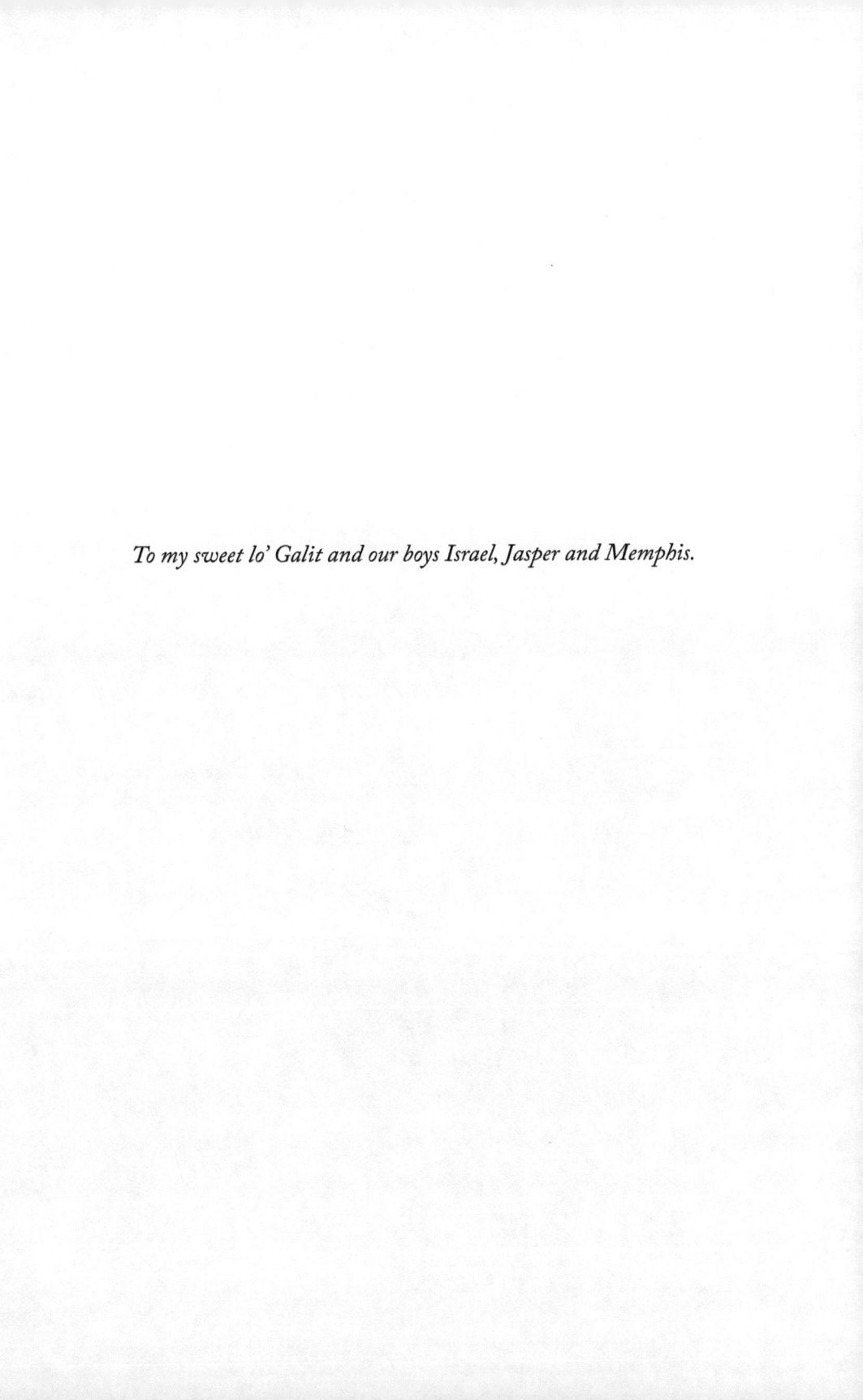

To my sweet lo' Galit and our boys Israel, Jasper and Memphis.

ACKNOWLEDGMENTS

This story is for the playground Nons – foreign or domestic - forced to find identity, companionship and peace from within first; whose pains and barbs make the melodies and beats of the new American song; whose hard-fought discoveries create the hues and tints of each new American dusk; and whose grit and resilience are part of the concrete that makes the American Playground.

Special and hearty thanks to the best pal a foreigner could have, Steve Mac, thanks for never laughing at my many stumbles; EM Cannon for being my first and constant champion; Helen, Lotfy, Naz, Babs & Shizzy for bringing the crazy with so much passion, humor and love.

Thanks also to Chris Heiser at Unnamed Press for his patience and early efforts; Glen Edelstein at Hudson Valley Book Design for being so much more than just an outstanding artist; and Kristen O'Connell who helped navigate the terrifyingly confusing straits of 21st Century independent publishing with confidence, calm and grace.

And of course, a never-ending Thank You and Shout Out to the Charles E. Young Research Library at UCLA, a glorious sanctuary that employed me as a student and in whose stacks I first discovered the straightforward beauty of Bukowski, Fante and all the greats who helped me see the light.

Let us have more oceans, new oceans that blot out the past, oceans that create new geological formations, new topographical vistas and strange, terrifying continents, oceans that destroy and preserve at the same time, oceans that we can sail on, take off to new discoveries, new horizons. Let us have more oceans, more upheavals...
Henry Miller, *Tropic of Cancer*

"Be just what you is, not what you is not. Folks what do this has the happiest lot."
Mr. Wizard, *Tooter Turtle* ·

PART I

IN THE BEGINNING, *they finally loved me. Teacher gave me boss jobs when she took smoke breaks, asked me to do numbers on the chalkboard. She put me in English with the smarty pants kids. Learned their Aleph Ba and had seven words: Man, Woman, Boy, Girl, Love, Play, School. Classmates loved me too, my shoulders squared, neck locked, breathing fierce like a Captain. Ramin picked me for soccer. In my hard black shoes, I made the same tough skid-and-scuff sounds on the asphalt as the Olders did, digging for the ball, attacking shins and ankles just like they did. Even Shideh invited me to sit with her at lunch, touching my long black hair, telling me I looked like George, the best Beatle. I shared my orange soda and Kalbas sandwich with them all. The Olders, who had seen everything under the sun, knew my name. Some afternoons they'd invade our class when Teacher was on break and appoint me their Special Soldier. They'd have me line up my classmates for inspection, roust them from their chairs, stand them up, necks locked. I'd order them to stand until further notice and if they didn't obey, I'd discipline them with a pinch of the flesh at their throats or order them to hold their book bags over their heads - a little trick the Olders used on me once. I felt superior and nobody said a word when Teacher got back, not even Ramin. Teacher would thank me for taking charge, stroke my hair, her hands running through my bangs, her fingernails gently scratching my scalp. Tingled. "You're my star," she'd say and I'd feel the heat from her hand on my head and purr for her like a*

1

little lion. I'd look out at Ramin sitting at his desk, hands clasped, neck locked, my pinch mark still rosy at his throat. He'd still pick me for soccer; Shideh would still sit with me at lunch. That's how good it was going for me in second grade at New School in Tehran. I had made it! Then we left.

Second Grade. Second Semester.
First Monday. January 1971.

"That Arab won't make it through the week," she tells Moses in a warm rasp. A perfect Amrikayi: jade green eyes, crinkled bronze skin, burnt gold hair curling at her shoulders like paisleys on rugs Baba sold at bazaar. She smells western, charred Nescafé, sugar and tobacco, like the stewardesses. Exciting! I have my seven words, but the way she shakes her head, shifts her eyes from me to Moses, is how I get her gist. She is talking about me. I am the Arab.

Under bright buzzing lights, their flag hanging next to a poster of Apollo 13, I study their faces; different, not just from mine but each other: Freckled, pasty, shiny, brown, smooth, black. Hair gold, orange, brown. Eyes blue, grey, olive. None like me. They play while Moses talks to teacher. A bucktooth freckled kid pops up, rears back and fires a tight ball of paper across the desks. Direct hit. A pink imprint on the cheek of a startled blue-eyed kid with brittle yellow hair. Laughter. Bucktooth-and-freckles sits back in his chair, a cool smile on his freckled face. Must be their leader; the one I need to work on.

Outside, the winter chill gives off the same smell of burning diesel as the airport did the night we landed. Gonjeshk playfully flit through the bare branches of trees lining the fence. On the street, a car rumbles. Fordmostang. Really! The driver's jet pilot sunglasses reflect the haze rising from the smoker between his lips as he waits for the light. His radio plays the same song from the airport. *"My sweet lo', ooh my lo', I really wanna be with you..."* I am here! Amrika!

I give Bucktooth Leader a nod so he knows I have him. He snarls. I need cowboy pants and sport shoes like them. We don't have any, even if I could run out and find the house.

2

"Up there," Maman said this morning, pointing her slick polished nail across the street to a lone palm at the top of the hill. "Our yard. See how close?" We were meeting the principal. Precious was more scared than I was. Maman was showing him how close she'll be.

In the principal's office, Maman in a smart, cream-colored two-piece and perfumed air, gaped up at the majestic figure. "Mashallah! Baba was right," she whispered as he clomped toward us, broad shouldered in heavy black shoes and a dark suit. "He is indeed big as Moses."

Moses took Maman's tiny hands in his boulder-sized palms, to explain things. Maman took her hands back and explained things to Moses. Then she took Precious, flashed the signal – double-blink-lip-bite – and walked out, leaving me with Moses, her elegant scent lingering.

But did she also explain things about me to Moses? My Amrikayi name? Which class to take me? Heart pounding and tightlipped, I mumbled to him, "Two. Kelass Two."

He didn't look like a messenger of God to me; just a dangerous Amrikayi in a tall black suit. He could do whatever he wanted to me. Steal me. Deliver me to a wrong class. Lose me.

"Kelass two," I bleated, pleading but calm, not wanting to make him angrier than he already must have been, his steely glare fixed on the door Maman had walked out of. She never showed me the way to Albatross Lane. *Really wanna go with you, but it takes so long my lo..."*

"Where?" Teacher, Nona Lee, had asked Moses when he led me into Room 7.

"Purr-zha," Moses trying to sound like he knows. "Where cats and oriental rugs are from?"

"You mean E-ran?" Nona Lee asked. "With the king?"

"She said Purr-zha. She said second; she said he knows English. He's yours."

That's when teacher said the thing about the Arab not making it. But just wait till I get in with their top dogs; with freckle-faced Bucktooth Leader. She'll see.

Maman's probably home now, boiling rice in salt and butter for katteh, searing shank, frying onions. Four days in and her pots have been clanging and rumbling like she's marking the kitchen, painting the walls with her cooking: orange turmeric, green dill, red saffron.

Room 7 smells white – milk, sugar, cream filling. Makes my stomach churn with pain.

Fastest way is the hill. Looks dangerous. She's probably on the phone pouring her heart out to Sweet Lady in their secret tongue, elegantly streaming her smoke to the ceiling. Home…

The squeeze on my arm makes me flinch. Moses - well-fed Amrikayi, chiseled, sunburnt face from cowboy movies - lowers to face me. His hair is the color of weathered straw; wavy lines etched across his boxy forehead. In a deep tone, pointing a craggy finger at me, Nona Lee, the other kids, he declares Commandments. When I learned their Aleph Ba, their words were easy to read. But rolling out of their Amrikayi mouths sounds come fast curved garbled no space no clarity no breaks. "Yermothersaid" is all I get as Moses rises and turns, the clip-clop of his shoes echoing as he walks out, oblivious to the gonjeshk songs or the freewheeling roar of the Fordmostang as the light goes green. Moses leaves me too, now alone, in front of them.

"Come," Nona Lee carefully enunciates with her warm rasp, takes my arm.

I clench. Maman gone. Moses gone. Only teacher now. And them.

"Come," she says again, this time with a smile and a slight tug. "It's OK."

I give in. She tries for their attention; they're in the middle of their carefree chaos. I try remembering words and names Maman told me, but nothing is in my head except "Arab."

"Children," she announces with a smile, not loud enough. Pink erasers are flying now. Screaming, rumbling desks, screeching chairs.

"Kids! Attention please." Her smile getting flat.

Yelping, darting and ducking.

Now sharp-eyed and grim, she leaves my side – I feel a chill where she was standing. She walks to the wall, puts her hand on the light switch, stares out. They don't notice.

"Freeze!" She flips the switch. Room dark. Silent. Still. She slowly flips the lights back on, then off again. Even the buzzing stops. "Freeze."

New word! Stops them mid-movement. Statues. A game they are all in on… or has she actually put them under a spell like Amrikayi TV

4

show *The Bewitcher*. Amrikayi teachers have *Samantha* powers? Stopping time by turning lights off and yelling the magic word? In the darkness Nona Lee returns to the front and stands beside me.

"Lights Off means…" she chants, waiting.

"Lights Off Means Stop Look and Listen," they chant. "Take Your Seats Let the Leg of Your Table Touch the Leg of Your Chair." Spellbound, they move back to their seats. Chair legs screech across the floor, clang against the steel legs of desks. They sit up.

You did this; the incantation, the darkness, the spell. They were having fun, now they're in trouble because of you. They'll remember it and want revenge. Wouldn't you?

Stiff in their chairs, necks locked, hands clasped, they wait for instructions.

Nona Lee walks to the light switch, "Your undivided attention!" Flips the lights back on.

Everything is good again. They exhale, slouch, unclasp.

"We have a new classmate, from a new country," she announces in a friendly voice, like she was never mad. Maybe everything really is easier in Amrika, even forgiving.

They study me, tilted heads and crinkled noses. I stare, wide eyes, hot cheeks. Trying to remember the words…names…my new name… what was Maman saying this morning?

"This is," looks at the book in her hand, squints. "Mishel Man – what is that, dear–"

"Michelle?" Confused whispers and playful snickers.

"Help me, dear," she holds the book, "What is this," pointing her lacquered fingernail.

I look at the page and make out the sequence of letters on the line she's pointing to. My first and last names, Farsi words in Amrikayi letters! Feels odd, out of place. Foreign.

"Say this for me, dear."

It'll sound Farsi. They're already laughing at the Outside name Maman said they won't laugh at because it's not as odd as the Inside name we use at home. She was wrong!

"Dear, your name." Now tapping her foot, lips tightening, warm air from her nostrils hitting the back of my neck. She's losing patience.

Whisper in her ear, use Amrikayi curves like Maman does. "Mnchri-an... MnCHERRYin." Not harsh Farsi – slanted "Maa-noo" hard "Che" long "Ree-Yawn."

I look up at her, shrug.

"Dear," Nona Lee insists, tapping the page. "Just say your name to the class."

I interrupted their fun; now all eyes on me. My turtleneck, a hand-me-down of rough wool, is prickly against my warm neck, cheeks starting to steam up, white lights a constant buzz above me. The book, her fingertip on my name, avoid eyes and faces. Try not to overheat.

"Uh," can't hear myself over my heartbeat. "Mish... uh..."

"Right here," she won't take her finger off my name, "what's that? You read English? Let's read together, *Mmm* - you know your name, don't you dear? You can just tell us."

I pretend to be figuring out the letters. Don't want to say it. It's not my name. Not here. That was me for school in Tehran, my outside name there. Not here. "Yes. Uh...Mish-"

"Dear I know that," she is frustrated. "Your first name is Mishel, I know; it's your last-"

"Girl's name!" Bucktooth Leader, hands unclasped, blood-caked elbow hanging on the back of his chair, confident as a cowboy. "Where'd you say he's from? 'Cuz it's a girl's name."

More laughs. All unclasped hands and slouched backs now; sitting easy and cool.

Maman told me my Amrikayi outside name this morning, but I can't remember anything.

Should've taken the hill. Don't let them see panic. They'll pounce. Wouldn't you?

"Now hold on. Mishel can be a boy's name too." A deeper voice breaks the silence - brittle yellow hair with chalk blue eyes who got hit with the paper ball. "In France."

She told you to memorize; Amrikayi Mishel... Maman said Amrikayi Mishel is--

"Shut up, Kelly," Bucktooth Leader, orders. "He's not French."

The kid sitting beside the leader, a swath of silky dark hair slanted over one eye and a wicked smirk, chimes in: "Kelly smelly with a big fat belly made outa jelly!"

They chant: "Kelly smelly with a big fat..."

Brittle Yellow stays quiet in his chair, his chalk blue eyes glaring as he shakes his head.

"Enough," interrupts Nona Lee. "Thank you, Kelly," she says, trying to regain control. "But Mishel here isn't from France. Tell your new friend Kelly where you're from, Mishel."

Whoa! She's putting you with Kelly, the guy they're laughing at? Kelly? Kelly! Kell!

"Kell! My-kell!" I blurt, hoping it's right. "My mawther say My-kell?"

"Michael?"

"My-kell." I got it right!

"Michael," she announces with a tobacco smile and a shine in her jade green eyes. She crosses it out in her book and corrects it. "Children, meet Michael."

Kelly smiles at me as Nona Lee walks me past him to my seat. I ignore him.

"OK, Michael," she says, "so what do you want to be called? Michael or Mike? You want Mike? Mike can be your nickname! You want a nickname?"

They picked your names: Inside for family; outside for Guweem at school; new outside for Amrikayi. She's letting you pick. "Mike." Fast and flashy, like Fordmostang. Slick racing stripes. Amrikayi! She's letting you. Her jade green eyes. Be her lion, purr for her.

"Yes," I say. "Mike."

"Mike?"

Snickering, giggling, whispering: "Me-shell!"

My first day at Pinnacle Palace Elementary. I am Michelle.

The new house is cold. I'm working my stiff pink fingers pulling up socks and shoelaces when Maman, barefoot in her purple robe, pops in to hurry us up. Still hasn't asked how it went yesterday after she left me. The rough laces dig into my tender palms as I pull.

"You are right," she's telling Baba in the kitchen, "he's like Moses."
Even in her robe, Maman is naturally elegant with her high cheekbones
and hazel eyes, stirring milk and honey into our farina. "Amrikayi are
all so big," pouring it into bowls. From another pan, she fishes out two
soft-boiled eggs for Baba. "His hands," Maman goes on, "big enough to
hold the Tablets of Adonai." She places them in the rooster egg holder
and two slices of toast on a plate.

Smelling like his French cologne and tobacco, Baba ruffles his
newspaper in response.

I warm my fingers over the steam from my bowl of Farina as Baba
lays down his paper to expose his clean-shaven face and furrowed brows.
The teaspoon looks tiny in his thick hand as he taps his egg, picks shell
shards off the top and leans in to slurp the goo before it spills down the
sides. He scrapes butter across his toast, making sure to cover the entire
surface before sinking his teeth in with a crunch. Finally, he looks up at
Maman who is still working the stove.

"So?" Crunching, slurping. "What did he say about keeping them
in their grades?"

"He said they should go down a grade because they don't know the
tongue."

Back behind his paper, Baba washes down his toast and egg with
his hot tea. "And?"

That's when Maman starts bragging about her first battle in Amrika, and how she won it. I don't know what she told Moses yesterday
in his office, but I know Maman will do and say whatever she needs to
get things done, hazel eyes fixed on her subject, eyebrows arched, using
local dialect to pass as Them - Guweem, Amrikayi – if needed. We
learned early to stay out of her way when she's working; if we try to be
heroes – blurting out an omission we think is a mistake - it could ruin
things. Maman doesn't make mistakes; her intentions become clear in
time. Yesterday she used Amrikayi dialect - curved words, soft lilts – to
impress Moses.

"You think I'd let a dehati Amrikayi send my babies back because of
English? I said '*No, ser, my boy wery esmart, he under-estand English*' and
before he could answer I said '*tank you ser*' took Saeed and walked him
myself to the first-grade class. Moses koor khoondeh."

8

Baba is amused, crunching, slurping, scraping the inside of the egg-shell with his spoon to get every bit. "Did you take over and teach the class for them too?"

My fingers are too cold and stiff to grab my spoon so I bang it to the table. Fed up. "You could have walked me!" I yell. "Mishel is a girl's name. I forgot my Amrikayi name. You left me there! Teacher said 'Mishel' in front of everyone. The wrong name!"

"You wanted them to put my precious Saeed back a grade?" Maman says, finally sitting to have her own tea and toast. "I had to take him or they'd put him with the babies." She blows on her tea, cracks a sugar cube with her teeth and holds it as she takes a quiet sip. "Besides, Mishel is a good outside name," she offers. "Baba used it when he stayed in Paris."

"You moved us to Amrika, not Paris," I yell, needing them to see my anger; knowing they won't. "In Amrika it's a girl's name. They laugh!"

"If they dare," Maman says dismissively, taking a small bite of toast. "They can get lost. Mishel is Mykell in Amrika. Everybody knows. Don't worry, My-kell jan. I have you."

"What about me," Precious chimes in, looking up from his farina with his cotton ball cheeks and tiny teeth. "Don't I get an Amrikayi name?"

"Your name is perfect inside and outside, precious," Maman says. "Saeed means Happy and Lucky. Jews, Guweem, Amrikayi, they all know. Did your classmates bother you too?"

"They said Sid to me," Precious whines, trying to muster anger so he can be included.

"Seed? Seed yanichi?" Maman looks up at Baba, wondering. "Did they laugh?"

"I don't know," Precious says, confused about how he should feel. "But they smiled."

Not wanting Precious to pull attention away as usual, I grab my belly. "My stomach!"

"Is Seed a name," Maman asks Baba, ignoring me. "Or were they making fun of Saeed?"

"Can't go to school," I breathe, twist myself up until it hurts for real. "My stomach, ow!"

Baba drops his paper, pushes aside his drained tea glass and plate of eggshells. "Don't be a baby," he orders, brushing crumbs off his tie. "Be a man," as if nothing has changed for us since last week. "Almost noon," his favorite phrase to rush us, "let's go."

I memorize the route as Baba drops us off in the drizzling rain. *Down block, right, right, school. The hill is faster, but dangerous.* On the playground, Precious runs to join his new classmates. I stare across the blacktop: Bucktooth Leader and his Second-in-Command, Wicked Smirk, lean against a beige stucco wall, hands tucked in the back pockets of their cowboy pants, talking to a few others. Brittle Yellow in a blue windbreaker, barks commands in a voice as deep as a crow's caw to two uninterested boys - one with a red scarf and cowboy boots; the other in a green army jacket and black boots; building hills and burrowing tunnels in a boxed-in space full of sand. I can barely hear the gonjeshk songs over all the yelps on the yard and duck into the bathroom by the beige stucco wall. Getting in with the top dogs may be tougher than I thought.

The bathroom walls are unevenly layered with blue paint that is both shiny and dull. The air smells like piss; the floor damp with mud and pulped paper towels. At the sink, I try to quiet the voices in my head: Ramin, Shideh, Maman, Baba, new ones. The mirror is cracked, dried boogers on its edges. Is that me? Brown skin, black hair, lips pursed, nostrils flared, lonely mole on my jaw, eyebrows slanted diagonal like airplanes taking off from opposite directions ready to crash into each other - a dark triangle above my panicked eyes. This is me in Amrika.

I turn the faucet, wait for the water to get hot, stick my fingers under the stream to loosen them, close my eyes, head tipping back, mouth falling open, fading... *WAIT!*

A rush of cold air blows in with the outside noises as the heavy door pushes open.

Open your eyes, shut your mouth, straighten up and pretend-wash your hands.

The kid with the green army jacket and black boots, two sinks over, turns his faucet. I stare ahead, pretend-reach for the soap, check him from the side. Thin, so pale he's almost purple, flat black hair surrounds his face like a chador, light blue eyes with pink rings. I should leave but…another second of warm water on my hands. He runs water over his hands too, doesn't pretend-reach for soap, no pretend-washing; lets his head fall back.

"Ahh," an easy open smile. "Good *something-English-something-English*? Yeah?"

He wants to be friends. Careful. Remember him?

Yesterday, Buckteeth, Wicked Smirk and some Olders chased him, threw bread and balled-up foil at him, laughed at how he ran. But he was fast and they couldn't catch him. "Polack!" they yelled as he tried to look defiant, hand on hip, elbow out, chin jutting, blue eyes fixed on them, lips forcing a smirk, looking winded but keeping his back stiff, neck locked.

"What was your name again?"

They'll chase you too, call you names too, if you run with him. He's in here to escape, to warm himself too. Likes warm cozy water too. But friend? Ally? Does he even have wisdom?

I have to know who to run with, but also who to avoid. Standing beside the kid they call Polack, our hands under running water, chasing warmth, we close our eyes, let our heads fall back, bracing for the bell. I don't answer him; memorize the way home. Left, left, end of block.

In the beginning, there were pots. Large, wide pots, rumbling and gurgling. Heavy lids trembling. Familiar smells hovering. Freshly plucked chickens bounced in pots of boiling water yellowed by turmeric as swirling ribbons of sliced onion danced with bobbing garbanzos. Dried limes, finely chopped fenugreek and leeks simmered in pots; okra, yellow peas and sour grapes melted with spicy stewed tomatoes in pots. On the counter, the radio played all day, music from around the world. "Comedian's Gallop" for morning news as we crunched buttered toast and drank hot milk with honey. The "Cazacho" marched us out as we grabbed our books and headed to school. Maman fluttered around her city all day, cool and breezy, card games and chic

lunches. But every afternoon she stood barefoot at the stove, her heels flung in the corner, tending to her pots, singing with the radio, still chic like a brisk city breeze, hints of perfume and hairspray lingering around her. We did our sentences and numbers at the table, but when certain songs played, like the sweet melancholy of "Those Were the Days," Maman would leave her pots and join us for a tango, clasped hands and pressed cheeks from the dining room to the kitchen, spinning us until we laughed. When the song ended, we returned to our pages and she to her pots. When Maman agreed to leave Tehran for Amrika, she insisted on bringing her pots; wrote her name on the steel sides and lids with red nail polish so they wouldn't get lost; so we would never forget who we were or where we come from; so our new kitchen would rumble with our sounds and smells through the steam from her pots.

February 1971

There was swaying and jostling, the tortured sound of creaking wood. Lots of us inside, sitting cross-legged on the wooden deck of the dark boat lit by our laughter. We were clapping, singing a song we all knew with easy confidence from the pits of our stomachs, full-throated, in harmony. But when the waters got rough, she got nervous and lost her smile, which made her face shadowy. Still, not wanting to spoil the joy, not wanting to scare the rest of us, she kept singing. Suddenly we were no longer on water as the hull, lifted by a wave, tumbled and plunged down, not back on the sea but on dishes, platters, ashtrays, saucers. Even as we continued to sing and keep the harmony, we only heard porcelain and glass crashing beneath us as the vessel dropped and tottered. That's when she could not hold herself any longer. That's when she started screaming with panic, yelling toward the bow of the boat, "Where have you taken us? Where is this you have steered us to?"

When I open my eyes, Precious is on the floor by his bed, still asleep. Outside our room, Maman is screaming, "Where is this, then, that you brought us" as footsteps run up the hall.

"Don't come in here," she screams when I make my way to the kitchen.

"Wear shoes, you'll cut your feet," Baba says.

Both in pajamas and slippers, on their knees, picking chunks of broken dishes off the floor. Cabinets flung open. Salt and pepper shakers on their sides. Rooster egg holder fallen, beak chipped.

Maman is a mess, on her hands and knees picking chunks of broken dishes, trying to piece them together, sobbing "why did he bring us to this jittering nation? All day alone, I don't know their tongue, abandoned. Take us back. The streets of Tehran may not be paved with diamonds but at least they don't tremble under our feet!"

Baba mutters to himself as he sweeps the smaller shards. Last time I saw him holding a broom was Tehran; he was trying to kill a lizard in the stairwell. It was awkward, the broom an unfamiliar object in his thick, clean hands as he tried to shake the stubborn lizard off the bristles.

"Wake Saeed," Baba says. "Get dressed, walk to school." Baba doesn't give morning orders. He usually hogs the bathroom, shuffles his newspaper, tobacco smoke seeping up from under the door, before emerging clean shaven in his suit and tie, smelling like a fancy airport.

"Let's calm down," Nona Lee yells over the chatter. "We can talk about the earthquake after Morning Routine. Now who wants to lead the Pledge of the Lesions?"

The morning's shaking has riled Room 7 but when she asks who wants to do the Pledge of the Lesions, their hands jut and poke the air like normal. The winner winds his way through desks and chairs, hiding an excited smile as he stands in front of their flag ready to lead their Morning Prayer. Even an earthquake that makes plates come crashing down and kids cluck like chickens doesn't stop their Morning Routine. I still haven't learned the words.

"Flag salute, stand and face the flag, place your right hand over your heart."

We face the flag hanging limp in the corner, its stars and stripes hidden in folds.

"Begin."

"*I pledge the lesions to the flag of the yanighted-staytsuva-MERica into the public for widget stanz one day should underdog invisible with libidee injustice ferawl.*"

"Now who wants to man the record player for Morning Music?"

Hands go up. The winner lowers the needle on a record. "*This land is your land; this land is my land from calla four ya to new year I land...*" "*Uh-MEH-rica, Uh-MEH-rica, I see you're shining, see...*" "*Uh-MEH-rica, stand the sider, and guider...*"

With hand still on heart, I watch their lips and teeth; I replicate their motions. Buckteeth, crusty-eyed, snarls. Brittle Yellow crows in his low voice. Cinnamon Hair in cowboy boots and red scarf stares out in sacred salute to a glorious place of Honor beyond the ceiling panels, hand clutching heart, chanting each word to an all-powerful Amrikayi God as imaginary jets fly for Him, the song sung for Him: "*God Bless Uh-MEH-rica, my own, sweet home.*"

"Who is ready for Curney Vens? We have a lot to discuss after this morning, don't we?"

For Curney Vens only Big Mouth Patricia raises her hand. Her white sandals slap the floor as she walks, like she's splashing puddles. She holds up a neatly cut news clipping taped to a sheet: helicopters, muddy soldiers, palm trees, brown women in triangular hats crying.

"The earthquake is important," Big Mouth Patricia, nose up, eyes closed, "but I prepared this last night. Curney Vens!" like a teacher. I memorize, recognize some words from TV news – Laos, Nixon, Vietnam. When she's done, she scans the room. "Any questionzer commons?"

I raise my hand; my own Morning Routine. To avoid Polack (real name, Pincus) and because I don't understand Curney Vens, this is when I usually warm my hands in the bathroom.

"Mike M.," says Mrs. Lee. "You have questionzer commons?"

"Twalette."

She tilts her head, stiff paisley-shaped hairdo slanting, lips thinning, eyes narrowing. I have seen that look, from when she loses patience with them. For me she usually has a soft smile, a nod, patience. She has me. Not today. They are all shaky today.

14

"Again?" she asks. She reaches in her desk for a blue slip. "Make it fast," she says, not smiling, handing the blue slip over. "You're a pain in the neck, you know that?"

I've upset her. They are looking, giggling. My arm is still raised, getting heavy.

"You can put your hand down," she says, annoyed. "I see you; we all see you."

Not like this.

In the beginning, I ran with Shideh and Ramin. Ramin had wisdom; he knew things the others didn't. He told me I turned seven when my tooth fell even though Maman said I was six. "When your tooth falls, you're seven and get wisdom," he explained, his sharp blue eyes shining, hand on my shoulder. Shideh was bossy. She lost her tooth the year before – top, front - so she got wisdom before either of us. Even in her little dress and shiny black shoes, she could beat us in a foot race. She looked straight at you when she talked, never letting her soft brown eyes get lost in her black hair which she tied over her head like the crown of a tree. We'd meet up before the bell, hide in the bathroom, do things. Playful, secret things. One morning, we formed a circle, our underwear at our ankles, staring. She called it the "Show It" game. As we tried to make sense of what we were seeing, Shideh broke the silence: "You can touch my Shame." That's what grownups call that part of a girl: Her Shame. She turned to Ramin. "Not you." I looked down at Shideh's Shame. It looked like nothing: the curve of an elbow, a shallow dimple like on a chin or the back of a knee. I was curious, but not enough to touch it. I didn't get it. Still, she had picked me over Ramin, so she got it. And she had wisdom. Ramin, eyebrows up, turned to me. "Why not him too," I asked. "Armaniyeh," Shideh said. "Am not," Ramin objected. "Torkam!" Then, to me, "Tell her." "Torkeh," I said, "look at his eyes." "What's it to you," Shideh asked me, "you're not Armani too, are you?" "I'm not Armani or Tork. Never mind," I said, reaching for her Shame. "You never mind," Shideh said, bending to pull up her underwear. "You're both out." "But I'm not like him," I objected. Ramin gave me a hurt look and turned to leave. Before he could, the heavy door pulled open, sucking the rancid air from the bathroom and hitting us with harsh sunlight. We looked up, squinting at the grownups.

15

I don't do shits in the blue bathroom. No doors; they see, they point. Brittle Yellow (real name, Fertig) did last week. Baba had been taking his time again, ruffling his newspaper and clearing his throat to signal he's in there, like the smoke seeping from under the door wasn't enough. So I used the blue bathroom, trying to finish fast before anyone came. Wouldn't come, moved slow, refused to drop. I pushed, grunted, eyes bulging. The bathroom door swung open; a rush of cold air hit the bottoms of my dangling feet. I raised them, held my breath as footsteps squished toward the stall. Ass getting cold, legs getting tired from holding them up, I leaned out beyond the stall to see who came in, where he went. A deep, hollow breath at the back of my neck. Looked up to see a hand clasping the top of the stall, and the brittle yellow hair and chalk blue eyes of Fertig creeping up over it, watching me squirm and struggle to hide, the way a cruel kid watches a fly with a broken wing struggle to escape the shadow of the landing hand.

"Hello, Sports Fan," said Fertig, pink face and chalk blue eyes peering down. One hand clasped the top of the stall; the other held a plastic bag full of pink and white cookies.

What did he want? He knew he had caught me and was holding me in his glare. Was he waiting for me to cry? To admit doing a shit, trying to hide it? To beg him to go? Was he waiting to watch me clumsily wipe myself with the wad in my hand, knowing I was no expert at the disgusting Amrikayi way of cleaning? Goose pimples grew on my ass and the smell of shit and piss swirled around us. He didn't seem bothered, satisfied to be looking down at me.

"Hello," I finally said looking up at him, at his mercy.

"And what have we here," he propped himself on the top of the stall with his elbows and took an elephant-shaped pink cookie out of the bag.

God is going to turn him into a monkey!

Maman's laws: Wash your face every morning; stray cats pee on it when you sleep. Never leave clipped toenails unflushed, or scissors crossed - it causes divorce. And never eat God's bounty in a bathroom or He will turn you back into the original monkey you used to be.

"I am in here," I was hoping he would understand, "doing twalette."

"I can see," said Fertig, mouth full of cookie, "Shouldn't do that here," he said, taking out two more and popping them in his mouth. "No doors. They'll see you; they'll point."

"OK."

He wasn't done. "You Mike?"

"Yes, Mike," I said, my neck getting stiff from looking up at him, waiting for him to go.

"Kelly Fertig, at your service."

Kelly Smelly with fat belly make from Jelly...

"I know."

"Okay, nice to have met you, likewise, I'm sure." His fingers unclasped the top of the stall, he jumped down, sneakers slapping the muddy tile, and he skipped out.

That's why I don't use the blue bathroom to do shits. I use it to warm my hands. As I run the water, trying to understand the shaking that rattled my dreams, the door bangs against the wall and they blow past me, yelping, already sweaty, metallic glints of sun bouncing off teeth. They run faucets at full blast, pull paper towels so hard from the metal dispenser it rattles. "Earthquake!" They work expertly, folding paper towels into squares, poking holes at the top, puffing air to make them puff out, filling them with water and slamming them against the ceiling. They explode, water splashing down. "Earthquake!" Metallic laughter, hand slaps. Then again, water soaking the once serene bathroom. Flattened paper sticks to the ceiling then falls back down, smeared to a pulp on the bathroom floor by rowdy, savage sneakers. Amrikayi Olders are here!

My chance to team up, be allies. I imitate their words and tones like Maman would as water-filled-papers slap the ceiling and rain down on the bathroom floor. "Yeah, O'right!"

Even bumping into me as they rush the faucets to fill fresh pouches, they don't see me.

I mix in and they don't do anything to stop me, so it's like I'm with them. "O'right!"

The door swings open, this time slow, filling the blue bathroom with bright sun. In the doorway, the tall silhouette of rugged Moses looking like he just returned from the mountaintop to see his failed flock in mid Sin. It gets so quiet I hear echoes of yelps, water dripping from the ceiling. A heavy silence. Not the peaceful, warm-water-on-back-of-hands silence that filled the bathroom before the Olders stormed in, but a ringing silence like you hear after a slap on the ear.

Moses clip-clops in his heavy black shoes, sidestepping puddles of pulpy paper, surveying the mayhem. As he does, he has to dodge a wet square that drops from the ceiling just missing his shoulder. His craggy face gets pink as he points a long, crooked finger at all the disappointment before him. "What *is* all this?"

Standing before him, the Olders look like children, small like me, scared eyes searching for answers, eventually landing on the dirty floor in shame.

If not for the anger and tension, I would appreciate how Amrikayi Moses smells – breezy talcum powder, sweet tobacco probably from a suave pipe after a jaunty ocean adventure, rugged but un-itchy turtlenecks at elegant marinas lined with bobbing white boats, crisp white sails snapping in the wind, preparing to carry first-rate travelers. But there is anger; there is tension.

"You boys," announces the weathered but air-conditioned Moses, "are in trouble!"

A new word. I can tell by the way it comes out of his mouth it is not good. It makes the Olders widen their eyes, open their mouths and squeal.

"But why, Mister Haley," the harsh metallic glint now barely hiding under panicked lips.

"It was like this when we got here. From the earthquake! Why are we in trouble?"

"What did I do, Mister Haley? Why am I in trouble?"

What and *Why*. Thought they were interchangeable. *What* the formal *Why*. But *Trawbl*? Confused, lost, so… not sure how it got there, in my hand: Squared paper towel, full of water, ready to be slammed at the ceiling. I should drop so Moses won't see; I don't. Should separate from them; I don't. If he sees me holding it, standing with them, he'll think we're together. Maybe they'll think it too. Something tells me I should drop it. Moses, towering over me, a monument.

"You?" He says it with a sneer, like he's been waiting. "Over there," he commands, his big hand shoving me in with them. Me! With the Olders!

At the end of the movie, he was so mad, white hair, long beard, flowing red robe, raising the tablets over his head, throwing them at those he led out of bondage; mad messenger of a mad God. Ready to punish. Will he remember me from that day with Maman? Will he be merciful?

"Get the hell out!" demands Moses, holding the door for us to exit into the unforgiving light. Head down, I turn to go when I feel his forearm slam into my gut like the wooden staff he wandered the desert with, used to turn water into blood, to bring frogs and darkness. To punish.

"Wait!" He commands, surveying the floor one more time. "Clean this up!"

"Remember me, Mr. Haley?" I ask, pleading. "I was with my mawther?"

"I remember you," says Moses. "And your mother." Wagging his large finger, "I was right; you need to go back a grade. I'll call your mother and set her straight."

Maman will drop her lids! The clatter will echo in harmony with her wail to Adonai. She'll pull off her shoe and aim for my head if she gets a call saying they're sending me down too. She's still mad about Precious being sent down after the tambourine fight. It was his turn, he explained as he dodged Maman's shoe. A kid took it from his hand, shouted a nasty sounding word, so Precious banged the tambourine on his head.

"No, I should please stay in second. I was doing twalette. I not with them." I stare at the Olders, hoping they'll understand this small betrayal. I won't be their fierce Captain. Not today. But, except for a metallic sneer from one of them, they don't look my way.

"Clean it up!"

We get down on the damp floor; that stale pee smell up close. As Moses looms over me, my hands on the floor, his hard black shoes step on pulpy paper towels, close enough to step on my fingers. He walks out.

"Let's split," the Olders get up, wipe their hands on their pants, step over me and head for the door. One of them looks down and I expect a "we got you, kid" or a "you're with us."

"You missed a spot," he says, the metallic glint returning with his sneer. They laugh.

I look up and laugh too like we're in on the joke together, still hoping to make inroads, we're in it together, laughing together, not just them laughing at me. They exit without so much as a nod, leaving me in the blue bathroom on my hands and knees picking up pulpy paper towels. It is quiet, peaceful, my hands are warm. I think about *what*, *why* and *trouble*; I'd ask Maman about them later. Then, panicking again, I pray to Maman's Adonai that she won't get a call.

In the beginning, the hard and salty Olders ran the school. They played rough, kicked and tripped each other for laughs. During soccer, they were so fast their arms and necks pumped and churned like gears on a train. Nobody appointed them but they were bosses of the youngers. If there was a commotion or dustup, they'd rush over, sweaty and wide-eyed, ready to take over. "What's the news here," they would demand with the confidence and expectations of police. And things would die down. I followed the Olders, fetched for them, offered them bites of my Kalbas sandwich. One day before the bell I ran over to say "What's the news" and learn more of their words, which I would imitate later. One of them, Fardin, slapped my cheek. It stung and made a sound so big everything before and after it was black silence. I pretend-fell to the ground, not sure if I was hurt, clowning or fishing for sympathy. I was embarrassed and hid my hot face in my hands. "Now why'd ya have ta smack the kid, Mister?" another Older asked Fardin. "He's a good kid, Mister. That was unmanly." That's how Olders measured things, "Manly" or "Unmanly." "Kid needs to know what's what," Fardin explained as I stared inside my hands, my palms so close I could smell my sweat. Feeling pressure from his comrades, Fardin lectured me righteously about the Armani and Tork. I hid in my darkness, waiting for the humiliation to end. The others, stifling snickers, took mercy. "Leave the kid alone, Mister. With us, Mister, with us." That's when I knew I had them. I stayed on the ground, hid in my hands until Fardin finished. As they left, one of them muttered "don't worry, kid, we have you." When I knew I was alone I got up, brushed my pants off and walked to class, the contours of Fardin's hand rising hot on my pulsating

cheek. But it didn't hurt. I pretended it wasn't even there, looked around to make sure nobody saw. I'd be fine. I had the Olders, and they had me.

They're doing Clean Up Time early. Busy picking up books, erasers and chalk shaken loose from the earthquake. They share sounds, innocent chirps, entitled trills, they dart freely around their classroom. They weren't just yelled at by the principal; they won't be dodging shoes later. They aren't hot and prickly in wool hand-me-down sweaters. They are air-conditioned cool, winter fresh in the place they belong, doing things they are allowed to do. I want to forget the steamy piss smell of the bathroom, be air-conditioned like them. But they started without me and, as usual, I have to jump into the middle of it and find a spot for myself.

Under the sink is the cabinet with cleanup materials. I open it, reach in to grab a sponge but there is only a new one left, still wrapped. I can use it to sop up pencil shavings, eraser crumbs and chalk dust off desktops and the floor.

She appears as sudden as *Jeannie* in a pink puff - a blonde and blue Amrikayi blur.

"What! Are! You! Do! Ing!"

Her pink lips form each sound to make sure her words are under-stood. The red barrettes holding her blonde hair shake as she points her tiny finger. She is concerned. Important. Wonderful. Perfectly Amri-kayi like the doll Shideh left behind one afternoon when Maman was out and she had come to play. Shideh's doll had coarse gold hair, cold pale skin and three-dimensional crystal eyes as blue as the Amrikayi sky. If I laid her back, her eyes would close under blonde-lashed lids. If I sat her up, they'd open. Laid her back, close. Sat her up, open. Eyes so bright they lit up the closet where I took her after Shideh left. And she was quiet, no pull string in her back, her only sound a faint click when her eyes opened and closed. I tried laying her back but keeping her eyes open, to see the mesmerizing blue staring at me as I twisted my small lips over her cold pink ones, the way grownups on television did it.

But Jodi S. is no doll. In her simple dress with pink and yellow flowers, shiny black shoes and thin white socks with lace at her narrow ankles, she smells like bubble gum and shines her blue Amrikayi eyes on me to light me up and expose me as she waits for me to confess.

What or *Why*? Which one should I use? *What* is a question; *chee* in Farsi. *Why* is the slang, cool version. Same as *I'm* is the slang, cool version of *I am*. I want to sound cool for Jodi S., her cheeks so close to mine. Her breath, her attention. I take my time. *What* or *Why*?

"Why," cool smile, ignore the prickly-wool-sweaty neck, be air-conditioned.

"Because! You! Are! Not! A-llowed!" She's getting pinker. Pointing at my sponge.

Loud? I thought I spoke cool and easy. "Why?" Still smiling.

"Be! Cause! That's a new sponge! You need permission! Per-MI-shun. Understand?"

I don't, but nod anyway, hoping we can clean together while it's still Clean Up Time.

"OK." For sure that is a slang, cool word. "Yeah." Slang, cool. I unwrap the sponge.

"Ummah!"

I didn't think it was possible, but her eyes get even bluer as she holds her cheeks with her hands, her mouth round with shock. My smile frozen, I keep peeling the wrapper off the sponge.

"Ummah!" She's back to pointing at my sponge. "You're in tr-ruh-bbl?"

That word again. Moses said it to scare the Olders – and it worked. I wish I could lay Jodi S. back so her blue eyes would click shut. She's loud, difficult, talks fast, nothing like Shideh's doll. I don't know what she's saying, so I stop with the cool slang version and get real.

"What is?"

Too late. She has already turned to go to Mrs. Lee who usually sits at her desk at Clean Up Time. Jodi S. points, says "Michelle *something something* perMIshun!"

Still Mishel? What happened to Mike? Not even My-kell? Been a month.

Mrs. Lee looks in my direction. I figure I should put the sponge back in its wrapper and in the cabinet. I pretend to be busy wiping the counter with my hands, being helpful.

"I just spoke with Mr. Haley, Mike," she is firm, tobacco and sweet coffee on her breath.

At least she said Mike.

"You go to the bathroom during curney vens to play and make trouble?"

Trouble, definitely bad. Every time someone says it, they're either angry or terrified.

From the corner of my eye, the brittle yellow head of Fertig slow-shaking as he walks over. "I've warned him about the bathroom, Mrs. Lee."

"Mrs. Lee, the sponge?" Jodi S., arms folded, flashes Fertig an annoyed look like he's intruding. "Is Michelle allowed to use new sponges?"

"OK, thank you, Jodi S.," Mrs. Lee says. "Mike, you used a new sponge?"

"I just do the Clean Up Time," I say, holding up my palms to show the dirt.

"Liar!" yells Jodi S. stomping her shiny black shoes against the floor.

Trouble, the new word, echoes in my head.

"I may need to be with Mr. Haley when he calls your mother."

Maman's never home. This morning, after sweeping broken glass from the kitchen floor, she probably took Baba to work like she's been doing. She'll shop for tape or glue. She doesn't even pick us up anymore. Still too scared to take the rugged hill – I walk, left-left-end-of-block, crawl through the doggie door, make a ketchup-cheese pita, warm a can of beans, watch Wise-But-Naughty Rabbit, weekdays at 3 Channel 11, then Holy Girl who flies. So let them call.

"Mike's in tru-ble," sings Jodi S. She and Fertig, normally not allies, nod each other. But when Fertig flashes a smile, Jodi S. stomps away, arms down, fingers out, shoes slapping the floor as she joins her friends. I watch them clean with joy. They get to. It's their right.

I have the rest of the school day to wonder if they will call, if Maman will be home, if she'll be waiting when I get there, steaming lids on the floor, shoe in hand.

At least she said Mike.

She is at the kitchen table, calmer than we left her this morning. The cassette player next to her is playing a song about a regretful bird whose wings have been bound by Love. On an issue of Zaneh-Ruz magazine lays a sheet of thin slate-blue Par Avion paper for air mail letters. Her eyebrows are sharp, cheeks glowing from the heat of dinner on the stove, she is writing furiously. "Don't make beans," she says without looking up. "We have beans with dinner."

I make a ketchup-cheese pita. On the stove, sweet and tangy sheft-eh-berenji simmers in a pot with dried limes, prunes, tomato paste and red beans. I sit by her, take in her perfume, wondering if she is quiet because she is still shaken up from the earthquake, or if she got a call from school and is holding her fire for later. She raises her head, eyes shut, belts out the final verses of the song on the cassette player. When it ends, she opens her eyes, finally seeing me.

"Had you a good day," in playful Amrikayi, going back to writing her letter. No call from school. It is cloudy and cold outside but cozy in the warm kitchen.

"I had the good day," I respond. "You are writing the post?"

"From Azar I got the new Zaneh-Ruz and new songs. I'm writing her back, telling her how nothing is stable in Amrika, not even the ground." She pulls another sheet of the Par Avion paper and slides it over, "Do you want to write to your friends?"

Been a month. Have any mates asked after me? Did any notice I left? I know Shideh's address. I pull out my pencil, enticed by the slate blue sheet, never noticed its vast emptiness. No lines or borders, wide and blue as the ocean it will fly across; waiting to be written on, a story, history, message. Maman hits rewind, lights a smoker, filling the kitchen with the sultry aroma of matchstick sulfur and fresh-lit tobacco. I think about what to write Shideh.

"Is there a difference between *What* and *Why*?"

"Yes, my love," Maman answers, writing feverishly on her sheet, eyes sharpened.

"They're not different versions of the same word? You don't use them the same way?"

"No, my dear." Rolling her pen point across the sheet with confidence. "*What* is when you want to know something," she says, patiently looking up. "*What* is Chee."

"And *Why* is the informal version, no?"

"No. *Why* is when you don't understand the reason somebody does something, or something is a certain way and you ask. *Why* is Chera."

"*What you are doing?*" I start on my sheet to Shideh, showing off my Amrikayi. "*Why you did not asking of me?*" I wonder if she knows that *What* and *Why* are not the same. I switch to Farsi, tell her about Amrika's love of squares, everything has four even corners - orange cheese, white bread, toilet paper. I tell her they have tomato paste in bottles, how they pour it on everything and how much better everything tastes with it. I tell her I miss our games and ask her to write me back, not sure if she will. Shideh with the cold stare, pressed lips, short answers; she had wisdom but I could never tell what she was thinking, even when we played our secret games.

A soft tap on paper. I look over. A droplet smears the ink on her sheet, absorbs into its fibers. She wipes her cheek with the back of her hand, keeps writing. I take another bite of my sandwich, not worried. Maman cries – airports, parties, letters on slate-blue Par Avion sheets. Now, earthquakes. I consider cheering her up, distracting her, asking if she knows *Trouble*. But her eyes are focused. I let her be. I'm a bit homesick myself. I'll ask her about *Trouble* later.

When we finish our letters, Maman twists her smoker into the ashtray and pushes on the kitchen table to lift herself up. She goes to her pot, ladles tomatoes and beans over the sheftehs to keep them moist, puts away dishes she washed – the ones that didn't break - clapping them softly on top of each other, sweeps bits of plates and teacups from under cabinets. When she is done, she looks out at the afternoon sun breaking through the clouds, lays down on the rug to warm herself under it. Solid ground at last. "Walk on my back," she says. "I need energy."

I take off my shoes, stand on Maman's back and walk along her spine as she groans, her bones cracking under my feet. I still have questions, the meaning of *Trouble*, and new math. Mrs. Lee furiously taps the board with her chalk, scratching out numbers and symbols, too fast for me to catch, another new tongue to learn. I know +, - and =. But not x.

"What's x, Maman," I ask as she lay on her stomach, cheeks resting on her hands, her feet, swollen and bruised from tight high heeled shoes, turned in. She's already asleep, breathing steady, a faint whistle from her nose. "What's 2 then x then 2? It isn't adding?"

She lifts her head, wipes her mouth, cheeks already folded from sleep, and clears her throat, "What are two twos" she lays her head back down. So simple. A clear explanation while resting after restoring order, learning songs, cooking dinner, thinking a hundred more important thoughts. Still, she offers key truths, shines her warm light on me, pulls me out of darkness. I stare in awe, her back gently rising and falling – a gonjeshk at rest, a rare sight, on the Persian rug in the kitchen of a new, jittery country.

Every day, left-left-end-of-block, crawl through doggie door, hope she's home, hoping that before Precious or Baba come, I can take in her perfume-and-tobacco scent, listen to her adventures in Amrika by the light of her fiery eyes, basking in their warmth. Maman is finding her way too; looking for solid ground. I leave her to rest, deciding not to ask her about *Trouble*.

In the beginning, we were raised on the art of Pazirayee - hosting with elegance and grace. Strangers or acquaintances, expected or not, were entitled to a glass of tea, a dish of sweet dates, a bowl of pistachios, trays of honeyed pastries, peeled and salted cucumbers, bread and cheese and grapes – no matter what burdens a host is carrying inside. On the cold wintry night before we boarded the BOAC, Maman hosted one last time. Grownups held drinks and smokers, made promises, exchanged addresses and hugged, bawling so hard snot from their noses mingled with drool from their lips, gumming up their hairspray stiffened 'dos. Late into the night, we were allowed to stay up with them among the half-empty platters of lamb with dill-and-lima-bean rice, greasy plates, drained cocktail glasses. They sat on the rug in suits and dresses, leaning on cushions, sipping tea or scotch. Maman sat cross-legged as we rested our heads on her thigh. She sang their favorites, her head swaying,

eyes closed, nodding with a bittersweet smile. They were under her spell. I could feel her controlling the power of her voice, raising it from the pit of her stomach, pushing it through her lungs, heaving it from the back of her throat, a howl that awed the silent room lit by the orange glow and grey haze of smokers. Maman took Sweet Lady's advice; agreed to fulfil her duties as wife and mother. Baba had been gone since Fall. She pulled us from school during winter break, packed our things. We would meet Baba. She would give Loose-and-Jealous, Amrika a try. She would be closer to New York where Sweet Lady was. Maybe she would make a life there as full as the one she was leaving behind. But first we would be their guests. And Maman prayed for elegance and grace from her hosts.

March 1971

"Wanna comover?"

"Comover?"

"After."

"After?"

"After school. You wanna comover after school?"

I'm waiting for Fertig to say something I can hold on to.

"My house." Then he uses his hands. "You (points at me). Come (waves me in). My house (fingertips together like a triangle roof). After school (points to his wrist). Yes? I live down there," he points to the street behind the fence down from the Hill.

Nobody has invited me before.

"Yes." Maman won't care; she'll be busy making the Purim feast, lentil-rice and rosewater Halva. She's been thinking of Purim since we landed. She says she's like Esther, preserving our Persian-Jewish traditions in the shaky dehat of Amrika.

Fertig lives down from school between the Hill and Texaco. He has his own housekey on a chain around his neck. When we go inside, amazing smells! A sweet haze making my nostrils widen and point up like the cartoon dog sensing fresh baked pie. So much better than the musty smells of boiling chicken, searing meats and frying greens choking our house. I want to float along on the vapor trails of these gorgeous new smells, let them lead me to a better place, an Amrikayi dehat place. Smoky. Sweet. Peppery. Buttery. I hear giggles and chirps.

"I brought a friend," Fertig bellows as we enter, sounding as bossy as he does at school.

"OK honey," the voice sings melodically. "Come get something to eat." Their kitchen is yellow like ours but a lighter shade like feathers on a playful canary. At a glass table with two straw placemats and four bamboo chairs with green-and-pink-flowered cushions sits a green-eyed Amrikayi woman with wavy light brown hair, playfully twisting the curly cord of a phone around her clean, clipped fingernails. Her hair flows over a soft, light blue men's shirt, top buttons undone, untucked over light brown men's pants, cuffs rolled up to her smooth ankles, bare feet with clipped toenails uncomplicated by polish, callouses or swelling from constantly being jammed into tight high heeled shoes. She is air-conditioned cool.

"C'mon in, honey," she says in a hushed tone, placing a hand on the receiver. "Who's your friend," tickling the air with her fingertips to greet me. "Mike."

"Let me call you later, sweetie," she says into the phone as she hangs up and gives me her full attention. "Hi, Mike," she walks toward me, leans forward, the front of her unbuttoned shirt falling open as she places her hands on her knees, "dju like something to eat, hun?"
I want to hug her, alone, pull her in with both arms, press my head against her long, bare neck and purr for her. I want to stay with her in her kitchen. That sweet smoky scent, peppery haze, buttery aroma, her clean rosy cheeks and easygoing feet. She is light and simple, just like they always say about Amrikayi women. Golden. Blue. Unworried. "Kelly, honey, I made a BLT you can split with Mike while the cookies cool."
"Want half?" *Kelly Smelly with the Big Fat Belly Made Outta Jelly*, who they laugh at, who eats cookies in the bathroom oblivious that he'll be turning into a monkey, who talks like he knows it all even when nobody listens. This is his kitchen. That's his Maman. "It's *biyelty*."

"Biyelty?"

"BLT. B for Bacon. L for Lettuce. T for Tomato. Ever heard of it? You like bacon?"

"Baking?"

"Not baking, bacon. Bacon? You know bacon?"

Smells so good, smoky, sweet. Trying to make sense of what he's saying. He opens the sandwich and shows me dark brick-and-pale colored strips of foreign meat I have never seen.

He tries to find words to explain what is basic to him. "Pork? Pig? Oink?"

Toorah says no Pig. Maman warned about Pig and Amrikayi. They like it. But it's Sin; worse than turning into monkeys. There it is. I'm looking at real Pig. Smells so good; making my mouth water. Sinful Pig. Delicious, sweet, smoky Sin. But Sin just the same.

Can't complicate things. Can't make a scene. Can't make a run for it and disappear.

"Can't," I say. "I not . . . can't."

"You don't like BLT?"

"Because, I am… not-"

"You're not allowed to eat pig, right?"

Hide!

"No. Yes. Pig is t'rific," I say fast, "I just not…hungry."

"Are you a Jew?"

"Kelly sweetheart, we don't say 'Jew' honey. It's rude. We say 'Jewish' remember? And yes, some Jewish people don't eat bacon, you know that. Dad explained it."

"That why Dad left? Because you made him eat bacon?"

"Your dad loved my BLT, thank you very much; shouldn't discuss family matters in front of guests." To me, "Mike, hun, it's ok if you can't have bacon. Have a cookie." Back to Fertig, "And I didn't force Dad to…I was just trying to find my…to exercise my…never mind."

Complications? She needs help? Her own son doesn't get her?

"Take a bite," Fertig says, holding out half the sandwich. "Watch," biting into his half. "You know you want to. My dad's a Jew and he ate bacon; nothing happened."

Except divorce, like Maman said. Smells good. Wish he'd stop talking about Jewish rules.

"Kelly, honey, leave him alone, if he isn't allowed, he doesn't have to--"

"Is OK," I say before she finishes. "We eat it, sure," I take the sandwich, study it, side to side. One corner has more bread and lettuce, less Pig. I aim. I'll bite, avoid Pig, they will be satisfied and stop talking like I'm a foreigner forced to live by ancient laws. I bring it to my mouth, open wide - smoky peppery Pig aroma, cold mornings on the prairie, cowboys shoveling spoonsful of hot vittles from tin plates. I sink my teeth. Toasted bread scrapes the roof, damp lettuce, tomato, mayonnaise – then something tough, chewy…sweet. Delicious. I clamp down, hold, exhale through my nose, crushing the smoky taste against the roof with my tongue, chew slow, eyes roll back, "mmm" escapes, heavenly… not Pig…sweet…smoky…not Sin …floating…lifted by the aroma like Cartoon Dog… floating … like the Holy Girl … heavenly…

"S'good, right?" Fertig's elbow nudges my rib. "Take another bite, I won't tell."

Open your eyes. You're going to Hell. Monkeys. Divorce. Sin!

"Havta go!" I swallow. "My Maman making the Special dinner because it's--"

Don't say Purim!

"But you just got here," complains Fertig. "Don't we wanna play?"

"Havta- havta go," I say, feeling nauseous. I give the rest of my Pig sandwich back to Fertig. Thin strands lining my tongue, slivers, fibers… Pig hairs? "Havta go!"

"Mike, honey, you wanna take some chocachip cookies? Just made 'em. No bacon, I promise," she runs her index finger across her partially exposed chest to make an "X" then holds up two fingers, "cross my heart," she says with a smile and wink, like it's our secret.

"Go ahead and take some," says Fertig. "She makes chocachip cookies all the time."

She takes four soft cookies from a full sheet on the stove, puts them in a plastic bag, expertly flips a flap to close it. She bends down so close I smell clean light lemon on her skin.

"Take these with you, honey."

"No, thanks."

"Sure? I made plenty. It's just Kelly and me."

"OK," I say, taking the bag from her. I'll throw them away later on the way home.

"Come over any time, sweetie," she says. "Kelly is with his dad on weekends but we'd love to have you over after school any time."

"You said don't discuss family with guests, why tell him about weekends at Dad's?"

"It's OK, sweetie," says Fertig's mother. "Divorce is nothing to be embarrassed by."

Amrikayi tell family secrets to strangers - Divorce, Pork, Sin - all free and easy, while I try to figure out how to keep my Pig Sin from Maman. He walks me to the door. I breathe the fresh cool air outside, hoping to dissipate the smell; the peppery, smoky wonderful smell of Sin.

"You sure you have to go?" he asks, his usually salty ocean blue eyes soft for once.

"They're waiting. My mother make special dinner tonight."

"OK," says Fertig, looking down. "Don't worry," he says, "I won't tell about the pork."

He knows it's a sin too!

"No, it's OK," running out, "we eat Pig!" Outside, a purple dusk pushes the innocent sun down behind the trees, swirling out layers of shiny orange clouds across the sky. I feel sick. I run for home, hoping for Purim to cleanse me. I scrape Pig fibers off my tongue with my teeth, my spit, but they're embedded. The sky goes from orange-purple to dark. No time for left-left-end-of-block. No choice but the treacherous hill. I jump into the spikey bushes, prickly shrubs. Climb. Pretend wild animals, lizards, roaches, poison vines are not crawling on me. No pricks or jabs at my calves. Climb. Scrape. Spit. Shudder. To the top, the palm tree. Home.

If you don't talk, she won't smell Pig; doesn't matter, Sin happened, even if Maman never finds out. Only chance is atonement. Yom Kippur. Months away. An eternity.

Maman is lighting candles in the kitchen even though Purim doesn't have candles. She's been lighting them all the time lately, chanting prayers for her dead father, her mother, rocking back and forth, eyes closed, cupped hands scooping the flames toward her, entranced. She sees me. "Where did you go? Even Saeed didn't know where you were."

"Nowhere," I say, sucking fibers off my tongue, swallowing to get rid of the smells.

"What's wrong," she comes to me, "you're white as chalk. Did you eat? Your heart is racing; you're sweating. Did you find someone to play with? What happened?"

"Nothing," I say, mouth tight so nothing seeps out. "Played, friend's house. Ran home."

"A friend's house? You made a friend? Who? Did they feed you? What did you eat?"

"Nothing."

"You look sick, my love. Are you going to throw up?"

"Nothing."

She studies my face, her mouth closed tight, her eyes sharpened, her nostrils working. "Have some halva," she says, bearing down on my eyes, "it'll sweeten your mouth for Purim."

She knows!

I rush to the table, put a chunk of dense halva in my mouth, chew, another, letting the sweet amalgam of rosewater and saffron smother the Pig. But...too sweet, water, heart pounds, sweat turning cold on my face. I run to the faucet, fill a glass, large gulps, fill, but before I take another swig it comes rushing out, heave after painful heave. I can't hold it. I watch it pour out, yellow halva, pink tomato, green lettuce. As Maman runs to me, shrieking, holding my head, I feel assured that nobody could possibly see the purple bits of Pig, the hints of sweet savory Sin.

April 1971

"Who is?" Maman clutches her blouse when she hears a knock. She's making kuku for Passover. In Tehran, our door was never locked; she knew everyone who walked in. In Amrika, she has become suspicious of every sound. She has made no friends; everyone is a stranger.

"Shelly. I'm Shelly. Our boys play together."

Her boy is Kersh; lives down the street. Cowan lives across the street. Kersh and Cowan go to Pinnacle; they play with Precious. Maman says Precious, with his lighter skin and fairer hair, could pass for Amrikayi. She beams when she says it. He has more friends than me. When he isn't running on the playground with his friends, he's on our street with Kersh and Cowan. I stay inside and watch TV. First the Wise-But-Naughty Rabbit, then Holy Girl who flies.

Maman peeks through the door hole. I go to hide out in my room.

"Our boys play together. I brought a kugel for Pesach."

"Pesach?" Maman loosens her grip on her blouse. "You are Jewish?"

"Yes. Shell-lee," slower, louder. "My Brian plays with your Sid. I brought Kugel."

"Who is this dehati you've thrown around our neck, now, O Adonai," Maman mutters, opening the door to a dark-haired lady with the plump round face and soft lips that form an easy smile. Wearing a wide-brimmed floppy sun hat, she holds a plastic container. When she steps in, she immediately sniffs and wrinkles her nose. "Oh! You're making ...dinner?"

"Kuku," Maman says, "vid the egg and all the many greens."

"OK," Kersh's mom forces a stiff, flat smile. "Interesting. Smells... so... exotic! I should go," she says, "just wanted to introduce myself; enjoy the Kugel."

"You make the Kugel; I make the Kuku!" Maman laughed. "Do you like to have tea?"

"Ooh, tea? My ex only liked coffee; such a bore. I always wanted to try tea, so exotic."

"Ex?"

"My ex-husband. I'm divorced."

Maman clutches her blouse again.

"What type of tea do you have?"

"The Persian tea," Maman says, sharpening her eye. "We are Irani from Persia."

Maman's English isn't good, but they talk. Women, especially mothers, must share a secret tongue that connects them beyond country or culture. She doesn't bother with the curvy tones she reserves for Amrikayi. They talk, whisper, even laugh. When their voices get loud near the front door, I come out to see them. "Nice to have finally met you!"

Maman sees me in the hallway and her expression changes. Double-blink-lip-bite. In her best round, curvy mock Amrikayi, "Oh you are wery velcome, wery nice to meeting you olso, mm hm, ya," like she wouldn't want me thinking she enjoyed chatting with an Amrikayi dehati; like she only did it to be polite to an unexpected guest. Kersh's mom doesn't notice.

"Enjoy the kugel," she says. "You can send the Tupperware back with Sid whenever."

"Wait," Maman says, her hosting instinct taking over, "take Kuku!" She goes to the kitchen and brings down one of her good plates from the cabinet.

"No, really," Kersh's mom pleads, "I shouldn't; I'm dieting; it's your family dinner."

But Maman has already lifted a large chunk of the thick green Kuku out of the frying pan. She slides it onto the plate, wraps it in foil and forces it into Kersh's mom's hand, "Kuku."

Baba coming home early on a school day is weird. He rushes through the front door, drops a department store bag on the kitchen table and walks into the living room to hand me an envelope. "You have post," he says as he heads down the hall. "Now go get ready!"

"For what?" It is a slate-blue Par Avion letter. My first post in Amrika. My old name scribbled on the front, with our Amrikayi address. I am really here. I unseal it.

"*Mishel my bell!*" in English, "*Where went you? I run up to play on you but see no man woman boy on you apartomun. Teacher say you Amrika go. Amrika mod is? You mod are in Amrika? You George-of-the-Beatles are in Amrika? My stomach little little for you. My stomach little for our play. You Tehran come? One day I Amrika come.*" She switches to Farsi, "*Do you have new Amrikayi friends? You know what? Ramin really was Tork. They returned to Torkyeh. Our friends are leaving Tehran. Are you enjoying Amrikayi school? You understand them? Talk like them? You know in Amrika they only say Mishel to girls? Tell them you are a boy, Mishel my bell. Write to me again. It has been my pleasure, Miss Shideh.*"

Picturing Shideh's face with the new ones is hard. Skin dark like mine, eyes brown like mine, heavy like they've seen more than they have, hair black as a thousand-and-one nights tied up like the crown of a tree, voice thick from repeating ancient words and myths. Unlike the new faces, snow-white skin, sun-gold hair, ocean-blue eyes, joyous yelps in a modern tongue. Their stories, their myths, start with them. Mod. I put Shideh's letter in my closet, wondering if I look heavy and dark to them; if I can ever be light, Mod like them; if my myth can start with me.

Baba is waiting in the kitchen, a bowl of water, black comb and scissors set on the table.

"Sit," he orders, "we need to get you ready for tomorrow."

"What's tomorrow?"

"Free pictures at school. See how smart it was to move here?"

Maman walks in. "You disrupted our lives, moved us to this shaky land for free photos?"

"That's just one benefit," Baba says, sliding his thick fingers into the scissor holes. "Amrika has big cars, big stores, big opportunities for anyone who wants to take them."

"You know scissors?" Maman asks, hands on hips. "Since when do you know scissors?"

"Never mind," he says, "I know."

I reluctantly take a seat as Baba dips his fingers in the bowl of water and wets my bangs.

"Careful," she warns, "his hair is delicate. He's our George-the-Beatle, don't ruin it."

But Baba loses control fast. Can't keep the bangs even; snipping side to side, zigzagging up, above the bridge of my nose, eyelashes, eyelids, eyebrows. Determination popping his eyes.

"What are you doing?" Maman yells. "Watch it, you're going too high!"

"Velemoon kon," Baba barks, forging ahead, refusing to admit he may have stepped into foreign territory, "This is how Amrikayi haircuts are. Short in front, long in back."

Maman shakes her head, amused by Baba's odd behavior ever since we got here. "Woman's work. In Tehran you didn't do woman's work. You want to scrub our socks next?"

35

Baba, too focused to answer, keeps trying to even out the bangs until he reaches the top. My forehead. That's when he steps back, squints, pretending to study his handiwork. "OK," he nods, attempts to twist his natural scowl into a smirk. "And that…then…is…. that…"

"You ruined his hair!" yells Maman. "It was beautiful! Silky! George-the-Beatle."

I run to the mirror by the front door. Is that . . . me? George-the-Beatle replaced by box-headed Herman on *Munsters*, weekdays at 6 Channel 5. I shut my eyes, wait, open. Still Herman, short bangs like a row of thin black teeth on the short end of a plastic comb. Panic.

Baba freezes his face to look unworried, chin tucked in, shoulders back, chest out, trying to make it look like he did a good thing. He breaks into French, knowing we may not understand but also knowing what we all believe: Farancavi are better at fashion than Irani.

"Viens ici," he yells to Precious coming in from playing with Kersh and Cowan. He sees my dark sweaty face in the mirror, Baba standing at the kitchen door holding scissors.

"Ha!" he yells, "Now I'm George-the-Beatle!" Precious thinks his light skin makes him look more Beatle-y, even though everybody knows George is the dark Beatle.

"You have light, curly hair," I remind him. "You can't be George! George is mine!"

Precious points with a tickled laugh, "Look at your front, Herman Monster."

Baba ignores my pain, brings the shopping bag from the kitchen. "Attends," he stays with French, pulls out a jacket. "Try 'dis on for the size," switching to terrible English.

A grey jacket with red and navy checkers like *Mannix* Sunday nights at 9 Channel 2, starring Mike Connors who Baba loves because he is Armani. Armani are practically Irani for Baba now that we're in Amrika. Mannix is one of us. On Sunday nights as Baba and Maman play Rummy on the couch, Baba will recognize the theme song on TV and perk up.

"Armaniyeh!" he says. "Maneex Armaniyeh!"

The first time he said it, Maman blew smoke to the ceiling with a laugh. "In Tehran, you gave Armani crooked-eyes," she reminded him as she arranged her cards, discarded and stared at him. "Now you're one with them? What a change!"

Baba sipped his drink, picked up Maman's discard and slipped it into the fanned-out cards he was holding. "In Iran, our differences separated us," arranging his hand, "in Amrika, they connect us." With that, he laid his cards down in sets until he was done, paused like he was waiting for applause. "Count your damage," he ordered Maman.

Now he slips the Mannix jacket on me, tugs the sleeves, straightens the lapels, smooths the shoulders. I pray he knows what he's doing, the well-travelled Farancavi-educated adult who dragged us here. Is he Mod or just loading more ancient myths on my shoulders? I like *Mannix*. Not because Mike Connors is practically Irani, but because he's a Mike! *Mike* Connors hangs from the helicopter; *Mike* Connors races his convertible sports car through the streets of Los Angeles, punching criminals through doors and windows; *Mike* Connors wears a grey jacket with red and navy checkers. But do the kids of room 7 know and like *Mannix*? Will they recognize the jacket and think it's Mod? Am I "Mike Mannix" or "Mannix Manoucherian"?

"La piece de resistance!" is a gold scarf with paisleys. Baba twirls it into a fluffy rope, wraps it around my sweaty neck and pushes the ends through a gold ring he slides up to my throat. He tucks it inside the lapel of the jacket and gives my bangs a tussle to make them seem wind-blown. But the bangs are too short to be tussled so it's just Baba slapping my forehead.

"Et voila!" Baba beams with the pride of certainty, "vous etes suave et debonair comme Alexander Mundy a la It Take a Teef! Regard," he yells over to Maman who is now standing in her bathrobe, a hand covering her mouth. "Robert Vagner!" Baba yells. "It Take a Teef!"

"I don't want this on my neck," I yell, tugging at the scarf.

A debate about the scarf breaks out as I stand at the mirror, almost in tears.

"C'est un foulard," insists Baba with a sense of adventure.

"That is a choker," titters the angling Precious, "like the mom on Partridge Family with Herman Monster hair." He runs back out to play, like he won.

"It's dashing," Maman tries to convince me, "Robert Vagner."

Three feelings: Hope, as in, hope the kids in Room 7 love *Mannix* and *It Takes a Thief* as much as Baba. Doubt, as in, doubt I'll make it through the day unnoticed. Fear, as in, terrified of being exposed as the dumb foreigner who took Picture Day too seriously. Hope. Doubt. Fear. In the mirror, dark ancient eyes stare back, shoulders burdened by hand-me-down myths, wide brown forehead - no hair to hide behind. Hope doubt fear. Hopedoubtfear. At the kitchen table, sweat beads on my forehead, my trembling lips. I am Herman Munster.

Maman sits beside me, picking slivers of hair stuck to my forehead with her nails. "You are a guest in their country," she says. "Even Amrikayi know to be gracious to guests. Like your friend's mother who brought the food today. Yes? You will be fine. You look handsome."

Can I trust them? Do I look Mod? Amrikayi? It's been a weird afternoon. I make a honey sandwich and head for the TV; first Wise-But-Naughty Rabbit then Holy Girl who flies.

"H'yur! 'Trow it!" Yelling outside. Precious playing with Kersh and Cowan. Light-skinned, fair-haired Precious plays like them, runs and spins and throws and catches like them, screams like them. "H'yur! 'Trow it h'yur!" in a hoarse rasp, just like Amrikayi. And they throw it to him! He has learned their games, their sports words. They play with him, sweaty, hair stuck to cheeks, chewing gobs of pink gum. They call him Sid. I stay inside, hiding my short black bangs, my sweaty brown skin, curtains drawn.

In Farsi, Rabbit is Khar Goosh - "Donkey ear." But Wise-But-Naughty Rabbit is no donkey. He speaks Amrikayi with a savvy confidence and the best words, "Mac" "Stinker" "Doc." He gets the better of Mean Duck, Nervous Pig, Genius Coyote, all while staying air-conditioned. Even under the gun of Angry Cowboy or Stupid Hunter, Rabbit shows moxie, an ability to escape jams, leaving them holding the dynamite as he takes his carrot to his cozy hole.

"H'yur! 'Trow it!"

At the commercial, I nudge the curtain aside. Precious waving his hands in the air, feet jittering side to side, as Cowan chases Kersh who is scrambling, holding a brown pointy ball, avoiding Cowan's lunges. "I'mopen!" he yells. Through the sliver of curtain, I stare.

Go with them. Get out, play with your light-skinned brother and his Amrikayi friends.

"They're in the middle of their game," I argue with voices I don't trust anymore. I like it inside, watching Wise-But-Naughty Rabbit beat his foes, and Holy Girl who flies over the chaos.

Let 'dem stinkers play 'der games, Doc. And never mind Maman. I have you.

At dinner, Maman tells Baba about Kersh's mom.

"What does he do," Baba asks, referring to Kersh's dad without mentioning him, even though Maman has been talking about his mom.

"Lashoon," Maman says. Only Baba understands Maman's code words. "Poor soul, two boys and she's laughing, sipping tea like nothing. Mashala. I gave her Kuku to take for dinner."

Baba shrugs as he shakes salt on his Kuku, cuts it with his fork.

"Lots of women are doing it," Maman nods, slicing and serving Kuku to Precious and me then taking a seat. "Even in Tehran. It was in the Zaneh-Ruz Azar sent me."

"They're ruined after it," Baba forks another hunk into his mouth, "the women."

"La*shoon*," Maman insists in code, slowly chewing her Kuku, looking off somewhere past the ceiling. "How do they do it alone? Takes strength doing it alone."

I'm only thinking of tomorrow; wondering if my hair will grow out, even a little, by then.

With stiff cold fingers, I wet my bangs as Baba rings the scarf up my neck. We walk in the spring air, burning diesel my only comfort. Precious is playful; Maman didn't let Baba near him after butchering my hair. At the bottom of the hill, the lone palm waves as the blacktop lies in wait across the street like a lion with jagged chain link teeth and a concrete tongue. In I go.

Nowhere to hide on the unforgiving playground. If you want to not be seen, avoid eyes, look down, be invisible. I start along the orange hoops of basketball, to the tall brown walls of handball, sidestepping the yellow boundaries of foursquare. I slip past flipping pigtails, skidding sneakers, flying elbows, exposed shins, avoiding hardened wads of loogies spat with competitive ferocity. The smell of eucalyptus leaves churns my stomach as sweat beads my forehead. I want to perch with the gonjeshk, protected and warmed by a community of like-feathered comrades, watching the humans below, their small dirty hands clutching iron bars, swinging skinny arms, fingers clawing tunnels in cold sand, heartless conquerors. In I go.

The back fence beside Room 7 is where the sad kids - more conquered than conqueror - wait for the bell. I avoid them too, slipping into the blue bathroom to stare in the cracked, booger-stained mirror: Dark eyes, brown face, lonely mole on my jaw (it's not a freckle if it's only one); eyebrows forming the triangle of fear; Herman Munster head and hair. They like long hippie hair, not army hair. The Holy Girl from TV would float above all this. Wise-But-Naughty Rabbit would put on a wig and lipstick and charm his tormentors.

Foist ting's foist, Doc. Ya gotta shrink dat forehead! Shorten dat gap between bangs and eyebrows. Tilt your head in. Blur lines. Blend. Find a sucker – dat's "gracious host" to you, Doc - someone welcoming; a soft target who gets your humiliation, has no appetite to be cruel. A loser like you, Doc, but an Amrikayi loser because an Amrikayi loser is still an Amrikayi, right? Stand beside him like you're pals. You don't get to choose a lifesaver when you're drowning, Doc; you grab whatever helps you stay afloat and you hold on. I have you, Doc.

The morning bell jars my eyeballs into focus. I straighten up, walk back out to their chaos. I hide in line, slow-march through the door. Blend, blur, head down.

Find a sucker and be his pal.

The cinnamon haired kid they call Dud. Lazy gummy smile coated by a film of spit he's not good about swallowing. Stringy hair off his forehead hides his freckles and green speckled eyes. Cowboy boots and … a red scarf! For Picture Day he greased his hair and combed it back to expose his watery eyes and peanut-shaped head. Dud is like an old sweater carelessly tossed in a corner: musty, crumpled and mostly forgotten - until it gets cold. My soft target.

Your lucky day, Doc. You found yourself a sucker – er, new pal.

I stand beside him. "Look! Both esscarf," pointing to our necks.

He lights up, starts flinging cowboy words off his tiny wet teeth. A wad of spit works its way from his gums to the corner of his mouth, a white clump he wipes with his sleeve. My ears can't catch most of it but there's no ridicule in his twang. Then he undoes his scarf and waves it like a flag, holds it up like a parachute, over his mouth like a cowboy bandit. He's excited.

Plan's woikin', Doc, keep it up. Make like you're interested.

I pretend-listen, like it's important. If anyone sees, they'll think we're discussing something heroic; that they underestimated me; shouldn't have laughed at me that first day; I am rugged Mannix, elegant Robert Wagner, being heroic with my comrade, the Amrikayi Cowboy.

Second bell! I start for my seat, relieved. So far, so good.

You made it, Doc! You fooled 'em! Except...wait... what's dat? Over der...

At the doorway, hands in front pockets looking smug, is Wicked Smirk (real name, Worm), staring with the eye that isn't covered by long bangs that used to look like mine. Like his pals, he hasn't dressed or combed special for Picture Day. We lock eyes and he smirk-nods, points his dirty finger at me and Dud who is still floating his scarf over his head.

"It' the Flying Non," shouts Worm, "and her Mexikin boyfriend, Beaner Boy!"

"Flying Nun" is Holy Girl who flies. In the show she has a friend who wears a scarf like mine; Carlos. Carlos is brown like me, which – aside from being able to fly – is why I watch. Carlos looks like me. But Worm says it like it's bad. Maybe it is.

Run, Doc!

I try stepping away from Dud. We only had a strategy for a bad haircut, not for being brown. I walk to my desk, pretend not to hear the laughter, deep in thought, important things. When I think they're not looking, I wipe sweat off my big brown forehead. No Robert Wagner. No Mannix. Only Carlos, the ... Beaner Boy? I don't get the joke, but I get the gist.

"Carlos is actually American aka Puerto Rican," Fertig informs me at recess. "But the idea's the same, your Puerto Ricans and Mexicans eat beans, ergo Beaners. Nobody's saying you eat beans; just that you're brown like a bean-eating Mexican aka Beaner. That's the joke."

"Eating beans is funny? Why? Why Mexicki is funny? I not Mexicki."

"Mexi*can*, Beaner Boy," Fertig claps my shoulder with a sniff of satisfaction, "you're not Mexi*can*," looks over at Dud and Pincus, winks and chuckles. "But you do look like one."

I am Beaner Boy.

PART II

IN THE BEGINNING, *Maman wore a tweed two-piece on a crisp fall morning. She smelled exciting like matchsticks and black pepper. Said we're going out, gave me a present - a box of colorful clay, hefty in my hand. She told me to bring it. We drove on the cold grey streets, parked in front of a concrete yard surrounded by tall, bare trees. Kids were playing. We walked across to a room in a grey building where more kids talked and laughed. I stood by Maman, one hand clutching my box, the other holding hers as she talked to a lady with black hair pulled up in a ball. Maman spoke in a tone I'd never heard, like outsiders, like the Guweem - a brisk, joyful tone brimming with unfamiliar confidence. She told the lady I was ready. The lady asked my name and Maman announced "This is Mishel." I froze; I am Essagh, I thought. My hand got moist, nearly causing the box to slip. Maman felt my other hand sweating in hers, looked down at me, top teeth quick-tapping lower lip, quick blinks. The lady wondered if I was too young. "Did my husband call," Maman asked, pretending, a careless windswept confusion in her new tone. That's when she pulled the box from my sweaty clutches. "For the class," Maman said, "from Mishel." A smile lit up the lady's face, until she caught my face, flush from betrayal. She squatted, her face hovering above her slightly parted knees; her grey skirt hiked halfway up her leg. She stroked my hair as I stared into the dark triangle between her knees, my sorrow a perfect cover. "Mishel dear," she said, stroking slow, "welcome to kindergarten." I drew my*

*glance up from her knees, thighs, loose white blouse, gold Shah coin on
a chain dangling at her bosom. I stiffened my neck as she stroked, felt
a purr coming on. A nudge! Maman's knee in my rib. "Thank you,
Miss," I said, head down. She stood up, my box in her hand. "Look
what Mishel brought," she announced. I watched the dirty-handed
strangers unwrap and open my box, pulling row after row of my clay,
squeezing. They thanked Mishel – my outside name. I looked up at
Maman who tooth-tapped her lips again, double blinked, then left.*

Third Grade. First day.
September 1971.

"*Cherokee pee-pul, Cherokee tra-hab.*" I hum my song in front of
Room 13. Still hot, summer was just yesterday, our first in Amrika. We
got a black transistor radio and I found 93KHJ with Real Don Steele
who plays the best Amrikayi songs and uses the best Amrikayi words.
I had the radio at my ear all summer, memorizing. The playground was
open. Maman dropped Baba off in the mornings and drove around
all day learning the streets and stores, in the afternoon she'd be on the
phone with Sweet Lady. I was usually on the hill, climbing vines like
Batman or sitting on bumps watching cars go by and the action at the
playground across the street, radio at my ear. "*Cherokee pee-Pul! Cherokee tra-hab.*" It's Boss!

On extra hot days I went to the school library where it was cool
and quiet. Sometimes kids ducked in to avoid beatings from Buckteeth
(aka, Speed) or to do God's Eyes and Lanyards with Yard Teacher. I'd
sit on the shag carpet, hiding from Beaner Boy jokes and waiting for
my bangs to grow out. I looked at books. One had a kid on the cover
who looked like me: brown skin, sad eyes, black hair bound by a colorful
band. *Navajo.* I opened it to see who the kid was. Indians! Bad guys in
cowboy movies. But they look like me, a cooler Amrikayi version. After
that, I noticed them everywhere – TV, posters, magazines – Indians are
cool. *Billy Jack* was full of brown Indian kids getting bullied, like me.
They were the good guys in that movie. I could be like them, Navajo

instead of Beaner Boy. Aztec. *Cherokee pee-pul! Cherokee tra-hab!*

Even glorious Amrikayi Mrs. Mendelsohn dresses like Indians. Her thick blonde hair flows past the fringes on the back of her suede Indian vest, Indian moccasins, turquoise Indian rings. On this stifling hot morning, she lines us up before the bell as I fantasize dancing to *Cherokee People* with her, purring for her. New year, fresh start. I'm here from the beginning. In the crowd of classmates, I hear a familiar voice humming a familiar melody…

"*Cherokee pee-pul…*" I look over matted mopheads, sun kissed faces and ocean-washed blue eyes in search of the voice humming my song. Near the back of the line, I see a shag of light brown hair bobbing in rhythm. Bucktooth Leader, aka Speed, the one they all want to be friends with, who can be mean but never gets in trouble for it, who nobody makes fun of. "*…Cherokee tra-hab.*" He knows the rest of it too: "*so proud to lee-hiv; so proud to daaaa…*"

Probably listens to Real Don Steele too. Dis is your chance, Doc. Fresh start. Go!

I jump out of line and head for the blue bathroom. In the mirror, bangs grown out, brown skin tinged rosy gold from summer. I'll make them forget Beaner Boy. From my pocket, I pull the thick blue rubber band from yesterday's groceries, it held broccoli. Like the Navajo kid on the cover, I stretch it around my head - tight, pulls my hair, indentation in my forehead. Stretch, adjust, line it up. Practically Navajo! Practically *Cherokee Pee-pul.* Practically Amrikayi.

Outside, I sidle up to Speed, bobbing my rubber bound head, trying to remember Real Don Steele's cool radio words or words I've heard Speed and his group use on the playground.

"Hey," Fertig says from behind. "No cuts."

Ignore him, focus.

"*The Cherokees* is boss, man!" I nudge Speed with an elbow, get his attention.

"What?" He turns, tilts his head at my headband, sneers yellow buckteeth at me; from the golden crust at the corners of his mouth, I see he probably had crunchy delicious Amrikayi cereal for breakfast. Up close, his freckles are smooth, not raised like my dumb mole. Lucky. Gets freckles, buckteeth, sweet breakfast! His clothes have that harsh piney detergent smell mingled with sour sweat from playing, running with the confidence of being allowed. They all have it. It is all theirs; for them. With air-conditioned cool, he shakes his head and turns away.

"Beaner Boy no cuts! No ifs ands or buts! Get back here," Fertig orders.

What a maroon! Ignore him, Doc. Try spicin' up yer woids to the cool kid.

"*Cherokee Pee-pul,*" I sing to the back of Speed's head, "It's boss, you shet man?"

"What'd you call me," he shoves my chest, both hands, pushes me into Worm.

"Watch it, Beaner Boy," Worm shoves me back into Speed, swipes the curtain of hair from his eye to get a good look. "What in the world is that on your head?" he asks with a laugh.

"It's my - I'm Cherok-"

"Watch where you're going, Beaner," Speed with a punch to my gut that bends me over.

"I'm Cherok-" but can't breathe or straighten up, need to pretend my gut isn't twisting.

"What? You're choking?" smirks Worm. "That rubber band is choking off oxygen to your brain, Beaner Boy?" He pulls it, snaps it against my forehead. Stings. They laugh.

"I warned you," Fertig straightens me up as I land on him. "No cuts, no ifs ands or buts."

Second Bell? Been ringing a while? Shoving. Bent over. Spinning. Lovely Mrs. Mendelsohn chatting, laughing with Mrs. Lee. At me? Kids in line, tittering. At me? Gonjeshk flitting in the thick green summer leaves, chirping, laughing, maybe at me? I try to straighten up. Maybe they're all laughing at their own sunny joy; their trouble-free innocence, knowing who they are, why and where they are? Second Bell won't stop. Hot but shivering. Ringing but dull. Laughter is theirs; they own it; their right …Chirps, Titters, Trills, Bell, Spinning…

When I open my eyes, I see up. A portion of the sun blocked by Fertig's big face looking down over me; Pincus, Dud, familiar Mrs. Lee, angelic Mrs. Mendelsohn…orbiting, spinning.

"You OK, sweetie?" Glasses pulled back to hold her wild blonde hair, leaning over me, suede vest falling open, bare arms close enough to smell spice, tobacco, mint. Lovely *Jeannie*, weekdays at 5 Channel 13. Don't want her to see me like this; can't purr for her like this.

"OK." I rub my forehead, finger the indentation where my rubber band was.

"Lookin' for this," Fertig asks, twirling the rubber band with his index finger.

"Give it," I say, disoriented but aware enough to be embarrassed by them looking at me.

"Not so fast, sweetie," says Mrs. Mendelsohn as I try to sit up. "What's your name?"

Sweetie!

"Yes, I'm Cherok--"

"Man'cherian," offers Fertig before I get my chance to tell her who I am.

"Are you Mishel?" asks Mrs. Mendelsohn, searching her book. They all have the book.

"You're no Indian," Fertig twirls my rubber band. Girls nearby skip rope, chant rhymes. Pincus swipes the rubber band from Fertig, stretches it from his pinkie past his thumb to the tip of his index finger, points like a gun at Speed and Worm. As they run elegant slants and sharp cuts in a heated game of tag, Pincus shoots my Cherokee headband at them and we watch it land quietly a few feet away, trampled by the sneakers of the jump-rope girls. "You're Beaner Boy," Fertig continues as Mrs. Mendelsohn puts a check next to my name in her book, "not Cherokee."

"Billy Jack is Indian. Cher is half-breed. So, me too." I point to Pincus's army jacket, "Is he soldier?" I point to Dud's boots, "Is he cowboy? Are you Columbo," pointing to the crumpled blue windbreaker Fertig wears daily. "Is this Amrika land of freeds and braves? I can be Navajo like Billy Jack or half-breed like Cher or Cherokee People like the song, if I want."

"Give it up," smiles Pincus, "they're never gonna call you Cherokee."

"You are aka Polack," I remind Pincus. "He is aka Dud-"

"-cuz m'name's Dudley," says Dud, "a *Lee* after a *Dud*, see? Just a basic aka, no harm."

"They get good aka's," I ignore Dud, "Speed. Worm. Why I can't get aka Cherokee?"

"Cuz you're not an Indian, Beaner Boy," says Fertig.

"I'm no Mexicki too," I insist. "So why they get to say Mexicki or Beaner Boy to me?"

"Mexi*can*! And they're Pros, they do what they want."

"They are what?"

"Pros."

"Pros?"

"It's third grade, Beaner Boy. You know who they are," Fertig says. "Pros are your basic cool kids – long hair, fast runners, throw far, pick teams, say shut up whenever, throw stuff without getting in trouble. Even if they do, they make it look cool. They're your Pros."

Dud and Pincus share a nod, shrug, waiting to hear more of Fertig's playground laws.

"Now Pincus and Dud here," Fertig goes on, "they're your basic Nons. Around here, you're Pro or Non and don't need to be told which. You just know. You're your basic Non."

"No. You're your basic Non; I'm your basic Pro."

"Not *my* Non, just Non," Fertig corrects me. "My dad says Indians are aka *Indians* because when Columbus set sail on the ocean blue, he was looking for India, made a wrong turn and landed here and since Columbus didn't wanna admit he was lost, he called them Indians. You're from Eye-ran, closer to India Indian than Cherokee Indian. So maybe aka India."

"You think I'm Hendi? I'm no Hendi."

"Or go by *Injun*, like in Tom Sawyer," says Dud. "You'll still be a Non though."

They call him "Dud" - if they call him. They hold their noses when he walks by; throw food. He never says a word. He just watches them through stringy strands of his cinnamon hair, forces a gummy smile as he waits for them to move on.

"Werzidat," he'll mumble to me under his breath.

"Werzidat?"

"The Frito. Werzidat? Werdit land?"

Since the scarf incident, my friendship with Dudley aka Dud is me picking off food they throw at him. Otherwise, I'm not like him.

Pincus aka Polack, spooky smile, jet black hair, pink-ringed blue eyes, purplish pale skin – is a happy ghost. He and Dud whisper in code, tell jokes only they get, laugh when they get laughed at. Even Fertig can't figure them out, snorting along but obvious he isn't in on their jokes and is only laughing to stay in the mix. Pincus is like nobody else at school, me included.

Your basic Nons. Why am I thrown in with them? It's a new year. Fresh start!

"Now, your main Pros are Speed and Worm," Fertig continues. "Both are runty but feisty, ready to fight or yell to scare you off. If Speed ever puts up his dukes, they all take his side. That's how you know you're a Pro. Everybody takes your side no matter what."

"They prolly take his saad cuz they don' wanna be next," says Dud.

"Irregardless," says Fertig, "Pros rarely fight. Small kids are too scared and big kids don't bother because Pros are too fast and feisty to catch. Pros always win."

Fertig is the leader of the Nons. No freckles or buckteeth, but with his yellow hair, brittle as it is, and blue eyes, pale as they are, he looks like your basic Pro. Why isn't he? Is it the windbreaker? Pros don't need them; their skin glows with sweat, adorned with blood-caked scabs on happily scraped elbows and knees. Windbreakers are for trembling Nons with runny noses, wet coughs, black socks, hard shoes. Nons need protection from the elements; Pros don't.

Maybe it's how Fertig talks, his deep voice making heavy, engraved-in-wood words like he's doing the *Six O'clock News*: "Hello, Sports Fans, looks like another long line in the Caff today. Let's do our darnedest to not cut. No cuts! No ifs-ands-or-buts!" Pros don't talk like that. They use rapid-fire Amrikayi cuss words that burst from their seething teeth, rattle off their tongues like machinegun bullets. *"Fack!" "Facker!" ""Shet!" "Bowshet!" "Anss!" "Ansso!"*

Or maybe it's the aka. Fertig aka Kelly Smelly. "It was one time," he explained. "First grade, Room Two," nodding like a salty, burdened grownup. "It wasn't me, but they pointed at me anyway," sad nod at the ground, "so it's my aka. For now," exhale. "Someday I'll do something to change it," chalky blue eyes narrowing. "Something big. I'll show them."

But what is big enough to get Pros to stop calling him Kelly Smelly or me Beaner Boy? What cool cuss words would we have to learn?

How many scabs will we need? What heroic act, personal risk? Taking a bullet to save a classmate? Getting bit by snakes, like *Billy Jack*?

We go to Room 13, first day of third grade. Stand by our desks for *Pledge of the Lesions.*

"Whoa!" Fertig loud-whispers from behind as we clutch our hearts and face the flag. "It's *one nation under God*," he pronounces, "not *one day should Underdog*. Never fear," the leader of the Nons assures me, a pat on my shoulder, "We'll make an American outta you yet!"

In the beginning, animals roamed. In the backyard, frogs jumped from puddles to pebbly creeks. We caught them, stroked their slick green backs, watched them leap off our laps. Frogs didn't scare us. Ducks flew in and out of the yard. We let them hop on us, quacked with them, tapped their bills, their shiny green feathers. They were tolerant, but not friendly. Sometimes they'd snap their bills and waddle off. Ducks didn't scare us. Chickens ran wild in the yard and the road out front. They clucked and pecked at pebbles, the claws on their skinny wrinkled feet scratching at the dirt. Sometimes their feathers, light and soft as spider webs, floated where they had just been. Sometimes they were dinner, lying on the kitchen table, ready to be plucked and boiled. They'd flap for their lives and although they couldn't fly, they were fast. Sometimes they got to keep living. They were nervous and mean, but chickens didn't scare us either. Just sheep. Sheep didn't come around on their own. They were brought in at the end of a rope pulled by a bearded holy man in a white robe. When sheep showed up, so did new faces, lit by the gleaming purple dusk. They'd huddle over a steel tub full of water as the holy man lured the sheep with sad lilting melodies, enticing it to drink. When it leaned in for a slurp a hand held its neck and a long blade waited. There would be a struggle, pulling, confused bleats of desperation, pleading and, eventually, surrender. Unlike a frog, duck or chicken, a sheep never has a choice. With sheep, there would be a last breath; a final, vulgar bray petering out from the gash across its woolly neck before its entire body went limp. And there would be blood, clouding the water; blotting the coarse wool around the gash; soaking into the dirt; splattering on the blue and white cuffs of the holy man's robe; dabbed with a thumb on the forehead of a humbled guest of honor. Sheep

scared us. When Baba was leaving for Amrika, they brought one. Baba forced a smile, quickly wiping the blood from his forehead as he tried to exit the tight circle of well-wishers.

December 1971

Dark clouds overhead and that smell of eucalyptus leaves on the tall trees surrounding the playground gives me a nervous stomach ache. We're doing tetherball after lunch, an Amrikayi playground game. Last year I watched; this year I line up because you don't need to get picked for tetherball. You wait in line; you get to play. It's an easy game and I've memorized the rules:

The ball-on-the-rope is tied to the tall pole. Punch ball-on-the-rope and rope goes around until the ball hits the pole; you win. You punch one way. Guy you're versing punches other way. Only punch. No Holds. No Bus Stops. No Puppy Guards. No Ropies. If something goes wrong, you chant "Fawl Tio!" Game stops, situation gets examined and fixed. Play on.

I'm up, versing Speed, leader of the Pros, and before anyone says "Ready Set Go" he grabs the rope and flings the ball over my head sending the rope hurtling around the pole. Fast.

"Fawl Tio!" I chant. "No ropies! Fawl Tio!"

Nothing. Like I'm invisible. They cheer Speed on as he keeps smacking the ball around the pole, almost to the end of the rope. Nobody calls it, that he ropied to start the ball going.

After two more Fawl-Tio's I have to bus stop - catch the ball and hold. Had no choice.

Speed stomps over, sneering with perfectly Amrikayi buckteeth and freckles I wish were mine. He rides pop-a-wheelies on the black-top, against the rules, his light brown hair flowing behind him like the Amrikayi flag on Four-the-July. He plays Lilleeg ball and rock-a-roll drums. Knows all the words to *Cherokee People*. Still, ropies aren't allowed.

"No ropies!" I repeat and chant again. "Fawl Tio!"

"Don't you be goin' an' callin' Time Out on me!" Speed yells before starting a rant where, except for "*Facken*" which I hear plenty, I can't recognize any words shooting out of his mouth. The rest of them surround us and, led by Worm, start chanting "No T.O! No T.O!"

Energized by their support, Speed comes at me, a blur of sweaty knuckles and elbows; a storm I won't survive. I need to wait it out. I wrap my skinny brown elbows around my head like a helmet, tuck my chin, hands clasped at the back, biceps covering my ears so all I hear is my body. I wait for the storm to pass inside my cocoon.

Outside I hear taunts; sweaty kids yelling for my blood as Speed's knuckles pound my wrists and elbows. Charley's Horses will come soon, bruises right behind, but I'm safe for now. Even though I'm comforted by the gonjeshk songs in the stomachache trees, a human ally would be good. Pincus and Dudley are no help; they don't fight, prefer sitting under the stomachache trees, sharing secret jokes. Fertig? He only butts in where he's not wanted but is never around when you need him. I stare into the darkness as fists beat against my boney fortress.

Then I feel it. A jab breaks through, bangs the side of my head. I see the white of my own eyeball go black. Head feels like it might drift away. Shouts rise as I try to steady my neck, shouts as I force my spinning eyes straight. Shouts I sink in, drown in… Black.

"Breakitup! Breakitup!" Fertig's bellows break in. "He's had enough." I open my eyes.

But Speed only stops because he's tired from the punching, not because Fertig said to.

I get up. Heat from the blacktop seeps through the thin soles of my shoes and soggy socks, stinging the bottoms of my damp feet. Speed, Worm at his side, stands next to Fertig. Pincus and Dudley come off the fence to see what's up - can't tell if they're my allies, like Worm for Speed, or just waiting to see what happens next. I try to see straight, ignore the headache.

"You ropied," I finally yell, trying to calm my breath. Then I raise my voice high but not so high that it quivers: "No ropeeez! Ropeeez is Faaawwl Tio *gat-dammit sunvagun facken!*"

Worm giggles first. The others follow with snickers as I hear my own words smattering off their lips, in my accent. Pincus and Dudley chuckle too but more like they're trying to figure out what I said. Fertig stands silent, arms crossed.

Speed ignores my carefully worded complaint. He gets close, smells like warm oranges and sour candy: "No bus stops, Beaner Boy! Get off the court! Learn this: O.U.T. Yer out!"

I look out at the simmering crowd, shaking their heads, disgusted, muttering about how Nons and foreigners should learn the rules. I am both. And I know the rules. From watching, listening, memorizing. I want to scream back: *I know it the goddammit rules, fackens!*

"I did bus stop cuz you did ropie, so--"

"—that does it! I'll see you at the flagpole at 3!"

Flagpole at 3. Their ritual. After the bell they gather at a worn patch of grass by the flagpole, their flag hanging droopy on a rope at the top. I saw my first fight there last spring. Olders. Giants. Stanley, bulging blue eyes and frizzy orange hair that must've broken teeth on every comb that tangled with it, was a gravelly-voiced loner with muscles rippling from the cutoff sleeves of an old sweatshirt. Smiley was a big, pale, brown-haired kid with thick glasses. Word was his dad, a chauffeur who smiled for a living, taught him to smile at bullies. So they bullied him for smiling, aka Smiley. A normally timid kid, he finally lost his smile and yelled "Fine!" after Stanley's third shove. Like two bull elephants fighting to the death, they grappled under the flagpole, twisting, pulling, leaving their feet and hitting the grass with thuds that raised so much dust their giant bodies disappeared in a sunlit cloud. When it settled, it was Stanley who stayed down, blood trickling from his head, soaking into his frizzy orange hair.

They gather under the flagpole at 3 to see fights. They don't expect cracked heads or actual blood. Stanley got sent home to recover; Smiley got expelled. Neither was seen again.

"Now hold on," Fertig steps in. "Let's leave the flagpole out of this. That's penultimate. What's the point of the flagpole at 3 when you already let him have it here?"

They turn away, start walking to class. Speed and Worm leave too, shaking their heads.

"Penultimate?" Worm shakes his head as he walks away.

"Beats me," shrugs Speed. "What do you expect from Nons?"

"That's right, folks," Fertig tells the backs of their heads, "keep moving, Sports Fans." He does a Satisfaction Sniff like Barney Fife of *Sheriff Andy*, weekdays at 5 Channel 11, thinking he's saved the day. He doesn't realize they are moving on because the bell has rung, their hisses and titters hanging in the afternoon breeze. Fertig gives me a Disapproval Stare like Sheriff Andy gives his son Opie when he's done something wrong, like "I taught you better than that."

It's not supposed to be like this. On Amrikayi TV, like *Sheriff Andy*, when kids cheer the bully for shoving the new kid, something happens. One kid stands up to the bully, defends the new kid. One kid does something big, heroic! Maybe at great personal risk. The bully gets shamed into learning a lesson about dignity or honor. We can tell he's changed by the change in his tone, kids patting each other on the back, saying "No heart feeling?"

I don't need Fertig. Rather run with Speed and Worm, smell like oranges and sweat, on the winning side of the rope, not forced to learn "O.U.T." I walk past him, pick up my jacket and drag it behind me. Head throbs from the bump. I wish I was better, rising above, floating like grownups on TV using *Lifebuoy* soap. He follows, snapping disapproval with his tongue.

"Didn't need your help," I say, looking straight and keeping two steps ahead. "You think you did something big? You think they stop aka Kelly Smelly to you?"

"You'd be getting your ass kicked at the flagpole if it weren't for me. I risked a dogpile for you, Beaner Boy. You're welcome, that's all I'm gonna say."

A slight breeze dries the sweat off my neck, gets the flag on the pole to flap. There won't be a fight there today, that's true. But next time I'll do it different. Next time I'll be better.

Lunch is over.

The hill across the street from the playground is a rugged slope of overgrown shrubs, vines and dirt bumps. From the sidewalk it creeps up to the ridge lined by the backyards of Albatross Lane. From the playground, I can see the lone palm in our backyard, swaying like it did the day Maman first pointed it out. Some mornings we're late and I use the hill as a shortcut, my cold stiff hands grabbing onto the rough vines as I lower myself. When the bell rings at three, I scramble up the hill to get home. Some afternoons I sit on a bump to watch them on the playground. With distance their yelps sound small, like gonjeshk songs. The hill is my turf.

I bolt at the bell. Dark rumbling clouds cross the playground as I pass girls singing jump rope songs, boys picking teams, the tall brown walls of handball, orange hoops of basketball, to the street. The sun peeks through as I approach the hill ... lightning? Metallic glint hits my eye, menacing, too close to be from the sky. I look around, nothing. Start up the hill. Glint.

"Wait up! Hey, Beaner Boy, I said wait!"

Becker, a coldblooded fourth grader with dark curls and dead black eyes that lock no matter which way his neck swivels. His mouth bulges with jagged metal so thick his thin lips can barely close, forcing him to breathe through his half-closed mouth like an angry ape.

"Beaner Boy!"

He's had it in for me since that day in the bathroom with Moses and the Olders. On the playground, I catch him staring, like he sees what others don't, I'm trying to get away with something, I'm a fake. He lurks and circles, fixed on taking me down.

Stay calm. Make like you're in a rush and scram, but don't run. Never run.

"Man, I have to go to my house, Man, so..." I say from the base as I turn to the slope.

"Got a Mexikin joke," he says, running faster, crossing the street as I hesitate.

Well what're you waitin' for, Doc? Get movin'! But steady, cool.

"Man, I'm no Mexicki. My dammit mom's waiting, so..."

He gets close enough to catch me if I run; starts a riddle about a Mexicki and a bicycle.

"Yeah, I a'ready hear this joke, Man, so..." I climb, focus on the lone palm.

"Better watch out for Smiley, Beaner Boy," he sneers.

"Smiley?" I ask, confused.

"The Non who got expelled for cracking Stanley's skull last year; he roams this hill, cracking skulls with rocks. Surprised you ain't been attacked."

We're halfway up. Becker's metallic sneer glints from the muffled afternoon sunlight. I smell the damp golden weeds; soft dirt under my feet.

"I never seen Smiley. Maybe a different hill; maybe you mistaking."

"Nope. This is Smiley's hill. Everybody knows. You never saw him?"

"Nope." I've been lied to plenty in my life, I know what a lie looks like.

"Siddown and I'll tell you about it."

Friendly request? Threatening demand? What does he want?

Do what he says, so he won't chase or tink you're scared. Maybe you'll be friends.

We sit on bumps, stare out at the playground.

"First close your eyes."

Starting to breathe heavy, nostrils widen, stomach churns. Stay calm.

"You have to close your eyes to pass the test."

"Test?" Heart thumps. Test?

"Can't be with the cool kids if you don't pass the test. You're cool, aren'cha?"

"OK." Breathe. Crouch. Ready to run.

"You ready?"

"Y-" before I finish my nostrils get jammed with hunks of thick, cold mud. Packed in. Can't breathe. Becker laughs like a mad scientist, punches the boney ball of my shoulder.

I dig mud out of my nose, picking, blowing. Jump up, turn, Becker laughing as I casually claw up the hill, trying to not act panicky. If they sense panic, they chase.

"Wait," he yells after me. "That was part of the test! Now come look at this!"

I turn to keep an eye on him, sore from the punch and short of breath. Keep climbing.

Becker climbs too; his cupped hands holding something. "I got this for you." He opens his hand to a grey salamander squirming in his palm, kept in place by a dirt-caked finger pressing on its back. Aware of its situation, its tiny hands and feet claw at Becker's palm in a desperate, useless effort to escape. Its body thrashes to stay alive, but its dark eyes are cold and lifeless.

"You want my pet salamander? I need to get rid of it. My hamster tortures it."

I stiffen. Insides shivering, I start running, scraping my knees against dry shrubs, pricked by weeds catching my pant legs and socks. But I can't shake him and run out of breath.

"Sit," he insists. "You gotta see my pet salamander. Isn't it cute? But I can't keep it."

We sit, the salamander still in his palm, calmer; its narrow body moving; tiny tongue flipping. It has stopped clawing, maybe accepting its fate, awaiting an outcome it can't control.

"Keep it away from me!" I pant, trying to hide the pleading tone in my voice.

"Fine," he says. "You don't want it, so I'll show you a trick. You'll love this!"

I wonder if the salamander is praying, if it has surrendered and is getting itself ready for death. Or is it just a stupid animal? Its round eyes unmoving, no more pleading or prayer in them. If I take it from Becker, I can save it - this squirmy, slimy, terrified creature.

"OK, Beaner Boy, you don't want this little guy, so..." Becker holds its head between his fingers, points its face at me. I stare into its cold dark eyes; its mouth closed. It all unfolds at once: salamander's face between Becker's muddy thumb and finger, squeezing, mouth opening; gap between its beady black eyes growing like an expanding balloon; thumb and finger squeeze until they nearly touch; Becker's braces glistening in the afternoon sun; salamander's face, mouth, eyes disappearing behind a thick brown goo oozing from its forced-open mouth... A tremor runs from the pit of my stomach to my ears as I jump and charge past Becker.

"Don't you want a turn?" yells Becker. "I have another pet salamander right here," he says, reaching down in the dirt to dig up another innocent creature. "Your turn, Beaner Boy."

I flip myself over the fence and land down onto my backyard.

"You failed," Becker with a cool sneer wipes his salamander goo fingers on his jeans. "Thought you weren't a Non, guess I was wrong. I see you, Beaner Boy. I know you."

If I could've saved it but didn't, did I kill it? Poor, stupid salamander. Sin? What is the punishment for witnessing cruelty, for cowardice? I watched it struggle. Atonement between me and *Adonai* is on Yom Kippur. Cold dark eyes looking up at me, waiting. Was it a test? Could I have been a Pro if I killed the other one? Maybe I'll get another chance. Next time. Shudder, mud oozing from its mouth; glinting metal teeth. Shudder, churn.

In a rumbling dark, dead black eyes shine, a gaping mouth with metal teeth chases as I flounder up a river of mud. Dazed and frantic, my eyes open to darkness and rain pelting the roof. I hear Maman in the hallway.

"Is it still night?"

"It's a storm," Precious yells, jumping out of bed to join Maman. "It's day but night!"

"This deluge will cease everything," Maman in her purple robe slaps her hips in panic, hair mussed, flips the switch up and down until the lights come on. "What luck! But schools can't open in this darkness. You can't go anywhere."

"We're staying home?" Trying to hide my excitement, pretending to be mad like Maman at this damned deluge forcing us to stay home and avoid the jagged fangs of the playground.

Baba sticks to his routine; on the toilet ruffling his newspaper, smoke creeping up from the bathroom door. He comes out shaved, suit and tie on and sees us in the kitchen barefoot in our pajamas, slurping cereal while Maman fries eggs.

"What are you doing? Almost noon, get dressed."

"Are you crazy," Maman asks, "it's pitch black." She slides the spatula under the eggs and lays them on our plates. "They can't go to school. It won't even be open!"

"This is Amrika," Baba reminds Maman, "they have lights. Get dressed," he orders us.

"You can't leave me alone in this tempest," Maman says.

"Will the house slide down the hill?" Baba, irritated, sits and waits for his toast and tea. "Will it be nighttime forever? It's rain. It doesn't rain in Tehran?"

Maman pours tea, places toast beside the butter and sits. As Baba crunches and slurps, she takes small bites, chews slow, staring at the tablecloth, sipping her tea. When Baba finishes and gets up, she lifts the yellow receiver from the wall. She'll talk to Sweet Lady all day.

At least there's no playground on rainy days – no lining up, getting shoved and mocked for not knowing the rules. No Becker. When it rains, we stay in, play Concentration, Thumbs-Up-Seven-Up or sit by the bookshelves, reading and chatting on pillows. I have Shantay.

There's no blacks in Iran; I'm the darkest we have. Whenever I walked in on Maman and her friends playing cards, they'd sing "*Black one, black one, don't come to our house; we have a bride-in-waiting, she won't like it.*" I'd slink out, pretending to not be embarrassed. Amrikayi Blacks are not much darker than me. They get treated differently. Every morning most of them step off a bus called Normandie. Every afternoon Mrs. Mendelsohn yells "Normandie!" and they line up. Certain words or jokes are specifically about them and it's obvious they don't like it because they either get quiet or mad; if they get mad and fight, they get sent to Moses. Most stay quiet, closed, not involved. They don't raise hands. They answer questions in low whispers or shrugs. They ask to use the bathroom in mumbles, staring down. But not Shantay.

On the first day, she sat beside me. "Sap'nin'" her accent is like Dud's Texas cowboy, but fuller. She leaned in, her face so close I could see where the deep brown of her eyes ended and the creamy whites began. She had dried egg yolk at the corner of her mouth; told me a joke: "Adam tol' Eve his was a snake. Eve tol' Adam hers was grass 'n headlights. One naat Adam wakes up 'n tells Eve to turn on her headlights cuz his snake's crawlin' 'n her grass!"

When you don't understand but don't want to come off as stupid you say "I don't get it."

"His snake? Her headlights 'n grass? Y'don' gidit?"

I wanted to be friends. I could see she had wisdom. Egg yolk at corner of her mouth meant she likes runny eggs, same as me. Maybe likes to sop it up with bread like I do. Maybe we're cut from the same odd-shaped, cozy blanket. At least we're both brown. "I get it," I lied.

Shantay is all nerve and energy; her face glows when she talks; her voice like the best Amrikayi radio music. In class, she sits at the edge of her chair, cheeks high like royalty, almond shaped brown eyes darting, braids bouncing, her smooth flat nose sniffing out opportunity like class is a game of jump-rope and she's waiting for her opening to jump in and sing her rhyme. When we came to Amrika, everybody looked the same. I couldn't tell them apart. It's when you get to know them that you can tell them apart. I know Shantay. She smells like coconuts and sugar, and never calls me Beaner Boy. I have her and she has me.

The classroom is steamy and loud today, everyone talking about the storm and playing indoor games at lunch. The door opens and in walks Mrs. McLean, Room 14 - fourth grade.

"Well I wonder," she says with a big smile on her pale round moon face, her frog-green eyes twinkling, her plump hands resting on her knees, "if you Room 13 kids would enjoy having visitors from my Room 14 to share Rainy Day lunch. What do you think?"

"A terrific idea," says Mrs. Mendelsohn walking to join Mrs. McLean. "It would be fabulous having your fourth graders join us for lunch and teach us a few things, right class?"

Before we can answer, in through our door come the fourth graders of Room 14 with their squishy sneakers, throwing their wet raincoats into our coat closet, laughing at the lessons on our blackboard, pointing to our drawings and mobiles, collages they remember from last year like big brothers visiting old bedrooms. Olders, taller, sweaty necks, shaggy hair under the white fluorescent lights, glinting off their jagged metal... menacing ...teeth...

His bulging mouth and cold eyes scan the room and land on me. Our eyes lock; he flashes a silver smile, nods. Friends? Was the salamander sacrifice an initiation? Does he have me? Do the Olders have me?

The classroom steams with hot chatter as the rain falls in heavy drops outside. Shantay and I head to the window to watch. We grab the sunflower pillows on the orange shag by the bookshelf, pulling books. She likes hard books, *Phantom Tollbooth*, *Tom Sawyer*. I like easy, *Chicken Little* and *Little Red Hen*. She says we should read big kid books to learn big words. I say little kid books are cozier on rainy days, like being under a blanket.

"You read baby books?" Becker's face hangs over us like a glaring streetlamp.

"Hey man," I look up at him.

He nods, turns to Shantay, "can't you and your friend here read?"

"We jes' talkin' and lookin' at pictures, thank you," says Shantay, face turning from Becker, waving him off with the back of her hand - without a hint of fear.

"So you can read real books?"

"Excuse me?" Shantay turns to Becker. "Yeah, we can read, dum-dum. We in third!"

I wish she wouldn't call him dum-dum. An Older; wouldn't want to choose. She bends her neck toward him, cocks it, pushes her chin out. He throws sharp eyes at her. My stomach...

"He's doing joke," I tell her, then to Becker, "Right, man? We just read for fun. Ok?"

"Why it's ok?" says Shantay. "It ain't ok. He don't know me. I ain't jivin' wit' him."

"Beaner Boy reads English?" Becker smirks, ignoring Shantay. "You know these books are in English, right, Beaner? Not Mexikin."

I turn to Shantay, then Becker. "Sure, man, but I tell you a'ready I'm not Mexicki."

"Name's Myko, dum-dum," Shantay yells at Becker, "an' he ain't no Meskin. He Araybyan. Right, Myko? Y'all even know where Araybya is, dum-dum?"

Dum-dum again; I should say something.

Keep yer trap shut, Doc. Watch and loin.

"Where the rich sheiks and Araybyan Nights and oil come from. Y'all heard of it?"

Stomach twists, caught in the middle. Becker the Older, maybe sacrificed a salamander to initiate me; Shantay, my cozy, egg-yolk loving comrade. Don't want to choose. I whisper to her, "Don't say to him dum-dum. Also, I am Irani from Persia. Not Arab."

She leans in to me, whispers warm in my ear. "They ain't the same?"

"No."

"But I'm closer, right? Araybyan is closer than Meskin? He a dum dum, right?"

I stare.

"Right?"

"I don't get it," I say in a panic.

"You're confused," interrupts Becker, "Beaner Boy is a beaner. That's why he's Beaner Boy. So, Beaner Boy," he turns to me, "*can* you read English, or just looking at pictures?"

"It's just for funny," I look up at him, back at Shantay. "Rainy Day lunch reading, OK?"

Shantay shakes her head, disappointed. She isn't scared of him. The other girls, the other black kids, they all have her so she can talk like that to Becker. Who has me?

She has you, Doc. Remember?

Becker pulls a big book from the shelf, thin pages, no drawings, opens it randomly and brings it down to me. His dirty salamander finger is pointing to a spot in the middle.

"Quarter says you can't read that word."

I look where he is pointing. A long word, letters clustered together at the tip of his dirt-caked finger – chew scabs at the edges. Nine letters, twice more consonants than vowels, every third letter a vowel. Never seen it; can't rely on memory. Have to use the foolproof way – letter by letter, sound it out. I can win. A quarter, their biggest coin, heavy, thick, their first king on it, the one with the wig. Father of their country.

"Take the bet!" says Shantay. "You know that word," she says. "Here we go, Myko, here we go!" she chants, clapping her hands. "Here we go, Myko, here we go!"

I don't want to disappoint her. Stomach bubbling.

First part, "spa," easy. Last part, "etti," also easy. The middle "gh" … the rule is "gh" makes "f" like "laugh." "Spaffetti?" No. But "spaggetti?" "Espagetti" in Farsi. So, new rule, sometimes "h" is useless, like "ghost." Another pointless use of letters Amrikayi put in their words; you have to accept their rules, even when they don't make sense. "Spaghetti."

You got it! 'Dem's the rules, and you win!

"Spa-ghetti!" I breathe, try to sound casual. "Spaghetti," I say again, looser, like I knew it all along, didn't spend time figuring it out letter by letter, word-rule by word-rule. Like "dumb of you to challenge me with such a word; maybe hard for you so you think it's hard for me." That's what I try to sound like when I say "Spaghetti!" a third time. Exuberance seeps out but not enough to spill the "Spaghetti you *facken shet ansso fack*" I feel inside. Stomach easy.

"Y'all can pay up now!" Shantay points at Becker. "Y'all got that quarter wit'cha?"

Becker glares at her, nods at me - a nod I know well; Maman does it when I do something bad but she can't do anything about it in the moment; like the time I stayed in the movie line with her instead of sneaking in while she sweet-talked the ticket-taker to distract. Precious went under the velvet rope, excited to carry out Maman's plan. I stayed put, afraid of getting caught. The nod means, "I'm dealing with this idiot ticket-taker now and can't do anything but will deal with you at a more convenient time; when I do, be assured it will be with appropriate measure." That's the nod Becker does as he reaches into his pocket to find the quarter he lost to me.

"Das'right," Shantay keeps it up, "Dat'll be twenny-fye cint, mm hmm! Pay it up!"

Becker ignores her, but for how much longer before he does something that will force me to choose sides? He stares at the ceiling, feeling inside his pocket. Checks his other pocket with some force. It scares me because he could decide to hurt either or both of us out of frustration.

"I'll owe you," Becker flashes his metal. "OK, Beaner Boy? My spic buddy?" Smile or sneer? Can't tell. Friends? He has me? Because he lost to me? What's 'spic'?

Don't ask so many questions, Doc. Seems like you got the upper hand today. Leave it.

Can't I be friends with both? Shantay smiles at me, her eyes richer; a sweet, deep brown like the classiest marble in the bag. Her smile, warm and soft. She sees me. Like this. She has me. At least Shantay has me. But Becker?

"Sure yes," I tell Becker, feeling generous. "Pay later, man. I have you."

He tilts his head in confusion.

Shantay and I don't talk the rest of the afternoon, but as Mrs. Mendelsohn reads *Island of the Blue Dolphins*, we glow with warmth, bask in each other's air, lean toward each other. I sneak looks from the side of my eyes. By the time the bell rings, we can barely talk.

"OK, Myko," she mumbles meekly. "See you tomorrow?"

We're dark, sloppy egg eaters. Becker hates her. What do Pros think of her? My cheeks feel hot as I gravitate toward her, her coconut skin.

Careful, Doc. They're all watching.

"Tomorrow."

⚽ ⚽ ⚽

Maman doesn't like us to wear t-shirts to school, especially if they don't fit. "Only derelict hamalls or Amrikayi wear undershirts with nothing over them," Maman says. "We wear undershirts proper, under a shirt." She feels the same about cowboy pants. Before school started, I asked her about buying Amrikayi clothes. She looked up from her latest Zaneh-Ruz, "I shit on their cowboy pants and cotton shoes! You are dirty cowboys? We are Amrikayi?"

Maman prefers shirts with buttons, collars and cuffs. Most of our clothes are hand-me-downs from Maman's big sisters; that's how Sweet Lady raised them. When your husband dies and you have five girls to raise, you get maximum use from your clothes. Our clothes have been worn by our oldest cousins to our older cousins to us. Most of my clothes are older than me. But like the green, red or yellow khoreshts Maman cooks for dinner, like the Hebrew prayers we chant before bed, like gondi on Shabbat, hand-me-downs are tradition, who we are. In Tehran, it was normal. In Amrika, it is shabby and embarrassing – just one more thing I need to hide.

So when Maman went shopping at a new discount store on La Cienega before school started and bought a box of t-shirts, it was weird.

"For Rosh Hashana. Seventy percent off," Maman showed off to Baba. "Like free!"

"Certainly," Baba replied with a salty smirk. "Like profit. Mobarak!"

They are an odd shade of pale, odd-sized, splattered with images of crooked stars. Maman wouldn't know that Pros also wear odd-sized t-shirts to school.

"That's what they're best at," Fertig had explained during one of his daily lessons. "They wear what they want, the larger the better, down to the knees. It works for them. I can't. My Mom says I'm too tall for that silliness. Being well-built is both blessing and -"

"- their moms say is OK to wear big shirts?" (If I don't interrupt Fertig once in a while, he'll spend all recess talking about why he can't be a Pro and how he's better off as a Non.)

"Moms? You still don't get it, Beaner Boy," Fertig chortled so hard his misted my forehead. "They don't care what their moms think. They wear what they want!"

Today is my turn. I slip on a star-shirt; it flows to my knees. Cool, Mean, Lowdown. Bucktoothed (practically), freckled (if I had a hundred more moles instead of just the one); growl their cuss words, their way. "Faw-cken she-yit! Anss! Muth-facken-titi-sacken-tubaw-betch!"

"Take it off," Maman says, standing in the doorway. "I bought those for when you grow, when they fit. Wear the green and yellow checkered one," she orders me. "It's clean."

"Can't I wear this?"

"No."

"Why did you buy them if we can't wear them?"

"I didn't know they were so big. They are for under sweaters. They don't fit yet. I may send them to your New York cousins and they can send them back when you two get bigger."

"Hand-me-ups? Can't we ever wear new stuff? These have stars on them, which means they were made to be worn over, not under anything. I can tuck it in if you like."

Maman turns to the kitchen, ready to interrupt Baba's morning and have him settle it.

"Fine," I say.

When she goes, I tuck the star-shirt into my pants, put the checkered shirt she wants over it and button up. Cool. Mean. Lowdown.

I memorize a joke to tell my new pal Becker. He'll tell the Olders and Pros. Pincus told it to me. I don't get it but Becker will. Sargeant Friday from a TV show I haven't seen: "Dark night. I am with my secretary, driving my police car on a case. Raining. We get a flat. I pump. She pumps. I pump, she pumps. Then we get out to change the flat." That should get me in.

In the bathroom before the bell, I unbutton Maman's checkered shirt, peel it off, untuck the star-shirt, tie the checkered around my waist, check mirror: eyes not too scared; no triangle of fear eyebrows; nose not flaring in panic; lips loose and easy. Cool. Mean. Lowdown. Pro?

On the playground, I try a Pro sneer, chest out, show off my new shirt. A couple of them look. But … laughing. Now pointing. They do this thing with their fingers: one index finger shaving the top of the other index finger, chanting: *Beaner Boy and Shantay sittin' inna tree.* I've heard it before. Nobody named in the chant is ever happy about it, so I know it's not good. I focus on the joke, looking for Becker, maybe even Speed, leader of Pros. He'd like it too.

Shantay walking toward me doesn't look happy. Don't feel like seeing her. Yesterday's sweet connection has vanished. She looks weird - braids aligned, old rubber bands replaced by new ones with red balls. Lips shiny. She looks unfamiliar, not warm – no dried egg. I'm eager to find Becker and tell the joke before I forget it. I try to avoid her.

"--Ess-cuse me!" She has an angry rhythm in her step, one shoulder back, the other jutting forward, pointing a finger at herself. "D'ju tell people you go wit' me?"

I hesitate. Tilt my head. Yesterday we were mates; now...? "I don't get it."

"Don't play wit' me! Why they singin' 'k-i-s-s-i-n-g' 'bout us? What you said?"

She's so mad it's like she's pretending, like being named in the "k-i-s-s-i-n-g" chant makes her more important. I'm the one wearing the large t-shirt. I'm the one who doesn't care what Maman thinks. I'm Pro, not her. But I play along, acting riled. Rumors and gossip happen when you're a Pro. Can't be helped. This is me now.

"This is the *hell*!" I shout at Shantay, voice cracking. "This is the *goddamit*! The *shet*!"

"What you told ever'body?" Shantay demands. "What you told 'em 'bout me wit' you?"

I tug on my star-shirt, make sure it's down to my knees, tighten my lips around my teeth so they look like buckteeth, tighten my face. Chin out.

"I don't do *shet*!" tapping my chest with my finger. I call up words I've heard Pros use when they're hot, words I've been hearing Baba use lately when he and Maman fight and he wants to add legitimacy by yelling in English to show he's figured it out and she still hasn't.

"I never in this *goddamit hell* life say those *shet* stuffs!" A rush of heat on my cheeks.

"Did you curse?" Mrs. Mendelsohn opens her door. "If you use that language again, I'll send you to the principal. Is that clear? I thought you two were friends. What happened here?"

Shantay and I cold stare each other. I hate her shiny lips, the red balls at the end of her cleaned up braids. The bell rings and we go in without another word.

Still raining. I practice sneers and jaw-juts, waiting for Mrs. McLean to bring her class again so I can strut over to give Becker an elbow nudge, tell him the joke. Pros will see me with an Older, joking, elbow nudging.

"Want me to teach you cards," Fertig stands over me, shuffling a deck.

"No," my eyes fixed on the classroom door.

"You're just going to sit here watching the door?"

"Yes."

Fertig moves on, shuffling, looking to bother someone else. Dudley and Pincus share whisper jokes. The Pros lay palms on their table, slapping the backs of each other's hands. Their ruckus gets so loud Mrs. Mendelsohn has to go over. Everyone watches; all eyes on the Pros, always. I tug on my shirt, make sure it's long; I tighten my lips inward, bucktoothy...

You don't wanna read wit' her, Doc?

Forget Shantay! I could care that she's on the other side of class playing Flapjacks with her friends. Laughing loud, pretending to be having fun without me, I could care, or... I could care less... or, wait, how does it go? I couldn't care less . . . can't remember which you use when you want to say you don't care, but whichever it is, I don't. I *goddamit* don't the *shet*! I keep watch over the classroom door, rehearsing the joke. But Mrs. McLean's frog-green eyes and moon face never

67

show. I consider telling the joke directly to Speed and Worm.

Easy, Doc. You got the joke memorized, but what about delivery? It's all in the delivery.

Maybe not. Wouldn't want to mess it up. Wouldn't want them to see me like that. I stay at my desk and pretend to be thinking important things, in case anybody is watching.

When the bell rings I don't say "see ya" to Shantay and she ignores me too, runs to her friends to get on the Normandie. The hill is too muddy so I walk the long way with Precious in tow. Still Mean and Lowdown, in no mood to chat with a first grader; worse than a Non.

"Didn't Maman say to not wear that shirt without something over it," he asks.

"*Goddamit anss*, I wear what I want," I yell in full-throated Pro-tinged Amrikayi. We don't use Amrikayi cuss words at home. But today I could -- or couldn't -- care less.

Precious stares up at me – fairer face tilted; lighter brown eyes confused. "You're not supposed to say bad words," he reminds me in Farsi. "Maman said. Baba will be furious."

"It's not of your bizwax, *ansso!*"

Dat oughta shut his trap, eh Doc?

Maman is in the kitchen cooking dinner so I slink down the hall to take off the star shirt before she sees it. Precious heads in the other direction. "He wore the shirt you told him not to, Maman, and when I told him he wasn't allowed he said Amrikayi bad words, over and over!" Then he yells down the hall, "Did you think I'd let you get away with it?"

I storm back up the hall, shirt untucked, flapping in a breeze created by the force of my storming, a Lowdown strut. "*Fack* to you, *anss!*" I scream, pointing my finger. "Not of your *bizwax, facker ansso tuba beetch!*"

"Then *Facker* to yourself, Mester *fack ansso*," Precious unleashes his own Amrikayi cuss words with force, like he's been waiting, holding his fire to stick to family rules. We both let loose everything we have been holding back. This is our first fully Amrikayi conversation.

"Chee?"

Almost forgot about Maman, but Precious and I are too far gone, unleashing anger that has probably been sitting inside us for months.

"*Fack* to you!"

"You're *shethead*!"

"Stupid *jackansso*!"

"*Facken mother sacken tubal betch*!"

"Basseh," screams Maman. "Basseh digeh!"

We grab, pull, sweat. The green veins in his soft, pale neck bulge, his light brown eyes widen as he screams in the hoarse voice he uses when he plays. Maman between us, separating, making sure we don't tear each other apart. She drags us down the hall, throws us on our beds, pulls off my shirt, tugging until she finds a snag and tears into it with her fingernail.

"This is why you don't wear undershirts. Only the hamalls talk like this. When I tell Baba he'll tear both of you apart. We talk like this now? We've gone and turned Amrikayi now? We are Irani! We don't talk or act like Amrikayi! He will tear you to bits, just wait. Now put on a proper shirt and both of you sit here and wait for him."

I sit on my bed, panting. Precious on his. We don't look at each other, both sweaty, catching our breaths, wondering how bad it will be when Baba gets home. When I hear the front door, I jump up to close our door. Precious and I stare at each other in fear, no time to maintain a feud. Maman's voice is muffled but she immediately starts in. Our door opens. His face is shadowy from the long day. Thick dark brows furrowed. Black glare. Flashing his furious "F" - sinking his big upper teeth deep into his lower lip "FFF". His anger is unpredictable.

"What have you been saying?" He towers over me.

"Nothing!"

"*Fack*!" shouts Precious. "He said *Fack*!"

For that bit of tattling, Precious gets Baba's thick palm across his cheek. "Khaffekhoon!" he thunders, turning back to me. But soon as I see his hand go up, I know where it will land so I dash. He manages to clip the back of my ear as I bolt out of the bedroom, up the hall, Maman, Precious and Baba stumbling behind. It's a sweaty blur, Precious and I evading Baba, running around or behind furniture, contorting to avoid his wild swipes, yelling "No!" or "He said it too!" as Maman, sharp-eyed, clutching her blouse, keeps asking Baba the same important question which only enrages him more: "*Facker* yanee chee*?* *Facker* yanee chee*?*"

When it's over, everyone is beat. My rosy hot, tear-stained cheeks puffed, huffing for air as I lay crumpled in a corner behind the couch while Precious whimpers in spasms on the chair. In the kitchen, Maman ladles steamy white rice onto a platter and tomato-okra khoresht into a serving bowl, dishes and silverware clanking down on the table. Baba goes to change, returns in his slippers and striped pajamas; everything back to normal but quieter, like after a thunderstorm.

At the table, silence. Maman pours khoresht over rice. Precious pours water for me and him. Baba digs in. We eat. Chew. Swallow. Again. "Water," Baba grumbles and Maman lifts the glass pitcher, pours. "Hrrmmph," is his "Thank you." It's Maman who breaks the silence with the question she never got an answer to: "*Facker* yanee chee." That does it.

"Basseh!" His heavy hand grabs the edge of the table, flips, letting fly white rice, red khoresht, water pitcher, cups, dishes, silverware jangling, all crashing down onto the Garden of Life design of the Persian rug. Baba roars hot, profanity laced words - spit and rice fly off his teeth, eyes bulge, face red - about Maman repeating a vile word even after he ignored her the first four times. As he thunders on, Maman, Precious and I get on our knees, cowering and cleaning. Maman, looking less elegant than usual in her purple robe and bare feet, picks rice flecks and okra chunks with her long, manicured fingernails in silence. Dark clouds rumble in my heart; thunder pounds my head. Stomach on fire. I did this. Mean. Lowdown.

"See ya next year!" Fertig goes table to table, even to Mrs. Mendelsohn's, waiting for them to get it. Last day before Christmas vacation. I'm still feeling low from last night. Outside, the rain finally let up but it's still wet so Mrs. Mendelsohn is having us play inside, arts and crafts, games, running around; an all-day Rainy-Day Lunch before our two-week break.

"Get it?" Fertig elbows me. "When we come back, it'll be 1972, but today it's 1971! So next time we see each other, it'll be next *year*. See ya next *year*. Get it?"

Like everyone else, I ignore him, staring across the room. She looks normal today. Still has the fancy rubber bands tying her braids, but her lips are un-shiny, smile easy, laughing with friends. No longer pretending to be a grownup in a Saturday afternoon black-and-white movie about affairs with men in hats. She moves past me, back and forth, grabbing sticky letters and shiny stars for her poster, ignoring me each time she passes. The fourth time, she looks my way.

"Oh hey, Miko," she says with a quick smile, keeps moving.

Hearing her normal tone, I exhale. She turns, faint smile on her perfectly un-shiny lips, a trickle-finger wave. I smile back. She whispers to her friends, walks towards me.

"So whatchu doin' for Christmas?"

I don't know if she knows about Hanooka and I don't know how to pronounce it in Amrikayi. It'll sound weird out of my mouth if I say it to her the way we say it at home.

"Wanna hear a joke?"

"You got a joke? Finally! Your turn." She smiles big. "OK, hit me."

I haven't seen Becker since I beat him at spelling, so I'm probably not going to tell it to him this year. I'm too scared to tell the Pros. I won't tell Fertig; he'll lecture me on how to tell it better, who the real TV characters are, the history of flat tires. I might as well tell the joke to Shantay; at least when she explains it to me, she won't act like she's above me. I tell it.

"Get it?"

She throws her head back, eyes shut, mouth open so wide her royal cheeks disappear as she sends a hearty chortle to the ceiling. "Ya'aah gid it! First dey pump, den dey fix de flat!"

She notices my flat smile, my outside-candy-store stare. "Want me to explain it?"

Afterward, she goes back to her poster: Rainbows. Peace signs. Stars in a smoky sky. "Pollution Solution" in bubble letters. I stay at my desk, watch Pros trip unsuspecting Nons for laughs. Nons get up slow, rub their knees, force a laugh. Even say "No heart feeling" like it was their fault the Pros tripped them. Shantay runs past me to get stuff from the arts and crafts table. "Hey Miko" she says each time she passes, "I pump she pumps! Gid it?" Feels good, warm and happy to be back to normal with her. Being Mean and Lowdown can be tough.

"Beaner Boy," Worm sits beside me in Shantay's chair, so close I smell the peach shampoo in his silky black hair. It isn't every day Worm - a trickster who snickers like Muttley the wicked prankster dog on *Whacky Races*, weekdays at 3 Channel 9 – talks to me. Not since he named me "Beaner Boy." Maybe they're finally seeing me.

Stay cool. Breathe. Not too eager.

"Hey."

"Say, I got an idea." Even when we're in the middle of a rainstorm, Worm's face still smells like the salty, sweaty sun.

I look for a perfectly Pro word: "Terrific!"

His dead eyes makes me think I used it wrong, but the smirk stays. "Next time Shantay runs by," he whispers, "stick your foot out to send her on a trip." His chipped front tooth makes his smirk extra wicked. "She'll slide across the floor! Hilarious!"

"I don't get it."

"Like *The Three Stooges*, Beaner Boy. You know *The Three Stooges*, right?"

"Yeah, I get *The Three Stooges*. I love them. But Shantay probably doesn't get them."

"Everyone gets *The Three Stooges*. She'll laugh."

"Is this for sure?"

"Oh this is for sure, Beaner Boy. Trust me! She gets it. She's gonna get it. I just sent Fertig on a trip and he's still laughing." Worm points to Fertig on a chair rubbing his knee and getting ready to stick his own foot out to send Dudley on a trip. I want to believe him. I want him to stop calling me Beaner Boy. I want to do something big. Be a Pro before next year.

Don't do it! We only trip 'de enemy. She won't get it.

She's never mentioned *The Three Stooges*. She might get mad. Like when they step on the back of your shoe so it comes off and everybody sees the hole in your sock - the Flat Tire. Or the one where as you take a step, they kick your foot up from behind and you land funny. Their foot goes under yours, makes your foot go up. Gets me in with the Pros. They'd see me, floating high like *Lifebuoy* soap...floating...

floating? My foot…Worm's dirty sneaker under it, kicks it up…wicked snicker…lifting my foot, pushing it…out…Shantay gliding by…I see her. *Thwack!* "Oomph!" Her mouth falling open…hands out to break her fall… tumbling… spilling stars, red balls on her rubber band braids rattling… Shantay splayed on the floor.

Wicked giggle like he's being tickled. "Wupsee!" he whispers, evil Muttley snicker.

Shantay doesn't get up right away, staying on the floor for long seconds.

"Good one, Beaner Boy," Worm laughing, patting my shoulder. "Nice trip!"

Shantay sits up, cheeks wet, eyes crinkled, head tilted at me in disappointment.

Mrs. Mendelsohn jumps from her chair. "Well help her up," she yells as she runs over.

I'm frozen, eyes fixed on Shantay. I see Mrs. Mendelsohn pick her up, put her on a chair with her leg sticking out. "You OK, sweetie?"

They look my way as Worm whispers, "Beaner Boy tripped her." Shantay wipes tears from her cheeks, tells Mrs. Mendelsohn her knee is sore. Like this, they see me.

The only safe spot to stare at is down, the floor, eyeballs drying out staring at the tile, scuffmarks, paper bits, pencil shavings, stars - eyes throb to the pounding of my guilty heart. Yom Kippur is the day we think of those we hurt. We dress in silence, walk to temple, confess, ask forgiveness. We don't need to explain our Sins or why we did the bad things we did. We all have the same reasons, same Sins. They're written in the Book. We recite them in alphabetic order, repent the same way, because we all Sin the same. So why can't I apologize to Shantay?

"You listening?" Mrs. Mendelsohn has been talking. "Why would you hurt a friend?"

The chattering and chuckling. White lights buzzing on the ceiling. Shantay catching her breath in fits and starts. All to the pounding of my guilty heart. I avoid Shantay's eyes.

I can tell on Worm; it was his idea, his foot lifted mine and pushed it. I could get him in trouble. Big and heroic? Great personal risk? Would telling on a Pro get me in? Or I can cover for Worm; he'll owe me; and that'll make me a Pro; and lose Shantay for good.

'Tink fast, Rabbit.

"She was running," I hear myself say, eyes still fixed on the floor. "I didn't see her."

"You stuck your foot out right in front of her," says Mrs. Mendelsohn. "Go sit in the corner," she orders. "That's how you'll spend your last day before Christmas break."

I sit on the Trouble Chair in the Trouble Corner facing the wall as they go back to their innocent trills and joyful shrieks, their sounds, their right.

"So, why'd you trip her? It hurts getting tripped, you know." Fertig saunters over, shuffling a deck of cards. "You were trying to make friends with Worm, weren't you?"

"Not of your bizwax," I simmer, "Go lost." He seems to enjoy it when I mess up.

"Beeswax, not *bizwax. Get* lost, not *go* lost." Fertig's booming voice sounds annoyed for a change, "At least say it right for cryin' out loud. Never mind. See you next year. Maybe."

I'm bent over on the Trouble Chair, holding my stomach. Next year there will be no purring for the lovely Mrs. Mendelsohn; no playing with Shantay. No more corrections from Fertig.

On Sunday, January 16, 1972, a crew of Amrikayi cowboys in a colossal boat killed a group of dolphins. Or were they in a tank? I'm not clear on that part. Starback, I'm hearing, the courageous captain of the conquering cowboys, "whipped greasy dolphins." I'm hearing. The cowboys "creamed those jived . . . cookies?" I hear. One year in, and I'm still trying to listen.

It's all over the playground this morning before first bell. Excitement. Everybody, Pros, Nons, Olders, all talking fast as white puffs of brisk morning air burst from their mouths. New words dart and whirl around the blacktop circling my ears. One year in, and I still need to catch and turn new words over, under, sideways, inside and out. Still need to listen and memorize.

"Slaughter." "Starback." "Cowboys." "Dolphins." "Greasy." "Zonk."

Chatter. Phrases. Tones. Accents. The way words leave mouths; lips under teeth over tongues. I plan on repeating it exactly like them.

One year in, but on the cold hard blacktop beneath the grey diesel-and-eucalyptus sky, I am still standing behind their crouched backs, trying to breathe the air they breathe, expel the words they expel; still leaning at their huddled packs to better glimpse their excited faces, to find mine among theirs - brown neck, large nose, eager ears burning to break their codes teeming with secrets, their language of inclusion.

A Super event. Amrikayi football. Slaughtered Dolphins versing Champion Cowboys. The famous Doozie Defense with Captain Starback's rifle creaming cubie greasy stuffed zonks.

"They stuffed Zonk like a cookie."

Cookie? You sure dat's right, Doc?

"That Zonk's a jive cookie!"

"Starback deserved that MFP."

That's toothpaste, Doc. "Colgate with MFP!"

Nodding important, I stare at their marble cheeks, find an opening, wedge my way in.

"Yeah, Starback sure needed that MFP, oh man! Dirty teeth!"

They stop. Turn. Tilt. I wait. Clap on the back? Slap-me-ten? "O'right" or "Righton?" They turn back to their wonderful chatter in perfect blue cowboy pants and worn-in sneakers.

"Oh he needed MFP o'right," I try again, "Fluoride! Colgate is best! Oh man! Righton!" I extra-chuckle, I clap my hands together and rub, never daring to clap any of their backs. I over-chuckle a little, almost lose control, teary-eyed.

Easy on the chuckle! Wait for a nod, a glance, an "I hear ya, man."

"MVP, Beaner Boy, not MFP," Fertig from the back fence, that annoying sneer when he catches me using words wrong. We haven't talked since "last year." "MFP is fluoride in toothpaste. MVP is Most Valuable Player, awarded to the best player after a game. Did you watch *Super Bowl* yesterday? I watched with my dad at his bachelor pad. It was penultimate!"

I haven't missed him, pretend I don't hear him, or care. Still, I take note, memorize.

"Yeah, *duh*! I watched Super Ball," I lie, turning to get back to the huddled Pros, but the bell rings and they break up. I was almost in, if only that *jive cookie* Fertig hadn't barged in.

"Let's head in, Little Buddy," he guides me by my shoulder. "I'll explain at lunch."

The food in the steamy Caff may smell rotten but is Amrikayi enough for me to always be hungry for it. Orange cheese melted on pale bread grilled in rancid butter; orange spaghetti warming in steel pans; shredded potatoes sweating in plastic bags poured under hot orange lights. The smell hovers, an odor so ingrained in the Caff nobody notices how nauseating it is; because it is theirs, and I want some. I want to eat their food, chirp their words, know their facts.

"You kidding me? Super Ball was great oh man, stuffing Zonker! You saw?"

Nothing. I'm talking to backs of heads. Fertig approaching; I keep talking, mingling.

"Ain't that a kick in the head? Cubie the Starback MVP slaughters the Zonker."

I keep my face away from Fertig and turn to face the metallic glint.

"I didn't know Mexikins knew football; thought you guys liked soccer," jagged smile.

"Yeah, but I'm not Mexicki" chuckle to soften him up. "You betcha I get football. Yesterday's Super Ball! Zonker's greasy Dolphins got slaughtered," I offer. "Jived dammit."

"Super *Bowl*," says Fertig. "Super *Ball* is a synthetic rubber ball with space-age bounce."

"Let's bet on tonight's game," says Becker, ignoring Fertig. "Dolphins can come back but I bet the Cowboys win again. How about dubbler-nothin' on the quarter I owe?"

All morning I listened. It all included the word "yesterday": "Cowboys creamed Dolphins *yesterday*." "Starback was MFP *yesterday*." "Doozie Defense slaughtered *yesterday*." I pretend-saw it myself, on my pretend-color TV. Yesterday! Like the rest of them.

"But Super Ball was...yesterday," I say, hoping I sound casual. "Cowboys creamed."

His hard eyes screw in, lips close over his jagged metal. He puts his hand on my shoulder and holds it so I can't move. "That was Game 1, my spic friend. Super Bowl is a best of three. Miami wins Game 2, there's a tiebreaker. You knew that, din'cha, Beaner Boy?"

76

My am what? Tyraker?

"Now hold on a darn minute!" Fertig keeps not minding his biz-beeswax. "Super Bowl was yesterday. Great game. Penultimate."

Becker looks at Fertig. "You're using that word wrong. Now get lost," he hisses. "I'm talking to my favorite spic friend and you're bothering us. Beat it."

Second time he said 'Friend' about me and corrected stupid Non Fertig. He has me.

"Beat off," I say to Fertig.

"It's a sucker bet, Beaner Boy," pleads Fertig. "He's taking you for a ride."

"You heard him," says Becker with a silvery glint. "Beat. Off."

"The Super Bowl is one game, Beaner Boy," Fertig insists.

"Beat off!" I am finished with leader of the Nons. Becker the Older, the Pro, has me.

"Your funeral, but I warned you. By the way, spic is a bad word." He goes.

"Where were we," Becker fixes on me. "Oh yeah, our bet. Now don't get me wrong, Miami's good, but I'm gonna bet Cowboys."

My am what? Lost again. His forehead cocked forward like a fist, mouth bulging, eyes fixed. I don't care. He owes me a quarter anyway; said 'friend.' Even if I lose, I don't lose.

"So, dubbler-nothin' means winner gets double the quarter I owe. I got Cowboys."

Once we shake hands, there's no backsies or redo's. "Sure you betcha man."

"Bet," Becker squeezes until my knuckles press on each other, making sure I get we're engaged in something official and painful. Then his bulging mouth gives way to his menacing metallic smirk. "Sorry, Beaner Boy, it *was* yesterday. Cowboys won. Can't believe you fell for it," shaking his head, holds out his hand. "So, dubbler-nothin' means you owe me fifty cents."

The stink of stale tater-tots hangs low in the muggy air inside the Caff. Nauseating.

"You're not planning on welching, are you, Beaner Boy?"

Looks like he took you for a ride. A sucker bet.

"You know what a welcher is, Beaner Boy?" His eyes now as grim as his mouth.

Don't say Grape juice! Don't say it.

"Means I'm gonna have to kick your spic ass if you don't pay me," he makes a fist.

"Not so fast." Behind Becker stands Fertig, arms folded, brittle yellow hair shining under the Caff lights, blue eyes staring. "Double or nothing means if Beaner Boy wins, you pay double what you owe; if he loses, you don't owe him anything. Either way, he doesn't owe you."

His lips cover his glint. "One o'these days, Kelly Smelly." Becker grins, turns, goes.

"That was close," Fertig chuckles, looking down at me. "Have no fear, Kelly Fertig's here. Next time listen," pointing his thumbs to himself, doing a Satisfaction Sniff. "Do like I say and you'll be OK. I'm your penultimate savior, Beaner Boy. Got it?"

I get it. As long as Pros call him Kelly Smelly, he will be glorious leader of the Nons, and I am a Non. His cushion will always be his Amrikayi superiority. He belongs, knows their words, their written and unwritten rules, and my Sins. As long as I am on the bottom, he will never have to worry about hitting the hard, cold ground; I will break his fall. My darkness, my ignorance of the words and rules will cushion his fall, allow him to tower over me, cast his yellow-haired, blue-eyed shadow. Fertig my sun, my light, my shade – my shield. I get it.

And until I learn it myself, I will let him; our unspoken pact. Nobody listens to Fertig? I will. Nobody praises Fertig? I will. We all need allies. Mine has to look like them, talk like them, understand them. Allies are key on the playground, especially when things get heated. And things are always getting heated.

I sit next to Dud now since Shantay switched seats. No more jokes or egg yolk encrusted lips. Just Dud, Polack, Kelly Smelly and me, Beaner Boy. We are Nons.

PART III

IN THE BEGINNING, *Maman wanted to stay. She was a Tehrani at heart and didn't believe those tales about Amrika – golden Cadillacs on boulevards paved with diamonds. She said Amrika is a dehat, a village, and she was a modern woman from a modern city, free to do as she liked. Perfumed and elegant, she drove her own boulevards, wisecracking motorcycle cops who dared to pull her over, haggling with grocers who dared to pawn yesterday's produce off on her, enjoying card nights and cocktails at chic cabarets in downtown hotels with friends. When needed, she used her Guweem voice to pass as one of Them, to prove to Them that a fatherless ghetto Jew was as good as any Guweem. She was happy. It was Sweet Lady who convinced her, after cracking eggs to see who cursed her and caused Baba to go to Amrika. She reminded Maman how lucky she was to have a man; how different things would be without one. Her modern city would be full of obstacles and dependence. There would be whispers, heads shaking behind her, not just from the Guweem but from our own. Tehran might be modern, but just below that surface of chic lies centuries of unforgiving tradition that looks sideways at a mother living without a man. Sweet Lady knows, having left Tehran for Amrika herself after Maman was married off. So Maman gave in. To preserve good fortune, to protect family, to save face so nobody would say Baba left us. She would not be like Sabya Moshéh. We would go to Amrika, where the sidewalks glittered and the sun, like everything else, was gold. She was bet-*

ting Baba would change his mind; that he would see Amrika was for Amrikayi - hamburger-eating cowboys, simple dehati addicted to the lazy conveniences of infidelity, fast food and divorce. Maman was betting Baba would realize there was no point in learning new rules and roads, making new food. We are Tehrani, Maman figured. We would be back.

Fourth Grade.
September 1972

Something Good. Something Bad. Coat of Arms. I copy the "Meet Me" project off the blackboard. Maman got us Bics, notebook paper and three-ring notebooks to start the year. Now I sink the firm Bic into my stack of paper, pressing on the top sheet, making an impression on the sheets below; same way I plan to make an impression on them this year. We'll show our projects to class, then to our parents at Open House before Halloween. They'll finally see me.

Something good. "I saved a little girl from Smiley Skull Cracker. It was a summer afternoon and I'm minding my own business on my hill, singing '*Brandy yu'ra fan gurl.*' The playground was full of kids picking teams and skipping rope. But I had important business on the hill. I'm sort of Hill Sheriff around here, carry a special Hill Sheriff badge. I knew the Legend of Smiley, but wasn't scared. Then I saw him holding a girl (don't know her, probably a visitor), getting ready to Skull Crack her so I picked up a baseball-sized rock and like left-hander Tommy John Number 25 of L.A. Dodgers, I threw a strike that hit Smiley right between the eyes, cracked his glasses and made him release the girl. Off he ran. I walked the girl down to safety and took off back up the hill before she could thank me. Hill Sheriffs don't need that."

Heroic, like Billy Jack helping the Navajo kids, at great personal risk. That should do it.

Something bad. So many. Can't write about Baba flipping the table, Maman's shoe, Becker's salamander, Kersh and Cowan liking Precious more than me. That's too much. I copy words of sad songs I hear on

93KHJ: "What they do! Smile in my face but all they wanna do is take my place, leaving me alone again, naturally. But I hold my head up, trying to take it easy. Told my motorcycle Maman don't get hooked on me; cuz we had our seasons in the sun."

Dramatic, like Keith singing to a girl on *Partridge Family*, Fridays 8:30 Channel 7.

Coat of Arms. They draw swords, crowns, baseball bats and dogs. I can't draw. Rodrigo can. Rodrigo used to think I was Mexicki like him because we're both brown. He taught me to trace the Turk from the Camel ads at the back of Sports Illustrated. With black hair, thick dark eyebrows and brown skin, the Turk looks like us, if we were Pros - smokers in the pocket of his denim shirt, thick moustache, Amrikayi beauty hanging on him. The Turk is my Coat of Arms.

October 1972

When Mrs. McLean asks "Who wants to show their project," I shoot my hand up. She picks Worm. Pros don't usually raise hands. They sit back and make fun of smarty-pants kids they'll beat up later at recess. But Worm raises his hand to bug the smarty-pants kids and show that Pros can be smart too. Worm has this beautiful Mom who wears tight dresses and high heels during daytime. One afternoon she showed up in a fancy car and fur coat. Pincus said "Her boyfriend got her that Jag" like it was bad. But we all stared at the car, at Worm's Mom, her bare ankles, slender arms. I don't think any of us was thinking it was bad.

When Worm gets up, the other Pros make funny sounds. He plays along, clearing his throat with a loud "A-Hem" holding up his Coat of Arms. Shaped like a police badge, two baseball bats crossed like swords, an ancient "C" above the cross, eight baseballs below.

"My coat of arms," Worm says. "I love baseball and the Cincinnati Reds. My favorite player is number 8, Little Joe Morgan - like me, he's small but mighty." Gap-toothed smirk.

"Perfect Mr. Wormeier!" says Mrs. McLean. "Now, Something Good, Something Bad."

He turns the page: "We played the Expos. I got two doubles and a homer. It was good."

He turns the page again. "We played the Athletics. I struck out three times. It was bad."

He closes his booklet and this time he tries to hide a proud smile, looks straight ahead.

"Excellent, Mr. Wormeier," Mrs. McLean twirls her hand. "You told us clearly and concisely all we need to know about you. Who's next? Mike M., were you raising your hand?"

I slink down in my chair, trying to be invisible. Got it wrong, again.

"Go without me," Baba says when he gets home. In his dark suit, crumpled shirt, red tie still pinching his throat, Baba may tug on his collar but never loosens his tie or undoes the top button until dinner is on the table. The only relief he allows himself when he gets home is to take off his hard shoes and walk around in his socks, a barely visible grin of relief on his face.

"What am I going to do there," Maman complains. "Isn't this why you came to Amrika? To attend these chic Amrikayi affairs?"

"Velemoon kon," Baba grumbles, sitting on the couch rubbing his feet. "Go. I'll fry biftek and pommes frites for when you get back."

Last year in his suit and tie he looked out of place, hard eyes, classroom lights bouncing off his bald dome. With hands clasped behind him, he quietly examined the walls, slow nodding, inspecting posters of the Apollo and art projects like he was studying something important. His stern glares, furrowed brows, black hair ringing his dome made him look like nobody else. When he asked Mrs. Mendelsohn about Picture Day, his harsh accent sounded angry: "Ven you said dey take de peek-chair?" It startled Mrs. Mendelsohn and the other parents who looked over, whispering. Maman coming is bad enough; Baba staying home is small relief.

Perfumed in a flowery blouse, flared gabardines, matching scarf and gold hoops, Maman will stick out too. She makes me wear a new shirt - gold and copper leaves in polyester, makes me sweat. Every Rosh Hashana and Yom Kippur Maman buys us new clothes for good luck, for a fresh start in a new year. Last year it was the star T-shirts; this year the leafy, sweaty polyester.

Their parents look as right as TV commercials. Dads in golf shirts and Sansabelt slacks brought to you by "Hamm's the beer refreshing, Olympia Brewing, Milwaukee, Wisconsin." They look comfortably humbled but confident, because it's all theirs. No furrowed brows or dark glares, no scowls of disapproval. Hi-C Moms in sleeveless blouses and checkered skirts chatting easy like Open House is where they are meant to be. All cool and airy, where they belong. Maman stares at them with a hint of fear, suspicion and desperate superiority, her eyes darting like a nervous bird that accidentally flew into human territory through an open window.

As they survey art projects and work folders, talking to Mrs. McLean and each other, Maman clings, asking questions in a nervous tone. I show her my desk, my art assignments. I try introducing Mrs. McLean but the line is too long, we stand beside each other watching them do cozy belonging, wondering how we can imitate them, do some cozy belonging of our own.

When she sees my "Please to Meet Me" project, I figure she'll glance and move on like she did with everything else, but the Turk's dangling smoker catches her eye.

"Een Cheeyeh?" Not a scream but enough angst in her tone that anyone within a few feet can hear us. My instinct is to calm her, keep her voice from traveling.

"This? Just an Amrikayi thing. Did it wrong. Let's talk to teacher, I think she's free."

"This hamall with the moustache is smoking? Is he supposed to be . . . you?" Her concern is about to rise to a panic that will cause her to not care where she is or who hears her. "Are you pretending to be this dirty Amrikayi cowboy?"

"Maman, Torkeh. From a magazine. I didn't draw it; my friend did. And it's all wrong." I try to pull it from her hand but she pulls back, and starts reading.

She turns the page. "Esmiley kiyeh? There was a girl on the hill?"

"Doesn't matter, Maman. It's wrong."

The more I try to calm her, the louder she gets. "Was somebody behind our house--"

"--Yes!" I cut her off. "The hill is dangerous. I climb it after school because you're always late picking me up. I'm lucky to be alive!" I know saving a girl and running Smiley off is fake, but Maman doesn't. She'll think I was heroic; she'll quiet down.

But she's not letting go. "Motorcycle Maman?" she turns the page. "You kissed somebody?" Maman reads Amrikayi better than I thought.

"It's from a radio song. It's nothing. I did it wrong; I told you."

"So smoking and kissing girls?" she asks, her voice loud enough to carry. "Is this what you're becoming? Oh, Adonai, where did he bring us?"

Thats when I hear it. We're speaking Farsi. Kids and parents watching and listening, nowhere to hide, lights buzzing, Maman glaring, sweat rolling down the sides of my face. And all around me is their chatter – joyous, air-conditioned chatter of the innocents, who belong, who are not hostage to misinterpretations.

Tink fast, Rabbit. Everyone watchin'. Make it woik, Doc!

"Lighten up, Mom," I say it with an Amrikayi twang but there's terror in my eyes.

"Chee? You called me what?" Some turn to look. Worm's moon face, so close I can touch his cheek. My chance. Worm, always there to trip me up. He'll see me, like this.

"Wasn't smokin'," twang, side eye Worm. He misjudged me; I am bad, lowdown; Pr--.

Maman does it lighting quick. A thunderous clap that rings my ear, ricochets off the classroom walls, careens through the show-and-tells. My hot cheek stings where her fingers landed and as I rub, my eyes catch Worm's - round like he just saw mighty Joe Morgan strike out. No snicker, or smirk. I can't look away, so I give him a firm face, harden my trembling lips, swallow my humiliation, blink to stop my stinging eyes. I stare a stare that screams:

"Hey Mister Ansso! You enjoy making fun but can't handle my *Something Bad*. It waits for me every day; worse than your strike-outs. Go! To your sexy Maman; your perfect class project; your fancy freckles and long hair. Don't look at me! Don't see me! Not! Like! This!"

I turn to Maman, armpits stinging, lips pursed, puddles in my eyes. Since we arrived, I've been trying to learn Them, run with Them, see myself in Them, get Them to see me while she worries about us becoming cowboys and what Tehrani's will think of us when we go back.

I wanna scream at her too: "Can't you see over there is finished?"

I wanna shake her: "Can't you see here is where we are and will be?"

I wanna plead: "We need to find ourselves here; get on with becoming Amrikayi. See?"

Maman takes my hand, smiles at Mrs. McLean, a graceful bow of her head, and we go.

Worm may have been shocked yesterday, winning me a sweet dose of temporary pity, but today it's the sly grin and wicked gesture, scraping one index finger over the other, code for "Busted by your mom!" He elbows Speed, they shake their heads. They all saw.

I keep to myself, avoid eyes, hoping nobody else saw yesterday's humiliation.

"Come with us to the Halloween Carnival," Fertig nudges. "It'll get your mind off that doozy of a smack your mom put on you yesterday."

Evil pumpkins with missing teeth, witches riding flying brooms, skeletons lying casually on haystacks - all over the playground. On Halloween, the wicked and dead are fun because when you belong, even scary and wrong are jolly and right. They're all in on the joke, happily blindfolding themselves, hands behind their backs by choice, sticking their heads into barrels of icy water to spear apples with their teeth.

Pincus holds a roll of tickets. "Look what I found," a nod to Dudley.

"I'm not sure you should keep those," Fertig rubs his chin, gives Pincus the side eye.

"Don't worry," says Dudley. "He'll split 'em even-Steven, now shut the heck up."

"Well," Fertig figures, "I suppose I can go along for today, seeing's how it's Halloween."

"You found them?" I ask. "And you get to keep them, not give them to lost and found?"

Pincus and Dudley smile at each other, look to Fertig.

"It's the Finders-Keepers Rule, Beaner Boy, part of American juries prudins."

"Position's nine tens o' the law," Dudley nods.

"We're keeping 'em," Pincus says plainly. "You want in or not?"

On my second turn at toss-rings-at-Coke-bottles, I win a kite. Besides Ben Franklin in our history book and TV commercials, I have never seen a real kite - a strictly Amrikayi toy. Having one gets me closer to being one. But it's not a kite; it's a box with a picture of a kite full of kite ingredients: an odd shaped sheet of white plastic with blue stripes; two sticks; a ball of rope; and a sheet of instructions with numbers, letters and drawings telling me how to build a kite. Everything in Amrika comes with written instructions and "assembly required."

"Assembly is part of the fun," Fertig says. "Read the instructions. Want me to help?"

I don't want Fertig coming over to smell our house and then blab to everybody. I run off the playground, cross the street, climb the hill. I don't bother with the instructions, use the box pictures: cross sticks, tie, slip ends through loops in sheet, attach string where sticks cross. Kite.

"What's that," asks Precious when he comes home.

"Whataya think it is, Precious? My new kite. Won it at the carnival; built it myself."

"Stop calling me Precious. You shouldn't have that in the house. It's bad luck."

"Umbrellas in the house are back luck, not kites. Learn your Amrikayi laws, Precious."

"We're Jewish, genius. You brought a Christian kite to our house. Bad luck."

"I won this at Halloween; hit three Coke bottles, assembled it myself," I add for TV drama effect. "It's not a Christian kite. It's my Amrikayi kite."

"It's got a big blue cross on the front," Precious turns it to show me the blue T. "Crosses are Christian. Stars are Jewish. You should throw it away. Bad luck."

I remember Baba's beatings when we used our fancy cuss words, so I keep it simple.

86

"Imbecile," I tell Precious. "Those are racing symbols, not a Christian cross."

"Idiot," Precious tells me. "Racing has stripes, not crosses."

"Ignoramus," I tell Precious. "Why would they give Christian kites at Halloween?"

"Jackass," Precious tells me. "Maybe they're brainwashing you to turn us Christian like Maman said they would. And it's working because you brought a Christian kite to our house."

"I'm going outside to fly my kite. You can come watch or you can stay inside."

Outside, Precious standing skeptically by, I run down Albatross Lane pulling the kite behind me, letting the ball of string unspool as it jerks and tugs in my hand like a wild animal. Kersh and Cowan stop shooting hoops to watch. No mention of a cross; they ask for turns and I quickly hand it off. Now maybe they'll think twice before liking Precious more. When Precious says he wants a turn, I make like *Little Red Hen*: "I bet you do."

When it's my turn again, I stiffen the slack as the kite floats in the afternoon breeze, then let it run to make it go higher, like Sister Bertril, peaceful above us, our chaos, the skeletons and witches we celebrate. We all look the same from up there.

Yelling wakes us. Baba's thundering bellows; Maman's wailing. It's dark and we can't make out the muffled words behind their door, until that word is uttered. Only Maman uses that word and when she does it has a dark, harsh tone. Maman only utters it about other people.

"Tallagh!" She screams. "I'll do it, like the Amrikayi!" She threatens. "I'll dooo iiit!"

Baba roars and commands her silence, which never works on Maman.

We sit up in our beds, in the dark. I hear Precious weeping in whispers.

"Told you! Christian kite!" he sobs. "What's going to happen to us if she does it?"

He's my little brother, counts on me. I can tell from his whimpering he is past blaming me for ignoring his warnings and is looking for the comfort he usually gets from Maman who just screamed that threat. I brought the Christian kite to our house.

"I'll fix it," I finally say, knowing what has to be done. "Don't cry, Saeed, I'll fix it."

I crawl out of bed in the dark, feeling for it on the carpet. When I find it, I poke my fingers in the plastic sheet and rip. I snap the sticks in two then four jagged pieces, ignoring the scraping at my palms. Gritting my teeth, I push, crack and rip until the thing in my raw hands is no longer a cross or a kite or kite ingredients. The garbled, muffled yelling keeps up as I open the backyard door, carrying my Amrikayi toy, the offending carcass of Sin, across the damp grass in the cold fall night. I rear back and throw it over the fence, watching pieces of Sin scatter on the cold patchy hill that brambles down to the street which separates me from the playground where they play their games at full speed with full rights by rules they know, rules they made, rules they don't always apply to themselves but which always cause me to stumble, tempering any sense of wonder and hope with doubt and paralysis, freezing me in my tracks. I throw the Amrikayi toy out of our house to stop the tears and hollering, because in this house Halloween is no joke and scary things are no fun. I take a long, pleading look at the dark starless night sky, a deep sniff of burning leaves, firewood, coming of winter. Almost made it; so close.

"Done," I tell Precious in a reassuring voice, holding steady so I don't start crying too. "Kite's gone. Stop crying. It's gonna be good now. Stop crying, Saeed."

"Are you sure?"

"Positive. Now sleep. The sooner we sleep, the sooner things go back to normal."

The yelling stopped when I got back in but I only notice now. In the dark, I stare at the ceiling, pray to be forgiven. Maybe I'm not as ready to be a real Amrikayi as I thought.

December 1972

In the Impala, Maman's brown hair flutters in the wind coming from her cracked window. I sniff deep, waiting for that smell of burning jet fuel as we get closer to the airport.

Baba peers through the windshield to study the big green freeway signs. His hands grip the wheel like he's trying to convince someone that he's being extra careful. I lean over the front seat to reach for the radio dial but Baba catches my hand.

"Leave it."

Last night, when we asked about Maman's trip, they paused. Maman mumbled their secret code "Lashoon" and Baba shrugged. "Trip."

"For what," Precious asked.

"Visit," said Maman.

"Not long," added Baba.

"What are you gonna do there," I asked.

She looked at Baba but I couldn't pick up their signals. "My friend's mother died."

That was a lie; Maman hadn't cried. When someone dies, even if they're not family, Maman slaps her thighs in grief and wails up to Adonai. Her eyes and nose get sloppy, she wipes carelessly, sleeves, hands, napkins, because she's too upset. She lights a smoker and an extra Shabbat candle. None of that happened. Also, Maman lies all the time.

But at the airport Maman does cry - an airport cry, not a somebody-died cry – quiet and dignified. Her nose doesn't run; tears roll with slow elegance under her chic sunglasses and down her cheek. At Departure, Baba is extra attentive, handing Maman her ticket and a wad of cash. Baba runs her suitcases to the entrance of the plane as we hold Maman's hands.

I stand stiff, shoulders back, trying to be the Man Baba always tells us to be; trying to smile. But it feels forced, more like a sneer. I realize I'm making fists at my sides. She comes in for a hug; her damp cheek and heaving shoulders pushing into my neck. I'm too big for her to lift; she picks Precious up and he holds her neck; they rub noses. Baba kisses her, formally, both cheeks, and they say things to each other in whispers. I guess they know what they're doing. She wipes her eyes under her glasses and walks onto the plane. The door closes behind her.

"OK, bebee!" Baba breaks out his rarely used Amrikayi slang back in the car. He rubs his palms together with a big clap, rolls his window down to casually rest an elbow on the door, like a movie star. I sit in front and when I reach to turn the radio on, he doesn't move to stop me.

"What do we men want to do," he asks. "Just us men for the next one or two weeks."

"I thought it was a short trip," says Precious. "Won't Maman be back for Hanooka?"

"She'll be back," Baba says, keeping his eyes on the road. "What should we do?"

Baba usually acts excited only when Maman complains that he's not excited enough - a discount she finagled, talking her way out of a ticket, good grades. It's usually fake excitement, clownish shrieks that shake the house. Today's excitement isn't fake, but definitely forced; he's making up for something. Precious and I don't spend much time with Baba without Maman. He doesn't like movie theatres or popcorn, preferring black-and-white movies on TV and pistachios. He gets bored watching us ride the donkeys at La Cienega park and doesn't play sports.

"Let's go to brunch!" But Charley Brown's is for special occasions – orange leather booths, wood-paneled walls, big windows overlooking clean white sailboats bobbing peacefully in the marina. They get Bloody Marys; Maman loads her bag with blueberry muffins. "Ask them to bring another bucket," she nudges us as giant, leggy servers with luscious hairdos glide across the carpet in miniskirts, stockings and high heeled sandals, carrying buckets of muffins. Doesn't feel right without her. Baba, wide smile, needs us to go along with his plan. "Should we go?"

"Can't wait! Blueberry muffins," I look back at Precious to make sure he's on board.

"We won't be able to take any home-"

"- It's fine," I interrupt before he finishes. "Let's go, I'm hungry."

Baba orders steak and eggs and a Bloody Mary. He takes deep long sips, then orders another. He lets us get waffles with whipped cream and maple syrup. We fill every square with the smoky, woodsy better-than-honey elixir, acting like it's no big deal, like we have syrup all the time. But it is a huge deal. Everything today is a giant, weird deal. Almost an emergency.

"Who's going to wash our clothes and make our lunches," Precious asks.

"Don't worry," Baba takes a swig of his red peppery drink. "Iran Khanoom is coming."

Baba doesn't call her Sweet Lady. We finish our syrupy waffles and ask the tall, lovely waitress for another bucket of blueberry muffins, excited. Sweet Lady is coming.

Before anything is the smell. Before my groggy eyes adjust to the pre-dawn blue through the window, before my ears prick up at the creaking of the linoleum in the kitchen, before my feet touch the carpet, I smell her. Fragrant jasmine petals and black tea steeping in a pot of boiling water; butter melting in a pan; eggs crackling over the sweet smoke of chopped dates frying; the perfume of Pond's cold cream. Sweet Lady has arrived.

"Where you going," asks Precious from his bed when he hears my sheets ruffle.

"Go back to sleep." I want to be first to see her while the house is still blue. But Precious smells it too and jumps out of bed. We race to the kitchen.

Maman getting on a plane and the awkward brunch afterward made me nervous. Sweet Lady's arrival makes my heart skip. But it also confirms that something is off. Not an emergency, but important, like Yom Kippur when food, TV and lights are Sin; visitors sleeping over, pulling pajamas from overnight bags; bedsheets on couches; feeling in unlit hallways; candles casting tall shadows that dance like ghosts. It's a solemn event, but we make light of it too; we're in it together. It's exciting, but not normal, almost emergency. Something is off.

"Good mornen," Sweet Lady says, "had you good nigh-nigh?"

"Why did Maman leave," Precious asks without hesitation.

"Oh, she went to see a friend," Sweet Lady replies, handling the spatula, making sure the whites cook evenly over the dates and the yolks don't burst. She doesn't look up.

"Did her friend die," asks Precious.

"God forbid," Sweet Lady pokes the dates with the edge of the spatula, shakes the pan gently over the heat to make sure the butter singes the ends to make them crispy.

Precious and I exchange glances. Tallagh?

"Maman said she's going to a funeral," I tell Sweet Lady, burying the tremble of my voice in my chest. "She said her friend's mother died and she went to help with the funeral."

She turns off the heat, the crackle of eggs slowly waning, pulls plates from the cupboard.

"Don't be such a fuzul, little one," Sweet Lady says, a grin highlights the dimples in her meaty brown cheeks, the mischievous grin she gave to her baby girl. She expertly slides the spatula under the eggs and onto our plates. "Her friend's mother, yes." She lays our plates in front of us and pulls a Winston from the pack on the table, lights it. "She'll be back," as she exhales that first puff of smoke. "Now eat your eggs, wash the cat pee off your face and brush your teeth."

As we devour our eggs, joyfully sopping up sweet date-tinged yolks with our bread, Baba gets off the living room couch covered in rumpled sheets and a blanket. Whenever Sweet Lady visits, Baba grudgingly is on his best behavior. He grunts out five deep knee bends.

Sweet Lady - a sturdy woman with thick ankles and a hefty bosom that nursed five girls before she had twenty-five years – has married off all five and knows how to handle her grooms.

"Sopeh shoma be khayr, Manoucher Khan," she says with a confident but respectful lilt as she rests her smoker in the ashtray to slide the spatula and plate two eggs for Baba.

"Sope be khayr, Iran Khanoom." Grudgingly.

"I wouldn't worry," Fertig leans against the cold fence before the bell.

I wasn't worried. I thought I was showing off - trip to airport, brunch.

"When we got divorced, my dad left, not my mom. Moms don't leave. So you're fine."

Tallagh, like Maman warned. Pig sandwich? Christian kite? Open scissors? What caused it? Me? Sweet remnants of fried eggs and dates swirl inside, burn my belly.

"They're not getting divorced," I keep a casual tone. "We had brunch after the airport."

"My dad takes me to IHOP every other Sunday, asks what my mom is up to. Even with the penultimate assortment of syrups, it's depressing. He gets the couch and I get the bed in his bachelor pad in Reseda, where it's hot and sticky and I have no friends."

"We stayed up to watch Columbo and played cards," I say, trying to convince us both that our Sunday was a special occasion; that something wasn't off; no emergency.

"My dad played cards too, at first. I loved going there, like camping. Now he makes frozen pizza, opens a can of beer and we watch wrestling. I can't tell if he fought to get me or if he got stuck with me, but I can't wait for Sunday night so I can sleep in my own bed."

Pizza and TV don't sound bad, Doc. Like honest to goodness Amrikayi. Divorce? Hm...

"You really think they're divorcing?" For the first time, I need Fertig. I'm terrified but, maybe, excited too. Do I want him to say yes or hope he says no? He's one of Them; he knows.

Fertig rubs his chin, "You said your grandma is here. Did she make breakfast?"

Don't talk about the fried eggs with dates or sopping up yolks. He won't get it.

"Corn Flakes," I blurt out. "Essential part of complete breakfast. Four-to-five vitamins."

"That's *fortified*, Beaner Boy. Now, is that your mom's mom?"

"Yeah."

"Then I'd say probably not. Your mom goes on a trip; her mom comes to cook. If your dad isn't cooking dinner, you're fine. Dads have to learn cooking when they get divorced."

"It's Bouillabaisse!" Baba - in pajama bottoms, his bare feet in slippers, a faint smile on his lips and a glass of whiskey on the counter beside him - stirs a ladle in one of Maman's pots. "We made this in Paris from fish scraps the fishmonger didn't want at the end of the day."

"I thought you only cook your vegetable omelet for special occasions."

"Iran Khanoom needs a break. She has been cooking and cleaning all week."

In a panic, I turn to see Sweet Lady on the couch, her thick, stockinged legs crossed, watching *I Love Lucy* and smoking a Winston. When she sees me, she gives the double-blink-lip-bite, then a sharp side eye to Baba as she blows smoke. She's staying out of his way tonight.

Even when Maman is around, Baba and Sweet Lady are only polite with each other, short smiles, quick nods. She calls him "Manoucher Khan" and he calls her "Iran Khanoom," politely passing the wine cup on Shabbats. Since she got here, they have kept the formality, meaning plenty of low grumbles from Baba and double-blink-lip-bites from Sweet Lady behind his back.

We've been playing Rummy and watching TV after dinner while Baba quietly reads, but I know he's getting restless because he forces us off the couch earlier each night, laying down the sheets. Tonight he is easy, sipping whiskey, cooking fish soup for no reason. Maybe for good reason; maybe Fertig is right. The idea of divorce, the smell of fish boiling in tomatoes, garlic and saffron, the smokers and whiskey, it churns my stomach and makes me want to vomit.

"I can't eat fish," I remind Baba. "I faint, remember? Can't we have normal food?"

"You won't faint," he takes a pull off his glass, stirs the pot. "We loved it at my old rooming house in Paris. C'est magnifique! If you faint, I'll catch you."

"If Maman was here we would be eating normal food and you wouldn't be cooking fish."

"Is he going to faint again," Precious asks, almost excited.

Baba places a big steaming bowl in front of me.

"I'll faint if I eat fish," I warn Baba again with more urgency.

Maman used to drop to her knees with a shriek, desperately fanning me with her hands. She'd order Precious to fetch water and sprinkle it on my face as I lay limp, dazed, eyes half open. Maman bought it. Baba never did. I'd peek at him standing over us, picking fish from his teeth with a fishbone, shaking his head at Maman for being so gullible. Still, it was a house rule: I don't touch fish, eat fish or have fish oil. But Maman's gone and Baba cooked.

"You'll eat this," he commands. "You'll like it and you won't faint."

"Can't I make a ketchup-cheese pita with a can of beans?"

Baba finally looks over at Sweet Lady on the couch, like he has no other options; she is the only other grownup who can understand what he is witnessing. "He's like a Mexicki," Baba chuckles, takes another sip. "All he eats is tomato paste, cheese and beans."

Sweet Lady gives a half-hearted shrug, blows smoke, watches Lucy's mischief.

"Mexicki neestam!" I yell. "Ketchup Mexicki neest. Loobya Mexicki neest," breathing hard, lightheaded. Sweet Lady can't stay forever. Will Maman be back? Is this Tallagh life?

Baba loses his smile, furrows his brows "This bouillabaisse cost me money and time."

"You said it's made from old fish scraps nobody wants," I remind him defiantly.

He puts down his drink, eyes dark, kitchen light shining gold on his bald dome. He flashes his furious "F" - things could get hot fast. "How would you like a double-sided across the face," he asks, holding the back of his hand in ready-to-swing position.

Precious brings his hands up to cover his eyes. I turn to Sweet Lady. She does a double-blink-lip-bite, signaling that she has me.

Baba makes a quick turn, catching her in mid-blink-bite.

Sweet Lady, expertly pivots from lip-bite to a pretend-sneeze.

Baba isn't fooled; lets her know the jig is up: "You will kindly cook nothing tonight," he instructs in a hard tone normally used on us, never on Sweet Lady. "This is dinner tonight."

"Yes sir," she says in a sarcastically stern tone, the fake salute of a soldier giving in to his clueless captain. She is pushing it, knows Baba is seething. But Baba knows she will comply.

"And if it isn't any trouble," still glaring at Sweet Lady, "no more interference."

"I said something?" Sweet Lady asks, her manicured nails on her massive chest.

"You think I don't recognize your blinks and gestures?"

"As God is my witness, Manoucher Khan," Sweet Lady vows with a holy breath, "I am here at your service while my girl is away. I am here for the kids. Would I interfere?"

"You talk with her daily, long distance at great expense, which we will set aside for now," Baba says, picking up his glass of whiskey and taking another, longer, sip; this time with less joy and verve than before, squeezing it down his throat with a sneer. "What's she doing?"

"Lashoon jeloye benechi," says Sweet Lady. Their secret tongue.

Baba sneers, takes another sip, turns to me. "Tonight, this is dinner. For everybody."

"Fine," I scream. "You'll see. You shouldn't force people to faint because you ate soup made from old fish in Paris or because you feel bad."

"Feel bad? What do I have to feel bad about? Eat your soup before it gets cold."

"Lashoon" I yell, "Benechi! I have ears, I hear. I know what's going on."

"OK," Sweet Lady steps in, bites on her lip to hold back a smile. "Keep quiet, little one."

I dig my spoon into my bowl of fish soup; nobody stops me or screams "Don't!" I lift the spoon to my mouth, hold my nose for effect, pour the soup in and try to swallow it whole to avoid tasting it but still do – oily, oceanic, gamey, fish! I heave, swivel my head with my neck, eyes up, down, back. For my grand finale, I let my head drop back, exhale and go still. This is usually when Maman screams, kneels down to hold me in her arms and orders Precious to fetch water. But as my head dangles over the back of my chair, as my half-open eyes gaze the room, nobody is moving. Precious isn't fetching water. Sweet Lady looks confused.

"Breathe, little one," she says, putting a morsel of soup-drenched fish in her own mouth, her red polished nails glistening with flecks of pepper and garlic chunks. "Breathe, azizam."

Baba, unmoved, dips the spoon into my bowl and holds another load in front of me.

"That's right," he grumbles. "Now another. It's good for you. Brain food."

"No," I finally yell, straightening up. "I don't eat fish and if Maman was here she would tell you. I don't want you cooking for us. You're not cooking for us every other Sunday."

"You were faking?" asks Precious.

"If it takes a hundred black years," says Baba, "you're eating that soup. Now let's eat!"

Sweet Lady eats a spoonful, looks at me. "Delleshess," in English. "Eat, little one."

"Not bad," Precious says to Baba, then looks at me. "Try it, faker. It's pretty good."

"Hundred black years," Baba sneers, gets up to pour more whiskey. He gets another glass from the cupboard, drops ice cubes, pours and hands it to Sweet Lady. "Salamati."

"Salamati," Sweet Lady says, raising her glass to Baba before taking hearty sip.

They eat, dipping bread into the tomato base, slurping, chewing. When Sweet Lady starts gathering the empty bowls, Baba, pulling another needle-sized fishbone from his mouth to use as a toothpick, orders "Leave his. He isn't getting up until he finishes."

"Of course," Sweet Lady says, taking all the bowls but mine. When she's done with the dishes, she passes me at the table with my cold fish soup. "Take it, little one," she whispers, laying down a ketchup-cheese pita. "Nooshe joon," she says, her soft hand on my shoulder as she passes. Nobody sees me better than Sweet Lady.

She joins Baba and Precious in the TV room, grabbing the cards for Rummy. When she pulls a Winston from her pack, Baba flutters two fingers at her so she pulls one for him too.

"Obliged," he mumbles, the smoker dangling in his lips, hands cupped around them.

"Please," she says, lighting his, then her own.

"Two weeks it's become, you're waiting for what?" Sweet Lady's voice is the first thing I hear in the freezing darkness. Outside, the sky is just starting to get light. Our final weekend of vacation. We had Hanooka, Christmas, New Years, all without Maman. We talked to her a few times long distance, asked her to bring presents. School will start Monday without her.

"She's not staying," I hear Baba mumble dismissively. "Everybody is running away from there, with all that's going on. Even her friends are coming here, don't worry."

"Why don't you go there, have a nice visit, then bring her back. Think of your boys."

"I'm not thinking of them? This is why I'm taking them before school starts."

"How will that solve your problem? You need to go get her."

"Velemoon kon!" Baba finally spits, tired of the badgering. Over the past two weeks, Baba and Sweet Lady have dropped the stiff, pretend-respect talk for more honest and informal exchanges. "I said I'll address it when we get back, didn't I?"

Baba's footsteps stomp down the hall to our room.

"Get up," he bellows. "Before the sun gets too high. We're going to ski."

The Impala is already packed - blankets, pillows, jackets, sweaters, two grocery bags full of pita bread, orange cheese, salami, apples, pistachios, pumpkin seeds and dried mulberries.

We get dressed in the pre-dawn light, pulling our warmest sweaters over our pajamas and double socks so thick we can't tie our shoes. It's frosty out, the sky still a deep blue as we crawl into the backseat and huddle under one of the blankets. Sweet Lady waves goodbye.

"God keep you safe," she says to us as Baba backs the Impala out of the driveway.

"Isn't she coming," asks Precious.

"Don't worry about her," Baba says. "She'll be fine. She needs some rest."

The streets are empty as Baba idles down Albatross Lane, makes two rights to Pinnacle Palace Ave past the playground that has been hibernating for winter like Yogi Bear, to the Texaco station. The tip of the sun emerges behind us like a shiny yolk as Baba rolls down his window to talk to the attendant. When Baba has to ask strangers for things he needs, his accent gets thicker: "Please. Veech vay is to the Big Bear Lakes for the eskee?"

"Takin' yer boys skiin'?" the guy asks with a smile. He pulls out and unfolds a huge map with blue and red lines going in every direction, swaths of green, beige and blue, numbers and symbols; like hieroglyph-ics. "Take National to the Ten to the Two up through the Angeles till it turns into the One-Thirty-Eight down to the Eighteen and 'fore you know it, you're in Big Bear."

It's hard to believe Baba got all that, but he fills the tank, grudg-ingly pays a dollar for the map and bends it against its natural folds so the directions stay open beside him. The Ten freeway is an ex-panse of smooth, grooved grey; six wide empty lanes running behind and ahead as far as we can see. Baba's foot is barely on the pedal but the Impala hums at seventy-five as we zoom east in the cold, quiet morning like we are a hundred feet above the world, soar-ing. From this elevation, not hemmed in by everything down there – bumpy potholed streets, big metal traffic lights, one-ways, dead-ends, supermarkets, parking lots, shoe repair shops, rows and rows of single-story houses and fenced-in concrete playgrounds where mad children scream all day - I get a fresh view of Los Angeles. Float-ing on the Ten, surrounded by lush green treetops, golden foothills dotted with green shrubs, snowy purple mountains looming in the misty distance shining under a crisp blue sky and a cold sun. I roll my window down as cold wind fills my nostrils, eyes squint, cheeks frosty. I huddle in a blanket, smelling pine, morning frost and gaso-line. Precious has fallen asleep as Baba hums an ancient Persian melody about tortured devotion. We pass signs for Dodger Stadium, Glassell Park and Eagle Rock, I fall asleep too.

When I wake up, we're on a narrow, winding road deep in the snowy foothills I saw from the Ten, surrounded by tall pines and low walls of dirty snow. Baba pulls to the side overlooking rows of trees bent under the weight of snow, for buttered pita and fruit. We take turns peeing on the slushy embankment. Around ten in the morning we get to the wooden ski lodge at Big Bear.

"OK, bebee," yells Baba in his awkward vigor. "Let's get some fresh air and ski!"

Last time we were in snow was in Tehran. I take deep whiffs of the sweet pine and smoky cold air on the way to the ski shop, trusting Baba to know what he's doing.

"Ve need de boot," Baba says with a jolly nod and smile to the guy behind the counter.

"No skis or poles?" asks the guy studying the three of us.

His brows furrow fast, his loses his jolly smile and I get scared. "How much?"

"Twenty per day for the set of skis, boots and poles; seven for just the boots."

"How much?" Baba repeats to show the guy he's not believing that price.

"That would be sixty for three sets, sir, or twenty-one for three boots."

"OK, only boot, OK?" Baba waves the guy off like he's trying to put one over on him.

"You have your own skis and poles? I can measure the bindings for the boots."

"C'man," says Baba, getting annoyed. "Ve don't need, OK?" as he takes out his wallet, pulls a few bills to pay for the boots and walks out knowing we'll follow.

I look up at him, still hoping he knows what he's doing. But... "Don't we need skis?"

"Of course," he says without looking at me, "Why pay that guy when there are skis everywhere," he says as he bends down to help us with our boots.

The boots snap tight around my ankles, heavy and clunky, forcing a Frankenstein clip-clop walk as we crush snow, squeaking with each step, a sound that makes my skin crawl.

Baba stops in front of the lodge where skiers plant their skis in the snow, cheeks pink from the cold, eyes wild from flying down slopes, white air bursting from their mouths. Their steps are energetic; their boots don't seem clunky; even their squeaking sounds right. The lodge smells like spicy chili, charred meat, salty fries, rich cocoa, whipped cream and marshmallows. It is made from logs with large picture windows where they sit at tables sipping drinks, watching other skiers groove down the mountain they just conquered. A wide wooden deck lets them sit outside to take in the crisp mountain air. Like paradise; birthplace of the air-conditioned cool.

"Here," Baba points sheepishly to rows of skis sticking up out of the snow. "Take."

People come and go, sticking their skis in the snow, leaning them against the wall, tying them to racks while they take their well-earned chili and hot cocoa breaks in the lodge.

"I think these skis belong to those people," I offer. "We can't take them."

"No, my son," Baba chuckles at me like I have no understanding of the world. "Those are for everybody," he explains. "Whoever needs, takes and uses, then they put them back for anyone else to use when they're done. Just take a pair and put them on. Go ahead."

"But they are not ours," I insist.

"Are you Ke-ray-zee" Baba barks in Amrikayi but with the same dark scowls and facial gestures he uses when speaking Farsi. "It is ess-kee! So go ess-kee!"

"But what if other people want to use them," I whisper plaintively, looking around to make sure nobody hears us. I don't want to get caught again.

Baba dismisses me with a backhanded air-swat, like I'm too scared or unindustrious to accept how things work in Amrika; that everything is up for grabs here. That's why we came. Everybody gets a fair shot in Amrika as long as they are willing to reach out and take it. He pulls a pair of skis from the snow, drops them on the ground and squats to grab my unwilling ankle. His bald dome gets purple as he struggles to stick my unwilling boot into the binder, determined to teach us what it means to be Amrikayi; to be go-getters; to—

"—Scuse me, kid, I think you have the wrong skis."

He is talking to me because I am the one standing with my boot on his skis.

"Those are my skis," he says, a perfect Amrikayi smile framed by red apple-for-the-teacher cheeks. He looks high school age, tall, square shouldered, breathing in an athletic 'I'm getting ready to attack the mountain' way. He has an easy, controlled air, standing on firm, familiar ground, a confident twinkle in his grey eyes. Light brown curls creep out from a black knit ski cap with a patch of an elephant on skis. He's wearing a navy long sleeve under a beige t-shirt that says "Go Climb a Rock." A real Amrikayi.

At my waist is Baba's bald purple dome, ringed by his jet-black hair. He is kneeling uncomfortably in the snow, struggling to jam my boots into the skis.

"Dad," I tap his shoulder, trying to sound Amrikayi. But I'm a baby: "Daddy?" A dumb foreigner: "Ay Dadee!" Unindustrious coward with no idea how Amrika works. Keep tapping, desperate to avoid the word I don't want to use, the one more embarrassing than getting caught trying to slip into someone else's skis. But it's no use.

"Baba!"

The guy's smile widens, probably amused watching foreigners struggle to understand the Amrikayi. "Where are you guys from? What language is that?"

"It's cool, man," I curve Amrikayi twang. "We're from L.A, man," tap Baba again.

Baba finally looks up, annoyed, dark brows furrowed like he might explode.

"I think you've got the wrong skis, sir," the guy says without a trace of fear, or doubt. "These are my skis, sir," he enunciates to make sure Baba understands. "Yours. Must. Look. Like. Mine. These. Are. Mine. Sir." Points to a space just below the tip of the skis. "My name right there," he says, pointing to a grouping of gold letters etched into the skis.

Baba rises defiantly, shoulders back, chest out, studies the guy up and down. Clenches his jaw. I brace, praying he doesn't explode. "Is your eskee?"

"Yessir," the Amrikayi says with a humble smile. "Is my eskee." He looks over at me, winks as if to say, "It's OK, kid, I don't mind speaking your Dad's foreign tongue."

I smile back, shrug like "Yeah, my dumb foreigner dad doesn't get how things work 'round here. What a Non! Him, not me. Hardly know the guy. I'm not with him. Let's be friends. Let's ski. Take me with you!"

Baba exhales, chest deflates, shoulders slump. "Oh. I think anybody can take."

"Anybody can take?" He tilts his head, a confused smile that turns into a quick snort. "No, sir, we ain't Soviet. Rental shop over there," pointing to the place we just left, "is where you can rent skis, poles and bindings – everything you need - from that shop."

"Oh," Baba turns his head to the ski shop like he hasn't seen it before. He leans the skis over to their rightful owner; brows unfurrow, face softens like I haven't seen before. "OK," half-bowing an ancient, humble "please forgive me" bow, hand on chest. "*Dezolay. Pardon.*"

"Have a good one!" He walks with his skis to an empty spot between the lodge and slopes. With an easy grace, he drops his skis on the snow, stabs his poles in, steps into the binders, bends forward like a swan to flick his bootstraps shut like he's flipping a light switch. He straightens up, pulls his poles from the snow and glides away. No hitch. No obstacle. No doubt. That's Amrika. For him. For them. He wants us to have a good one. No heart feelings.

I wish I was his friend, his cousin, his little brother. Him. Light and trouble-free, standing tall in a world where I want to be. I don't want just to have a good one; I want to feel so right I can tell someone else to have a good one. I want Baba to teach me that. I know he can't. I hoped Baba knew what he was doing but as I watch him, deflated, motioning us back to the ski shop, I wonder if he even knows why Maman left or if he can bring her back.

Baba gets boots and skis for himself too and one lift ticket we take turns using; we have to go up in the chair alone; ski down alone; hand off the ticket. We take the easiest hill right in front of the lodge. But even the easiest hill is steep with plenty of bumps and curves.

When it's my turn, I stand alone at the top, staring down at the steep curves and bumps, stomach twisting. Baba and Precious cheer me on from below: "Come on! Do it!" All alone.

I stick my poles in the snow and push, stammering, knuckling around bumps, leaning on my poles, carefully bending, slowly twisting, lumbering and hurtling downward, doing anything I can to avoid falling. It is only when I reach the bottom, relieved as I watch Baba and Precious take their turns, that I look up at the hill's slope, bumps and curves and realize I just skied this glorious mountain! Struggled but survived…and never fell. Did I have fun on the way down? Did I feel excitement hurtling down? Or was I too busy being scared, too scared of falling?

Baba falls. He struggles to get back up, tries to keep his skis from sliding down the hill. His cheeks get so purple they shine through his whiskers. He hasn't looked this energized since the days when we first arrived from Tehran. He gets up, chugs, glides down, white mist bursting from his mouth. He falls again and again, but doesn't seem bothered by it, making excited "Eep!" and "Aah!" sounds as he tumbles and picks himself up. He looks almost athletic in his red-and-white sweater with the giant snowflakes – a hand-me-down he kept for himself and managed to squeeze into. His smile is as wide and white as the snow.

As the lodge gets ready to shut down, Baba is feeling like a sport and agrees to hot chocolates. We stick our skis in the snow, like real skiers, and walk to the lodge. Baba gets in line and we find a table outside on the deck. A chilly breeze lifts the powdery snow off the treacherous mountain, off the thick tree branches. Warm in multiple sweaters and zipped up jackets, we sniff the piney air like maybe it belongs to us too. Baba's hot chocolate smells minty and sharp. In our chairs on the deck of the wooden ski lodge, we sip and stare up at the big, white mountain we have just climbed and, in our own ways, conquered. My chest feels big. I feel like yelling to my friend, "Hey, Man, we had a good one!"

"Does Maman ski," Precious asks.

Before I can picture Maman, elegant and perfumed with her shiny nails and dangling earrings trying to snap shut those bulky ski boots, Baba drains his minty cocoa and gets up.

"It's getting too dark to drive home," he says. "We'll have to find a motel."

We return the skis and head to the car, excited about staying in a motel. But after driving around and finding no rooms, Baba changes plans. We have blankets, pillows and a bag full of cheese, fruit and nuts. Baba parks by a curb on the main road; we lock the doors and crack the windows.

"Don't forget to say your Sheman Israel," he says, leaning a pillow against his door and unfolding a blanket as he stretches out on the front seat.

"Why do we have to pray tonight," asks Precious. "Aren't we allowed to skip when we're not sleeping at home? Maman usually does it with me."

"Say it," Baba says. "Prayer is even more important when you're away from home."

I say the Hebrew part out loud and my secret wish part to myself, like at home. But Precious says his secret wish part out loud. "Please bring Maman home soon so she can ski with us next time," he prays, hands clasped together. "Amen."

"Amen," Baba says from the front seat. We never think Baba listens to anything we say.

"Is she coming back," I ask.

"Of course," Baba says. He yawns, loud and long like a tired lion.

"It's been so long," says Precious. "Are you sure?"

"She'll be home," Baba says.

"Why'd she go," I ask.

"To help her friend, like she said."

"The one who died?" I ask, trying to get at the truth.

"She has things to take care of," Baba says from the front seat.

He sighs long and deep. Then he's quiet. Everything gets quiet after that and, figuring we're done talking and are going to sleep, I say "Goodnight" but get no response.

"Don't worry," Baba says minutes later, breaking the long dark silence. "She's not mad at anybody. Nobody did anything wrong. Everything will be fine."

We don't respond and it gets so quiet I can hear the yellow streetlights buzz outside. The car windows frost up. A smell of rotten eggs floats inside; Baba cracks his window further.

Precious and I look at each other and giggle.

"What're you laughing at," Baba asks as he rolls the window back up.

But we can't stop. "Nothing," I manage. "But can we keep our window open, in case?

"In case what?"

More giggles.

"OK, quiet down and get some sleep."

We can't, whispering until we fall asleep. Baba cracks his window every few minutes.

School starts Monday.

January 1973

We are warm and sleepy in our pajamas when the cab honks. Baba at the door beside a suitcase wearing the grey hat with the black band and red feather he wore when he left Tehran. Hasn't worn it since. Amrikayi men only wear hats in movies and are never happy about it, usually caught up in unpleasant business involving saloons, money or crazy dames. And guns, always guns. Baba looks caught-up too, prob- ably over money he has to pay for a taxi to the airport, or that crazy dame, Sweet Lady, who browbeat him into going back to Tehran to get that other crazy dame, Maman. He thought she would be back by Hanooka. On long distance she keeps saying she's coming, but never when. Unpleasant business. Baba's hat confirms it.

"How long does a funeral take," Precious asked last night when Baba said he was going.

"Bad luck to talk of such things, little one," Sweet Lady said before ritualistically biting both sides of her hand and spitting to ward off the bad luck Precious brought with his question. "May you always be far from such things."

When the cab honks a second time, Baba straightens our shoulders up man-style and hands Sweet Lady a wad of cash which she tucks inside her bra. They kiss awkwardly, both cheeks. She hands him a bag of pistachios, dates and walnuts for the long airplane ride.

"Be good boys," he says with no smile and grim eyes as he turns toward the waiting cab.

"Pleasant journey," Sweet Lady says, watching him get in the cab. "God protect you."

Something is off. Sweet Lady's normal face is a smiling one - crin- kled brown eyes, wide laughing lips, bright teeth lighting up her brown cheeks. Her normal way is warm and playful. Even her double-blink-lip-bite comes with a smirk like it's all dangerous fun. But lately it's been different; sober eyes, sealed lips and serious words. The kitchen has no smell of frying butter, dates or eggs, no tea brewing. The kitchen is cold, with Sweet Lady leaning against the yellow tiles, eyes fixed, dialing the operator again, long distance.

There's a box of cereal on the table. She covers the mouthpiece with her hand, "have Komepress," which is how Sweet Lady pronounces "Corn Flakes," which is her name for all cereal – Fruit Loopies, Sugars Pop, Captain Crunchy, King of Vitamins. They're all Corn Flakes to her because in Iran Corn Flakes is the only cereal. Komepress is Sweet Lady's breakfast of last resort when there is no time, or in an emergency. And the good thing about emergencies is sometimes we get outside food - Kentucky Fries Chickens, Mickey Doonalds, even Pizza!

"He is coming," she exclaims to the phone. "Of course, azizam," she reassures.

"Is that Maman," I interrupt, trying to keep my voice from shaking to hide the panic. "Can I talk?" I try to sound demanding. "I want to talk to Maman!"

Sweet Lady puts her hand on the mouthpiece again. "Get ready for school, little one." No smile, no blinks, no dangerous fun. All business, like she is our boss now, not the playful partner-in-crime and whose visits we look forward to. Maman is gone, Baba is gone, Sweet Lady stands alone, in her stockinged feet and cash wadded in the strap of her bra.

"I wanna talk too," yells Precious, clumsily pulling the cord and caus-ing the receiver to slip from Sweet Lady's hand, dangling and bouncing off the kitchen floor with a series of clangs.

"What are you doing," she says with a sharp tone we have never heard from her. "I'm talking, can't you see? This isn't baby games here! Eat your breakfast! Immediately!"

It was like an unexpected clap on the ear. Sweet Lady angry. She pulls the phone up by the cord and continues talking. We pour the ce-real and milk. She eventually relents, handing the phone over. Maman sounds fine but distant; still won't say when she's coming back, which is suddenly important. When we leave for school, we don't even say goodbye as Sweet Lady, still talking to Maman. We climb down the hill, neither of us saying a word because maybe neither of us wants to say what we're thinking, because saying it might make it come true. I bite both sides of my hand and spit to ward off bad luck like Maman taught me, just in case.

"Your mom back yet," Fertig asks as we huddle by the back fence before the bell.

I'm still feeling hyper from the morning, don't want to fill him in on how we are almost Amrikayi like him now - Baba gone, Maman gone, cereal for breakfast and Sweet Lady taking over. It's kind of embarrassing, how even divorce isn't Amrikayi when we do it - our grandma moving in to be our Mom. For a second I feel bad, ignoring Fertig, then I remember I don't need approval from Nons. I can act however I want around them. Nons don't count.

At lunch, my stomach does the slow boil, maybe I have malnutrition. I rarely eat Maman's lunches, chucking them before anyone sees. They don't contain any Proper Nouns: Oscar Meyer, Underwood, Best Foods, Kraft, Wonder, Hostess - as seen on TV. We get plain, foreigner lunches, small letter ingredients. It's embarrassing.

Sweet Lady knows even less about Amrikayi lunches than Maman did. Trying to get a head start on the day because Baba was leaving, she made lunch last night, using Maman's routine: pale, flimsy non-Oscar-Meyer meat, wilted lettuce with a dangerous shade of copper singeing the edges, clumps of hard butter spread by force in a pita. Snack is an orange with tooth marks, to help start the peel. And it's all packed in a large Von's bag, the top half cut to make it look like a normal-size lunch bag. Only to clueless foreigners does a cut supermarket bag pass for a normal-size lunch bag. To Amrikayi, it's an obvious, sad attempt at passing for normal.

Amrikayi have lunchboxes with pictures - Partridge Family, Superman, Johnny Quest. If they use paper bags, they are white with yellow smiley faces on them. It costs a quarter for a stack at Von's. Maman scoffs, "Why pay for bags when Von's gives bigger ones for free with groceries? Only simple dehati pay for free bags." I wait until after school, make a ketchup-cheese pita and a can of beans at home. But at lunchtime, the slow churn of malnutrition.

Fat Guillermo is lunch monitor. Five minutes before the bell, he gets to leave class and comes back pulling a red wagon full of lunchboxes and smiley-faced bags. Sometimes he reads the names off the bags and comments on what's inside as kids come up to get their lunches.

"Fertig!" he'll scream. "Sliced carrots and celery with Fig Newtons, boring!"

"Dudley! Peanut Butter and Frito's. DisGROSSting!"

I don't put my name on mine and when Fat Guillermo calls out "Von's" with a heartless chortle, holding it up for everyone to see, I sit tight and wait until everyone has gotten theirs.

At lunch, the benches bustle like the Tehran bazaar where Baba worked. They're all looking for deals. Frito's and Fruit Rolls go fast. Laura Scudder's BBQ chips get interest. String Cheese and Cheez n' Crackers are throw-ins on bigger trades. Main targets are Wonder bread sandwiches with Underwood or Oscar Meyer, Amrikayi cheese and Best Foods, or Skippy with Smuckers Grape. Ding Dongs, Twinkies, Fruit Pies are prizes. Trading is brisk and I'm a spectator; my mystery-meat in pita with butter clumps and orange with bite marks have no value.

The real Mexicki - Rodrigo and Fat Guillermo - have fried tortillas stuffed with meat, cheese, beans and shredded lettuce. Rodrigo holds one out for me.

"Quieres taquito?"

"Rodrigo," making sure he understands. "I. Not. Mexicki. Already tell you this."

"Se que no erés Mexicano," Rodrigo says with a big smile, still holding out the rolled tortilla. "Pero quiero enseñarte ya que todos piensan que erés Mexicano."

I stare.

"He's joking with you," says Fat Guillermo.

Fat Guillermo is lighter skinned than both me and Rodrigo, like a small teaspoon of Bosco in the milk. His light brown hair is neatly combed and parted to the side. He speaks better English than me or Rodrigo and wears sweaters with diamond designs on them and grown-up men's shirts underneath; probably why he gets to be lunch monitor.

"Go ahead and take a taquito, Mike, they're tasty."

I take it, hold it, turn it over. It feels greasy in my hand. "Thanks, Rodrigo."

"Yerry."

"Yerry?"

"He's saying Jerry," says Fat Guillermo, chewing a taquito. "That's his new name," wipes grease off the side of his mouth. "And my new name is Guy."

"Doesn't Guy mean boy? Are you changing your name to Boy or is Jerry and Guy the American translation for Rodrigo and Guillermo?"

"Me gusta Yerry," says Rodrigo/Jerry. "Ess cool. Como Tom y Yerry cartoons."

"I like Guy," says Fat Guillermo, "Guy is a fun name. Try it. Say Guy to me."

"I don't get it," I say. "You're going to tell everybody to call you Guy?"

"Well, Jerry's gonna call me Guy," he says, turning to Rodrigo/Jerry.

"Jess," nods Rodrigo/Jerry. "Y Guey gonna calling me Yerry."

"Dices Guy, Rodrigo, no Guey," Fat Guillermo/Guy says to Rodrigo/Jerry. "Mi nombre es Guy, como Chico, no Guey. Y tu nombre es Jerry, no Yerry. Dilo J-J-Jerry, no Yerry."

Fat Guillermo/Guy leans in, like we're sharing a secret. "Call me Guy and you can be co-lunch monitor with me. You get to leave class early; get your lunch first. French Benefits."

I don't care about the first two. But ... "What's French Benefits?"

"That's when you get free stuff just for being lunch monitor. Like they do in France."

I like the sound of that. Free stuff sounds better than anything I have in my Von's bag.

Fat Guillermo/Guy hands me one of his own taquitos. "Here, try mine. My mom's taquitos are less greasy that Jerry's mom's."

I bite into one. Crunchy, cheesy, chewy – delicious! It opens up my tongue and teeth, my lungs fill with new air like they'd been closed until then. I must have been starving. I eat the other taquito as slow as I can.

First thing I see when I pop my head through the doggie door is Sweet Lady's thick ankles. She's still leaning on the counter, phone in hand like we left her this morning, urgency in the air - cold stove, tired eyes, near-full ashtray on the counter. Important things happening; sometimes that means no time to cook; outside food. Emergencies can be good sometimes.

When she sees my head pop through the doggie door, she tucks the phone between her neck and shoulder and pulls a pot from the cabinet. She pours rice, water, salt and oil, starts the stove then does a fast teeth-on-lip signal and shoos me toward the door.

"I'm making dinner, little one, go play," like I'm in her way. We are definitely having an emergency. But not the good kind, no Kentucky Fries Chickens, Mickey Doonalds or Pizza.

At dinner, we sit at the table shoveling raisin-and-lentil rice, chewing in silence. We rarely see Sweet Lady eat; she is normally in motion, chatting, joking, doing hair, painting nails, smoking, cooking and serving. It's like seeing her for the first time, chewing with the left side of her mouth, missing an upper tooth on the right, cheeks wrinkled, a splotchy dent normally hidden in the folds of her laughter shaped like a foreign nation on an ancient map. Her hands are spotted, her teeth are like old stained dice. But her small brown eyes are clear like a baby's. You can't see people until they are still and most people are only still when they are sad, in thought or sitting to dinner. I see Sweet Lady tonight. Maman isn't here for her to gossip with, or Baba to banter with. She hasn't asked about our day. Tonight she is still. Precious looks like he might ask her something, lifts his head, takes a breath, maybe about Maman's return or Baba's arrival, then thinks better of it, exhales and asks for water.

Fat Guillermo, hair combed and parted to the side and wearing a grownup man's shirt under a beige sweater, pops up as usual when the clock hits eleven-fifty-five.

"Time for lunch, Mrs. McLean," he says, sweet and proper.

Moon faced Mrs. McLean has told us many times that she used to be an actress, taught to launch her voice from the bottom of her stomach so they can hear her in the cheap seats.

"So it is. Gracias, Senor Guillermo!" she proclaims. "I discharge thee to your duties."

Fat Guillermo looks at me from across the room and motions for me to get up. I stay put.

"Did you know I go by Guy now? Sort of a nickname for Guillermo. Might be easier."

"I would have guessed Bill."

"But also Guy," looking over at me again. "Everyone calls me Guy now."

"Duly noted, Senor Guillermo, I shall mark that in my big book."

"Guy."

"Got it," she says, now flat and less theatrical.

"Also, I need help with the lunches."

"You need what?" She looks annoyed now, scratching her curly hair with a pencil.

"The wagon is heavy." He motions at me again to get up as hands shoot up by kids who want to be co-lunch monitor. "Oh Oh" and "Me Me" pops all over the classroom. In the back row, Speed, Worm and two other Pros sit back, arms folded, buckteeth out, wondering what all the fuss is about and taking advantage of the distraction to have their own chats about cooler, more important things. So who wants to be a stupid lunch monitor? Not me. Forget it.

"Mike M. told me he'd like to help," says Guy, ignoring the noise.

"No, it's OK," I blurt out.

Mrs. McLean tilts her head like she is seeing me for the first time. I keep mum, avoid her eyes, tuck my head between my shoulders to get invisible. I don't want her to connect me to Fat Guillermo in front of the Pros; to have them see me like that. But she stares until she forces my eyes up to hers. A smile forms on her lips. She thinks I'm being shy.

"You, good sir, are hereby dubbed Co-Lunch Monitor. Let it be so!"

Hands go down with exhales and harrumphs as Fat Guillermo claps with joy, "Goodie!"

I reluctantly get up and we walk past those who didn't get picked and the Pros talking about cooler things that I can't hear, even as I lean in on my way out.

We pull the empty wagon to the benches and toss the lunches in. Fat Guillermo opens a lunch bag, sticks his face in, inspects.

"What do we have here," pulling up a Kraft Cheez N' Crackers. "French Benefits."

"Guillermo, that belongs to somebody."

"Belonged. And call me Guy, remember our deal."

Sounds dumb, having your aka be what you are, a guy. And how come he gets to choose his own aka? He's a Non like the rest of us. But you can't argue with a loudmouth.

"Still belongs to somebody."

"French Benefits, remember? You look in bags, see who has lots of lunch items, sneak something they won't miss. This guy has a sandwich, grapes, Fig Newtons, string cheese; he won't miss a Cheez N' Crackers. So, French Benefit. See? For being lunch monitor."

"You don't get in trouble if you get caught stealing?"

"First off, it's not stealing. It's French Benefits for being lunch monitor. Second off, they don't notice if you take from full bags. Third off, don't take big stuff. Fig Newtons, string cheese, Cheez N' Crackers. Not stuff that can be traded or remembered."

Guy slides the Cheez N' Crackers into his own lunch bag and looks through other lunches. My lunch is bad as usual: soft apple, thin slice of damp purple meat called Pastrami with dark green lettuce and butter chunks on torn bread. I'll toss it later.

"Go ahead!" he insists. "Find something you like. It's fine. French Benefits."

How is he so sure? And why does he insist that I do it too, like if I don't he'll make trouble. Maybe it's so he won't be the only one, so we can share the burden of his Sin. I open a bag, peek in. Strange meats, foreign breads, foil-wrapped odd-shaped items, vegetables, fruit cups, yoghurt, olives, pita (like me!), boiled eggs that smell like farts. Some lunches look as foreign and odd as my homecooked Persian dinners. Feels wrong, peeking into somebody's Inside life; they'd be embarrassed if they knew. Maybe some of them aren't so different from me; maybe some of them are... Ooh! Hostess Cherry Pie! Thank you very much.

"Jehannam!" Sweet Lady screams, throwing the glass of milk at the counter. It smashes, glass flies, milk splatters, my heart pounds. Never seen her do that. She tried soft pleas, but I refused. She tried reason to convince me my growing body needs vitamins, I refused. She tried the threats Maman uses, but Sweet Lady would never raise a hand on us. Plain white milk - no sugar, honey or Bosco - is where I draw the line. But I didn't expect her to throw the glass. Her patience is wearing thin. Long distance calls; time with Baba; taking care of us. Thin as a dime.

As I watch the glass shatter and the milk rain down on the kitchen floor, I realize we're barefoot. Precious and I carefully step out of the kitchen to finish getting dressed as Sweet Lady continues spitting curses and bitter words under her breath while sweeping shards and slivers of milk-soaked glass from the floor. She's using words I've heard Baba and Maman use, but never from Sweet Lady's mouth. On the way out, we avoid her; she doesn't say goodbye.

"You think she's gonna be taking care of us forever," Precious asks on the hill.

"Shut up, Precious." I'm staring past him at the lone palm in our backyard as I hold a wet vine in my freezing hands, lowering myself down the muddy hill. "It's only been a couple days. And who cares? Maybe it's better with them gone. Cool Amrikayi are all divorced."

"Don't tell me to shut up. Don't call me Precious. They're not divorcing. You shut up!"

"Who collected lunches yesterday," demands Mrs. McLean minutes before the lunch bell. She's using her army general voice, can't tell if she's playing. Fat Guillermo is absent. Maybe the jig is up on French Benefits and he stayed home to leave me holding his bag of Sin.

Stay outa dis. Let the fat kid take the rap. Pros don't like lunch monitors anyway.

I keep my head down, stomach cooking, ass sweating as she scans the room with her frog green eyes, until she lands on me and again forces my eyes up to meet hers.

"It was you, wasn't it, Senor Miguel? You were in charge of lunches yesterday."

Talk exactly like the fat kid talked yesterday, and don't mention French Benefits.

"I was…Co. Vice. Lunch. Monter," I say, hoping it sounds Amri-kayi-official enough.

"And where is Senor Guillermo, today?"

"You mean Guy, don't you Mrs. McLean," Fertig in his thick voice, always butting in where he doesn't belong. "He's Guy now, remember, Mrs. McLean?"

"Yes, Mister Fertig," she gives an annoyed head-tilt to Fertig. "I remember, thank you."

"Guy is not present today, Mrs. McLean, remember?"

"Yes, Mister Fertig, I remember." She looks back at me. "So it was you who brought the lunches yesterday, Senor Miguel?"

Pros are watching. Don't say another woid. You won't take 'de rap.

"With Senor Guy absent," she goes on, "will you need your own Co-Lunch-Monitor?"

She don't suspect; you're in the clear.

I'm about to correct her, tell her I'm not Mexicki, when hands go up, faces looking at me. "Oh oh pick me!" I get to choose. I'm the boss. Satisfaction Sniff. But not for long:

"I'd be happy to help Mike bring in lunches, Mrs. McLean," offers Fertig, standing.

"So it shall be," Mrs. McLean, not looking up. "Now go and gather those lunches!"

"Looks like we'll be working together," Fertig says to me with a wink.

"Just for today," I remind him. I get to be Fertig's boss for a change. "And I am boss Lunch Monter; you're just worker Lunch Monter taking orders from me or you're fired, got it?"

"She said *Co*-Lunch *Monitors. Monitors*, Beaner Boy. So you can't really order me."

Just for that, I decide to not let Fertig in on French Benefits. We pile lunches on the wagon; I'm on the lookout for Cherry Pie. On the TV commercial: Fruit Pie the Magician beats evil ghosts - with a Hostess fruit pie! He rewards the kids who helped - with a Hostess fruit pie! It is both weapon and reward! *Apple. Berry. Cherry.* Need that sweet, tangy Cherry to settle the churning. Gonna find one, bite into its flaky buttery crust, let the syrup flow. I'll lick, suck, savor its gooey redness, its cherry lumps, let it coat the angst, soothe the chaos inside me. Fat Guy's Rules: Don't leave a bag too empty; don't wrinkle bags; don't take anything obvious.

And what do we have here? Jackpot!

This bag has a peanut butter sandwich and an orange to go with the pie. Taking it violates two of Guy's Rules.

Now 'dis shouldn't be a bodder at all, brudder. Just rearrange. Use yer noggin.

I look inside other bags. Heavy ones. Three have a bunch of things. Carrots. Celery with peanut butter. Fruit cups. Apricot Rolls. Twinkies. Oreos. Nutter Butters. Nilla Wafers. I switch items around, bag to bag, redistributing, weighing, so they look equal, fair, no signs that something has gone wrong, like they all still have plenty of food and tradable items. The snacks all look the same; nobody's gonna remember which one is theirs.

Nobody'll be the wiser, eh Doc?

"What in Sam Hill are you doing, Beaner Boy," asks Fertig.

I don't know how long he's been standing there.

"Not your beeswax. You're not a real Lunch Monter, so you wouldn't get it."

"*Monitor.* Are you taking things that don't belong to you?"

"French Benefits," I put the lunch bag in the wagon, keeping the pie in my clutches.

"French what?"

"You won't get it. It's for Lunch Monters. French Benefits. We get to take stuff."

"You mean *Fringe* Benefits? You're taking people's food as a fringe benefit?"

The way Fertig describes it sounds different from how Fat Guill-ermo described it.

"Once in a while," I explain to Fertig in a cool whisper. "It's pen-ultimate."

"You started as lunch monitor yesterday," he says with husky-voiced logic.

I give Fertig the side-to-side-coast-is-clear look so he feels like he's being included. "Lookit, it's just small stuff. Fat Guy says it's OK and he's been Lunch Monter all year. You can take too." Yes, I want him to share the burden of my Sin. "Go ahead, Co-Lunch Monter. But follow Fat Guy's Rules: nothing big, don't wrinkle the bags, and hurry it up."

"Well," says Fertig, rubbing his chin like he's rubbing an old beard and thinking things through, "I suppose I do have a weakness for apri-cot fruit rolls."

"Sure you do. So go ahead."

"Just a strip off a roll, that oughta be OK," Fertig setting his own limits.

"Make it fast," I say and before I'm done saying it Fertig is rifling through lunch bags until he finds one, unrolls it, rips off a huge strip, rolls it and throws it back in the bag.

"Ready!"

"Let's go," I say.

We don't talk, handing out lunches as they open their bags and get ready to trade. But it goes bad as soon as they look inside, then look up, confused by what they see.

Jeff K. holds up a bag of Nilla Wafers, a "what the heck is this" look on his face.

Todd M. studies the Nutter Butters in his lunchbox.

Barry G. notices his bag of Nillas being held by Jeff K. and compares it to the sealed pack of Oreos he's just pulled out of his bag. He smiles.

Fertig uses the little red plastic knife to dig out orange cheese from the orange cheese compartment of the Cheez N' Crackers in his lunch. The strip of apricot fruit roll sits beside him on the bench, ready to be wrapped around his finger and sucked.

I unwrap my Cherry Pie, start in. Chunks of buttery crust and chewy cherry melt on my back teeth, lumpy and glorious in my mouth.

I squeeze the thick sweet cherry goo between my tongue and the roof of my mouth, hold it, make it last as long as possible before letting it ooze down, tangy cherry stinging the back of my throat with pure joy.

"That's my cherry pie!"

Facken Anss Shet!! On my first bite?

"Beaner Boy's eating my cherry pie," Big Mouth Patricia, pointing at me.

"There's more than one Hostess Cherry Pie in the world, Patricia," says Fertig, looking over to give me a round-eyed gaze. A "what did you do!" look.

"But that pie is mine," Big Mouth Patricia declares, pointing at the pie in my hand.

I stare back, mouth full of sad, un-swallowed glory, being held on my tongue, waiting for clearance. "This is my Hostess Pie Cherry," I say, not convincingly. "From my house."

"No way," she yells. "You never have snacks. I'm telling." She leaves the benches.

Try to swallow. Throat tightens. Tongue thick with crumbs, sugar granules feel like they may choke me, give me away, refuse to go down.

She walks back with Yard Teacher, pointing at me, jabbering her big mouth.

"Hey kid," Yard Teacher says to me, "you steal her snack?"

Yard Teacher is tall. Curly brown hair pours out from under a white Gilligan hat. Bulging blue eyes. Bumpy sunburnt nose. Long throat, a big lump in the middle. Blonde moustache. He means business and I'm not sure it's a good idea to lie.

Big Mouth Patricia, skinny arms folded, dark curly hair spilling from the same red scarf Dudley wears, like the poster in class of Rosie the Amrikayi worker from Hitler's war, confident and strong. She waits for her justice, because she's entitled to it. But her justice is my Sin. I would gladly switch with her – expecting justice like it's a right, touble-free.

I'm still holding the offending pie. The corner wedge I'd bitten off is spilling its sweet, forbidden, cherry goo onto the wrapper, and my finger.

"I brought this from my house," I tell Yard Teacher, looking around for Fertig.

Fertig has moved on. Finished his Cheez N' Crackers, rolled the stolen apricot fruit roll around his finger, sucking like he was born with it, finally minding his own business.

"From my house," I say again, looking away from my accuser and the authorities.

"My name is on the wrapper, dummy," expectant, foot tapping, arms crossed, fingers on her right hand playing piano on her left arm, Wilma Flintstone style.

Yard Teacher grabs my wrist, the one attached to the hand holding the pie, brings it up to study the wrapper. "Patricia Room 14" in black marker. Looks at me. I look at the wrapper. Must've missed it; didn't think anybody would put their name on a wrapper. But when you bring a Hostess Cherry Pie, I guess you should. I look around to see who else is watching.

"Where'd you get this?" asks Yard Teacher.

"From my lunch bag. Gee, I thought it was mine. Somebody musta took my Hostess Cherry Pie. I'm telling! Did somebody take my pie?" I look around, for effect.

"Stop. You never have Hostess," yells Big Mouth Patricia. "You always have the same thing: a weird round sandwich and fruit. When did you start bringing Hostess? What a liar."

"OK, give her back her pie," says Yard Teacher.

I look up at Yard Teacher. The sun behind his Gilligan hat silhouettes his face as his blue eyes shine down on me. *You're lucky,* I want to tell him. *With your light brown hair and blue eyes, groovy moustache and Gilligan hat; a grownup Amrikayi, standing where you belong, above me, above all this; trouble-free, probably living in a bachelor pad, playing rock records, eating Kentucky Fries Chickens, Mickey Doonalds, Pizza. Can't you show some mercy?*

I look at Big Mouth Patricia. Her fists now at her hips, elbows out, legs apart, like an A. *You've had plenty of Hostess Fruit Pies. Probably all the flavors, even boring Apple. With everything going your way, on your turf, your Rosie the Amrikayi worker scarf on your head. Can't you show some mercy? Or at least not yell so loud so everybody doesn't see me like this?*

"Forget it," she says. "I don't even want it now."

I can't tell if she's being nice. My lips flatten to an almost smile.

"You got your cooties on it," she turns her head and folds her arms, "You can have it."

"I don't have the coolies. Here," I hold the oozing pie out for her, "take it."

"Why don't you give her something from your lunch bag," says Yard Teacher.

"No thanks! I don't want his cootie apple or chewed up orange," she yells. "Forget it."

"I can owe you," I say. "I have Nillas at my house. I'll bring Nillas tomorrow."

"You're in a lot of trouble, kid," says Yard Teacher.

I do it because it shouldn't be only my burden. Fertig, laughing too easy, enjoying the apricot fruit roll on his finger too much, sucking like he's trouble-free and without Sin. Not fair.

"He did it too," I point. "Look!" Loud enough to freeze him. "That's not his apricot!"

We look at Fertig, who looks back, caught in mid-suck, shaking his head.

"Beaner Boy ordered me. He's Chief Lunch Monitor; I'm just a temporary."

Then it all falls apart: "That's my Oreos," Jeff K. yells across the benches at Barry G.

Barry G., crumbs on lips and mouth full of cookie, yells back, "Cuz you ate my Nillas!"

"Who took my Fritos?"

They are all yelling, pointing. Yard Teacher looks around.

"You guys were lunch monitors today," Yard Teacher says to me and Fertig, "let's go."

We follow Yard Teacher. Fertig whispers "You gonna tell on Fat Guy, the ringleader? Don't take the fall for a ringleader. Why tell on me and not him? Aren't we better friends?"

After getting chewed out by Mr. Haley, we walk into class. Mrs. McLean has already started reading from *The Pearl*. They all look, snickering and whispering:

"Hands in the Hostess cookie jar."

"Caught Cherry-Red-handed."

"Kelly Smelly and Beaner Boy: Snack Burglars."
"Frito Banditos."
More aka's.

All I want is to make a ketchup-cheese pita, a can of beans and watch TV in peace, away from their playground, their games, their voices. Precious is outside with Kersh and Cowan. I pop through the doggie door, face to face with Sweet Lady's thick ankles. We haven't spoken since the milk incident this morning. She is still working the phone; doesn't even nod. Her brow is sweaty. She's pleading, trying to convince, throwing her head back in frustration. I go to the fridge and she puts her hand on the mouthpiece, motions me to leave the kitchen.

That does it! I slam the fridge, slam the kitchen door, open the front door and slam it too. Kersh, Cowan and Precious are shooting baskets in Cowan's driveway; in the distance the faint singsong of Ice Cream Man bounces toward Albatross Lane. I go back in for a dime; Ice Cream man is our routine. We can at least keep this, can't we? From behind the kitchen door, I hear yelling. I open a crack: her tired face heavy, cheeks shiny like she's been crying. We lock eyes.

"Wait outside, little one, how many times should I tell you," hand on receiver.

They never notice us enough to order us out of a room; today she's already asked me to leave twice. Not much time before Ice Cream Man leaves. In the kitchen, more yelling, strained words, plaintive tones. The jingling ice cream truck melodies go on loop; it is parked and doing business. He's pushing down on the slots of his change belt, handing out coins along with Sno-Cones, Astro Pops and 50/50 Bars. Soon he'll decide there's no more customers and drive off.

Sweet Lady's shiny black handbag is on the table by the front door. Inside it, a jar of Pond's cold cream, a red book of names and numbers scribbled in Farsi and English, a red-white-and-green pack of Red Rooster spearmint gum from Iran, and dimes. Unattended.

I got caught stealing today, but I know right from wrong. It isn't stealing when she hands over a dime every day. We sit together afterwards, I offer her some. "Try this," holding a cola flavored Bottle Cap, "it's like Pepsi!" She doesn't like Amrikayi candy, lights a Winston, crunches a square of Red Rooster with her good tooth, sips her hot tea sweetened with rock candy. She puts her feet up and we watch her afternoon programs about doctors, secret lovers and abandoned bastards as our dinner simmers. Usually. Not today.

Today she's busy and Ice Cream Man's music is slowing down. Soon it will fade. Maman and Baba are gone, no telling when they'll be back; Sweet Lady's handbag. Like an emergency. On Yom Kippur I'll confess, beg forgiveness.

On the table by the door, in the mirror I catch a glimpse of myself in the act. Dark. Wide-eyed. Sinner. Kitchen door closed. Ice Cream Man jingle looping. Sweet Lady on the phone, her voice a high pitch, her words stretching for emphasis.

"Be reeeeasonable ... kept his promiiise ... doooing his business .. . a nice houuuse ... kids ... school ... don't move back there ... disruptions ... everyone is leaving there too. . ."

We're moving back to Tehran?

Ice Cream Man's leaving. Get movin'.

Back to New School?

Take da coins!

I'd be leader of the Olders! Now part Amrikayi too! I'd run the whole show. I'd roar!

Hey Doc, maybe dey won't call you "Beaner Boy" over there neither.

Yeah!

Maybe they won't call you anything at all. Maybe they even won't remember you. Ever think o' that? Maybe they'll sing 'black one, black one' and laugh. Ice cream truck.

I take small, quiet steps, lift the handbag by its thick handle.

Slowly I toined...

To go down the hallway, out of sight.

Step by step...

Lift my knees high with each step, come down on my tiptoes extra gentle.

Inch by inch...

I'll open, fish out a dime, put it back on the table. She'll still be talking.

None the wiser. Like takin' candy from a baby. A dime, thin as her patience.

My favorite Amrikayi coin. Small, almost invisible. Thinner than the gaudy quarter. Twice as valuable as the dull nickel. I don't know who is on it; not their first king with the wig. Looks like Darren on *Bewitched*. The dime has power. Razzles; Milky Way; anything you want. But so small a grownup would never notice it missing.

Atta boy! Now snap it open and let's go – Wait!

The latch! Doorknob spring turning. Kitchen door pulling, sucking back the hallway air. Anchored by the thump of my heart, I freeze, handbag in my clutches. Turn.

"Oh my." Sweet Lady, eyes narrowed, meaty arm in midair, finger raised as if she was about to say something but was stopped in her tracks by what she saw. Her half-open mouth exposes the missing back tooth and crooked front teeth Maman and I inherited, a reminder that she is me and I am her. As she looks me over head to toe, I wonder what she sees: A dark boy, darkest of my people, black eyes, the large brown nose of a thief, the crooked teeth of a Sinner.

I expect the worst, having been caught stealing from an old lady, a grandma. That's bad in any country. They punish that everywhere. I brace for the shaming and damning; for the skin at my throat to be pinched and twisted; I wait for a cold, crisp slap across my cheek. Go ahead and lift me by the short hairs at the back of my neck and bum rush me out to the street where good, guiltless boys shooting baskets and licking sno-cones can see what a Sinner looks like.

"Now what is this, little one," Sweet Lady asks in a voice more puzzled than mad.

I can't look her in the eye. It has been a long, hard day I stare at the ground as my feet surrender to her, holding her bag out for her to reclaim.

"Ice Cream Man was leaving," I confess.

"Why, little one," she asks, her voice as warm as when she tells me to not eat before dinner, her tired eyes disappointed. "You could have waited," taking her bag from my clutches, snapping it open to fish out the dime. "This is nice?" she asks, handing it over. "This is naughty," she answers. "Don't be naughty. I have enough to handle. Tonight we'll break an egg and see who gave us the Bad Eye." She sighs, her entire body slouching like if she didn't have bones she'd crumple in a pile of sweaty flesh. Her heart is full and I made it worse.

I walk toward her outstretched hand holding the dime, the jingle music still playing but fading as the truck rolls away. I can still make it but I start bawling instead. Hard. Till I can't breathe. I try to catch a breath, to control it, but I can't. A long hard day.

"No," I whimper, "I don't want it." I throw myself into her heavy arms and bury my steamy face into the folds of her warm, layered neck. Her skin is thick, loose and soft. I burrow. She smells of Pond's cold cream, Aqua Net, sweat and boiled lentils from last night's dinner.

Sweet Lady pulls me in and wraps me, places a sweaty cheek on my head. "I don't forgive, little one. Adonai forgives. The easiest thing you can do," she says, "is be good."

She could have done anything to me, a dirty thief, a naughty boy. I deserve harsh justice reserved for those of us with dark insides. Instead, I get Grace. Finally.

"OK."

"Traitor!" Fat Guy comes for me before the bell rings. "You're fired as assistant Lunch Monitor! They called my mom, you Benedict Arnold!"

On an episode of *Brady Bunch*, Fridays at 8 Channel 7, Peter played Benedict Arnold in the school play; his schoolmates called him "traitor" for taking the part. I know it's an insult.

"Shut up your fat dummy mouth!" I yell. "You ain't no Lunch Monter neither!"

"Because of you, Benedict Arnold! Gonna kick your ass!"

Him? Kick my ass? He's a Non, as brown as me. Does he think they'll root for him over me? (Will they?) They all watch fights; that's why they gather as soon as they hear the magic words "kick your ass." Even the girls. Big Mouth Patricia, golden-haired Jodi S., new girl Lisa W., Shantay. I look to see if Shantay has me. Her hands cover her mouth as her shiny lips whisper to her friend; fingernails shiny red, suits her now. Does she see me?

"Too bad for you, Stinker," I yell as I think of more mean burns to snap him with.

"What?"

"Too bad you're a Stinker who stinks! I'm not fighting a Stinker cuz then I'll stink too. Take a bath, Stinker, and then I'll kill your *anss* but not get your Stinker Coolies on me!"

I hear giggles and look over again, but Shantay has turned and is walking away.

"Did you say Coolies?" He starts walking toward me and I don't move.

"It's a fight, it's a fight!" They chant. "Let's see who's the meaner beaner!"

"Lucha Libre! Which brown will go down?"

"El Gordo versus El Klepto!"

More laughs. More aka's. I don't see either of us gaining anything from this.

Bell rings and they head for class, leaving the two of us, fresh humiliations lingering over our heads. We unclench. With the crowd gone, I figure he'll see how pointless it is to fight.

"Flagpole at three!" he says, loud enough so they hear even with their backs turned.

The rest of the day, I try to be invisible but can feel their looks, hear their chirps, making me sweat. Even Speed and Worm chuckle. I envy them, breezy on the blacktop, flipping long hair, cool in soft sneakers, worn jeans, loose t-shirts – not sticky from nerves and fear of losing a fight to a Non. Losing a fight to a Pro is one thing – if you're a Non, it's expected; if you're a Pro, it's a battle. But losing to a Non?

"You'll be fine," Fertig says at lunch. "Try to get the first punch in, then cover."

"I know," I lie. Even Fertig's grating voice sounds breezy.

Three o'clock at the flagpole, the metal hook tied to the rope that holds the flag clangs against the hollow pole. Nobody here. Relieved … insulted. Nobody thought it was a big enough deal. Then again, I avoid humiliation with each passing minute, inching away from the flagpole, the lazy flag above me, inching toward the street, the hill, the lone palm.

You showed him; he chickened out. Now hightail it home. Go ahead, Doc, run!

At the top of the hill, I catch my breath, walk to the front, to Albatross Lane. And I stop.

It's them! With Precious and Sweet Lady at the front door, laughing, hugging. Maman crying in Sweet Lady's arms, hugging and swaying side to side. "Welcome, my girl," she says.

Baba is holding Precious, shaking him, mussing his hair with his big hands. He looks slim, a new moustache, bushy sideburns. A smoker dangles from his lips. Beige turtleneck, checkered slacks tight at the hips, flared at the cuffs, caramel leather ankle boots. A jacket is draped like a cape over his shoulders. Like Batman.

Maman glows, her soft brown hair grown out, corkscrew-curls falling around her, a brown midi-dress with red and yellow flowers and high heeled black leather boots up to her knees. She looks tall, stronger than she has been sounding on the phone these past weeks; her nostrils have regained that familiar flare of confidence she had before we ever came here.

They smell like breezy international travel - tobacco, perfume, cologne, gin, limes, black pepper, jet fuel, windswept adventure and unbuttoned adulthood. As they take their suitcases in, I watch with envy. They get to be grownups instead of being stuck in my sweaty playground life. They're not worried about getting busted for stealing, or into a fight with Fat Guy.

"I'm kicking your ass, Beaner Boy!" Fat Guy, pedaling his bike, labored and slow, huffing up Albatross Lane in a sweat. "I said flagpole at three, chicken. So we'll do it here."

"Who is this guy," asks Precious.

"Fat Guillermo," I say, "From school."

"He calls you *Beaner Boy?* Is that what they call you?"

"Some of them. When they're trying to be funny. I don't care."

"*Beaner Boy?* Even they think you're Mexicki?" he laughs. "Because you like beans?"

"Not because of the beans, dummy. Never mind. Don't they think you're Mexicki too?"

"No," says the lighter-skinned, fairer-haired Precious. "Why would they?"

126

"What do they call you?"

"Sid."

"Nothing else? No aka? What about ... what about when they want ... to be funny?"

"Sometimes they say *Oil Well*, but ... what's aka?"

That's not much better than Beaner Boy."

"I like it," he says. "Jed Clampett. *Black Gold Texas Tea*. Better than Beaner Boy."

"Come out here, Beaner Boy," interrupts Fat Guy. "We have a score to settle!"

Can't think. Heart beating. Is *Sid* more Amrikayi than *Mishel* or *Mike*? Is Beaner Boy a worse aka than Oil Well? Is Precious a Non too? Or just me? Fat Guy, his bike between his legs, hair uncombed, shirt untucked, fat sweaty slob - but he looks like he could actually beat me up. Precious is watching, probably loves that I am Beaner Boy and he is Oil Well. Gloater.

"Gidadahere, you dammit punk," I yell. "Get your coolies outta here, Mister Stinker!"

That was good. That should work. They all heard me burn him.

"I'm getting Baba," says Sid, tired of waiting for me to handle it.

"Getting who," Fat Guy asks. "Baaa Baaa? You got a sheep in there, Beaner Boy?"

Shouldn't have said those things on the playground. No escaping now.

"Gidadahere you ansso facken shet! Get off my property, tubbalard fatso!"

"Ha ha," says Fat Guy. "You're chicken! *Beaner Boy's a chi-cken!*" He sings, hands cupping his mouth like a megaphone. By tomorrow everyone on the playground will know. "Beaner Boy's scared to fight. He's chicken. He knows I'll kick his ass. He's--"

"Vat de devel is going on!" Baba, jacket still draped across his shoulders, chest out, shoulders back as the sun shines off his bald dome. "Who de devel are you?"

"I'm gonna kick your boy's ass," Fat Guy yells at my father without fear. Rude.

"Vat you're gonna do? You're gonna kick my boy? His ass? You use this bad vord? Ay gat dammit!" He looks at me: "What is this jackass braying about?"

Baba, brows furrowing, clenches his jaw and glares at Fat Guy. I should be terrified that he will unleash embarrassing accents and misuse words in front of everyone. Instead, I feel relief, comfort seeing Baba, his bald dome, his hard voice, our Farsi. Like, maybe, he has me.

"He wants to fight," I mumble in Farsi, low so Fat Guy can't hear.

"Fight?" Baba doesn't use a low tone. "What does he have to do with you?"

"Ew!" says Fat Guy. "What's the ugly language? Who's old baldy? Your dad?"

"Get de devel out from here, you sonvagun. Ay gat dammit!" Baba, simmering, moves toward Fat Guy. "Are you ke-ray-zee? Go to your house you gat dammit sonvagun!"

Fat Guy puts a foot on a pedal, rolls back, scared of Baba! With a surge of energy, I grab the rake on the lawn and run toward him, my chest and lungs full of power now.

"Get outta here you goddamn ansso facken tubaw betch I'll kick your anss!"

Baba tilts his head at me, then at Fat Guy laughing.

"Sure, Beaner Boy. OK. I'll see you at school. I'm gonna tell," he says, pointing his bike down the street, pedaling and singing out loud: *Beaner Boy the chi-cken; talks crazy lan-guage; needs crazy da-ddy and a broken rake to fight me*, hardy harhar..."

Baba shakes his head, trying to figure out what's happened in their absence, why an Amrikayi came to his door to fight. In Amrika, a man's home is his castle; Baba just defended his. We stand side by side in silence, watching Fat Guy disappear down the street. The sun winks behind branches as it sets across Albatross Lane, the winter sky a crisp dark blue. I'm still holding the rake. Baba's cologne, the smell of freedom, of unburdened grownups, lingers. Something warm and heavy, unfamiliarly gentle, rests on my shoulder.

"Sonvagun," Baba in his best English, squeezing my shoulder. "Come in," he says, "We're getting pizza."

The sounds from the kitchen this morning are boisterous, echoing with the festive laughter and long sighs of people catching up; no more tense whines or tortured urgings that engulfed the kitchen the past few weeks. I smell tea, toast and eggs as I run down the hallway with Sid, passing Sweet Lady's suitcase and handbag by the front door.

"Are you going to address that punk today," Baba asks with a playful smile when I walk in. He's crunching his toast and scooping up loose yoke from his shell with gusto.

Sweet Lady, leaning against the stove, reaches for the smoker Maman holds so elegantly between her fingers, takes a drag and hands it back. "Lashoon," she tells Baba, a tone of familiarity in her voice, an insider nod they didn't used to share. "They've taken a lot already."

He acknowledges Sweet Lady with a nod back and reaches for Maman's smoker for a drag too. The three of them nibble and sip their tea in peaceful silence, looking at me and Sid.

"Sit by me," Maman says, tapping the empty chair next to her. She turns to Sweet Lady, "Maman, please make your famous fried eggs and dates for them once more before you go."

Sweet Lady slices off a pat of butter, drops it in the hot pan and with a sigh of relief, rips a handful of dates, cracks four eggs, drops them in. They share the smoker until it's done.

"Fertig!"
"Dudley!"
"Vons!"

Big Mouth Patricia bugles names at twelve sharp. I don't mind being called "Vons" because today I have the best lunch in fourth grade. Baba didn't know how to buy Pizza, or maybe he was feeling extra festive when he ordered, so Sid and I each have three chewy slices from Piece O'Pizza. As trading starts, I find a spot on the bench and unwrap my bounty.

"Wanna trade?" asks Barry G. "A roll of Oreos for a slice."

"Nah."

"I'll give you my Frito's BBQ flavored and Cheese n' Crackers for a slice," offers Jeff K.

Today I could trade what I have for whatever I want, except today I want what I have.

"I'll give you four taquitos for a slice," says Fat Guy. "That's fair; four for one?" He looks at me with soft brown eyes, no hint of the bitterness or anger that ruled us yesterday. "C'mon, Beaner Boy, you like my mom's taquitos, remember? You owe me that, don'cha?"

"Fair," I say. "That's fair."

PART IV

IN THE BEGINNING, *I played the sad bride waiting to be married off to a man I did not love. On afternoons when Maman was out and Precious napped, Shideh came up to play "Jacqueline's Affairs." Sad Bride was to be married off to Rich Groom who assured "you will learn to love me." Shideh would bring a lace napkin from her house to pin on my head and a gold tube of lipstick from her maman's toilet table to make my lips pink. "Be sad." I'd purse my lips for a pout. "Really sad." I'd glance down. "Nod slow when asked questions; heartbroken." I played. She'd wear a jacket we slipped off a hanger from Baba's closet, slap her face with his French cologne and run his wetted comb through her hair to slick it back. "When do I get to be Groom?" "Next time," she'd say, adding, "what's the difference? We'll kiss." I'd shrug, accept my role. We did it Shideh's way; she had wisdom. "Jacqueline's Affairs" always ended with kissing. She put her little hand behind my head, pulled me to her and kissed, long and deep. We swiveled our heads side to side like on TV. She pushed her tongue through my tightened lips, swish it around my mouth; it was thick, slippery and salty. I didn't like it at first, but I trusted her and let myself go. We got caught when Shideh's maman saw lipstick on her lace napkin. Shideh told them it was my idea. Maman and Baba gave me sideways glares, bit their lips, meaning there would be punishment. Shideh's maman and baba gave me sideways glares too. Even Shideh glared, defiant, both of us knowing it was her idea. I didn't say anything. She had wisdom. At least she hadn't told them that I played Sad Bride; that I wore the lipstick.*

Summer 1973

"And she has a Benz under her feet," Maman shouts from the bed-room as she leans into her mirror to apply her lipstick, "so they must be substantial."

"Because he sells Benzes," Baba shouts into the bathroom mirror, trimming his moustache and nose hairs, folding his wine-colored tur-tleneck.

"So they get it at a bargain," Maman mashing her lips together. "It's still a Benz."

"And you have rugs under your feet; that's not bad either," Baba says.

The Levins live next door. Mr. Levin is bald like Baba and has a moustache like Baba - but the similarities end there. Blue-eyed Marty Levin strolls out each morning in his bathrobe and slippers to get the Times from his driveway with a big smile. Baba says he has a constant smile because he's in sales. Maman says "then why don't you smile? You sell too." "Rugs are investments," Baba says. "I don't need to smile." Still, Baba has been trying to be more like Marty. Cool smile, macho moustache, fancy turtleneck. He's trying to change, be mod.

Saturday mornings if Marty sees us on the street, he talks the way he thinks kids talk. But he adds grownup words like "fellas" - a black-and-white TV word. One time he bent over to pick up his paper and his robe slipped open. Kersh made a crack about the moon coming out early so Levin pushed his robe aside, exposing his pale butt cheek. "Slap me ten, fellas," he said, slapping his butt like a butcher slaps a roast. We weren't sure if we should laugh, but Levin obviously wanted it to be hilarious because as he hightailed it back in, he kept pushing a cackle like Burt Reynolds does on *Johnny Carson*, weeknights 11:30 Channel 4. Baba wants to be more like Levin, even started watching *Carson*. The Levins are coming over tonight.

Maman is itching to host and doesn't care anymore who her guests are, even Amrikayi. She is nervous because other than burgers and fries she doesn't know what they eat so she's making beef stroganoff topped with shoestring fries. She sprayed Lemon Glade to hide our house smells; now it smells like boiled chicken and onions with a hint of plastic yellow.

Maman bows when she opens the door. Her sweeping arms welcome them in as she guides them to the front room we never use because it's for guests we never have.

"Wery velcome," Maman says with a wide smile as the Levins tiptoe in, look around, try not to sniff. She kisses Mrs. Levin, who is clutching her handbag to her chest, on both cheeks.

"Oh, twice, ok," Mrs. Levin says with a jingle of surprise. "How nice, very European."

Baba, having planted the TV on a folding chair in our bedroom, yells "Mardee son-of-gun!" in a festive tone that is new to his voice.

"There he is!" Levin yells back. "How the hell are ya, Manny?"

Manny? I guess Baba abandoned Mishel after seeing how crappy it went for me.

When I go out there, later, pretending to get water, there is an awkward silence, broken by nervous ice cubes jiggling in sweaty cocktail glasses; forks trying to stab cubed cucumber and tomato clanking against plates; Maman blowing smoke at the ceiling, legs crossed, jittery ankle. But as the night goes on, I hear giggles, titters, a couple of explosive cackles from Marty Levin.

"That's insightful and hilarious, Manny! Persians *are* the same as Armenians to us."

"I say it for the buyer to feel good," Baba goes on. "In Persian is called *putting watermelons under his arms*, extra compliment make buyer feel especial so he buys!"

"Manny, you oughta be on Carson," cackles Marty Levin, "take that on the road, boy!" And I wonder if he's not putting watermelons under Baba's arms, trying to sell him a Benz.

But Baba is on a roll: "And the gaddammit stagflation! Vat the devel is the stagflation? What is all dis *shen* we hear? Infla*shen*. Rece*shen*. Stagfla*shen*. Is giving me the depre*shen*!"

Marty slaps his knees. Baba, pleased with himself, laughs so hard his eyes tear up and he coughs as Maman taps her smoker in the ashtray, watching them from the side of her eye.

When Maman turns out the lights after serving tea, dates and baklava, it gets weird.

"Marty," Mrs. Levin calls out, putting down her teacup and picking up her purse to place on her lap. Her face glows in a soft yellow from the kitchen light. "What is happening?"

"I sing for you," Maman says, clearing her throat.

"Oh, how nice," Mrs. Levin watches Maman sit on the couch, crossing her legs, her ashtray beside her. She leans back and tilts her face upward, her mouth toward the ceiling.

"Do you know *Close to you* by the Carpenters?" Mrs. Levin asks. "Such a lovely song."

"I sing Persian songs. You know Hydeh, Mahasti, Googoosh? Wery famous in Iran."

Back home, hearing Maman sing after dinner was considered a treat. She'd turn out the lights, they'd grab their drinks and ashtrays, prop themselves on cushions and couches, ready to take it in or even sing along if the mood struck, though nobody could sing like Maman.

But on this warm summer night in Amrika, the door to the backyard open to the dull Los Angeles air, Maman can't get comfortable. She clears her throat, closes her eyes, but can't find her voice. Mrs. Levin seems scared and Mr. Levin, his salesman smile frozen on his tight, pink face, jiggles his cocktail glass, eyelids open just enough to catch the glance from his wife.

"Well wouldja look at that," he taps Baba, holding his heavy steel watch to Baba's face. "Almost eleven. Gotta get home and watch the Watergate wrap-up and Carson, right Manny?"

Mrs. Levin perks up, both hands now on her purse. "Well, I don't understand this whole Watergate thing, but Rich Little is on Carson. Do you know Rich Little? The impressionist?"

"Who?" Maman's eyebrows rise to that angle where disappointment, embarrassment and defiance meet. She shoots a salty eye in Mrs. Levin's direction. "*I* don't know Leetell Reech" she says in her highbrow Amrikayi tone that means, "how should I know who is on your dehati TV shows?" She tosses in a smirk and headshake, like she's just a sassy foreigner being sassy.

At the door, Maman bows again, "wery velcome!" But as the door closes, "Bebaranet!" she spits, using the hand that ushered them in to dismiss them - too dumb for Pazirayee. "Let them take you! *Tom Colleens* kiyeh?" she asks nobody. "*Vatergate* cheeyeh? Dehati."

Baba, still wiping tears from his eyes, has a loose and easy smirk. He seems satisfied. "You wanted guests," he finally says with a shrug. "You had guests."

"I'll never be able to make friends with that woman," Maman says, looking at the door.

Labor Day Weekend 1973.

At first, I noticed them in the background, like gonjeshk chasing each other through trees or random balls being flung across the playground. This summer I saw them everywhere. Lying on driveways, slotted in racks, chained to streetlamps. Black, white, red, plain or with the extra bells and whistles: Doherty grips, Mag wheels, Motocross bars, Chopper tires, Banana seats with Sissy backs. Pros do the best stunts on them: Pop-a-wheelies. Hawks. Cross-it-ups. They stomp their brakes and screech across the blacktop, leaving black streaks. With chain-locks slung across their chests, they ride to Guild Drug for Milky Ways or the baseball diamonds at Rancho Park. I see them at the bottom of the hill leaning back on their Sissys or forward on their Moto bars, watching the cars go by, trading words to the coolest radio songs or salty jokes I'm never close enough to hear or Pro enough to get.

Only foreigners don't get bikes.

The first time I asked Kersh for a turn, the pink wad of bubble-gum froze mid-chew between his uneven rows of yellowy teeth. His mom yelled from their kitchen window "Share, Brian!" and Kersh resumed chewing, flashing a devilish smile. "Just joshin'," he said with a wink, swinging his leg off and leaning the handlebar toward me. "Here you go."

Kersh and Cowan have been sharing their bikes with us all summer. We do stunts on rickety ramps we built with planks on stacks of bricks on cinderblocks on milk crates. We roll down Kersh's steep driveway for speed and pedal fast before hitting the ramp. Mostly, we fly. Sometimes we come down bad, twist an ankle…bend a rim.

Yesterday I got the sense that Kersh and Cowan are getting tired of sharing: "Let's build a bike!" Cowan suggested after I bent Kersh's rim. "We can use spare parts from the junkyard! A Chitty Chitty Bang Bang Super Bike with wings and inner tubes!"

Kersh and Cowan are as-seen-on-TV Amrikayi, like in Cheer commercials: Matted hair, excited eyes, raspy voices. Cowan turns purple when he gets ideas, his neck vein matching his green eyes. Building a super bike seems possible when Cowan says it. Any idea seems possible when Amrikayi say it. Cowan calls it "American in-jun-you-witty" - a mix of Pilgrim know-how and Indian survival instincts. It means obstacles don't stop Amrikayi ideas – no foreign tongues, culture taboos or complex rules to trip you up. They're the ones making the rules. Amrikayi get to have wild ideas. A bike that flies? Yes! Mistakes get washed away with Cheer, leaving a sharp pine and lime scent that burns the nose. Obstacles, like stains, are for foreigners.

Kersh is definitely sick of sharing. On this steamy summer morn-ing before the start of school, we're double-pedaling to Bikecology to fix his bent rim.

"When are you getting your own bike," Kersh asks as we slowly grind along National.

"Today."

Sweet Lady left us envelopes. Mine was addressed to Mr. Monkel, which is how Sweet Lady says Michael. The card inside read "Grand-son" - a cartoon of a stooped-over white-haired lady hugging a pale kid with corn gold hair. In shaky hand she wrote, "Little one, try to be happy, always be good. It is easy." A crisp ten and three wrinkled fives were inside.

The rest came from the doreh friends. In Tehran their doreh friends played cards on Tuesdays, Thursdays and some Saturdays, taking turns hosting. Saturdays went all day, with kaleh pacheh cooked overnight in a big metal pot, the sheep's eyeballs and teeth still in its skull.

The doreh friends here are an Armani couple, a Tork couple, a Lob-nani couple and a Tehrani couple – they all lived in Tehran and speak Farsi so Maman doesn't need to worry about *Tom Collins* or *Rich Little*. Now she comfortably cracks jokes about that stuff with her doreh friends. I guess when you have trouble understanding a new culture, you crack jokes about it.

Yesterday they played cards and watched the Jerry Lewis Telethon. They ate tongue sandwiches with pickles and mustard, kaleh pacheh, boiled eggs with fried eggplant. They drank brown booze with Schweppes and Bloody Mary's. Maman sang; Baba cracked his Amrikayi jokes – his doreh friends preferred Persian jokes about suffering and stupidity over jokes about Nixon or Stagflation, which disappointed Baba and embarrassed Maman. They played Belote and Gin Rummy but by the time the Telethon had raised twenty grand and Jerry Lewis had untied his bowie, the women cleaned up and the men dealt Blackjack, letting us play. We sat at the table, jiggling Ginger Ale on the rocks, studying our cards with grave looks, rubbing our jaws in thought, like grownups. Baba looked relaxed, having moved on from their rejection of his jokes. Probably figured they just didn't get him. Maybe he had become too Amrikayi for them.

"Hit me!" Sid said with gusto.

Asad the hearty Lebanese was impressed. "This one's a little firecracker!"

"Quick as a spinning top," Baba said with a proud chuckle, looking over at Sid.

They were less impressed by my burdened-grownup imitation, muttering "stick" or "hit" with deep sighs. When the Telethon hit thirty grand, they celebrated, giving us five-dollars each.

This morning, Kersh and I wait outside of Bikecology until the door jingles open. Kersh asks the old man about his bent rim and I go to the bike I've been eyeing all summer. It's blue. It's called Senator. Not as cool as the Schwinn's everyone else rides, but for thirty-six bucks it is solid with chunky motocross wheels and sort-of motocross handlebars; good enough.

"'Bout time," Kersh smiles, yellowed teeth resting on a morning wad of pink bubblegum.

The old man straightens Kersh's rim for free since I'm buying a bike; even threw in a racing plate and numbers so it looks more Moto - Amrikayi get nicer as they get older, I guess.

I pedal as fast as I can on National, coast under the big leafy trees of Motor, singing *"Brandy yu'ra fan gurl"* a thick morning breeze pushing against my face. Got me a bike!

"Mobarak" Maman says when she sees me and Kersh standing beside my new bike. Sid, rubbing sleep from his eyes, looks surprised.

Who's the firecracker now, Precious? Who's the spinning top now?

Sid steps barefoot onto the driveway to study my bike. Maman runs back in, comes out holding two eggs. Kersh can only stare wide-eyed as Maman wedges an egg in front of each tire, wrests the handlebar from my grip and pushes my wheels forward to crush the eggs. Gooey yolk and shell pieces get stuck in the chunky grooves of my new tires but what causes Kersh's pink wad to nearly fall out of his mouth is Maman's chant to the sky in Farsi for all our neighbors to hear: "Cheshmeshoon-koor, ya-Adonai! Blind our enemies' eyes, Adonai. Amen!"

Cowan walks over from across the street, stares at the smashed eggs. "What the heck?"

Kersh whispers, "His mom just egged his new bike!"

"Jewish ritual," I avoid their eyes, wishing I could disappear, "you wouldn't get it."

"We're both Jewish," Cowan argues in his rasp. "Never egged bikes."

"Special Persian Jewish one, you wouldn't get it." I run in to get a rag.

"Did you see his new--" Maman starts to tell Baba, but he is bounding out the door in a new tracksuit. It doesn't have rows of stripes or symbols, just a lonely white strip running along the arms and legs. On his feet, new sneakers so white they'd get mercilessly stomped on the playground. None of it looks right. Baba belongs either in a dark suit, white shirt, solid tie and hard black shoes, or pajamas. His furrowed brows, dark eyes and black strip of hair ringing his bald dome don't look right in a tracksuit zipped to the top, every lump and roll bulging in navy blue. He slips on a bright white headband, pretending to not notice Maman frozen in mid-sentence. When he holds the doorknob to squat and do deep knee bends, Maman finally asks.

"Een cheeyeh!" her hand moving from top to bottom like she's surveying an alien. "What are you wearing? What is that around your head? Did you hurt yourself?"

He grunts with each squat - a combined hiccup and post-drink exhale, "Ep! Ah!" – exercise with a Persian accent. "This is an exercise suit for modern people who want to stay strong." He runs in place, knees high. "Ep! Ep! Ep!" like a soldier.

"Since when? I'm making a special omelet for brunch. You want to go out now?"

Out? Wearing that? Head him off at the pass!

Sid has run off with Kersh and Cowan to play Horse on Cowan's driveway. If they see Baba, we'll never hear the end of it. I run out before Baba, to distract them.

"Two-on-two!"

They're surprised to see me out there.

"I got Sid," Cowan yells first. He looks at Kersh with a victory nod.

Sid, the firecracker, the spinning top, smirks at me, shrugs a non-gloat gloat.

"Fine," Kersh shakes his head like he lost an unspoken bet to Cowan. "But we take out."

It's true, I prefer TV. Besides bike jumps, I don't play sports. But this year is different. Clean slate! Not only do I have my own bike, but I have been practicing hoops all summer.

"Gimme that ball," I intercept it from Cowan in mid-dribble, slap at it, bounce it between my legs. It bounces up, hits my balls, rolls into the street. They give chase with a groan. That's when they see Baba at our front door, a sour look, yelling in Farsi at Maman: "Velemoon kon!"

He steps out on Albatross Lane, pretending to not notice us, hands clasped behind him as he walks past the Levins' driveway, surveying like he's never seen our street. Sid and I lock eyes, competitive rivalry taking a backseat to shared panic. I pick up the ball and run to the basket in Cowan's driveway across the street, so they'd face me.

"Let's go!"

But they're gawking at Baba's awkward moves. Jumping jacks: slapping hands, closing feet, wrong sequence, "Ep!" Deep squats: arms out, belly bulging, "Ep!" like he's in pain, but it's a good pain. Left hand-to-right toe. "Ep! Ah!" Repeat. Then, in his white headband, fresh track-suit and stiff sneakers, Baba starts running down Albatross Lane like he's running uphill in a windstorm. They can't take their eyes off him.

"What's your dad doing?" asks Kersh.

"What's it look like?" I say. "Exercise. Duh! Shoot for outs, s'go!"

We're so mesmerized we don't hear Bucky's El Camino careen onto Albatross Lane, slamming his brakes. Bucky, who lives across from Kersh, sticks his head out of his window: "What the fuck you doing in the street, Arafat?" he yells at Baba. "Move, you crazy Arab!"

Kersh's mom sticks her head out of her kitchen window to see what's going on.

Cowan's big sister sticks her head out of her bedroom window; she has a crush on Bucky.

Mrs. Levin walks out to her driveway, wearing an apron and holding a dishtowel.

"Is that . . . Manny Manoucherian?"

". . . what's he doing?"

"Is that . . . is he... jogging?"

"Learn the rules of the road," Bucky yells, "This ain't Beirut!" He avoids our eyes, looking to Kersh and Cowan for backup. "You don't run in the streets here!"

Kersh and Cowan keep mum. Bucky teaches us things: Dodgers baseball, getting on base with girls, kissing like the French. But today it's like he doesn't know me or Sid.

"That's our dad," Sid yells, then looks to me, waiting for his big brother to join him.

But Bucky is an Older, grown-out army cut, moustache, jeans and t-shirt. He douses matches in his mouth; let me ride shotgun all summer, driving the streets in search of Pros so I could look cool driving with an Older, maybe even find The Arcade. Should I risk all that because Baba decided to jog in the middle of the street? Does Baba even need my help?

"I am jugging!" he yells at Bucky. "Is 'dis your estreet? Are you owner of 'dis estreet?"

"In this country, streets are for cars. You don't run in the streets here."

"OK, so is good for you to driving fast-fast in the estreet all the days?" says Baba. "You see the childs play but you go fast-fast? Son of a gun! Go slow in your gaddammen car, okay?"

He makes no effort to talk like them. His heavy accent is not the humble, bowing foreigner tone Bucky expects. For Baba, coming to Amrika was family duty. He came with expectations and goals, not humility. He doesn't see Amrikayi as his hosts, or himself as their guest. To him, Amrika is the Wild West, a frontier for anyone to get in on, set up shop and chase your fortune. He bows to nobody. Obviously, Baba has never been on an Amrikayi playground.

"Don't cuss at our dad! Fucky Bucky!" defiant Sid keeps it up, almost in tears.

"What'd you say, Oil Well," demands Bucky like he doesn't know Sid. "Say it again!"

Sid looks to me again, waiting for me to speak up.

"C'mon, Bucky," I try to keep it friendly. "You can't yell at a guy for exercising."

"I can't? You tellin' me what I can and can't do, boy?" Bucky flashes an "I dare you" smirk that makes his thin moustache look dangerous. One minute they're teaching you secrets, giving you free racing plates; next, they're sticking their chest out, clenching fists, ready to pound you. Amrikayi can be the most generous people - as long as they know you need them, that you're less than them. But if you stand up, try to be as tall as them, they turn. Hard and fast.

Sid swipes the basketball from me in mid-dribble and chucks it at Bucky. Not hard enough. Bucky catches it, turns and kicks it high, deep and far down Albatross Lane.

"That's my ball," Kersh screams at Sid.

"Why don't you all get out of the street?" yells Kersh's mom.

"Your dad shouldn't jog in the middle of the street," Kersh yells, watching his basketball roll down the street. "We don't do that here. We have sidewalks."

Baba has moved on. As Kersh, Cowan and Sid run down the street after the ball, Baba jogs back to our front lawn for more jumping-jacks. "Ep! Ah!" Doesn't care what Bucky, Kersh's mom or Mrs. Levin think. He knows and does what he wants, even if he does it wrong.

I get on my Senator and ride past them all down Albatross Lane, egg shells crunching between my tires and the asphalt, leaving a trace of goo like a giant, stupid, foreign snail.

At the bottom of the hill, I lean on my handlebars, Pro style, watching cars go by, rugged, a cowboy on his trusty horse. I see them; Speed, Worm, Becker and an Older in ratty jeans with a vague moustache and thick black hair parted on the side. They skid in front of me, raising a cloud of dust. We are equals now, on our bikes, on the street, watching the cars go by.

Speed, in jeans and a yellow T-shirt with footprints on the chest, rests his sneaker on his pedal. "We're gonna kick your ass, Beaner Boy."

"Why?" My ears pounding. I'm surrounded.

"Because, my spic friend," smiles metal mouthed Becker.

"Just on my damn bike here," I try to sound Pro, "didn't do damn nothin'." I've been in plenty of fights. But always for a reason. Never for nothing, for ritual like a dumb sheep or salamander. My ears pound so loud I barely hear myself ask to join their gang.

"Whataya think, guys," Becker sneers, "should we let Beaner Boy join?" He buries his fist in my gut. I squeeze my handlebar, one foot on the ground, the other on my pedal, hold my breath, ignore the pain. Becker studies my Senator. "Looks like he got himself a…what is that?"

The Older with the vague moustache steps toward me. I flinch. "This your bike?" he asks, polite like the policemen who pull Maman over. She'd know what to do. She'd use her wits, Amrikayi accent, charm – anything to get out of trouble.

"Yessireeba!" I squeeze out, holding the pain. "It's m'new -- baak."
What was that? Cowboy? Barney Fife?

"New?" They stomp and spit on new sneakers. What's the ritual for bikes?

"Yep," barely able to breathe, staying cool. "Just goin' -- for a -- li'l raad."

"You didn't need to punch him," he tells Becker. "Seems like a good kid. Cool bike."

142

It's already paying off! They'll take me to The Arcade. They'll stop calling me Beaner Boy. Motocross Mike. Cherokee. Keep holding breath to reduce pain.

"Yep, I raad fast," air in my gut coming back. "I do skids, pop-a-wheelies, endos..."

"Endos?" Worm cracks a smile.

"I meant crow hawks...I do crow hawks."

"Crow hawks? You mean a crow hop? That's basketball. Did you mean bunny hops?"

"You got egg on your tires, kid," Vague Moustache says. "Did you hop on a crow nest?"

She broke eggs to blind the Bad Eye of my enemies. But, her gooey ritual, ingrained in the grooves of my tires, has only opened their eyes wider.

"Let's kick his spic ass," says Becker impatiently.

"Dudes!" A new voice emerges from behind. "Do I detect the El Supremos?"

Pincus leans on an odd-shaped pink bike, same army jacket and boots he wears daily to school. He's only seen me, so when they turn around, his smile flattens out.

"Get lost, faggit!" says Speed gripping his handlebars. "We're busy."

"Doing what," Pincus asks in a confident tone. "Playing Ring-Around-the-Beaner?"

"Get lost or we'll kick your ass too," glints Becker. "Two for one, spic n' span!"

"You wish," says Pincus, sitting easy on a white banana seat. "You'd never catch me."

"You're on a girl's bike, faggit," says Becker.

"My sister's. So what? Still won't catch me, you razor-mouthed slow poke ape."

"Who's the faggit," Vague Moustache asks Speed. "He friends with the Mexikin?"

"I'm not Mexic-"

"-Non from school," Speed shakes his head, trying to impress the Older. "Nons, man."

"You guys still doin' that," Vague Moustache asks Speed with a chuckle.

Speed glances over to see if I heard. Then he does what Maman and Sweet Lady do: "*ix-nay, o-bray,*" in a secret tongue to Vague Moustache, who shrugs with a salty smirk.

"This faggit with you, kid?" Vague Moustache asks me. "You're friends?"

They've been chasing him since second grade, but never catch him. He holds his ground with a smile, sometimes a defiant glare. Hands on hips, slowing his breath so they won't know they've worn him down. All the chasing back and forth has created a ditch, a swamp of spit and venom that Pincus has made his, happily wallowing in it, cozy. None of us chose the swamp, but we're in it too. Are we friends? I bet if I hurl the new word – on my new bike - it would get me in. Pincus wouldn't care; probably used to betrayal. I'd say "No way, this Polack Fagger ain't with *me*" and they'd forgo any more ass kicking, let me ride with them. All eyes on me.

Speed, still trying to impress Vague Moustache, says "let's just kick both their asses!"

They get off their bikes and walk toward us, smiling like they're having all the fun.

"Punch it!" yells Pincus as he turns his bike around.

I stomp my pedal, follow Pincus crossing the light as cars honk and breaks squeal, to the other side of the playground. Left, sharp right, between two houses, through the alley. At the trashcans, he puts a finger up to his nose as we hold our breaths, his bright blue eyes on me. I avert; I didn't answer them, didn't say "Yeah we're friends." He noticed. Now's not the time. Their greased chains slink closer, chunky tires zip by. They talk like cowboys in a posse wondering which way we went. Worm says "forget it" and their voices fade, getting smaller until they mix with the cool trills of the gonjeshk. Gone.

We ride to the playground. Pincus knows of an opening big enough to squeeze our bikes through. We lean on our handlebars, stare at the emptiness. We ride, zipping across the blacktop, zigzagging around the orange hoops of basketball, tall brown walls of handball, harsh yellow boundaries of their games – unforgiving during school but powerless today under our chunky tires. Pincus doesn't bring up my silence. We leave skid marks, everywhere. When school starts tomorrow, they will gather before the bell to chat and catch up as Pros, relegating us back to our Non swamp. But I will look at this ground, see my marks, and know I am here too.

Fifth Grade
September 1973

"Let's team up," Pincus says after the new teacher, luscious Mrs. Parker, announces the contest. Sell the most chocolate turtles, win a bike. Second is a scout knife with a screwdriver. Third is a t-shirt. Wouldn't mind a t-shirt with writing on it; I think I can swing third place. I'm not much of a salesman. Sid is the firecracker, not me. But partnering with Pincus?

"We can't share a bike," I tell him.

"Who cares about a bike? I want that knife! I'll never sell enough by myself, but together we can maybe get second place. Whataya say?"

Yesterday they asked if we were friends; I stayed quiet. In second grade, he tried to make friends as we warmed our hands in the sink; I stayed quiet. Pros hate him. If I called him *fagger polack* yesterday I'd be partnering with Speed today. Or not. Pros don't join in; cooler to rest an elbow on a chair back, flip your hair and make fun of everybody else.

Fifth grade. Playground rules. Clean slate. Almost had them yesterday. "Nah."

He saved your skin yesterday, Doc.

"Maybe."

After school, Sid the firecracker is already at it, explaining the contest to Maman, recruiting her to help sell to her doreh friends at the next game. He'll win the bike, Maman and Baba will heap more praise on him for being their little spinning top. He will gloat.

Pincus may look like a paler, sicklier version of cool Amrikayi, but he knows how to talk like them. And he's a Non so he's used to doors getting slammed in his face. It could work.

"What shows do you like," he asks as we ride our bikes the next afternoon, turning onto a new street in a neighborhood on the other side of Circle Park; foreign territory for me.

"I watch all of them," I say, looking up at the tall leafy trees, noticing there are no houses on this new block. The street dead-ends, just like Albatross Lane, except the end of this street is the back of a big, grassy golf course. "No houses here," I say, "let's try another street."

"I like Mary Tyler Moore," Pincus says, ignoring me. "What's your favorite?"

"Bob Newhart," I say, feeling safe enough to share TV fantasies. "I want to marry Emily; she's a beautiful smart-alex. Let's try another street," I say again. "No houses here."

"Smart-*Alec*, Beaner Boy. Not *Alex*. Let's take a break," Pincus lays his bike down; his voice suddenly different, thinner, softer. "Let's play Bob and Emily," swaying shoulders, sexy style, approaching. "You're Bob," he winks, "I'm Emily. *Dinner's ready, Bob, want a scotch?*"

He looks different; a crooked, pretend-naughty smirk. His bright blue eyes, gentler but narrowed, sly. I'm gripping my handlebars, not knowing my role, not wanting to play.

"*C'mon, Bob*," Pincus calls in a flirty sing-song tone, "*let's kiss*," leaning in, gently kissing my cheek, caressing it with his own cheek. "*Now you kiss me, Poopsie.*"

I jerk my neck to pull back so I can see him better. Pincus squeezes his shoulders together and wrinkles his nose, flirty, shuts his eyes and puckers a pouty smile.

"*C'mon, Bob*," putting his hand on my shoulder.

I jump on my bike hurtling toward the dead-end the fence the golf course - Wrong way! Sharp turn. Confused Pincus straight ahead! Standing by his bike, playful naughty smile gone. I blow past him, knowing I disappointed him; and he rides much faster than me.

Pedal, Doc. Don't look back. Go!

I turn right – did we turn left onto the dead-end? Unfamiliar

146

neighborhood; Pincus leading; relied on him. Albatross Lane is... on the other side of Circle Park, and Circle Park is...

Uphill ... we had coasted down a slope, so I have to go up ... keep pedaling, uphill ... look back to see if Pincus is following ... all clear. At the top of the slope ... Circle Park!

Almost home. Getting chilly but I'm sweaty from pedaling; sun still up; still daytime.

Don't worry, Doc, you'll be home in pa-lenny of time, you're on de right track.

Circle Park connects to five streets, like spokes on a bike wheel, all going in different directions. One of the spokes leads to the playground and home. Which one? They look alike: Patches of green grass, tall trees with yellow and orange leaves; a hodgepodge of houses – Spanish, German, Greek, Storybook; front lawn to sidewalk to lawn strip to curb to paved street to yellow line in the middle - and a mirror image on the other side.

Sun starting to set, sky getting orange...but it ain't purple yet. No need to worry.

The late summer air lingers with scents of wilted jasmine rising as evening approaches. Their sweet perfume reminds me of summer nights in Tehran, where I knew my universe - streets, corners, Maman's hand in reach. I take a street on the spoke, go two blocks, wrong. Turn back. Next spoke, familiar. Ride slow, peer in windows – kitchens, living rooms. Moms clicking lights – yellow and warm. Refrigerators open, their light shining on Amrikayi brands I recognize from TV, trouble-free snack time. They get to. They have rights. Not lost. Glowing TV screens flickering Samantha, Star Trek...News? Already? The purpling sky, the balmy early-evening breeze shaking the weaker leaves off their branches.

Rustling leaves, scraping branches, but you ain't scared, fifth grader; you got wisdom.

But where am I? From the side, a flash, a silver flicker in the dusk. I turn. Nothing.

Go back. Dis ain't de right street.

Darker now, purple and orange being drowned by velvety navy as stars begin to glitter and street signs get harder to read. Flashes of silver in the corner of my eye. What was that? No, nothing…everything is unfamiliar. Did I turn a corner? Inadvertently went on another street as I looked back to check the silver flash? Need to retrace my steps. Turned left, or right--

--Streetlights! Never seen that. When we're out in daylight they are off, thick glass vases hibernating atop rough pebbled columns they chain bikes to or scratch backs on. If we go outside after dinner, they are lit yellow, glowing, watching over the street like they were always lit. But on this unfamiliar street, they light up in front of me - all at once along the street, a whispering click, a soft buzz, like God flipped the switch and set rows of vases aglow. Takes my breath away. The street looks even darker, less familiar now. The breeze can't cool my cheeks, my pumping heart, churning stomach trying to convince me I'm lost, to panic.

Not just yet, Doc. Relax. Retrace your steps; you'll find your way.

Need to get back to Circle Park, start a new spoke. But which way? Did I turn a corner? Two? Circle Park uphill…after a left? The breeze swirls leaves, sways branches, casts dancing shadows on the asphalt under the yellow streetlights. That menacing silver glint again! A metallic flash, keeps disappearing whenever I turn around. What is it?

Let's face it, Doc, you're lost. No two ways about it. Time to cook up a plan.

It's a black door. There were other doors, other front lawns, other window-lit rooms with the warm comfort of refrigerators and televisions. But I am lost and this door is attached to the house closest to the corner. How could I know who is behind it when I ring the bell?

"Tell 'em we don't want any," a familiar voice spits from the other side of the door.

"Hush, Kevin," a voice replies as the door cracks open. "I'm sorry, we're not interested." Her flat smile and blank grey eyes are framed by a blonde hairdo that looks hard as a helmet.

Pincus did the talking. Tired and wary, I try remembering his words. I push my voice, it squeaks: "Scuse me, could I please borrow your telephone to call my mother, please?"

She lowers her powdered face, tired lipstick flaking across her lips, spearmint gum not quite hiding the tobacco smell. "Are you lost, dear," eyes, soft and warm, the concern inside them so sincere it makes my lips tremble. I *am* lost! She *sees* me...

Easy...

"Oh no, um, Miss, I am selling these chocolatey turtles here for school charity--"

"--Ooh I love turtles! What school do you go to, dear?"

"Pinnacle Palace, Miss, but I was--"

"--Kevin, this boy goes to your school! Are you friends?"

She opens the door. His face may be shrouded by dusky shadows, his voice maybe muffled behind the door, but his metallic sneer is unmistakable. Becker. Always around for my humiliations. A few days ago, he was threatening to kick my ass, forcing me to run for it with Pincus. Now, because of Pincus, I am delivered to his doorstep.

"Hey," I nod. Will he be at least pretend-friendly because he's my host?

"Who is your friend, Kevin? You didn't tell me school is selling turtles. I love those." She looks back at me. "C'mon in, dear, I'll get my purse, I want two boxes. Leave your bike on the front step, hon. It's safe there. My, what a pretty bike! Kevin, it's blue!"

Becker unseals his lips, flashing the protruding metal. "Selling candy is for lame-o's," he says, looking at me. "And don't bring that in the house; it'll muck up the carpet."

"He knows, Kevin," his mom comes back with her tiny purse, "You heard me tell him."

"Well Dad's always bangin' on me for my bike," he says in a thin whiny tone I've never heard before, "so I'm making sure...probably doesn't understand half what you're saying...why should he be allowed to bring his bike in and muck up the carpet when I get banged for it. . ."

"—Shut! Up! Already!" yells a girl coming downstairs; seen her at school, pointy elbows, knobby knees, sneers like Becker. "He left it outside so drop dead, Metal Mouth!"

"Alice!" their mom yells.

"Get dead, A-Lice!"

"Kevin! Now he'll think Alice has lice and he'll tell everybody! That's a consequence."

"He barely understands English. And why should I get a consequence? For what?"

"Shut up out there or I'll fix it!" In their living room lit by a TV screen showing news, I make out part of a coffee table, stockinged feet on top, the familiar sound of ice cubes jiggling in a glass being set down hard on a side table. It startles me, but makes them jump.

"See what you did," Becker's mom whisper-yells. "You riled him during Cronkite."

"She started it," Becker hisses, shifting his eyes toward me to see if I am listening.

I look down, try making myself thin, fade into the entryway, get invisible.

"Here's the money, dear," Becker's mom snaps her purse open with a sigh, "two dollars for two boxes, do you want to write down my name and address, dear?"

I reach into my back pocket, the other pocket, front pockets. The sheet with addresses must've fallen out when I escaped Pincus. He had the dollars, I had the sheet. I'll have to crawl back to Pincus. Becker watches my desperate search, flashing a metal grin as I avoid his eyes.

"Dear? Do you have a sign-up sheet or can I get a receipt?"

"He doesn't know what he's doing, Mom," Becker laughs. "Don't give him money!"

"I must've left it...I can give it to Becker—er, Kevin - at school. May I call my mother?"

"Phone's in the kitchen, sweetie, c'mon," then she glares at Becker, her boy. "And no more nonsense from you, got it? Now keep quiet and watch his bike!"

"Yeah, I'll watch his bike," he says, rolling his eyes.

I follow her to the kitchen where the waxy smell of spray-can lilacs is replaced by the heavy smells of baking beef, boiling broccoli and potatoes. It turns my stomach. I dial and when I hear Maman's voice, I want to cry. I exhale a shaky, quick whisper in Farsi "Maman come get me" then switch to English and louder, "Mom? I'm at my friend's house, Mom."

I ignore Maman's panic and hand the phone to Becker's mom.

"Can you please tell your address to my mom?"

She takes the phone. "Hi…he's fine…you live where? Oh, just a few blocks…terrific."

That word again - so modern, happy - taps her tongue, rolls from the roof of her mouth, flings off her lips - "tu-rri-ffick" – a warm cheer. She leans toward me, her large eyes, now more blue than grey, fixed on me; her lips, pink beneath red lipstick flecks, smiling.

"You hungry, sweetie? Can I get you anything?" Bends forward, hands on knees, blouse falling open…consider a sly peek, purr for her. I'm Bob, she's Emily. She handles her wicked son so well. Lay my bike on her front step. Is it safe? Head spins. Pincus swaying shoulders, approaching. Becker sneering metallic. Beef broiling, broccoli and potatoes drowning. Mint gum, tobacco. Cold sweat. Head too heavy for my neck, bobbing. Need to swallow.

"You feeling ok, sweetie?"

"No thank you yes good." Need to keep my eyes straight, my neck stiff…

Maman has honks for different situations. *Not Late* is a series of short blasts starting blocks away to make us think she's been there all along. *Sick of Waiting* is a heavy lean of two long blasts for when she has to wait longer than it takes to pluck eyebrows in the rearview. *Celebration* is a rhythmic trio – three short blasts, three times - for special occasions like when they crowned the Shah. Tonight, *Not Late* is a rising scream out front as the green Impala hisses to a stop under a yellow streetlight. Full of relief, I hold my tears by pressing my quivering lips.

"Don't forget my turtles," Becker's mom helps load my bike in the trunk.

"What happened," Maman asks when I get in, her eyes sharp with worry. Sid is in the front seat, turns around with a smirk. I don't want to tell her in front of him. Gloater.

"Selling chocolates."

"You're selling too?" She is surprised, already moved on from her panic. "I thought the school asked Saeed for help. Our doreh all bought from him."

"It's a contest for the whole school, Maman. They didn't just ask Precious to do it."

Un-dark, un-murky, light-haired Sid shrugs his shoulders, tilting his curls with a coy grin.

"But Saeed sold to the doreh. Who will you sell to? Amrikayi buy from their own."

"I don't need your doreh friends like Precious does," I glance over at Sid, my breathing back to normal. "I went to Amrikayi houses; sold plenty. Probably going to win another bike."

"Doubt it," Sid says with a confident smile. "Maman's doreh friends are asking their families too. How many did you sell?"

"So many that I lost count, more than you."

"Show me."

Ya lost de list, remember?

"None of your beeswax," I say. "I even sold two to my friend's mom just now."

Dat's a doozy! You got him on that one.

"You don't need to tell," Pincus says when I hand over the two dollars from Becker's mom. His army jacket and boots look tough; his gentle blue eyes and easy smile barely hide his worry. "We were just kidding around, for laughs. Right?"

What would I get for pointing, yelling "fagger polack"? Would it get them to stop calling me Beaner Boy? Would it make me a Pro? Fertig said it takes something big to get them to stop the aka's. To get in with the Pros probably takes something bigger - telling on Pincus, calling him words I may not even be using right. Pincus is the same class of shit as me. Not dark or foreign with weird house smells, but with something to hide, something we didn't choose but are made to be ashamed of, that keeps us in the shadows. He would hide me from Them. What would be the point of telling on him? I got enough Sins.

"I lost our list," I confess, knowing it's safe to tell him. Doesn't mean we're friends.

"The sheet with all the addresses on it?"

"Must've slipped out of my pocket yesterday, when I took off, after you did that--."

"--I get it," he nods, gives me a narrowed stare. "It's fine, I remember the houses."

Except Becker's. I didn't write it down. Bell rings.

"You owe me two bucks, Beaner Boy," Becker catches my shoulder. Last night, getting yelled at by his family, he looked small. Now the sun glints off his metal teeth, eyes hiding behind dark curls. He's a Pro, and Older, the playground light changes who you are.

"Your mom bought," I remind him, trying to see him as small as last night. "I'll give you the chocolates." Then, looking both ways like it's just between us, I suggest, "you don't have to give them to her if you don't want. Keep 'em. Get it?"

"Refund, Beaner Boy," Becker unimpressed. "Money back guarantee."

"Refound?" Pretend-thinking, like I know the word. "My par'ner handed over to class."

"Your partner? You need a partner to sell chocolate? Couldn't do it by yourself? Came to my house alone. Had to call your mommy to get you. Gimme my money, Beaner Boy!"

Pincus strolls by, sees Becker's clasp on my shoulder.

"He wants his mom's money," I tell Pincus with a shrug, trying to sound calm.

"This is your partner?" Becker asks. "Figures. You and your faggety partner owe me two bucks. Money back guarantee, let's go!"

"Sorry," Pincus with an easy smile that doesn't indicate sorry. "Your mom's money has already been turned in and counted as a sale for us. We're getting that knife. No refunds."

He knows the woid!

Pincus isn't done: "You can deliver it to your mommy yourself when it arrives, ok?"

Becker releases my shoulder to take a stab at Pincus but Pincus has already bolted, big smile on his pale face as he rushes though the door to room 17. I'm right behind him.

"He'll just come after us at recess," I remind Pincus. "He's an Older. A Pro."

"Couldn't care less," Pincus takes a seat at the back of the classroom. "Fuck the Pros."

That's why Pincus will never be one. But I think he used it right; "he couldn't care less."

October 1973

I left it by the rack behind the ball box on a pile. We're playing Caroms and after banging a shot off the side of the sand slope to flip my carom on its side so it rolls into the corner pocket, I go to get my Senator. The playground is emptying out. But I don't see it.

I check along the fence, behind the rack, other side of the ball box. Nothing. I walk back to the Carom tables and close my eyes, hoping it'll be different when I open them. It isn't. Keeping my head down, I scan the playground to see if anybody's watching. If somebody pulled a prank, I wouldn't give him the satisfaction of seeing me panic.

"You lose something?" asks Yard Teacher.

"Just lookin' … for my jacket," I say not looking up.

It would be just as embarrassing if my bike got stolen as it would if it was a prank: dumb foreigner doesn't lock his bike. I check shrubs, hedges along the fence, bathroom entrances. I back up to the beige stucco wall, scanning the blacktop, not wanting to believe it.

Doc, your bike has been pinched, pilfered, purloined! You was robbed!

Before I know it, empty silence. Screeching sneakers, barks for balls, singing to the beat of rope slapping the ground, gone. Even the gonjeshk have fled. And in the aftermath of another brutal school day, under a muffled orange sky, I see the playground in a new light, an exhausted caretaker - Maman after guests have gone, sitting at the kitchen table curling smoke upward, saucer as ashtray, staring off blankly. The playground isn't so bad; doesn't judge, is mostly fair, and while it can't account for the misdeeds of its guests, its gates are open to everyone. I breathe in the late afternoon air, walk the blacktop, sweaty neck, racing heart, stomach burning – always in trouble. I squeeze through the fence to the sidewalk, warmed by the exhaust of cars, their red and white lights guiding me in the dusk. Gonjeshk shrieking to their trees. I take the long way.

Baba will ask if I locked it. Maman will threaten to call the cops, force me to go door to door demanding my bike from our Amrikayi thief-neighbors, figuring one of them stole it. She'll shame them, teach them about dignity by confronting them, head held high. My head.

I'll stop by Kersh's or Cowan's. They can't build me a bike but maybe a "Gee that's tough." I'll let their pity wash me, cool me down. When you're wandering in wilderness, no solid ground to stand on, a sweet dose of pity does the trick. I won't be getting any at home.

"They stole my bike," I yell as I walk through the front door.

"What folly!" Maman in her Guweem voice, in the dining room with her doreh, table littered with cards, drained teacups filled with pistachio shells, date pits in ashtrays with lipstick-stained filters, cassette player playing a song they sway and sing along with, the new Googoosh.

"Well come in then, dear!" she exclaims in that high-pitched playful tone of carefree Guweem like she's not bothered by the tragic news. Her tone would be different if her doreh weren't here. She'd have her burdened Jew tone; nothing carefree about it. But the sly nod she gives as I walk in tells me she plans on using that tone later, after they leave. For now, Maman is an easygoing Guween who takes bad news in stride. "Say Hello! Have a chocolate! Have a *Tom Colleens*!" They laugh out loud at the inside joke.

Two boxes of the chocolate turtles are open on the table among the cards and teacups.

"Look what sweet, generous Saeed brought us," Maman says, "a gift because of all the chocolates we bought from him to help your school. Go ahead, take one. Nourish your soul!"

Precious shows up behind me, a satisfied smile on his face.

"Where'd you get those?"

"They were in our closet. I must've miscounted the boxes I sold and had extras."

"You didn't miscount, idiot, those were mine! I'm supposed to deliver them!"

"You sure? I didn't think you sold any." Swiping his light brown curls aside with a finger, he pulls a wad of bills from his pocket, peels one off and offers it up. "Here. A refund!"

I try to not dwell on how it is that even Precious knows the word. "You took two boxes."

"Did I?" He peels off another bill and hands it over. "Musta lost count."

I hate to ask, to validate his gloating. "Where'd you get all that money?"

"I told them it's two dollars a box. You won't be the only bike owner much longer."

"You grace us with your presence," Maman bows to the ladies as they leave. Dinner simmers on the stove, Baba will be home soon and her tone will go back to normal. But for now, "your footsteps on our eyes, with joy, you are welcome."

"They should bury this donkey under dirt!" Maman yells to the ceiling. She's talking in her normal tone now to her almighty Adonai. But as she checks her pots, she has already pivoted to plotting: "Don't say anything to Baba," she says, her manicured fingers holding one of the old star shirts as a rag to wipe the table. "He will tear you to pieces."

"He'll cut your head off!" Precious chimes in. "It's OK, I'll let you ride my bike."

His key in the lock tumbles my insides. Maman starts in as soon as he enters: her card game, who won, who is a bad guest for never bringing even a stem, who invited them to dinner.

"And did you hear? They stole *this* one's two-wheeler."

Baba, dark suit, crumpled white shirt and suffocating tie, mutters about working hard only to be punished; I am revenge for his Sins. His exhaustion is my salvation as he sits on the living room couch, pulls off his tight shoes, rubs his tired feet over his black socks.

"Who is telling jokes on Johnny tonight," he asks nobody as he reaches for the TV Guide.

Maman winks at me and goes to the stove to start serving dinner.

"Tomorrow," she tells me, ladling tomato and okra khoresht, "you steal one of theirs."

My loins get tight and sweaty all over again.

"Certainly," she confirms, remnants of confident Guweem in her voice, "they steal from us," placing a platter of steamy white rice beside the khoresht, "we steal from them. That's fair."

"From who," I ask in protest as I place plates beside forks and spoons. "I don't know who stole my bike. Who am I supposed to steal from?"

"Them," she points to the world outside our kitchen window. "The Amrikayi mules who think they can take your things. An Amrikayi stole your bike so you steal an Amrikayi's bike. And if you don't steal a bike, you'll be dealing with me. Understand?"

All night in bed, wide eyed, I consider my options. Stealing is not out of the question for her. She's good at it, fearless and bold. She does it with excitement, a hint of her continuing distaste for Amrika. "Take that!"-style. I have seen her make a pack of Winstons disappear in the sleeve of her jacket at Von's just for fun - double-blink-lip-bite. Maman means business.

"You should make a list of the usual suspects," Fertig tries to sound like a TV cop. We're shooting caroms after school; the scene of the crime.

"A list of what?"

"Usual suspects. Culprits who may have committed the crime; who want to hurt you."

"An enemies list," Dudley offers.

"You think somebody stole it because it was mine? Maybe he just wanted a bike."

"No offense, Beaner Boy," Fertig prepares to shoot his carom over the grass bump to roll into Hole Four, "but if somebody wanted a bike, they wouldn't steal yours."

Precious rides over on his new bike. An orange colored job named Trident.

"Coming?" he asks, circling, copying my pop-a-wheelies, making sure I see.

"I'll come when I come," I say, not looking up at him, sliding the stick between my fingers to line up my shot. I may be a Non, but I'm still a fifth-grader. "Now get lost."

"Kersh and Cowan wanna build a clubhouse with the bamboo we picked."

"Good," I say coldly. "Gonna finish my game. Leave! Exit!" I'm still an Older to him.

"We're gonna build it against the fence on the hill," still circling, refusing to obey his older brother's commands. "Don't you wanna come?"

"Not now."

"You can't be in our club if you don't help build our clubhouse." Circling, staring.

"I found the bamboo!"

"Still." Pedaling, now feeling more in control of the discussion.

"The club and clubhouse were my idea. I'm in the club."

"Yeah, but still." Trying another pop-a-wheelie that holds up longer than the first one.

"Still what?"

"Still gotta help build it if you wanna be in our club."

"*Your* club? Get outta here." I say it firm and hard; show him who's boss.

He points his orange Trident toward the fence, foot on the pedal. "Almost forgot," he says, pushing his foot down, "Maman said don't forget to steal a bike."

I freeze, pray nobody heard, line up my shot and smack the carom with my stick.

As he rides away, he looks back: "Maman said if you don't steal one, don't come home. And you can't hide out in our clubhouse since you don't wanna help build it. See ya!"

"You call your mom Maman?" Dudley asks looking at me with his head tilted.

"Not me! Just my stupid baby brother calls her that." To make sure they get my point, I yell out as Precious rides on the street beyond the fence. "Tell Mom I'll be home later!"

"Not if you don't steal a bike," he yells back looking straight ahead.

"And tell Mom not to forget tater tots! Mom said tater tots to-night!"

Precious shrugs and keeps riding.

"Did your mom just order you to break the law?" Fertig stares like he's owed an answer.

He never told about me on the toilet, or my Pig sandwich Sin. But does he pass the test? If They round up Jews, Irani, or Mexicki, would Fertig hide me or turn me in? Would he do the "they went that a'way" trick, pointing in opposite directions to save me? Can't risk it.

"Nah," I say with a dismissive wave, leaning in to take my shot, "he's just kidding."

But when Dudley leaves with Pincus and Fertig runs to the mon-key bars to tell a few third graders they're swinging wrong, I'm alone under the cold afternoon sun, looking over a pile of loose bikes behind the ball box. Bikes belonging to kids I know, some who have done me wrong; deserve to get theirs stolen. I am Authority. I inflict Justice. I'll steal one that's better than my crappy blue Senator. Schwinn Sting-Ray; Huffy Thunder Road. Casually lift it, hop on, ride out the back gate, disappear down the street, come up the other side. Perfect get-away. Make Maman proud; I'll be her courageous thief. First I have to steal one; to decide who deserves to lose their bike; who has been mean lately; who shall –

"--And what exactly do you think you are doing?" Fertig's cop voice booms from across the playground, finger raised, running at me. Han-dlebars in my hand; how'd that get there?

"Just looking at this bike - these bikes – thought somebody took mine by accident. Nope, this isn't mine," lay it back down, try to look like I'm thinking something important, deep.

"I figured you may feel forced to follow your mom's order," says Fer-tig. "I'm here to tell you, the law's the law and you" – points at me like Smokey Bear – "shouldn't break it!"

I walk off the playground. At the fence, I close my eyes, face to the sun, wishing it could warm me. I open, a silver glint. Becker, always at my worst. Crossing from the hill to the playground, wiping dirt from his hands. More tortured salamanders? I reach into my pocket.

"Here," I say handing him the bills from Precious. "Your mom's refound." I run up the hill through the vines and brush, turning him small with distance, above him, beyond him. Maybe I'll help with the clubhouse, sleep there to avoid Maman. Maybe I'll slip and break a leg. In the hospital, as Maman grieves, I'll say I fell dragging a stolen bike. She'll feel bad for pressuring me. She'll make chocolate pudding, thick like the Amrikayi do on TV.

Halfway up, I turn to see the playground, marveling at how easy it looks from up here. The geometry of the playground—a perfect rectangle of grey concrete, yellow line segments forming squares, circles, triangles—boundaries they understand. From up here, they are trouble-free, innocent, running, jumping, sliding, a synchronized dance inside their yellow boundaries, their geometry. Kickball. Sockball. Handball. Horse. Hopscotch. Flies-Up. Four-Square. Tag. Even their commands and complaints are music from up here. They belong down there with their joy like I belong up here stewing in my trouble, my boundaries, my churning stomach.

I keep climbing, my feet pushing pebbles in the soft dirt. If I get home late enough Maman will be too busy with dinner to ask. When I reach our house, I look up for the first time. At our back fence, Precious, Kersh and Cowan are tying bamboo with vines for the clubhouse. They don't need to hide. I keep climbing, over leafy ivy, past mossy trees with thick twisted trunks. It's quiet. Smells like mud and bark. Sometimes on the hill leaves crunch and I can't tell if it's the echo of my feet or if I'm being chased. Sometimes I hear birdwings flap against branches, berries falling from trees, my neck turning to see - but except for Becker's salamander, nothing scares me up here. The smell of mud and damp leaves calms me. No stomachaches. I want to yell from the pit of my stomach to the top of the trees towering over me. I'm so far up I can't see home, or the playground.

A tap on my head.

Eucalyptus nut. The ground is full of them; they drop like rain. Keep climbing. Another hits my shoulder. Doesn't feel like it fell, more like it was thrown. I know the difference. I peer up into the dense green above me – trunks, branches, leaves – all still. No breeze that would shake anything loose. Another hits my leg, makes me jump.

"Who goes there?" A voice, slightly high pitched and scraggly.

I look around, trying locate where it's coming from.

"Hey, you! Kid! Who are you? What're you doing here?"

Look left, right, up at the green canopy. "I live close to here," heart starting to pound.

"Close to where? This tree?"

"My house is there," I breathe, feeling faint, point a shaky finger toward my house. Who am I pointing for? Who am I talking to? I keep looking. Stomach starting to churn.

"How far can you throw?"

"What?"

"Anything. How far can you throw anything?"

"I throw high." Light headed... churning... still seeing nothing.

A slow, creaking rip! Leaves rustling, branches cracking. Twigs shiver. A thud! Shakes the ground under my feet, raising a cloud of dust and dried out leaves. When it settles, a figure emerges, straightening up before me: Big, pale, messy brown hair, soft brown eyes behind thick brown frames, easy smile. His loose, brown corduroys match his eyes. Ripped sneakers. His dirty t-shirt is blank – no footprints, alligators, penguins, letters or cartoons.

"At your service!" He holds out a eucalyptus nut. "OK, kid, let's see how far you throw this." He could beat me up; hands look like they've had fights; fingernails caked with dirt.

I take the nut. Smells like the stomachache tree it fell from. I've stepped on thousands of them, small and hollow, grooved shells. They don't go far; get held up in the air if you throw too hard, hit the ground after a few feet if you throw too soft. I ponder my options; he's waiting.

"Just messin' with ya, kid," he says, easy smile. "You can't throw these; too light; better for chucking at people, watching 'em spin around to see who's the wise guy." He has a chipped front tooth, says "s" funny. I can see his tongue slip through between his teeth on "s" words.

"Yeah," I look up at him, "too small for throws. Better for *chucks*."

Chuck is a voib, Doc. I chuck. You chuck. He/She chucks.

He bends down, pulls a good-sized pebble from the mud, wipes it on his pants and rubs it clean with his hands as he studies it. He shows it to me.

"Now this'll make a good throw. This one'll go." He holds it out to me. "Wanna try?"

It's a good throwing rock, not too smooth, little lumps which lodge in the fingertips for a good grip. I take it from him, get a feel for it, turn to face the bottom of the hill. I propeller my arm like Bugs before a pitch, reach back as far as I can and lob the rock high and far. I watch it fly over tree tops on the slope below, waiting to see where it lands. It comes down beside our backyard. Far. Barney Fife Satisfaction Sniff-Exhale.

"You call that a throw," he laughs. Not a mean laugh, not a burn; more of a josh, a friendly rib. He picks up another rock, wipes it on his pants, huffs a pretend-polish huff.

"Watch 'dis, puddin' head," he says in the voice of Curly from Three Stooges, reaching back so far his hand almost touches the ground as he flings the rock. It catapults over treetops, so high it becomes a dot in the sky, past our backyard, down the slope until we can't see it.

"Now that's whatchu call a throw!" His smile exposes his chipped front tooth as he huffs on his dirty fingernails, proudly pretend-polishing them against his shirt. "And you are?"

I've heard people say that on TV: "*Please to make your kwaintince.*" "*How do you do.*" "*Likewise, I'm sure.*" Never heard anyone say it in real life. In real life, you just know people, not by choice but because they're in your class, on the playground, in line behind you. Nona Lee read my name from a sheet of paper. They call me what they want, see me how they want. Still, there's something freeing in the question. "*And you are?*"

And I am? I can say any name I want. He's not at my school or in my family, doesn't live on my block. He doesn't know anything about me or my aka or where I'm from.

And I am? I am like anybody else, like everybody else. I am.

And I am?

"I am Mike." Exhale. *Mike.* Better than *Beaner Boy* or *Mishel* or *Non.* "And you are?"

162

"That's weird. I'm Mike too! But they call me Smiley. Pleased to meet you."

Loping down the hill to escape Smiley Skull Cracker, I do like how he calls after me.

"Mike!" he yells. "Hey Mike! Wait a minute, Mike!"

He's chasing, may crack my skull, but calls me by my outside Amrikayi name, so...

"I didn't crack anybody's skull, I tell ya," he yells from behind. "Come on, Mike!"

He's faster, grabs onto my shoulder. I hate myself for being so slow. If we were jungle people, I'd be lunch. I try to shake loose, but I'm out of breath and he's holding tight, saying "Hold on, kid, now just wait a minute, listen," in between my frantic pleas.

"I ain't gonna hurt you. If I crack skulls, how come cops haven't come for me? Think about it, Mike." He looks at me straight-eyed, without a thought of calling me anything else, clutching my shoulder not to keep me from running but to lean on me, to catch his breath, explain himself. "Just rumor. Know what rumor means?"

"Yes. No. What?"

In his Curly the Stooge voice, he yells, "It's sabatoogee! I'm a victim of soicumstance!"

I'm just trying to catch my breath.

"OK. Here's what happened. First, they made fun of my lisp. Know what a lisp is?"

"No."

"The way I talk. Can't say my 's' too good. You didn't notice?"

"No," I lie.

"I was born with it, can't help it. Then they made fun because I smiled when they made fun of my lisp. My dad taught me to smile when kids are mean because I'm big and can do damage. But Stanley made fun of my dad. Being a chauffeur may look funny - black coat, black hat, driving a limo, opening and closing car doors - but he works hard and since my Mom left we take care of each other. I couldn't let him get away with it. We met at the flagpole. His head hit the pole on the way down when we tackled each other. I felt bad when he didn't get up right away, but he started it. Yard Teacher didn't care, so I got expelled. It followed me to Pines. They point, call me Smiley the Skull Cracker. So I stay on this hill; peaceful here."

"What if you're lying? What if you're saying that to crack my skull?"

"Christians don't lie, Mike. Lying's a Sin," he bends down, finds a good-sized rock and hands it over. "Keep this and hit me with it if you think I'm gonna crack your skull. Deal?"

I figured they're all Christian, all non-Jewish Guweem, but this is the first time anybody said it out loud. I'm looking at a Christian: chipped tooth, thick glasses, easy smile. He could've hurt me by now if he wanted. Still, I'm not telling him I'm Jewish. In case.

"Whataya mean you're a Non? They still say Non?"

We are digging grooves in the mud with twigs, doing imitations of Yogi and Booboo, Fred and Barney. He does a good Booboo, a perfect Barney chuckle. While comparing the Stooges – him arguing Shemp is smarter than Curly - I dismiss Shemp as a Non.

"What do you think a Non is," he asks.

"Somebody who stinks, isn't cool. On the playground they think I'm Mexicki or I don't get their cool. They put me in the Nons, but I get their cool. I shouldn't be in the Nons."

"Mexican, not Mexicki. And who cares about them? You know what Non means?"

"Means you're not in the Pros."

"Pros?"

"Didn't you go to Pinnacle? You don't know Pros and Nons?"

"I know *Non* is short for *Nonsuit*. At Pines, the P.E. coach lists kids who don't suit up as *Nonsuit*. Nonsuits come to P.E. with bellyaches, runny noses, pink eye, doctor notes – excuses to skip P.E. If you're a Nonsuit regularly, you're a *Non*."

"I do P.E.," I argue, "I get the Pros. I don't belong in Nons. I should be in Pros."

"I'm tellin' ya, it's a made-up word. Meaningless. Don'cha see?"

"On our playground, it's real. And I'm just as cool as Pros. I'm no Non."

"Ever watch Tooter Turtle? Mr. Wizard tells Tooter Turtle at the end of each episode: *'Be just what you is, not what you is not. Folks what do this has the happiest lot.'* Get it?"

We get the same jokes, watch the same cartoons; if he was at Pinnacle, he'd probably be a Non; I'd probably avoid him. We'll be Hill Friends. We get up, lope down the hill.

Near the bottom, close to the street, Smiley sees an ivy-covered opening I never noticed.

"Let's explore it," his smile forming dimples in his cheeks. We push ivy aside, step into darkness. I tell Smiley I could use this as my hideout when bullies chase me.

"Nah," he says, "I'll beat the bullies up for ya."

"Bullies are on the playground and you're not allowed there, remember?"

He's a Hill Friend; let's keep it that way.

My hand hits on something cold and hard. Metal.

"You feel that?" Smiley asks.

Bulky, heavy, thin enough to grab. Familiar diamond shaped chunks of rubber. Treads. We pull at the round metal rim of what looks like a mangled wheel covered with vines, caked with mud clumps. We drag it out. My blue Senator! Muddy, handlebars twisted grotesquely out of alignment, rims bent like they were jumped on, racing plate cracked.

"My bike!" I yell. "It got stolen yesterday! My mom told me not to come home today if I didn't steal one to make it even-Steven with Them."

"With who?"

"With them. With the . . . doesn't matter."

"Shouldn't steal, Yogi," he uses Booboo's voice-of-reason but his eyes are direct. "Sin."

Maman warned us about Christians. That's the third time he mentioned Sin. He brought it up first when I told him about Becker and the salamander; said Becker would go to Hell – which is great news - but that I might too because I was too scared to save the salamander.

"Jesus is always watching," he had said. "He wouldn't let you get hurt when you're doing good. You shoulda stepped in to save a salamander minding his own business."

So maybe he's not Smiley the Skull Cracker, but is Smiley the judgmental Christian any safer? Would he hide me or turn me in? To school, police, Nazis? That's still the test. Would he ask his Christian God to punish me if he thought I Sinned? Even worse, would he punish me himself in the name of his Christian God. Sin seems harsher with Christians. Would my Jewish God save me from his Christian God or would Adonai also be too scared to step in, or would he let me get punished because I'm a dirty Sinner?

"Look at my bike," I say. "Wasn't it Sin for them to do this?"

Smiley lays the bike down on the sidewalk.

"The Lord works in mysterious ways," he smiles softly. "This bike can be fixed so you won't need to steal one. Let's get to work!"

"It's busted," I say, hoping for that sweet dose of pity. "This can't be fixed."

"Oh ye of little faith," his smile lighting up his face. "Dis busted bike is like pen-goo-wins," he says in a gruff cartoon voice, "and *Pengoo-wins is practically chickens*! Take a look. No cracks in the frame. Tires still good. Wheels not broken. *Looks woiss dan it is, Mac*. Let's get to makin' a chicken outta dis here pen-goo-win."

We pull leaves and vines off the frame, check for cracks, align the front wheel with the handlebar. Smiley hands me a big leaf to wipe mud off the frame as he tightens nuts with his fingers. He lines up the seat and slides it onto its pipe. We flip the bike, stand it on its handlebar and seat to work on the pedals and chain. Smiley lines the chain holes with the teeth on the chain wheel, using a rock to straighten a crooked tooth, then slips the chain on, cranks the pedal. We watch the back wheel turn. Smooth.

"Good as new," he smiles, the tip of his tongue peeking through his chipped tooth.

We test ride it down the sidewalk. The pedal is stiff from mud at first but smooths out after a few turns. We try pop-a-wheelies, hops, skids.

"Didn't think we could do it, didja," Smiley is happy with himself. He takes his big dirty hands from his hips and holds them out to slap tens. I don't care if he's Christian, Skull Cracker or Non. No stomach-aches with him. He's easy.

As long as he stays on the hill, right Doc? Hill Friends?

"Let's show your mom," he says. "She'll see fixing is better than stealing."

Hold it right there! Show your Maman? Think again.

She'll be cooking Shabbat dinner; musty rice steam, boiling gondi and abgoosht stench, our stink. She'll give him untrusting side-eyes reserved for Them because to Maman it's the Amrikayi who are the for-eigners, not us. She'll ask questions. I'll have to answer, in Farsi. He'll see us, hear us, smell us. He'll wonder what we are. But I can't come up with an excuse fast enough to stop Smiley from jumping on the bike so I jump on behind him and hold on.

You need a plan, Doc, and you ain't got much time. Try heading him off at the pass...

We get to the end of Albatross Lane and I hop off, run to the door ahead of Smiley. In English I yell "Hi *Mom*! We're here, *Mom*!" Amri-kayi enough for her to get it and, hopefully, play along. Smiley, in right behind me, gets hit with the waft of smells, takes a deep whiff.

"What is that?"

Why can't our house smell normal like plasticky lavender Glade, sultry cinnamon Pillsbury rolls, buttery Duncan Hines angel food? Ev-erything in our house is permanently stained with the indelible stink of fried fenugreek. "I don't smell anything."

Maman emerges from the kitchen in a haze of ancient aromas, clutching her ladle, her fiery hazel eyes screwed on Smiley who is so tall he blocks the light in our doorway; the tallest person ever in our house. When he landed in front of me on the hill, he looked Normal Amrikayi Tall, but in our house, he is Freakish Tall, stooping to avoid hitting his head on the door jamb.

"Een vebba kiyeh," Maman lowers her ladle, sharpens her teeth.

My cheeks get hot, throat tightens. Don't want him to hear us. But if I don't answer – fast – she'll ask again, louder, and raise the ladle.

In English, curved, cool and soft: "Mom, this is my friend! He helped find my bike!"

Maman in Farsi, high pitch, thick tongue and teeth consonants: "You found it?"

Me in English, casual, laidback: "Yeah, Mom, it was broke and we fixed it."

Maman in Farsi, dubious, dismissive: "This hamall? He found it? Fixed it? He couldn't help you steal a better one? He looks like a thief."

Me now in Farsi, sly, low: "Didn't need to steal one. Found mine. Fixed it."

Maman in Farsi, savvy and quick: "Maybe he's the one who stole it."

Me in Farsi, quick nip in the bud: "He doesn't steal." *Don't say Christian!* "It's Sin."

Maman in Farsi, seething, raising the ladle a little: "You told a gharibeh that I said you should steal? Khak-bar-saret! What is his name?"

Every Amrikayi is a suspicious gharibeh to her. Can't he be a good guy? I try a double-blink-lip-bite to signal that he's ok; wish I knew her secret tongue. Then I realize: to Smiley this is all a "Lashoon-Benechi" gibberish code he doesn't get. He's lost.

"This is Mike," I finally say in English.

"*My? My* yanee chee?"

Smiley, still in the doorway, watching. Maman, at the kitchen door, waiting. Me in the middle. I repeat, in a Farsi tone: "Myyk! Myyk! Like My-kell! Myyk, OK?"

She nods her "I'm gonna mess with you" nod, smirks. Maman the prankster, stirs hot tea with a spoon then quietly taps it on our unsuspecting arms to watch us flinch. Sheytoun.

"Oh! Myyk," in fake Amrikayi. "Velcome!" In Farsi, nodding, half-bowing: "Maymoon." English: "You are wery velcome, Myyk." Farsi: "Adonai, why do all the ikbiris fall around *our* necks," elegant smile, dignified nod, bow and sweep of her arm.

"Nice to meet you, Ma'am," says Smiley, giving Maman an innocent smile.

Looking up at him with the smile only we know is meant as a joke, she asks in Farsi: "He looks big as a bear but talks like a baby. Is he... aghab-moondeh?" Smirk, bow, nod.

I stay quiet, watching innocent Smiley get mocked. I should say something. Protect him.

Maman keeps it up: "What grade you are, Myyk?"

"Seventh," Smiley smiles a sweet, oblivious smile.

"Seven? You are big! Where is your eschool? How you are friend with Essagh?"

"Essa?" Smiley looks at me, tilts his head.

Hot spoon on my arm, waiting to see me flinch. Spilling my inside name we don't use with Guweem or Amrikayi.

"—Who is Essa?"

Maman's smile is warm and lovely, even when she's burning you.

Be just what you is, not what you is not; but save yourself.

"She means Mike! Essa (hide the "gh") is how you say Mike in our dumb language."

Maman pretends to pick something from her teeth with her sharp, manicured pinky, but she's just showing her fangs. A casual tooth suck, looking straight at Smiley, waiting.

"Pines," he says nervously. "I go to Pines."

"Pine?" In Farsi to me, "Chee migeh?"

"Pines Junior High School, Mom! It's where everybody goes after Pinnacle Palace."

"Yes, Ma'am," with a smile that exposes his chipped tooth.

"And look at his tooth, vebba!" covering her mouth in pretend shock. "All these beautiful, shiny-white blue-eyed Amrikayi with cheeks like apples and you bring home this broken vebba?" In English to Smiley, "How you are friend?"

"I met Essa on the hill," Smiley says with a wink and grin in my direction.

"You met this hamall in the dirt below our house? You can't find proper friends at school like your brother? Does he have parents?"

He just stands there, clueless, as Maman berates him. What's wrong with him? What's he smiling about? Getting hot, stomach starting to churn. He shouldn't have come here.

"Myyk, do you have mawther," she asks, devilish twinkle in her eye.

"A mother? Sure."

She looks at me, smiles. "How many?"

Armpits stinging. Say something good, you big dumb Christian do-gooder.

"Just the one," still with the confused smile. "But she left. It's just me and my dad."

"Oh ya?" says Maman, smiling and nodding.

"But if my dad marries his girlfriend then I'd have a step-mom. So, I guess that's two."

"If your mawther olso marries then you have two fawthers," she side-glances me.

"I suppose," he shrugs, "I don't know. Are you cooking dinner? Smells interesting."

Maman in Farsi, "Vavaylah. He wants dinner too?" Turning to Smiley, "We are Irani from Persia, Myyk," she checks to see if I flinch. "I make the Persian food for Shabbat," curving her mouth, rolling her tongue so her words sound extra Amrikayi like a TV commercial. "Is abgoosht vid the gondi," she announces proudly. "Do you like a try? You are wery velcome."

"Abgoo...?"

"Ab-goosht! Is chicken, limou Amani and nokhod soup. Gondi is nokhodchee vid chicken." To me in Farsi, "Tell him to wash those dirty hands if he wants to stay for dinner."

"Oh, no thank you. My dad is making special dinner tonight."

"Oh ya? Your father is cooking? What he is makes?"

"Sloppy Joes."

"Sloppy chee?" To me in Farsi. "Poor motherless Amrikayi, even their food is disheveled," then to the ceiling with a smile, "Oh, Adonai, where have you delivered us?"

"It's like hamburger," Smiley explains, "but looser and with barbecue sauce and cheese."

"Hamburger for dinner; albateh," she mutters. "This is where he has delivered us." To Smiley, "OK, Myyk, you are velcome." To me, "Put cookies on a plate, pour him a glass of milk if he wants. Use the nice cups." She returns to the kitchen, where she has set Shabbat candles for sundown. "You have post," she says, "from Shideh."

The crisp fall breeze cools my face as we finally go back out. He doesn't belong in our house; can't handle the heat. We're outside friends, Hill friends. We take turns pedaling down Albatross Lane, fresh whiffs of eucalyptus leaves, chimney fires and tailpipe fumes – trouble free. Orange and purple cloud ribbons streak across the sky as streetlights click like honey-gold lollipops and kitchen windows light up like warm yellow squares of soft butter. Smiley and I use the final rays of daylight to ride my blue Senator, doing pop-a-wheelies, jumping off curbs.

It starts in Farsi: "*Mishel my bell. You disappeared? I see how it is. Yesterday friends, today acquaintances? You thought so, koor khoondi, my dear. Because...*" Then in English: "*Your mother tell mine many friends in Amrika and they have doreh for cards. Maybe we come too to play again like before. You show me your Amrikayi friends so they be my friend. OK?*" Back to Farsi: "*May your eyes light with joy we are coming, arms and heart open. We will show the Amrikayi who we are. They will see us! Miss Shideh.*"

I put the letter in my closet with her others. On my bed, I open my notebook to a stack of paper, clean as a blanket of fresh snow, unmuddied by the dramas of Math, Grammar or History. Empty space for me to carve my story, burrowing sweet blue-ink grooves of new history into its bleached white fibers, creating my myth. I can write whatever I want. In English only:

"*What's happenin'? Forgot my Farsi been here so long. Hope you get it. Things are cool in Los Angeles (aka LA). Got a cool bike, it hauls when I do motocross pop-a-wheelies, crow-hops, cross-it-ups. My friends are aka Pros, hippies with long hair, like mine. We ride bikes and listen to cool radio songs. I look Amrikayi now. I'll probably be busy with Speed and Worm (that's my cool friends' aka's!) but we can play if your parents come for cards. Check you later. Bye! Yours truly, Dynamite Moto Mike M. aka Aztec (it's what they call me here).*"

The hill flattens when it reaches the side of our house, rises again at the dead-end out front. Smiley and I play and sing there. He doesn't laugh if I sing wrong; he sings along. We sing "*Give me lo' give me peace on earth*" humming the parts we don't know – the parts I don't know, he knows all of it. I get to sing as loud as I want with Smiley because he sings even louder. Smiley is easy.

Still, when our chatter gets personal, like his love of runny eggs, I hold back, wondering if maybe Maman isn't right. Maybe he is a vebba, a Non. Why am I friends with him?

"I like 'em good and gooey," he says as we swing vines in the air to get that whipping sound, "I dip my toast, sop up the gooey yolk." Then he looks both ways to make sure the coast is clear and, whisper-confesses: "Sometimes I even lick leftover yolk straight off the plate."

Just like you!

The option is mine: confess my own secret love of gooey yolks, or not. Cool Amrikayi like scrambled; I've heard them talk. I like runny; I'm a Non. He likes runny; do the math.

So you love gooey but Pros don't. So what? Your secret is safe with him.

"Really?" Salty headshake, mean side glance. He's probably a Non at his school; must be if he's playing with me; old enough to have better friends than me. So why share with him?

Let's face it, Doc, he's fun. On the hill you get to be yourself with him; he's easy.

On the hill, where I hide from the shit-inducing tension of constant trouble, working nonstop to get in with the Pros. On the hill, where nobody sees us singing or cartoon voices. But still...

"You like runny?" I give a dismissive chuckle. "Scrambled is cooler."

Smiley shrugs, picks up a fallen tree branch and swats it in the cold November air.

Oh, brudder, now you done it. Went too far and got him mad. Get ready to run!

"Let's play ball," the smile, the tip of his tongue slipping through his chipped tooth.

Close call. If dat didn't get his dandruff up, either he really is a Non, or he's a friend.

The branch in his hand is thick but crooked; even I know it wouldn't make a good bat.

"Doesn't look like much of a bat," I say, another dismissive side glance.

"Hank Aaron used broomsticks and bottle caps. If it's good enough for Hammerin' Hank and Roy Hobbs, then this magic hunka wood should be good enough for me and my pal."

"Hobbs?" On the hill, I sing the wrong words and he doesn't care. Still, I don't want him to know everything I don't know. We know Yogi and Booboo, Fred and Barney, Rocky and Bullwinkle. We know George is the best Beatle. But Hobbs?

"Hobbs, yeah, on Dodgers. Number 17."

"Number 17 is Paciorek, chowderhead. Hobbs is from the book."

Pheew! Just a book. No need to pretend being a bookworm. Not knowing books is cool.

"Right," cool nod, using Smiley to practice being Pro. "Dumb *Hobbs*. Hated that book."

"No, numbskull," his smile crinkles his eyes in pure joy. "*The Natural* is a book; Hobbs is a character. You never read it? It's about America's pastime. You can borrow my copy."

"Maybe," I say, playing it cool. "Let's play."

Smiley hands me the branch-bat and picks up a smooth rock the size of a walnut.

I stand at the dead-end, the hill's slope is our backstop; Albatross Lane, lined with parked cars, is our outfield. Smiley rears back, fires the rock past me so hard it lodges in the slope.

"My fastball," he says. "Can't touch it. Now for my super somnam-bulistic slow pitch--"

—A voice! A thick and familiar intrusion, like a traitorous belch exhaling the rotting truth of an embarrassing, undigested meal – unin-vited, unwelcome: "What do we have here?"

Fertig's brittle yellow hair and faded blue eyes are out of place on Albatross Lane. His hands are jammed into the pockets of his light blue windbreaker like he's working a case.

Stinking stinker; a boip that stinks up the joint, get rid of him.

"What're you doing here?"

"Y'know, Beaner Boy," Fertig ponders, taking a hand out from his windbreaker pocket to rub his chin thoughtfully, "you've been to my house but I've never—"

"—What'd he call you?" Smiley stretches up tall, a new rock in hand ready for the next pitch. Only this time it doesn't look so much like a baseball as it does a rock.

"It's OK," I say, in my heart a low roar I haven't felt since the old days at New School. Smiley has me. "Just a Non from school," with a snide, elongated emphasis on "school" to make sure it is understood how I, like all Pros, hate school, a place only Nons like, "*schooowel...*"

"OK," Smiley says, loosening his grip on the rock and turning to Fertig, "and you are?"

Like a pig sandwich at our Shabbat table or Maman's ghorme sabzi oozing green grease from a Partridge Family lunchbox at the benches, Fertig here is wrong. It's Sunday on the hill and the playground has popped in, probably to tell me I'm doing something the wrong way.

"That's just Kelly Smelly...with a big fat belly made outa jelly," I say dismissively.

"Now hold on a—" Fertig tilts a disappointed head at me, "—that was a temporary—" then abandoning his explanation, he turns to Smiley, "Kelly Fertig at your service," sticking his hand out to Smiley. "Pleased to make your 'quaintance."

He's ruining the atmosphere. Keep 'em apart.

"Why are you here?"

"Who's your friend?" he asks with suspicion. "Never seen him before. Seems older."

"You can call me Essa," Smiley says. "Essa is Mike in Persian. I'm Mike - like Mike here, he's Essa in Persian too, so you can call me Mike or you can call me Ess—"

"--No!" I hold one hand out to shut Smiley up and another to keep Fertig where he is, a traffic cop trying to stop a collision. I frown at Smiley; he shrugs, like "What I do?"

They can't meet. Fertig is playground, Nons, my work of becoming Pro, trouble. Smiley is hill, hiding from the cruel world, doing and saying what we want even if we don't know the words, easy. Hill and playground should not meet.

"Guess you could say I'm both mentor and best friend to ol' Beaner Boy here," Fertig reaches to give me an awkward shoulder grab, pull me in. "I mean, Essa! Right? Essa?"

"He's your best friend, Yogi?" Smiley asks in his somber Booboo voice. "I didn't know you had another best friend. I figured I was--"

"--He's not my best friend," I interrupt, "we go to school together. He's a Non."

"For now," Fertig corrects me. "They think we're both Nons."

"I thought *I* was your best friend, Yogi," Smiley's Booboo feels dumb in front of Fertig. Yogi-Booboo is hill; using it in front of Fertig makes me cringe, and angry.

"Beggin yer pardon, Cap'n," Fertig joins in, "your Booboo sounds like Droopy Dawg."

"Hello Joe," Smiley replies in Droopy Dawg, which I haven't heard before.

"Hello Butch," Fertig replies in kind. "Wanna hear my Foghorn Leghorn?"

Eh, what's up, Doc? Looks like deez maroons are becoming fast friends, without you.

"You need to go home," I tell Fertig.

"Hold up," says Smiley. "Let's have a meeting on the mound." He pulls me aside as Fertig waits, unfazed by my rejection, hands jammed in his windbreaker pockets, whistling.

"I think you hurt his feelings, Yogi," Smiley says, still in now-annoying Booboo, looking down on me with his soft corduroy-brown eyes, smiling through his chipped tooth.

"He's just a Non from the playground, can you stop doing Booboo for a second?"

"Nons aren't real, remember? It's all made up."

"The name may be made up, but the rest isn't. Pros run with Pros. Nons with Nons. I'm a Pro, not a Non like they all think, like him. Bad enough I'm stuck with him at school."

"Aren't you friends?"

"We go to school together; forced together at recess and lunch. He's constantly telling me what to do, what I'm doing wrong. I didn't pick him."

"Mister Ranger's not gonna like it, Yogi."

On Yogi Bear, Booboo is Yogi's Conscience. When Smiley says "Mister Ranger" he points up because Mister Ranger is his Christian God and Yogi is the Sinner. I am Yogi.

"Fine," I turn to Fertig. "You wanna play? You can be the catch."

"Catcher," Fertig squats. "It's catcher, not catch." He punches his right fist into his left hand as I stand in front of him holding the branch to face Smiley.

Smiley leans in, shakes his head, nods. Confused, I look back to see Fertig wiggling fingers between his knees, signaling to Smiley. Secrets already? Behind my back?

"What do you think you're doing," I demand. "Secrets? He's my friend. I let you play and you make secrets behind me?"

"I'm giving him signs," explains Fertig. "A catcher gives signs to his pitcher."

I look at Smiley. He nods, looks frustrated. "He's catcher, I'm pitcher. Same team."

"Then I'll be catch."

"Catcher," says Fertig, getting up and taking the branch from me. "It's catcher."

I squat behind Fertig as he wigwags the bat. Smiley leans in; I wiggle fingers between my knees. He plays along, shaking, nodding, straightens up, winds his arm like a windmill, lifts his leg, rears back and lets the rock fly.

A dull thud. I don't feel anything, but everything stops. Smiley stunned. Fertig frozen. Gaping black holes where mouths should be. Should I be hurt? A rock to the head means you get to be hurt. Warm blood trickling down the side of the head means you get to scream. You're allowed when you get hit in the head with a rock. I scream. So loud I scare myself.

Smiley and Fertig hustle me to my front door, my eyes wide open. I'm conscious, screaming, consider crying. I get to. I'm not thinking of Smiley; about him getting in trouble or being scared. I get to not think of him. I get to be hurt. They hustle me inside, into the kitchen.

"What's that smell," Fertig sniffs.

Now he knows too. He'll tell. I moan to distract him. "Owee!"

"That's how Persian houses smell," Smiley says. "Thought you were his best friend."

"Ow-wee-yow!"

Maman at the kitchen table on the phone sees sweaty Smiley and Fertig holding me up. Our eyes lock and I whimper, still aware enough to lean my head so the blood trickles faster. An about-to-faint neck

176

bob. She howls and drops the phone, yellow receiver hits the floor, bounces, dangles and twirls off the curly phone cord. Maman grabs me as Smiley and Fertig scatter.

"Chee shod," she screams, the pupils shrinking in her hazel eyes.

Play it up. Whimper. Eyes frozen, trancelike. I may faint. Maman always buys it.

"We were playing baseball," Smiley offers when I don't answer.

"Een kiyeh," Maman points her jaw at Fertig. "More hamalls?"

"—*He* threw a rock at Essa," Fertig points a shaky finger at Smiley.

Essa?

"Yeeoooowwwee!"

Maman flashes her rage at Smiley. "You throw it the rock?"

"No. Well, yes. We were playing," Smiley tries to explain, looks to Fertig for backup but Fertig looks away, does the minding-my-own-business pretend whistle.

Maman grabs the broom leaning against the wall in the corner.

I finally speak up. "Maman, nakon!"

Too late. She's chasing Smiley, sweeping the broom at his feet.

"Go out from here, crazy boy," she yells. "Dirty boy! Go out!"

"Maman!" I yell in Farsi. "We were playing! It wasn't on purpose."

"It was an accident," says Smiley, still with the easy smile, tongue through his chipped tooth, skipping to avoid the broom. "We're best friends."

Maman sweeps Smiley to the door. Fertig tiptoes away, not wanting to be swept off.

Say somethin' Doc. It ain't right.

"Don't Mom!" In English. "He's my Best Friend!"

Smiley's eyes widen. Fertig turns to me, tilts his head.

Grudgingly, "They're ... both my best friends, Mom."

Fertig grins as Smiley the Skull Cracker continues to dodge Maman's broom, running to the front door and out, up the slope, past bushes, shrubs, trees. Gone.

As Maman gets her car key to take me to the emergency room, Fertig stands beside me in the doorway, holding a paper towel wrapped around an ice cube he got from the freezer.

"Here," he hands me the ice, "press it on your wound. You might need stitches."

Stitches. Scarred. Rugged like Billy Jack. They'll all see it.

At the emergency room, the doctor doesn't do stitches; but wraps a white bandage around my head, my long black hair coming out from under it. "Knock 'em dead, Cochise!"

In the mirror: Solemn brown eyes, sweaty brown face, black hair matted under a band of white gauze, a stain of blood soaking through. *Cherokee Pee-pul!* I am Cochise

It's chilly as I walk the playground before first bell, past the orange hoops of basketball, the tall brown walls of handball, the suddenly unimportant yellow boundaries of their games. My warm skin, warm blood feel good. Gonjeshk singing for me this morning, fluttering over my shoulders like they're my wings. The lone palm dancing for me. I don't have to say a word; my headband will do the talking. This one fits; nobody dares pull it off. I stare out at a stern grey horizon, waiting for them to see me: damaged, bandaged Hero. My quiet upward gaze means I'm thinking things, important things, not small, childish things like Pros, Nons or—

"-'t's a pretty big bandage for such a small head wound," Fertig, the interrupter.

"Doctor's orders," I say, regretting yesterday's emotional decision to call him Best Friend. Today he's back to being that rancid belch, repeating the stench of a putrid meal I ate in a weak moment. "See ya," I say, changing course to a place he's too timid to go: the beige stucco wall next to the blue bathroom where Pros hang around before the bell. They'll see me.

Speed and Worm leaning back on the stucco; Speed gnawing on a red Cheez 'n Crackers stick with his buckteeth; Worm chewing pink bubble gum. In faded blue jeans and beaten sneakers, they take turns flipping their long locks, sometimes a quick whip of the neck, sometimes a broad hand swipe. I pretend to head for the bathroom. Slow. Wait. For a nibble.

"W'happened," Speed looks straight, leaning back on wall like a cowboy.

"Maybe he's trying to be Big Chief Ironsides again," Worm elbows Speed, "like that time with the rubber band from the produce aisle." He giggles. Worm, the spoiler.

Now's your chance, Doc. Let 'em have it.

I peel back a portion, show the bloodstain, gaze at the horizon, to a better, simpler time – a Scarred-but-Wise Cowboy time. Maybe that's why Amrikayi like cowboys so much. When you're in the right, righteous and heroic, being a cowboy can be pretty good, I guess.

Cochise was no cowboy, Doc. Neither was the Cherokee. Or Billy Jack. Or even Cher.

"You scratch a mosquito bite?" Worm still giggling; dumb baby.

"Nope," Cowboy exhale. "Rock fight; had to go to Emergency; almost needed stiches."

"Really? Almost?" Speed only uses that word if he's interested.

Maybe I should tell them about-

Dat's too far. Wouldn't be fair. Bad enough you tryin' to be a Cochise-killin' cowboy.

"Smiley," gaze at the horizon, check to see if they're looking. "Yep. Skull Cracker."

When I say it, it's like they all hear it. Gathering, whispering. Even Jodi S. and Lisa W.

"Looks like he got you pretty good," Speed pushes his foot off the wall to have a look.

"Yep," I say, Cowboy twang coming into me all its own. "Shore did." Sniff!

"That monster is still around?" asks golden-haired, blue-eyed, non-doll Jodi S.

As they study the wound, Worm trades his useless giggle for a righteous tone, "What a son of a-. He's a real son of a-." Solemn, sensitive, doesn't say the "bitch" part so they'll think "What a righteous guy! Too decent to say 'bitch.'" Worm is good; I could learn from him.

"Isn't it so dangerous on that hill," Lisa W. asks me, looking at me, seeing me. Like this.

"Yep, s'pose so," my jaw square, glancing up the hill - brave, wounded Cowboy-Hero. "But ah clamb that thar hill ever-day, ma house is up thar, see that thar palm tree?"

Confused head tilt from Lisa W.

Don't overdo it, Doc.

"Damn Smiley," Jodi S. tries to regain the attention Lisa W. took. She's getting taller, Lisa W. Back in fourth, she had a quiet smile, short hair as gold as Amrikayi wheatfields; green eyes tamed behind gold wire glasses. Her slouch made her seem shy. Now her hair is long, wavy, more lustrous than Jodi's. Hoop earrings; cherry lip gloss. "It scares me he's up there," Jodis S. almost managing tears to make up for Lisa W.'s new beauty. "He really is a son of a-!"

"I'd kick his ass if I saw him," says Speed, not to be left out of this important topic.

He fixed your bike, stood up for you. He'd hide you from Them, Doc.

"He's scum," says Worm, "leave scum be." Because Worm is better than violence.

You don't know that woid, do you, Doc? Sounds ugly, and mean.

"Damn scum," gripes Jodi S. "You OK, Beaner? Um, Mishel- Um- oh I'm so upset!"

Jodi S. Talking. To me. Trying to remember my name, my outside Amrikayi name.

He was Booboo, Doc. Your conscience. Mister Ranger wouldn't like it.

I am Yogi: desperate bear willing to Sin for every picnic basket that's in Jellystone Park.

Over by the monkey bars, Fertig leans against the back fence with Dudley and Pincus, half his face tucked into his windbreaker to keep warm, but eyeing me and shaking his head.

After school, I ride my bike to the playground. Maman said I can't take it anymore but the rock fight softened her. In front of the ball box, Fertig squares up a shot at the carom table.

"Heard your tall tale today, Pecos Bill," Fertig says, shaking his head as he aims his cue.

"What tall tale?"

"Smiley the Skull Cracker? Aka your best friend, Mike, Essa, or whatever his name is?"

"But he is aka Smiley the Skull Cracker."

"And I'm Johnny Appleseed," says Dudley with a wet gummy smile, "and this here's Paul Bunyon," pointing at pale, scrawny Pincus, who salutes with a finger to his brow.

"Smiley the Skull Cracker isn't real," Fertig says. "He's just a guy who got bullied and tossed out of school. Just another unfair aka like your Beaner Boy, or my Kelly Smelly."

"But he really is Smiley. And he cracked my skull."

"A scratch. I was there, remember? You made him a monster to get in with the Pros."

The sky is cloudy. In my sweaty palm, the handlebar of my blue Senator, all fixed up. He adjusted the seat too, for better pop-a-wheelies – "wheelies," he had said, "not pop-a-wheelies." Only he hadn't made me feel stupid. He just said it, like in passing, smiling, tongue through his chipped tooth like he was joyfully, innocently amused by my saying it wrong.

"But you said to get in with the Pros you gotta do something big," avoiding Fertig's eyes. I look to Dudley and Pincus, they shake their heads, like I don't get it. "I did something big."

"You said he's your best friend. Plus you could've included me. He could've cracked my skull too. If you hadn't switched to catcher, it would've been my bandage."

The playground starts to empty and, not seeing Yard Teacher anywhere, I turn from them and decide to race my bike across the blacktop. Fast. I can do what I want today.

"Off the bike!" Yard Teacher, behind the ball box. "Now walk it all the way back."

I get off, holding the Doherty grips to happily walk my blue Senator. A metallic glint flashes the side of my eye; a black chill at my shoulder. Dark curls bounce beside me.

"So you found your bike, eh?"

"Yeah," I say, confused, at first. When I figure it out, I look in his cold shiny eyes. "Yep," in Cowboy. "Found 'er up on th' hill, near-broken." I move my eyes off him, gaze upward. "Figured some lowdown stinkin' polecat musta stole 'er and trad to wreck 'er." Look down, twist sneakered toe in the blacktop, back up at Becker. Hard daggers. "But we fixed 'er."

He ignores the accusation. "We?"

I would have abandoned it, thinking it was beyond repair; chalked it up to the Bad Eye – even with Maman's egg ritual. I watched the salamander die, not knowing I could save it, thinking I'd get in with the Pros if I just shut up and let it happen.

"My pard'ner worked on 'er with me," I tell Becker. "Just needed some straightnin' out." I walk past him, almost brushing his shoulder.

"Partner? You mean that pink-eyed faggit you sold candy with?"

Pincus never panicked when they chased him; helped me escape when they chased me. But I didn't call him friend when they asked. But no, I'm not talking about Pincus.

"Smiley," floating toward the fence, above Becker and the playground like *Lifebuoy* soap. "Skull Cracker. You don't know him."

This Yom Kippur I didn't atone for the lies, the betrayals. Maybe that's what caused the war there; nobody atoned. There's always a price for not atoning. Next Yom Kippur, I'll atone, for this Sin and all the ones before it. But for now, I'm a Pro. Practically.

Spring 1974

Maman's *Celebration* honk goes off outside as we're having Fruit Loops watching *Pink Panther*, Saturdays at 9 a.m. Channel 2. But it's not the Impala's horn. We run out. An almost-sportscar – two-door, copper, black racing panels, "Mach 1" etched in white block racing letters.

Fordmostang! Maman behind the wheel, brown sunglasses, smiling, *Celebration* honk.

"Bring eggs," she shouts as the suddenly shabby green Impala hisses to a stop behind her.

Baba in tight gabardines, brown shirt with green paisleys, emerges, a smile widening his neatly trimmed moustache, his bald head shining like a star under the gold sun. "Look at this!"

We run past him. I flip the seat forward to force Sid in the back and sit in the passenger seat, check out the console. FM. Cassette! I roll the knob, look for the cool stations Pros like; the ones which light up the red "Stereo" light. That's when you know you have a cool station.

Baba heads in to get the Polaroid.

"Don't forget eggs," Maman shouts, loud enough for the neighbors to hear.

"We don't need eggs," Baba yells back from inside the house.

"We have to break the Bad Eye," Maman argues. "Blind the eyes of our jealous enemies; poke out jealous eyes that refuse to see us in our good fortune. Bring one for each tire."

"Four eggs to waste on you superstition?" Baba asks. "Amrika we're in now. Superstition they don't have. Our destinies are in our hands, not magic, not ritual. Eggs cost money!" Then he translates an old Farsi phrase to English: "Is money the grass for the bears?"

We laugh; it makes no sense in English. Baba winks at us. He never used to wink or act playful. He never used to wear shirts with paisleys like the hippies.

"In Iran we would have sacrificed a lamb, at least a chicken, for a new car. You can't spare four eggs? They'll give the Bad Eye when they see a new car under our feet; two cars? You want the Bad Eye? On our children's heads, we have to break eggs! One egg for each tire."

Sid stops smiling as their voices get loud, fearing what Baba may do next - table flip, Christian Kite, having to leave and bring Maman back. Or just stop being playful.

I tune the radio dial between 94 and 96; scratchy, radar sounds. I'm close, the guitar intro to "Smoke on the Water" fades in. I turn it up to cover their yelling.

"Nobody is going to give us the Bad Eye in Amrika," Baba insists, "everybody has two cars here. You know why? Because nobody throws eggs away for a ritual in this economy."

"When good fortune comes, you sacrifice," recites Maman as Sid covers his ears.

"It wasn't good fortune," Baba yells, "it was hard work." Shaking his head, he goes in, "I'll get your damn eggs. Oh Adonai, why did you ring this simple dehati around our neck?"

Maman lays one in front of each tire, starts the engine and rolls her new car slowly forward, her shiny new tires crunching eggshells, squashing yolk and goo into the fresh grooves.

"Blind Bad Eyes!" she chants, crushing eggshells. "Blind jealous enemies!" She puts it in reverse, bangs the Impala's front bumper, a metallic clank that draws Baba back out in time to see Maman pull her new Fordmostang onto our driveway, tracking egg goo and shell bits.

"Should've sacrificed a chicken," Baba mutters, finding his smirk and shaking his head as he drags the hose from the side yard and uncoils it. "At least we could've made abgoosht."

"Manny!" cries Marty Levin coming out to see Baba hosing egg goo off the driveway, "I thought you were gonna give me a chance to put you in a Mercedes, what happened?"

Baba's shy grin means he's thinking up a clever answer to soothe his upset neighbor.

"Ay Mardee sonuvagun, Nixon say buy Amrikan car to help Amrikan gas crisis so I buy the Ford, named after his new Vice President. I try buying Nixon but they say it has too many leaks. We have to be Yankee Doodool Dandee, Mardee!"

Marty howls, slaps his bare knee as Baba revels in the laughter he created; a perfect smoke screen to get Marty Levin off his back. And he's not done.

"In my country, 'doodool' means 'little penis'!"

Marty stops cold, smile frozen. Baba freezes too, hose in hand, water rolling down the driveway. Did he go too far? Amrikayi don't like foreigners mocking their symbols.

"What is that," asks Marty in a serious tone. "Is that . . . Schmuck? Schmeckle?"

Baba's smile comes back.

"Eshmuck eshmeckel doodool bobol, Mardee, anyway you slice it, it come up *penis*!"

It takes a couple of seconds, but Marty Levin howls again. "You should go on Carson, Manny. A real card, boy. A regular Norm Crosby with the malaprops."

With a humble bow and quiet smile, Baba wraps the hose. His eyes have a pleased look; it's been a good Saturday. Worth the four eggs.

Spring is a dizzying mix of sweet jasmine and warm asphalt. A lazy afternoon breeze drifts in through the window of Room 17, fondles my skin, brushes against the tiny hairs on my arms. Beside me, golden haired Jodi S., my desk partner, yawns wide and easy, her breath a warm exhale of strawberry bubble gum and cherry lip gloss. I get an urge to extend my joints, stretch my limbs, push my back, my pelvis out far as I can.

I talk to Jodi S. regularly. Since the Smiley incident I've made inroads with the Pros, including Jodi S. I repeat jokes Baba tells at night and she gets them, laughs – with me, not at me. She sees me. Still, when the bell rings she rushes out. Pros don't stay after anymore; they have cooler places to be; places I'll be going soon. Maybe with Jodi. The playground after school is for Nons and babies now; playing games, waiting for Ice Cream Man or rides home.

I don't stick around either. I may not be going where Jodi goes, but I'm not playing with Nons. Or eating hamess; it's Passover, again. Maman makes salami and lettuce on matza each morning, I toss it before the bell; can't risk being seen with matza. They'll point. When the bell rings I dash across the playground, cross the street and climb the hill to eat at home. I sit in front of the TV with a fried egg and cheese on matza, fearlessly swooping rich salty yolk with my tongue as it rolls down my chin. I'm actually looking forward to watching *Jeannie* and *Gilligan* reruns, episodes I've seen a hundred times but which have taken on a different look lately. Ginger's swaying hips; Maryann's tight shorts; even Mrs. Howell's lipstick, so red. And Jeannie – funny, bouncy Jeannie – smooth arms, long neck - is that underwear beneath her sheer, baggy pants? If I get closer to the screen, I think I can see her--

"--Why are you so close to the TV," Maman screams. "You want to go blind?"

I don't know why I jump back; why I pretend I wasn't doing something…bad. Was I?

You were tryin to sneak a peek at Jeannie's underwear, Doc. You know what you did.

"Go out and play" Maman yells. "Saeed is out there with his friends, go play with them."

He's with Kersh and Cowan, munching peanut butter and honey on matza. No hiding, no fear of getting laughed at, doesn't know about Jeannie's pants, just Over-the-Line and Flies-Up.

"Why can't you be like him," Maman asks. "He laughs, plays, joins with other kids."

I can't explain to Maman why Jeannie's underwear interests me more than Over-the-Line; why I won't eat matza in public; why her Precious gets along with others better than me. Maybe it really is because I'm darker, like Maman always said. Maybe kids in my grade aren't as friendly. Maybe I just prefer staring at Ginger's hips or Jeannie's neck to playing Flies-Up.

"Go!" Maman orders. "It's a beautiful day; get some air."

I take the hill back to the playground, stepping on the eucalyptus nuts Smiley challenged me to throw on that first day. Last time I saw him he was running out of our kitchen ahead of Maman's broom. The look on his face, part fear of getting swatted, part mischievous smile, part "ain't you gonna help me, Yogi?" At the entrance of the cave where we found my bike, I see butts of unfinished smokers in the dirt.

"They make out over there y'know," Fertig has been watching me cross the street. His hands tucked in his pockets of his windbreaker, Columbo ready to expose the ugly truth.

"What?"

"Smoke too," matter-of-fact nod. "On your hill. Smoke. Make out. Know what making out is, Beaner Boy? It's not even time for puberty. Know what puberty is, Beaner Boy?"

Dis guy never shuts his trap, does he?

"C'mere," he walks me to the stucco wall the Pros lean on and points to letters scrawled across the bumps in blue crayon: *SK+JS* and *DW+LW*. "Know what those plusses mean?"

"I know what a plus means," I inform Fertig, annoyed and wishing I'd stayed home.

"It isn't math, if that's what you were thinking," he says. "Plus means going. Worm (DW) goes with Lisa W. Speed (SK) goes with Jodi S."

I should've known. She laughed at my jokes. I had made inroads. It was all a lie.

"Kissing too," concern-nods Fertig, "that's what making out means; kissing and--"

"--I get it," I need to stop him. "I get what it means."

But I don't want to believe it, even after watching Bobby kiss Millie on *Brady Bunch*. I should've known, kissing is here now. Pros, always ahead, already plus. They already make out, smoke, give each other sea-shell necklaces and secret notes in fancy ink and bubble letters.

I thought I was in. Less gut punches; getting picked earlier for teams; joking with Jodi S., cracking wise with Pros: "Good one, Beaner Boy!" "You're not bad, for a Beaner!" But I'm no closer. Getting picked for teams is easy now that they've moved on. Speed goes with Jodi; Worm goes with Lisa. I don't go. No kissing or secret notes. Still a Non; invisi-ble. And not the good invisible – not "Gilligan-gets-struck-by-lightning" invisible where I get to sneak into changing rooms at May Co. to watch ladies unbutton their blouses, unzip their skirts that crumple to the floor around their ankles as they step over them, calves arched from high-heels, hips curvy like Ginger, panties small and shiny like Jeannie, bra straps stretched from the heft of what's inside. That's good invisible. I'm just plain old shitty invisible, where nobody sees you.

"Let's get Razzles," Fertig says walking to line up in front of Ice Cream Man. But it's still goddamn Passover for me. They're all at the truck, coins in hands, buying Astro Pops, 50/50 Bars, Razzles. For us, Passover is matza and eggs, matza and salami, matza and jam. All week.

"Not hungry," I lie, but I go with him, watching them chew and lick their hamess candies.

Mrs. Parker, locking up Room 17, runs a red lacquered nail across her cheek to sweep away a loose strand of her licorice hair, her Jolly Rancher lips glowing in the afternoon sun, caramel eyes behind gold-framed Foster Grants. No hamess on Passover because Jews cherish their pain; no plussing because Nons don't plus or go. I have Ginger, Jeannie, Mrs. Parker. She sees me in the ice cream line, waves as she crosses the playground, moving past the stucco wall full of secret mark-ings of love in blue crayon. They all go. They all kiss. Not me.

What would it be like to kiss Jodi S.? Her dreamy face coming at me, golden feathered hair catching my lashes, drenching my nostrils in Herbal Essence shampoo. Would she close eyes? I wouldn't. Need to see, make sure it's real. Would her lips be dramatic, like forbidden lovers on Sweet Lady's shows? Would she write me secret notes in pink bubble letters?

She goes with the best Pro, Doc. But maybe if she thought you was already going with a girl...

"Beaner Boy goes?" she'd wonder. "With who? Did we get Beaner Boy wrong?"

Now you get the picture. Make yourself wanted and they'll want you too.

Wearing my Bruce Lee shirt today. It's not long like Pros wear, but I stretched it with my knees so it hangs. I hide it from Maman under a hand-me-down green-and-yellow checkered shirt. She hates my Bruce Lee shirt; has tried hiding it, ripping it, even using it as a cleaning rag. I always find it, twisted up, torn, tinted green from being washed with the other rags. It's my best shirt. I brought a Shideh letter with me. I keep them in my closet for when I feel lonely. I can barely see her face now; just her hair bunched up over her head like the crown on a tree.

It's Free Reading but nobody reads. They write notes to pass under desks or pretend-accidentally drop on the floor to be picked up. I peek over, Jodi S. using her fancy fur pen to make fat letters with the swift confidence of a teacher. She blows bubbles, snaps them in her mouth. Flips her hair, sending whiffs of lavender my way as she puts the finishing touches on her note, folds it, pretend-stretches as if to yawn, drops it behind her. It falls silently in front of Speed's chair; he covers it with his dirty sneaker, drags it close, picks it up.

I pull Shideh's letter from my pants pocket. The paper is drab and limp, not like the crisp white sheets Jodi writes on. And unlike Jodi's fancy pink ink, the dull grey lead of Shideh's pencil lays dense tired letters in an inelegant mix of misspelled English and screwy Farsi, our ancient alphabet: "*Mishel my bell. You disappeared?*" Sullen, loaded. "*I see how it is. Yesterday close friends, today mere acquaintances?*" Sagging from guilt and melancholy. Who wants to receive such a note? Where is the excitement, the color? Where is the Mod? Nobody will care who gave me this note; nobody will wonder where it came from, what it signifies.

While they exchange their notes with excited whispers, I pull a clean sheet from my notebook, push down green on my 4-Color Bic, and start writing; controlling my own myth:

> Dear ~~Mishel Michael~~ Mike, Thanks for that terrific kiss last summer. I love your cool cowboy shirt. You have a cool ~~bicycle bike~~ dirtbike. Thanks for taking me on that ~~fun~~ cool ride. You're a cool dirtbiker. I loved smoking and you kiss good. Too bad I live far and can't meet your cool friends. Kids at my school are cool too, but not like you. I'm so happy I go with you, Mike. You're so terrific. Can't wait to kiss more. ~~I'm in love with you~~ Love, Shirley.

I fold it, slip it in my shirt pocket and go back to pretend-reading. When Jodi finishes delivering her next note to Lisa W., I casually reach into my shirt pocket and pull out the note.

"Well what the heck is this?" I pretend-ask. "A note?" Glance over to see if she's watching. She's not. Unfold, pretend-read, nod, side-glance, accidentally push to the center of our desk so she can get a better look at the girly green ink, curvy letters, stars dotting the i's.

Jodi cracks her book open.

"Yep, note from Shirley," I go on. "Shirl the Girl. We go, so..."

"Stop," says Jodi, staring at her book; her eyes a cool blue; her retainer a simple, thin line of silver across the top row of teeth. She is mean when she wants, like all Pros; they practice it.

"Stop what?" I ask, careful not to blow whatever connection I have built with her.

"You know what," she says. "I saw you write it, fold it, put it in your pocket."

"What? This note?" I wave the crisp white paper in front of her. "Oops, you weren't supposed to see that. Top Secret." I lay it back on the desk, in case she wants to take a look.

She doesn't.

"Just an old note, from a girl... I go with... you don't know her... not from here, so..."

"Oh really," cold blue, right at me. "Because it looks like the same green ink from that 4 Color Bic sticking out of your notebook. The one I just saw you write the note with."

"Shirley gave it to me last summer."

"I'm sure." Blue roll. "Which one, the pen or the letter? Like, really." Feathered flip.

She's on to you. 'Tink fast. Pivot!

"Yeah, *this* note," I admit, "I rewrote actually... ripped when I unfolded it," I flash Shideh's letter, "see?" Shove it back in before she can see any Farsi. My myth; I control it.

"Right," says Jodi, nodding, grinning – with me? At me?

"Really," I insist. "You don't know Shirley. She doesn't go here."

"I'm totally sure," she says with a skeptical smirk. "Let me guess; she's from Canada?"

Losing control of it, the sweet connection I made with her circling the drain.

Do somethin'!

"Not Canada, no!"

Then where? Say somethin'!

"Tehran," I blurt. "She's from Tehran." I say it in full Farsi style, hard "h" hard "r."

Too far, Doc.

"Where?" She giggles. "Tekh-rrron? What's that? I almost choked saying it."

At me? I pretend it's with me, that she still sees me, the right way. "Just kidding, she's-"

Not another woid.

Bell rings. Recess.

Girls are quieter about it. They don't scream in your face or punch your gut, but can be just as vicious. They flock, warming each other with hot whispers, flinty titters. When we get back from recess, it's obvious. Big Mouth Patricia hisses to Lisa W.; a question that's not a question; more a *Can you believe it?*

"Beaner Boy?"

"What was her name?" whisper-giggles Lisa.

"Shirley," snidely-whispers Big Mouth Patricia, "an old lady name."

"What's Tekh-rrron? Is that Arabian like every word has that scratchy 'kh-kh'?"

They break into their own secret tongue: "sithago crithageepitha-gee."

Except Jodi S., looking down, pretending - not very hard - to be busy writing. No gum chewing, no talking, just slow-shaking her head in that "whatever, this is so lame" kind of way.

"Benedict Arnold!" That's what I'd call her to her face, if she wasn't Jodi S. the Pro.

Look away. Give 'em a Deep Thought gaze; a Pretend Busy scowl; like you're above silly crushes and love notes. You could (or couldn't) care less. You're not even here, Doc.

But it's never the good invisible; never the kind you need.

Mrs. Parker stops at our desk after lunch. I tossed mine again because Passover is the longest week like Yom Kippur is the longest day – never-ending. "Can you stay after?"

Jodi S. looks at her, then at me. I'm confused, maybe from hunger. Mrs. Parker stares at me with her beautiful brown eyes and earnest red lips, waiting for an answer.

Can I stay after? You bet I can! Alone at last. To confess our love? She'll hold my little face in her experienced teacher hands, put her plump lips on mine. I'll sit by her, like I do every day, but it'll be different. When her skirt hikes up and I stare, like I do every day, she'll let me. I'll take my time, from her knees to the hem of her skirt that forms the base of the dark triangle between her thighs. No more hiding. No more pretend-adjusting her skirt when she catches me. Jodi S.? She's just a childish, gossipy traitor. I'm gonna purr for Susan Parker.

"Sure."

When the bell rings, I'm starving and pray to Adonai, source of my hunger, to not let my stomach growl when we're alone. I stay seated, wait for the idiots to gather their imbecile books and get out to pick their stupid teams for their silly playground games and line up for the candies.

"I'm here," I announce, heart pounding so hard I can barely hear myself. "You said--for me to stay--after?" Should I call her Susan?

She's at her desk, writing with her red Bic, slow scratching the back of her calf with the point of her black shoe. She looks up at me with her perfect face: Maybelline lashes, Revlon lips, Ultra Brite teeth. Her wavy brown Clairol hair bounces – *Oh she's got - Personality.*

"Terrific," she says, getting up, adjusting her skirt (wink!) and turning to the blackboard to copy what she's written onto her notepad. "C'mere," she commands, staring at the board.

I stare at her back, arched calves hard from standing on those heels; skirt clinging to her hips; blouse wrinkled at the waist. I get up, barely able to walk straight, woozy from the cling-clang of my heart swinging me side to side, hoping my stomach doesn't growl. I stand behind her.

"Start with these," she turns around, her soft brown eyes on me, handing me erasers. "Clear the blackboard, clap the chalk outside, come back and I'll give you more. Are you big enough to reach the top?"

Are we still pretending? Do we need to keep up this charade while people are in school so nobody discovers our affair? I play along, wiping her blackboard, clapping her erasers. I come back in. She hands me pens and pencils, points to a desk where a sharpener waits. I get to work pushing pencils, grinding until the tips are sharp. With a brown paper towel, I wipe excess ink blots off her pen points. I unclick her click-pens, recap her cap-pens, place them in her pen cup which smells like sweet pink eraser skins and lead.

"Finished," I announce with anticipation. "What should we do now?" And as soon as I say it, the air in the classroom feels close and warm, my heart pounds again, dizzy again.

She walks toward me, smoldering caramel eyes, engorged red lips, brown hair tousled like it has surrendered to the heat of a long day. Her once-crisp blouse, wilted and clinging, revealing the raised flower patterns on her bra. The only sounds are my pounding heart and her heels clicking on the tile floor of the empty classroom.

"I saw you yesterday," she places her delicate hands on my narrow shoulders, her lemon perfume stale from sweat, breath smelling of her sack-lunch sandwich that must've included red onions and parsley. Hungry. Woozy. "You looked like you needed something."

Her hands slide up my shoulders, stop at my neck, the smell of acetone and pencils on her smooth fingernails as she carefully fastens the buttons on the collar flaps of my green-and-yellow checkered shirt. I'm the sixth cousin to wear it. Precious will be next. The way Susan Parker fastens its buttons, smooths it with her hands across my shoulders and down my arms, makes the shirt feel like a perfect fit for the first time. Our shirt. No cousin wore it like I'm wearing it.

"Promise me something," she says.

Anything. Everlasting love. Devotion. I promise to protect her from intruders, massage her temples after the bell, run away with her. We will be outlaws in love.

"Promise me that if you need help, you'll ask. I'll help."

Won't we get kicked out of school? Won't her husband be mad? Maman warned how divorce is common here. I'll suggest Susan Parker get one, and promise to stand by her.

"OK."

"So what's your favorite candy?"

"My what?"

"From the ice cream truck."

"From the...?"

"Is it those Razzle Dazzles I see everyone chewing?"

Are we still pretending?

She's offering to buy you Razzles, Doc. You got her all wrong.

"They're a dime, right?" She reaches for her purse. "Now listen. I'll pay you a dime every day, as long as you help me clean my classroom after the bell. Deal?"

She looks earnest, concerned brown eyes and a hopeful smile on her red lips.

"You looked so sad yesterday," she snaps open her purse, fishes out a thin shiny dime, "at the ice cream truck, like you felt left out. Go on, take it."

My favorite coin; President Darren Stevens on it; buys anything: Abba Zaba Astro Pop Black Cow Slo Poke…so small a grownup would never notice it missing, worthless to them.

"It's not charity," Mrs. Parker says. "You earned it."

She thinks I have pride; that I would reject a handout, a sweet dose of pity. I just want some of what they have, do some of what they do; to be seen by them like they see themselves. Mrs. Parker isn't going to go with me; won't make out or smoke with me. She's not Jeannie or Ginger; or Jodi S. I close my hand on her dime. Can't even buy anything - goddamn Passover.

Outside, a stupid breeze across the idiot playground blows the stink of stale perfume and pencil lead from my woozy head. I take a lung full of air as swaying eucalyptus leaves dust me with their stomachache powder; careless gonjeshk mock me with their songs. The sun's glow, muted by the rising exhaust of afternoon traffic, warms my face. I close my eyes, crank my neck up to it like a desperate flower, a blood-orange universe through my lids. Then I hear it.

A crowd at the orange hoops of basketball. Pros, Nons, girls. Must be something big.

Full court. Five-on-five. Usually, it's half-court, one-on-ones or two-on-twos. An all-star team of Pros: Speed, Worm, Becker and two Olders – Vague Moustache, the one who rode with the Pros last fall when they chased me and Pincus, and a guy with frizzy orange hair and bulging blue eyes. They're playing a sad collection of Nons led by Fertig running up and down the court in his blue windbreaker, pointing. Fat Guy, in slacks and a sweater, hops side-to-side applauding for the ball. Dudley, scuffing the blacktop with his cowboy boots, and Rodrigo and Pincus walking up and down the court cracking jokes. The Pros do Globetrotter moves, swishing shots and slapping tens while Fertig, the only Non playing hard, barks orders at nobody, sneaking glances at the girls to see if they are noticing his important frustration.

Girls don't usually watch. They have more important things to do - making jump-rope rhymes or sitting cross-legged by the stucco wall having serious talks. But things have been screwy all Spring so there they are, watching Pros and Olders trounce Nons from the sidelines. Jodi S. and Lisa W., glossed lips shining, feathered hair flowing in the breeze, platforms under the flared cuffs of their bellbottom jeans; clapping at every basket. Suddenly they like sports.

Still feeling humiliated from the long day, I keep my distance. But momentum changes fast in playground games; it takes one player leaving to grind it to a halt. "This is a drag" Pincus says, slouching off the court with a shrugging Dudley soon following. Rodrigo's big brother comes to take him. Next thing you know, the game has stopped.

"Beaner Boy," Fertig bellows, waving me over. He doesn't want it to end. Playing with Pros, girls watching, probably thinks this is his Something Big.

"That the kid with eggy bike tires?" Vague Moustache nods my way with a faint smile.

"Yep," Becker grunts, shaking his head. "What a Non."

Vague Moustache gives Becker a slanted smirk, like he's confused by Becker's response.

"C'mon over, kid," he yells.

Then the other Older with bulging blue eyes and frizzy orange hair, waves too. Maybe my Something Big too. I start a sheepish walk toward the court, imagining whispering chatter, "Beaner Boy's gonna play!" I do a slow-motion Jerry-West-athlete-shuffle-jog, too important to care about them giggling "Shirley" and "Tekhron." Girls. They don't get sports athletes.

"What's the teams, dudes," Fertig trying to elevate himself to co-leader with the Pros. "Even with Beaner Boy and Fat Guy I only have three."

"I'll switch," Frizzy Orange offers in a familiar gravelly voice. Where have I heard it?

"You wanna play with Nons," Becker shakes his head. "Be my guest."

Frizzy turns to Vague Moustache, "They still do that here?"

"Oldie but goodie," Vague Moustache shrugs.

"Flipside, cuz; ixnay," Speed tells them.

I look at Fertig, as confused as me. One more barrier - their code.

"Four on four," Worm says. "Let's play!"

Fat Guy has used the long timeout to pull out a plastic bag of pink-and-white animal cookies, offering them around. Thinks he can get in the Pros using cookies. Idiot.

They swarm. I'm starving too but avoid, pretending to warm up. Still Passover.

"You don't want any," Fat Guy shoves the bag in my face. Smells sweet and buttery. I feel faint, starving. Only idiots pass up pink-and-white animal cookies. And Jews on Passover.

"Sure." I take one, shove it in my pocket for after Passover, keep warming up.

Fat Guy holds the bag out for the Older with frizzy orange hair.

"No thanks," says Frizzy. "Pesakh. We don't eat bread on Pesakh."

"You?" In the gold afternoon sun, Speed's buckteeth shine like fangs.

"Yeah, me," Frizzy says, looking at the rest of them. "You guys don't do Passover?"

They munch on their cookies.

"Nobody does Passover," he says, more like a statement than a question.

Keep yer trap shut. Stay out of it.

"We're Jewish," Worm says casually. "But we don't do that stuff. We're normal Jews."

Worm too? Kersh? Cowan? Half of Fertig? They're all Jewish, Doc. Jump in!

"No Jew is normal," Frizzy says in his gravelly voice. "We're Chosen. And once a year we honor our story. Enslaved for being Jews. Moses rains maggots and death on Egypt, forces Pharoah to free us so fast we don't have time to make bread. Forty years wandering the desert, never giving up hope of finding our Promised Land, where we belong. Smart and strong enough to build pyramids but Pharoah made us feel powerless and we bought it; didn't realize we had the power to rise up. Moses turned us on to that. Nobody knows the story of Pesack?"

I do; heard it all my life. We watch the movie every year, even in Iran. Frizzy's version sounds cooler. Our version paints Jews as weak and helpless, relying on Moses for everything. Frizzy's version makes them defiant rebels - Billy Jack, Black Panthers. He tells the story like he's proud of it, not worried about anybody finding out, or making fun.

"What about you," he asks me as I dribble on the other half of the court.

Me? The guy tossing matzo lunches in the trash, preferring to starve over being found out? I ate a Pig sandwich, chose Sin over confessing to what Frizzy just proudly admitted.

Becker, metal teeth full of pink cookie crumbs, sneers, "Mexikins are Catholic."

"I'm not Mexican," I tell the ground, dribbling, shooting, too pretend-busy to discuss it.

"You're Jew?" Frizzy studies my face. "You look Semite. You Arab?"

Where have I seen him? Bulging blue eyes, frizzy orange hair, gravelly voice. Older? Pro? He's giving me a chance to confess, free myself. Be my own Moses.

Careful, Doc, tomorrow he won't be here. Tomorrow it's just you and Them.

"He didn't eat his cookie either," Fat Guy notices, "so he's Jewish."

I pull the cookie out of my pocket and hold it out to Fat Guy. "I'm not hungry," I lie. "I don't even like these," I lie again. "But...yeah, I'm... a regular Jew." I keep lying. Abgoosht. Gondi. Candles. Broken eggs. Adonai. I'm probably the most irregular Jew on the playground.

"Let's get on with the game," demands Speed, brushing pink crumbs off his lips.

"Yeah," I yell, happy to agree with Speed. "Play ball, cuzbros! Time for grand slam dunks!" I don't hear how off it sounds until it leaves my mouth.

"You're with the Nons," Speed reminds Frizzy with a sideways laugh.

He is good; glides, dribbles, bounce passes to Fat Guy, who Speed shoves to the ground. Frizzy jogs over, muscles rippling from the cut-off sleeves of his sweatshirt, reaches down to help Fat Guy up. "You a'right?" like an Amrikayi superhero. Where have I seen him?

Picture the stars 'n stripes flapping over his head.

He grabs a rebound, dribbles past Speed like he's not there and goes to the hoop. Two! Feels good playing with someone who knows what he's doing. Glad I confessed to him. A burst of fresh air fills my lungs. We are Super Jews. Maybe even related! Maman says all Jews are related. Even Irani are Amrikayi when they're Jewish, so basically I am Amrikayi, practically blue eyed, freckled and buck-toothed!

Speed and Becker keep shoving us, yelling "out of bounds" if we dribble close to the yellow line. Frizzy motions us to ignore them, guiding us. Then, running parallel, he bounces one cross court; it lands right between my hands. A pass!

Four years I've been running up and down this blacktop. In hard hand-me-down shoes or once-a-year Converse sneakers, in position, arms flailing, yelling the right words: "Here!" "I'm open!" "Pass god-dammit ball!" Nothing. Today, without having to utter a word, I get it. Dizzy. Heart pumps. Insides jitter. Girls watch. Pros wait. And I have the ball. All eyes on me!

Don't do double-dribbles. Don't do traveling. Don't blow your big chance!

I glide past them, pull up at the top of the key, crouch low, spring up and fling – a high arching launch that descends slow, dropping through the hoop, jangling the chain like a bag of gold doubloons and catching the bottom of the net - a split-second of suspension - before dropping with a backward spin to the ground.

Two!

I pretend to ignore any applause as I Jerry-West-shuffle-jog up court, cool-nodding my teammates, ice glaring Becker as I pass him in slow motion, my nostrils big with air.

Frizzy steals the inbound goes to the basket Speed shoves on the way up shakes the ball loose. Frizzy hits the ground. Pops up; turns to Speed.

"That's a foul, you little shit! Taking two."

Never heard anybody talk that way to Speed.

"You wish!" Speed grabs the ball.

"Sorry, little man," Frizzy, unimpressed, grabs it back. "Foul!"

Then Speed says it, like he's talking to… a Non: "You don't like it?"

"You Don't Like It?" is a new burn. Goes like this: We yell foul, they walk over, ask in pretend-sympathy, "Aw, you don't like it?" and before we answer they bark "Lump it!" Then they cool-nod each other. They've used it so much, they recently dropped the "Lump it!" Now they just go "You Don't Like It?" with a menacing head tilt, and that's that.

We don't have a comeback for it. When they say it, we exhale, surrendering to self-evident truths: Pros are Pros; Nons are Nons. Pros are never in trouble; Nons, always. Pros have cool hair; Nons, mistake haircuts. Pros wear cool clothes; Nons, out-of-fashion ill-fitting hand-me-downs with stains so old nobody knows where they came from. Pros understand it all, talk with confidence; Nons are hazy, start sentences mumbling "Huh?" or "Um…" Pros know what they're doing; Nons do everything based on bad guesses and stupid hope.

Some days we sit under the stomachache trees by the back fence, trying to figure it out.

"What's *lump it* mean?" Dudley asked once, small teeth trying to muster some anger.

"Means *shove it*," said Pincus as he sharpened a popsicle stick against the ground.

"A variation on *Up Yours*," Fertig informed, pretend-puffing a Smart Guy pipe.

"Heck, they don't even give a guy a chance to answer," Dudley whined in his tired drawl.

One benefit of being a Non is, because we didn't choose each other we don't need to care about hurting each other's feelings. We are a league of losers, free to hurl brutal, ugly Truths.

"Why, Quickdraw," Fertig cracked, "you had a biting burn you were waiting to unleash?"

"Lump yourself, Kelly Smelly!"

"That's not how you use it," Pincus warned, examining his popsicle stick switchblade.

"Irregardless," Fertig continued, "it's rhetorical when they ask if we don't like it."

"We can fight," Pincus, testing the tip of the switchblade on his finger. "But none of us is gonna fight cuz none of us wants to end up at the bottom of a dogpile."

The Dogpile goes against everything we have learned on TV from *Sheriff Andy*, *Brady Bunch* or *Partridge Family*: bullies are stinkers; honesty is the best policy; two wrongs to make it right. On this playground, Fear of the Dogpile rules; and not just because of pain. As an expert on the Dogpile, I know pain isn't the worst part. With so many bodies piled on, there's plenty of cushion to soften the blows. A few kicks to the ribs, punches to the back of the head, you cover, curl up in your cocoon, wait for Yard Teacher. Pain can be hidden.

The worst part of the Dogpile is after: ripped clothes you can't smooth out; stinging knees you can't blow on; heavy breathing you have to suppress so they don't see you're rattled. The toughest part of the Dogpile is hiding the humiliation, pretending it's no big deal, as you walk away limiting the limp and hoping they believe it.

Still, when Speed hits Frizzy with the old "You Don't Like It," it sounds like an inside joke being told to an outsider. Frizzy doesn't get it; the phrase hangs between them like that Green Cloud of Bad Breath in the Listerine commercial. He seems confused or... busted? The way we were when we first heard it? Is he a Non too, like us?

What a maroon! What a tararaboomdeay! An ignoranimus! He's woice 'dan you!

Frizzy's silence makes Speed bold. He steps up to Frizzy's face, gets on his tiptoes. "You. Don't. Like. It?" Satisfied, he grabs the ball back and begins to turn.

You was wrong, Doc. You ain't related to him after all; but he's definitely related to you!

Then it happens. Frizzy, examining Speed like he's a new species of pest, barks as if he's being forced to state the obvious. "Yeah I don't like it!"

Yeah I don't like it!

Fertig and I look at each other, eyes round, jaws dropped.

Yeah I don't like it!

Clean. Simple. Light. As soon as the words leave Frizzy's mouth it is clear how weak, how hollow "You don't like it?" is. We just never heard it with our Non ears.

They've been takin' you for suckers! How did you miss it?

SHUT UP, RABBIT!

Maybe I'm dazed from hunger, woozy from Mrs. Parker's perfume lingering in my nostrils, still steamed from the humiliation of Jodi S.

and Shideh's letter – but the playground is in a different light. My hazy eyes scan the silent faces of Pros, suspended in a fog, the echo...

...*Yeah, I don't like it. Yeah I don't like it. YeahIdontlikeit.*

Speed's curled-in lips dampen the swagger of his buckteeth, his narrowed eyes darting side to side like he's checking to see if anyone smells the fart he cut. Worm, hiding behind his sweaty mop, has no witty reply. Becker, trying to close his mouth over the bulging metal, waits.

Bullies are stinkers.

"Let's split," Vague Moustache breaks the silence. "These guys are scrubs; still playing *Pros and Nons* from the P.E. days. C'mon, Stanley, let's ride to the arcade."

Picture Ol' Glory waiving over his head.

But Frizzy's bulging blue eyes are fixed on Speed, fists clenched, jaw grinding.

"Not worth it, Stanley," Vague Moustache warns again. "Remember your last tussle here, that idiot smiling kid? Let's boogie."

Frizzy orange hair, bulging blue eyes. Grappling...Smiley! At the flagpole! Stanley!

Ignoring Vague Moustache, Stanley pulls the ball from Speed's clutches and shoves him to the ground. It never occurred to me how light they are. Behind the screaming, oversized t-shirts and faded jeans, Pros are just as light and fragile as the rest of us.

They're all Sister Bertril!

Busted! Almost feel sorry for him, landing with a thud on the blacktop, unfamiliar territory, my territory. He has wandered into my humble home. *The Art of Pazirayee* dictates I should be a good host, serve him hot tea and honey cakes, no matter how I feel inside.

To get in with the Pros you have to do something big, remember?

As his host, I could take his side, gang up on Stanley. I'd be a Pro. But going against Stanley, my fellow Jew? We're practically cousins. He passed to me, made me look like a sports athlete as seen on *The Agony of Defeat* show, Saturday afternoons, channel 7. He invented "Yeah I don't like it!" Shouldn't I team up with the Olders like I did back home?

It's all a noisy blur as Speed starts to get up. Stanley lurches towards him sending both of them back to the ground, rolling, punching, raising dust.

Heart, eyes, ears pound. Hungry, humiliated. I know the rules of playground fights: No kicking. No biting. No clipping. I don't care. Like the spring in a click pen, I unclick. Uncoil. Lunge, hands open, arms out. I clip Becker as he's about to jump Stanley. His shoulders forward, head snapping back, gnashing rows of metal crashing together on impact like tin cans.

"Yeah I don't like it! Yeah I don't like it! I! Don't! Like! Beaner! Spic! Ass! Bitch!"

I'm not curving my words for a more perfect Amrikayi. Not thinking about a dogpile. Just pounding Becker amid a symphony of sounds exploding around us. Hoots and howls. Frenzied gonjeshk trills raining down from the stomachache trees. Chirps and cheers jingling like coins spilling from a broken moneybag on the blacktop. Bodies pull push tug shove.

Stanley and Speed have stopped, watching me and Becker go at it: His black curls in my face smell like peppery shampoo mixed with sweat. I feel him pushing up as I try keeping him down. A blunt object. His head? Smashes flush against my nose. Everything goes black. Eyes water. Too late to retreat to my cocoon. Push. Shove. But no dogpile.

With my flailing hands I grab his ears. The Olders in Tehran taught me that a tough ear pull teaches lessons. Clutching his ears, I pull his sweaty face so close his freckles rub up against my eyes. I smell the sharp piney scent of Zest soap. I release one ear, leaving a hand free to punch his greasy nose as his fist pounds the back of my head, blurring me. We shove, pull, elbow. Pincus is back on the court, in my periphery, his lips doing a "just mindin' my own business" whistle as he slips his foot behind Becker's foot, winks.

I push. Down goes Becker, me holding his ear, him holding my neck. Down I go too, landing on top, pushing down on him to lift myself. Becker, furious, trapped under my knees as I hold him down by his wrists, afraid to let him loose. He rumbles violently.

"Get this fucken Beaner off me!"

"Break it up! Break it up!"

"Yard Teacher!" Hands grab my shoulders from behind, pull me up, drag me off the court. "Yard teacher," whispers Fertig. "Let's go!"

Dizzy, breathing heavy, I straighten my pant leg as Fertig pushes me to the blue bathroom, through its door. Empty. Hot. Smells of sweat and piss. Catch my breath at the sink, stare in the mirror: Black hair and brown face tinted blue from the walls. I got the high cheeks Maman got from Sweet Lady. I got the fat nose Baba got from Papa. I am them, they are me, we are all here, Ancient to Mod, in this stinking blue bathroom. Thin rows of blood stream from my nostrils, running along the sides of my mouth, joining at my chin where a single red drop hangs. Drips. Blots the faded green fibers of my Bruce Lee shirt. Is it me?

"How does it feel, Champ?" Fertig, smiling, in his thick sports announcer voice.

I stare at Fertig. "I'm the one with a bloody nose."

"Who was on top at the end? You! They saw. You brought him down. Now repeat after me: 'I beat up Becker. I kicked his ass.' Say it! Get used to it, Champ."

Do I remind him of the Rules? No clipping. No tripping. No ear pulling.

He called you Champ. He's gonna tell 'em all. Let him do the talkin'.

Dudley and Pincus run into the bathroom.

"Yee Haw that was fun!" shouts Dudley.

Fertig into his fist: "Beaner Boy K.O.'s Becker! Film at eleven!"

Pincus studies my face, my blood moustache. "But Beaner Boy has the bloody nose."

"Inadvertence and happenstance, my good fellow," Fertig answers. "Beaner Boy was on top at the end, pummeling. I pulled him off to avoid Yard Teacher."

I twist toilet paper into my nostril, point my face at the ceiling.

"I've had it with their shenanigans," Fertig goes on, not talking into his fist anymore, standing tall, hands shoved in the pockets of his windbreaker. "We're taking control. And if anybody asks, I came up with 'Yeah I don't like it!' Me, got that?"

I'm thinking of Stanley standing up for himself, not knowing the rules of the playground so not bound by them; didn't even consider surrender.

"Stanley came up with it-"

"-'Scuse us," Fertig takes me by my elbow to the toilet stall; the one we met in back in second grade. He gets so close to my face I smell the hard-boiled eggs he had at lunch.

"You get to beat up Becker, I get to come up with 'Yeah I don't like it.' Kapeesh?"

"But Stanley-"

"-Fuck Stanley!" Fertig interrupts. "He doesn't go here. This is our Something Big."

"But Speed, Worm, Becker. They all heard Stanley."

Fertig's blue eyes look crazy. "In all that confusion, everybody remembers it their own way. Put it this way, Beaner Boy, didn't they also see what really happened with you?"

Keep your trap shut.

"Becker punched you in the nose! He was kicking your ass until he miraculously tripped, courtesy of Pincus. And you clipped him from behind. Another No-No. Clipped and tripped."

He saw all of it. He will hold it over me; that's his special skill. I'll either be Champ, under him, or Beaner Boy, a Non who got beat up by Becker.

"You can't just make up a whole new story," I argue. "We'll both get busted."

"Have you been paying attention? Stanley laughed at them for calling us Nons. The curtain has been pulled back. It's made up. The only thing that keeps it going is them sticking together and us buying it. Think about it, nobody officially designated us Nons or them Pros."

"You did!" I remind him. "You said we are Nons and they are Pros. You said we know which one we are without having to be told."

"Until we get in on it," he says, a glint in his eyes. "Those guys laughed when Speed called us Nons. We always believed it. Stanely busted it open. Now we get to be in on it."

It'll never woik, Doc. You shouldn't sell Stanley out. He passed you the ball.

"I just don't know if it'll work."

"Or," Fertig says, pointing his head to the world beyond the bathroom stall, "I can just tell everybody what really happened. Clipped and Tripped."

Then again...

Fertig has always been tall, but now he looks different. Like them, steely blue eyes, cheeks flush from the heat of the action. If I look close enough, I can make out a freckle.

Pengoowins is practically chickens, doc.

The piss smell, closeness of air in the stall, hunger, dizzy. His hand out, to shake on it. They'll see me. I am Champ. I am Cherokee! Pick me first. Girls will go with me.

But Stanley, Doc.

I'll atone later. In the blue bathroom, I shake Fertig's hand. We're not friends; just two fifth graders in a toilet stall. Maybe liars, or Sinners, but not Nons.

I leave the empty playground, float home, cool, air-conditioned.

Maman is sitting in her car, windows down, listening to radio, pen in hand and a piece of paper propped flat on the steering wheel. She's scribbling, singing: "*Oh, yes I am vize, but is veezdem boren pain, yes I pay a prize, but look how much I gave.*" When the song gets away from her, she throws the pen in frustration and pushes in the cassette, belting out a familiar Googoosh song. She sees me approaching, bloodstains on my Bruce Lee shirt, and screams.

"What did they do to you now?"

Surprised by my own calm breathing, I tell Maman I had a fight on the playground, defending a Jewish boy from bullies. You have to do big things in Amrika.

"So you're an animal now? A vulgar Amrikayi. What next? Eating pig? Smoking heroin? We shouldn't have come. No more playground. And take that shirt off. It's bad luck."

But she'll be busy figuring out her new car, finding new routes, learning new songs.

The next morning, a breeze meanders in the late spring air as we wait for first bell. Gonjeshk sing victory songs over my bruised shoulders; blossoms blush, their perfumes flirting with swollen membranes in my blood-packed nostrils; I can almost smell their sweetness.

At the beige stucco wall, Speed leans back, his hands hang loose from the back pocket of his jeans; Worm, arms folded at his chest, listens casually to Lisa W., her fingers resting on her hips, elbows out. Jodi S. listens, head tilted sideways as she brushes out her flowing hair.

Under the stomachache trees by the back fence, Fertig, hands tucked into the pockets of his windbreaker, talks to Pincus and Dudley about a new language he's learning, a new code.

"You use dots and dashes instead of letters - *dot dot dash dot dash* – to send secret messages. Gonna tell the Pros about it. We'll use it as our secret Pro code."

He looks different, legs firm, hips out, confident as a sheriff steadied by the heft of a belt weighted by guns and bullets. He wears a large t-shirt like the Pros, but with new-shirt creases, running past his knees. Fertig being so tall, it makes him look more like Scrooge in pajamas than Pro. He can't pull it off; like a pretend uniform of a team he's a fan of, but isn't on.

I avoid him, find a spot on the beige stucco wall, lean back, cool-nod Speed.

With a glorious bucktoothed sneer he turns away to finish talking baseball and rock music with them – as if yesterday we didn't share an afternoon of basketball and fistfights.

When the bell rings, Speed looks at the entrance of Room 17, seethes a cool "psshh" to show how bummed he is that it's still not summer. Here's my chance.

"Psshh!" I seethe-agree, shake my head, check to see if any of them heard me.

Nothing.

Inside, Mrs. Parker taps her chalk on the board, scratching out a formula, remnants of my attempts to clean it yesterday now streaking across in short, ghostlike arcs. I was such a fool.

"Psshh," I say again, loud enough for Speed's ears. "Another damn pop quiz."

You love pop quizzes. You get tens outa tens!

This time I get a nibble.

"Really!" Speed replies in their tongue, with me. Slow-shaking his head, gnawing on a red plastic Cheez 'n Crackers stick. "Damn shit-brick quizzes. She sucks!"

You love Susan Parker. Licorice hair, caramel eyes.

"Damn her!" I mumble, trying not to gush at the genuine connection I am having with the leader of the Pros. "Damn quizzes! Can't she damn stop? Gat facken dammit!"

"Tired of this shitbrick," Speed mutters, buckteeth clenching the red plastic, cool-nodding nobody, maybe me. "This school is just one big shitbrick, man."

"Shitbrick." I remember it from Billy Jack. Must use it. *Shitbrick Shitbrick Shitbrick.*

"Really!" I cool-nod Speed, fellow Pro, say it like him: "Rullee. Shitbreck!"

Pros hate school. They peel the covers off their workbooks, scrawl on the fuzzy white beneath "Skool Sux" "Prisoner Wormeier, Pinnacle Penitentiary, Cell Block 17." In the back, they lean their chairs against the wall, cracking sunflower seeds and inside jokes, singing the cool radio songs, "*b-b-b-bennian the jetssss!*" If they get in trouble, they don't care.

I want in! Their jokes and songs; scrapes and bruises; long hair, loose t-shirts, beat-up sneakers and worn-in jeans. Punishment. I want it all! To be a dirty Amrikayi cowboy. Today I am closer than ever. As Mrs. Parker writes the Transitive Property on the board - *a* is *c* even if *a* is *b* when *b* is *c* - I peel the top layer off my workbook. In jagged letters I write: "Skool Stinx! Prisoner Mike M. Pinnacle Penitentiary, Cell 17. Warden Parker." I draw a motorcycle, chunky tires, motocross handlebar turned, "Cross it up!" "L" linked with "A" like a Dodgers helmet.

"Dodger fan?" Speed walks by.

"Yeh." Short and cool. Don't gush.

"Who's your favorite catcher?"

I've memorized names, numbers and positions. "Catchers yeh, Ferguson 13, Yeager 7."

"I like Sanguillen on the Pirates. Better hitter than Fergie; better fielder than Yeag."

"Fergie sucks," Worm comes over. "Simmons is the cool hippie; long black hair flying out from under his helmet."

"Cards suck," says Speed, "bad as Expos. Only Phillies and Pirates in it now."

Pros chattering at my desk but I only memorized Dodger names and numbers.

Change subjects. Sing that cool song! From the FM stereo station.

"Ban Donna Run...oooh... Ban Donna Run...oooh..."

"You like Wings?" Worm to Speed, even though I'm the one singing the song.

"Really," Speed nods. "Wings are way more bitchin' than the Beatles."

Likes or doesn't like? Bitchin. Thought "bitch" was bad. Just nod.

"I like the new EJ," says Worm. "B'b'b' Bennian the Jetssss…"

"Jets," I recognize it. Jump in. "Jets! Woo ooh ooh woo ooh ooh. Jets!"

"Not Jet," Worm turns to me like I'm interrupting, "Benny and the Jetssss!"

"Those guys all do it with each other y'know," Jodi S. chimes in.

"Who," asks a shocked Worm.

"All of 'em. Bowie, EJ, Mick," Jodi serious-nods. "At parties they take drugs and do it."

Lost again; sang my FM radio song with no plan for what may come next.

"Ban Donna Run," I repeat, "Ban Donna Run." It worked once…

"That's not how it goes," says that annoying Worm, obviously the Fertig of Pros.

"It's 'Band on the run'," says Speed without looking. "You like McCartney?"

"Mickart?"

"McCartney." Worm gives a smug smile of disbelief. "Wings? Beatles?"

"Yeh. Beatles rullee good. George is my best Beatle."

"Your best?" asks Speed. "Beatles suck."

"George sucks," Worm waves me off. "Indian Swami crap. Wings are way cooler."

My George, dark like me. *"My sweet lo."* My Beatle.

Say, Doc, don't you wanna stick up for him if he's your George?

"Yeah, the Wing is way cooler now," I nod. "George rullee sucks now, Doc."

"Doc? Is that Gunsmoke?" asks Worm.

I don't know what that is. Frozen stare. Frozen stare. Headshake.

"Wild Wild West?"

I know that one, but hate the cowboy shows, all those angry men and their guns. Shake.

"Don't tell me you're imitating dumb Bugs Bunny."

See, Doc, they all know me, even if they don't admit it. Now let him have it.

Half-nod…half-shake…half-shrug…

"You still watch cartoons?" Worm's voice rises, like when he first yelled Beaner Boy.

"I thought you were talking about a western too," says Speed, "not a cartoon."

'Tink fast!

"I love cowboy shows. When the Warner Bros sign comes on, I think 'Rullee, a cool cowboy show is starting,' but it's a damn cartoon. Rullee sucks," gushing. "Bugs is so dumb."

Ya got me, Doc! Right in the heart (cough cough) gettin' dark (cough) goin' to dat great big playground in the sky. You're on your own now. You know who you are. Tough part is admitting it and not being a stinker. Don't be a stinker, Doc.

Mrs. Parker sees a crowd at my desk, walks over and notices my revamped workbook.

"Is this what you think of our school and your teachers, Mike? That it stinks like prison?"

"Just kidding around," I say, looking down to avoid her eyes.

"School is prison? We worked so well together yesterday, you think I'm a Warden?"

"Everybody does it," I say with a slightly defiant tone. "It's joking."

"But you like school, Mike, you do well on quizzes, pay attention in class."

Something stirs inside that I haven't felt since Tehran. It's OK to be a mean sometimes.

"Well you know, Mrs. Parker," I brush an imaginary moustache above my lip, conjuring the jive pride of JJ Evans from *Good Times* Wednesdays at 8, Channel 2. "What can ah say?"

Embers of giggles spark chuckles that ignite a roar of laughter.

"Class!"

Floating from their approval, I keep my eyes down, study the hem of her skirt.

"I'm surprised at you, Mike."

"Surpraz surpraz surpraz!" My Gomer Pyle, daily at 11, Channel 13. Their laughter lifts me, cools me. I am air-conditioned. I am Pro.

Fertig tries to get in on it: "Y'know, JJ is *Dot-dash-dash, dot-dash-dash* in Morse Code."

Silence. It doesn't matter what we agreed to, he's not taking me down with him.

"Sounds like robot Pig Latin," I loud-whisper to Jodi S. She laughs, they all do.

"OK, Mike, knock it off," Mrs. Parker yells. Yep, I won't be purring for Susan Parker.

"Sorry," my smirk confirming I'm not. All eyes on me. They finally see me, like this.

"Correct me if I'm wrong, but we had a deal," Fertig blocks my path to the beige stucco wall at recess, where I'm sure they're waiting to talk baseball and FM songs with me.

"Nobody cares about goddamn Morris Codes."

"It's Morse Code, you imbecile. Not Morris Codes."

"Whippie! Who gives a goddamn, you shitbrick? Rullee."

"I do. You shouldn't make fun of Morse Code. Allies used it to beat Hitler in WW2."

"Look at 'em over there," I nod over to Speed, Worm, Lisa W. and Jodi S., leaning on the wall, flipping their wild hair, hands in the back pockets of snug jeans, battle tested sneakers with stripes on the sides, cheeks rosy and vibrant in the golden light of a new morning. "Do they look like they give a damn about the Morris Codes or WW2?"

"I'm a Pro too. I care. What's the point of being a Pro if I have to pretend to not like what I like or like what I don't," says blonde-haired blue-eyed Amrikayi Kelly Fertig with ease.

"Whatever you say," I shrug. "Anyway, Jodi laughed at you, not me."

"She laughed at your crack; by the Transitive Property, you laughed at me."

"I'm allowed to make jokes. I have goddamn First Commandment like anyone else."

Fertig starts to say something, stops himself, gives the same look Mrs. Parker gave.

"Whatever you say, Beaner Boy," he says with a shrug of his own.

At P.E. I get picked before Fertig or Dudley. When it's my ups I grab a bat, step in the box and turn to Worm crouching behind the plate. "Simmons sucks!" I say, ribbing my pal.

The pitch comes, my hand gripping the handle, my stiffened wrists, the thick chords in my forearms – I swing hard. The ball jumps off the fat end of my bat; I feel it through my whole body. This must be what exercising power feels like. A flush connection on a full swing with all your might. That is Amrika! The ball rises in an arc over their heads, hits the ground and rolls to the fence. I hear cheering as I run down the line, base to base. They're screaming to go home as I round third base. In front of me, Worm stands, hands on hips. I leap like on TV, throw my right leg out, tuck my left leg in, land sideways, sliding across fourth base. I am in. I am home!

Baba doesn't eat eggs anymore. At breakfast, he sits down to half a grapefruit. Instead of two spoons of sugar in his tea, he drops two Saccharin pills. Butter and honey on toast have been replaced with cottage cheese on wheat. Maman keeps boiling eggs anyway, fishing them out of the water, placing them in the chipped rooster egg holder and putting them in front of Baba. And each morning he reminds her that he doesn't eat eggs anymore.

"You're dieting?" Maman asks. "For who, Shahbanu? I made them. Eat now, diet after news of my death." But as she watches Baba burrow a spoon into pulpy grapefruit flesh, she taps the loose skin under her chin with the back of her hand, quietly feels at her hips.

When they came back, he had a moustache and had begun growing the hair around his bald dome, combing it across. Now he clomps down the hall in fancy platforms, his white dress shirts and solid ties replaced by polyesters with orange suns and purple paisleys, three, sometimes four buttons undone to expose his soft chest as he reads his paper. Baba is changing.

"Baba is leaving," Maman announces, standing next to him. She is disheveled in her purple bathrobe, her damp hair held back with a thin blue rubber band that held green onions yesterday. Her eyes are red as she wipes her nose with her hand.

"Why say it like that?" Baba with timid eyes. He even stares different.

"How should I say it? You are taking your leave? Pulling yourself aside? Departing from your home and family to chase after more important work?"

"Where's he going," Sid presses his schoolbooks against his hips.

"He's going to be a joke teller. A clown."

"Why say it like that?"

"How should I say it? You are off to become Shahanshah of Clown Nation? Minister of Wit? Jester for the Taj? One night with the crazy neighbor and he wants to upend his life."

"It's not one night. We've gone to a lot of those lectures. Marty thinks I have It! Something special! Like Dreesen, Brenner, the funny ones on Johnny Carson."

"I piss on Johnny Carson! Who is Marty Levin? A car salesman!"

"A Benz salesman. And not anymore. He's leaving too, to manage me. *If you will gonna try, go all the vay*; is Marty's philosophy. Sometimes that means sacrifice."

Sid's scared eyes bounce back and forth between them, lips starting to tremble. He puts his books on the table under the entryway mirror. "Are you getting divorced?"

Maman runs crying down the hall.

"Idiot!" I smack the back of Sid's head. "Can't say that word!" In Farsi, Tallagh. We don't say it. Bad Luck. Other than the night of the Christian Kite, Maman only ever whispers it, with raised eyebrows and darkness in her breath like when she says Sin. Still, in my head I try it out, imagining how it will sound when I announce it to the Pros, cementing myself as one of them as we head into summer. At the Arcade: *Pshh, perunts gettin davoerced. I'll be at my dad's weekunds. Shitbrick.* "What're you crying for," I look at Sid, "I didn't hit you that hard."

"Ve not getting de divorce," Baba assures in choppy English. "Ve explore. In Amrika ve can be anyting ve vant it to be; I go, find my truth, who I am. Maybe the comedian."

"You will be a vagabond hamall who should feel shame for abandoning his wife and children to be a clown," yells Maman from the bedroom.

Baba looks down the hallway, shaking his head. "It is a new philosophy," he explains to us in Farsi, "new, like this country where anything can be. She doesn't get it." Then in English, "I try to be who I am, live in present instead of playing role put on me by my people. I try to go past my current vision to observe my pozeeshenality. Under-estand?"

Words like that keep pouring out of Baba's mouth; like the nonsense we hear on Sunday morning TV when we find ourselves awake so early even cartoons aren't on. I keep listening to see if I can grasp what Baba is planning; if he's actually leaving. And if it's permanent.

"…so ve are decide to try it on for size, see if it fit. To reelize our fool potenshell, ques-shen our role as voman and man. Maybe I be comedian. Maybe I be on Johnny Carson and you see and be pride. Or maybe I come back kooneh lokht."

The refrigerator buzz is all we hear when Baba finally stops, reality sinking in; real as the life oozing from Becker's salamander, forcing me to run and scream; or the blood trickling from my head from Smiley's rock, giving me a choice to run and scream. Which is this? Am I sad, or just allowed? Was it the pork sandwich? Christian Kite? I run to the bathroom, check for open scissors, unflushed fingernail clippings – wondering if I caused this, or if I could care less.

When I come out, they're gone. I hear Maman crying in the bedroom, Baba consoling her. Sid has taken his books and is whimpering outside. Something is off. Not an emergency, not a celebration, but exciting, like Yom Kippur. In the mirror by the door: Brown skin, non-freckle mole, brown eyes trying to stay calm, standing where I belong. It is me. Amrikayi me.

On the table beneath the mirror, a slate-blue envelope addressed to Mr. Mishel. I open it.

"*Mishel my bell! We are coming. To be together. See you in Amrika! Miss Shideh.*"

PART V

IN THE BEGINNING, *I arrived in the middle of winter, ev-erybody already warm and cozy. They started without me, learned words, games, ready for more. I missed a lot: screaming slap fights, skidding sneakers marking the end of a school year, salty playground games on gold hot summer days, sweaty walks home in the calm of a smoldering orange dusk. I missed the cool-down of a new school year, crispy-leafed mornings of first semester where clean lined pa-per, fresh blue point Bics and stiff textbooks confirmed a fresh start around the corner - blank page, sharpened tip of a Ticonderoga #2, sweet-smelling pink eraser yet to be stained with inevitable, for-givable mistakes. I missed the night of Scary Pumpkins, bobbing for apples, begging for candy door-to-door wearing bedsheet gowns and pointy hats, dragging broomsticks between legs down the moon-lit streets of a neighborhood full of classmates. I missed the feast of the Bronzed Turkey, tart berry jams, orange potatoes topped with burnt marshmallows. I missed their month-long festival of Papa Noel and Amrikayi Noruz. In the beginning, I was dropped in the middle of all that, watching them spin out, find their rhythm, their landing spots, chanting their poetry "Not last night but the night be-fore, twenty-four robbers came knockin' at my door!" and I won-dered where in all this could I find a gap to wedge into, an opening to squeeze through, a chair to sit on before the music stopped, because no matter where you come from, music stops, there is scrambling and someone is left standing, feeling lost and awkward for everyone to see, laugh at, pity or worse, not see. In the beginning, I went through that. I won't do it again.*

The most enduring hand-me-down Maman got from Sweet Lady wasn't a wedding dress, winter coat or ancient recipe for crispy tadeeg. It was superstition. Stray cats piss on you when you sleep at night; wash your face every morning. Eat God's bounty in a bathroom like an uncivilized monkey; He will turn you into one. An egg held gently between fingers while chanting names breaks when you chant the name of the one with the Bad Eye. Nail clippings left unflushed, scissors left open like an X – tallagh. These are rules we live by, handed down from Maman who got them from Sweet Lady who got them from... well, I can't go back that far. But I know this: The untimely death of her husband left Sweet Lady and her girls in a lurch – young Jewish widow, handful of daughters and no Man in a Guweem country ruled by men. Hand-wringing, chest-clutching, thigh-slapping panic was their normal as they tried to make sense of their predicament. Maybe for Amrikayi "superstition ain't the way," but for Sweet Lady, her girls and the Persian Jews living in the Tehran ghetto of Sareh Chal, it was the only way.

And that includes the legend of Sabya Mosheh who, the story goes, wandered the dingy streets of Sareh Chal in a shabby dress, and rags for shoes. Years earlier, Sabya's betrothed had gone to the bathhouse before their wedding, never to return. Sabya waited outside, hours, days, forever – for the entire town to see! Not smart enough to be humiliated or proud enough to be angry, Sabya grew old, despondent and crazy. Neighbors walked past her. "Sabya," they pleaded, "don't be a fool, there's no one in there for you." "Sabya, go home, get on with your life. He's not coming out." Sabya didn't listen. She was betrothed, devoted, full of faith. And alone. When Sweet Lady pleaded with Maman to follow Baba to Amrika the first time, and to return with him the second time, she raised the ghost of Sabya Mosheh: "What becomes of a woman who lets her man go, thinking he'll come back? She ends up wandering the streets in rags for the neighbors to pity." Every girl Maman's age knew the legend of Sabya Mosheh.

Maman was different. The baby of the family, she was a sheytoun, with fiery eyes, a wicked smirk and a never-ending supply of mischief up her sleeve. She rejected any idea of being less than any Guweem or anyone privileged with having a father. While most Sareh Chali's sent their kids to the new Jewish schools built by the French, Sweet Lady kept her girls in the traditional Christian school to ensure they learned English and mingled with daughters of well-to-do Guweem. That's how Maman learned to pass for one of them, to talk like them and eventually to lure them into her own clique. It was the 1950's, Tehran was modernizing and Maman led a gang of girls who secretly smoked and swiped gumballs from the local shop while charming free ice cream cones from the keeper. Maybe a fear of being abandoned did drive her. Maybe the legend of Sabya Mosheh had lodged itself in Maman's heart. But mischief was her way.

June 1974

"Hey Beaner Boy," Becker tilts his big forehead at me; still can't close his mouth over all that metal inside. Four years and still has braces. "Let's talk."

He puts his hand on my neck like I'm his salamander. Tomorrow is graduation; he'll finally be gone. Good writtens. But today I need to beware.

"Sure," I say as he keeps hold of my neck and walks me into the blue bathroom.

"Thought we should settle up; haven't talked since the fight; I'm graduating tomorrow."

That familiar smell of stale piss as he guides me toward the sinks.

"Ever heard of the Last Laugh, Beaner Boy?"

"The Last...?" I notice the sink - same one I've stood in front of so many times to warm my hands before the bell – is filled with water.

"Take a look in there, Beaner Boy. What do you see?"

I peer in. Brown paper towels plugging the drain. Pressure at the sides of my neck – being pushed forward, toward the sink, in. Plunge! My face in the warm water, bobbing for apples on Halloween but no apples. His hand keeps me down. I push my head up. Mouth shut; nostrils tight; push; up for air. His finger-clamp on my neck pushes me back in. Flopping. Splashing. Hair, shirt, floor, all wet. Only reason I finally get up is because Becker lets go.

Breathing hard, fast. Water drips from my face and hair onto my shirt. I turn. Becker standing. Metallic grin. He's breathing hard too. Hard on him too, holding me under. Took something out of him. He's trying to hide it, to breathe easy, keep his smile. Eyes sharp. Neck stiff. I catch my breath. Wipe my face. Fire my best words, everything I have:

"Facken fack your mother bitch. I fack yer bitch mom, mother-facker!"

"I see you, Beaner Boy," his metallic grin widens, chunky and sharp. "The real you," he does that sudden head-jerk-shoulder-jut bullies do when they want to make you flinch.

I flinch.

He smirks, breathes deep. It took a toll on him. Takes effort to torture people. He turns to go. "You better pray I never tell anyone about the real you. Enjoy sixth grade, Beaner Boy!"

I pull the paper from the sink, ball up and throw it in his direction as he exits. I dry my face, stare in the cracked mirror. Brown, wet, terrified. Me. Always me that way. Never them.

Good writtens.

Summer officially starts with ceremonial music; classical trumpets, violins and flutes. It moves at a strict pace, trudging with heavy horns to an end of crashing cymbals as Moses himself stands like a hunk of rough pink marble before every sixth grader, announcing full names, hints of honor in his tone making them sound important no matter how mean, meek or uncoordinated they really were on the playground. Pros and Nons are equals on Graduation Day.

Next June my name will waft from the speakers to rows of chairs filled with parents. Will Moses say "Mishel" as written in his book, or will he finally get it right? Will my hair flow in the warm June breeze as I float, classmates cheering me on, chanting my coolest aka? Cherokee Manoucherian? Moto Manoucherian? Will they ask me to sing, Maman and Baba watching proudly (will Baba even be there? Been a month since he left; offers to visit with a bucket of Kentucky but Maman says "Koor khoondi!")? Even light-haired, fair-skinned Precious would be in tears – from jealousy! – seeing me sing the Eagles (can't get more Amrikayi than the Eagles!): "*So often times it happens that we live our lives in chains, and we never even know we have the key.*" I'll show them. They'll all see me. Right, Doc? . . . Doc?

Nope. I'm a dumb cartoon, Doc, remember?

After Moses reads names, proud parents leave with their graduates as the rest of us cheer the last day of school. We run the blacktop full speed, singing "Schoo-ool 'Zout Fo' Summa!" unclipping notebooks, shaking dangling modifiers and long division remainders over our heads like a goddamn parade. Yard Teacher will make us clean up, but even that's fun because we all do it - except I look up and no Speed, no Worm – no Pros! Only Nons and baby graders … a lame event, actually, like who even rullee cares? School's out? Pshhh! Pros could(n't?) care less. For them school's always out. School being out actually sucks for me. When school's in, I know where they are – leaning at the beige stucco wall. I work my way to them, their circle, I listen, chime in. And I know where the Nons are, to avoid. But when school's out? I straighten up, staring past the playground, cars zooming in both directions. I wonder when they left, where, how to find them. The Arcade? Still don't know where that it, or what it is. Even Fertig doesn't know. The Arcade sounds like a goddamn saloon from cowboy movies – mean men, low growls, guns. An acquired taste. But…I like that stuff…now. That's me…now. Pro.

Maman's new honk is somewhere between *Celebration* and *Sick of Waiting* – three quick blasts in a row. Not that I give a goddamn – cuz it's strictly for Nons - but in Morse Code three quick blasts is "O" - as in "O, Adonai! What has become of us?" which is what Maman has been sighing to herself every night since Baba left. "Shame is on us," she cries looking up at the cottage cheese ceiling. "Our reputation is ruined! At least nobody substantial lives in this dehat of a nation to witness our shame; Adonai spared us that indignity."

"Seventy black years," Maman mutters as she does the dishes after dinner, "let him go be a clown." She followed him to Amrika, twice, and he abandoned her anyway. She won't again. He can have his Amrika; she will have hers. She didn't come here, twice, to end up like Sabya.

Her new O honk careens wildly across on the playground.

"Get in," she yells with panic as we run over so she'd stop. "There's a sale at Orbach's."

"Again?" whines Sid. "Can I walk home with Kersh and Cowan?"

"Those guys?" I say dismissively. "Pshhh. They're Nons, man."

"Why do you keep talking like that," he asks.

"Like what, Little Precious? This is how I normally talk, cuzbro."

"It's not. You sound like a jerk. Kersh and Cowan are fun; I like them."

"You're babies, cuzblood. Pros don't play baby games. Pros play at the Arcade."

"What's that?"

"What's what?"

"Arcade?"

"It's not Arcade, dorkus; it's *the* Arcade. You don't know what the Arcade is?"

"No."

"Yeah, you *wouldn't*."

"I just said I don't."

"Pshhh, yeah, you *wouldn't*."

"I just said I don't. You gonna tell me what the Arcade is? Do you even know?"

"I'll tell you what it isn't! It isn't for little Nons like you, so *fush* off."

"Maman! He said that word again!"

"I said *fush*! Are you deaf? I said *fush*!"

Maman isn't listening; she's got 93KHJ on and is excitedly pushing the car lighter in, holding its electric orange heat to the tip of the smoker tucked between her lips, exhaling a puff of smoke that fills the car with that excitement of fresh-lit tobacco and electric heat. Her song is on and she knows the words, mostly: *"Del-ta Dawn what's that flower you have on, could it be a faded rose from days gone by?"* The parts she doesn't know she goes *"Lalye-lye lalye-lye."* At the red light, she sings so loud the guy in the car next to us looks in. I try to roll up my window but she catches me. "Nakon!" she yells, reaching over to tap my hand off the handle. I slide down in my seat, trying to disappear, but that only make her sing louder, *"and did I hear you say, he was meeting you here today, to take you to his man-shun in the ska-ha!"*

"Relax," the guy smiles, our cars idling at the longest red light in the history of Los Angeles red lights. "Your mom has a lovely voice. Don't be embarrassed. Let her sing."

"O tank you, ser," Maman gives him a regal nod, "Wery velcome, ser." Then in Farsi with a wide smile, "Your face resembles the ass of a baby monkey, mister."

"What?" he's still smiling. Is he flirting? Is she letting him?

Maman hits the gas with a laugh as the light turns green, singing *"Del-ta Dawn..."*

At Orbach's, she studies the price tag on a silk blouse. "I've had my eye on this one but they're full of shit if they think I'm paying forty-five," and heading to the sale rack.

At the counter, the salesgirl asks, "Twelve-fifty? For a silk blouse? Can that be right?"

Maman plays dumb, "I don't know. This is vat the tag say. You have the sale, yah?"

The salesgirl stares at Maman. Maman stares back, a mischievous, almost playful defiance in her eyes, daring the salesgirl to make Maman's situation worse than it already is. My palms sweat. The yellow overhead lights make my neck sweat. Maman hisses in Farsi under her breath, "Look at this monkey with her crooked teeth and oily hair," then with a bright smile and flirty Persian accent she says, "Look how byoodiful is your hair! How byoodiful you are smile," laying her shiny lacquered nails on her heart. "From where you did get your byoodiful eyes."

The salesgirl blushes, touches her hair. "You're so swee-eet," she says, examining the blouse again. "This is a real bargain," she says looking side to side like she's sharing a secret with her girlfriend. "Good for you!" and rings it up.

I exhale and wipe my hands off on my pants, marveling at how Maman gets away with it.

In the car, humming *Delta Dawn* with satisfaction, she speeds home so her Precious can play with his friends. He's in the backseat, satisfaction on his smiling face too. I stare out at passing storefronts, searching for signs that might read "Arcade." I consider telling Maman the words, the *lalye-lye* parts she doesn't know: forty-one-year-old lady wandering the streets with an old suitcase after being abandoned by her man. Wipe that satisfied smile off her face.

Today I follow them.

All summer I've been riding my Senator looking for them so they don't forget me; don't forget I'm a Pro too now. In June I spotted Speed and Worm on National, but I hid between parked cars. In July, riding past the Rancho Park pool on Motor, I saw Jodi S., Lisa W. and Big Mouth Patricia swimming. I figured other Pros might be there so I paid the quarter, waded into the shallow end as they sang "Rock the Boat" in their bikinis and barrettes, close enough to smell the coconut suntan oil on their thin, bronzed arms. With no Fertig to correct me, Bugs to guide me or Baba to embarrass me, I splashed and jumped, hoping they'd ask me to join the singing, hoping they'd see me. Finally, Jodi did.

"Stop," she yelled. "You're getting chlorine on my hair!"

Her beautiful golden hair.

Today, pedaling past Guild Drug I see Speed and Worm again on National. But instead of making the usual right on Motor, they turn left. Everything we know is a right turn on Motor – pool, playground, Albatross Lane. I follow. No Fertig; no Bugs; no Baba. On my own.

Left on Motor is a dusty, deserted area. Grey, boxy stucco buildings separated by swaths of loose dirt and gravel. No sidewalks. Quiet enough to hear the breeze and lazy flies buzzing.

At the gravelly front of one building, they sit on their bikes, lean on their handlebars, roll back and forth, talking to an Older leaning against the back of a pickup truck. Speed in a denim shirt over tank tops, a white sun visor holds his brown hair and shades his freckled nose. Worm has an old Cincinnati Reds hat on backwards like a catcher. The building behind them has a door in front with a wooden sign above it: "Pinball, Air Hockey, Pong." Below that: "Arcade."

222

I roll out from behind the car, pedal full speed past them, pulling my handlebar up for a pop-a-wheelie, pretending not to see them. I get an inch up before gravity pulls my wheel back onto the crunchy gravel. I pop it again, and again, landing with pebble-crushing thuds, glancing over to see if they notice. They are busy chirping about Nixon, Watergate, Pete Rose. Then they point. At me? "*Oh hey fellas, didn't see you there... 'Sap'nin' cuzbros! Didn't know you shitbricks go here!*" I keep my trap shut, switch from pop-a-wheelies to skids, pedal full speed slam brakes skid quick turn-spin. Again! This time I try a long hard skid to raise dust in front of them - a splashy greeting. I slam my foot back on my brake, start my skid, back wheel scraping over gravel–POP! A painful sound of grinding metal.

"Smooth move, Beaner Knievel!" Worm elbows Speed.

Speed looks at me, shaking his head: "Hops like a Mexikin Jumping Bean."

The Older, with long wavy hair wearing a blue-and-white pin-striped mechanic shirt, crunches gravel with his boots as he walks over, kneels to examine my wheel.

"Rim's OK," a crumpled pack of Winstons in his shirt pocket. "Your name's Beaner? Bean? Listen up, Brother Bean, you're gonna need a new tire."

"Brother Bean!" says Speed. "That's even better than Beaner Boy!"

"I'm not Mexi-" but I drop it. I decide to go another way. "Chiiit! My ty-urrr," A funny Mexicki accent I heard on the radio. "De guy at de Bike chop is my friiind, he'll fix iiit!"

"Check out Cheech," chuckles Worm, his palm out for the Mechanic to slap him five.

"Quit squawkin'. I got an idea," the Mechanic slips one between his lips, pulls a steel lighter from his jeans, flips it aflame and lights up. "Let's drive Brother Bean to the bike shop; see if there's anything worth swiping," he orders. "Savvy?"

Squawk. Swipe. Savvy. Memorize his words.

He tosses my Senator in the back of his pickup. Speed and Worm hop in.

"Comin'?" asks Worm, elbow hanging over the low wall of the truck bed.

It feels like time has stopped. Squinting through the sun, I float on the lingering question. Worm and Speed asked me to join. Mark it down. August 1974. Number 1 on Casey Kasem's Amrikayi Top 40 is "Havin' My Baby" Paul Anka. The song playing on the Mechanic's radio is Number 40, "Rikki Don't Lose That Number" Steely Dan. But the song I'm thinking of is Number 37 Bo Donaldson & the Heywoods, "Who Do You Think You Are."

Who do I think I am? Who do they think I am? Easu? Mishel? Beaner? Who would Maman think I am if she saw me in the back of a pickup with these freckled bucktoothed Amrikayi? Couldn't care less! Pros don't care what moms think! Dad goddamn split Cuzbro--

-- The Mechanic's honk! Not *Celebration* or *Tired of Waiting*. More *Call to Arms*. A locomotive horn: hop on! Engine rumbling; Amrikayi waiting. I climb in, he peels out, churning gravel and raising dust.

"He remembers you, right?" the Mechanic outside the bike shop, bold and unafraid. Speed and Worm will be like him some day – cool and defiant, not weighed down by Fear, Superstition, Passover, Yom Kippur or parents. *Savvy.*

I use cool Pro: "Sold me my Senator, Broham. Didn't charge tax, even threw in a bitchin racing plate. He'll fershur give us a rullee good deal, Cuzblood."

"Good deal?" Mechanic chuckles. "Keep him busy, Brother Bean, we'll do the rest."

"The rest?" Eyes squint so he won't see my fear; sun hot on my head. "Rest of what?"

"Quit squawkin', Bean. Just take your time, show him the flat, keep him near the back."

Unafraid, cool, long hair, leather wristband. Gonna be your friend!

"Remember me," walking my bike in, "got a flat."

"Let's have a looksee, son." He is bald like Baba, but his dome isn't harsh. The hair around it is soft and grey. His eyebrows aren't heavy and dark like Baba's and his eyes crinkle at the sides from smiling, which he is doing as he comes around the counter to check my wheel.

"You really blew it out, din'cha? What happened?"

"Daredevil stunts," I say, remembering to keep my tone Pro. "Pop-a-wheelies, skids."

"Good for you, son," he says, squeezing the tire to check for the hole. "But you gotta remember, I sold you a Senator, not a Harley. You should know what your bike is and isn't. Now let's see if we can fix this gash maybe without you needing a new tire."

He looks up, sees them moving around the doorway. "Boys, please don't touch those!"

The Mechanic, Speed and Worm run, arms full: bike pumps, racing grips, plates, a wheel.

"Hey!" The old man runs after them but by the time he gets to the door they're gone and I hear the sound of the items clanging in the truck bed as the engine ignites, roars and fades down National, the high-pitched yelps of Worm and Speed fluttering in the breeze. They left me.

The old man stands at the door staring at the street, then bends down to pick up racing gloves, a lock and patches that were dropped. His bald dome is now pink as he mutters grizzly words like "sunza bitches" and "no good bastards" - words I couldn't have imagined coming from his friendly mouth. I lay my bike down and go to help. Guilty. Terrified.

"It's OK, son, I got it," he says as I start picking stuff up. "You see those punks?"

"I don't know them-" insides shaking, "I couldn't see, don't know what happened."

"You didn't get a good look? We'll need to identify 'em to the police?"

Police? Identify? Keep yer trap shut and stay cool!

"I just wanted help fixing my tire," I say, losing my Pro tone "Don't know them."

The old man looks up, stares at me a long time, gives me the up-and-down.

I stare back, round eyed. Does he see my quivering lips, my flaring nostrils?

His frown softens; forms a smile. "Bad upbringing. Weren't raised right. Delinquents and dropouts! Don't be like them, son. You seem like a good kid. Stay that way."

"I don't know them," my big eyes getting misty, biting down to steady my lips.

A silent stare, the kind Baba sometimes does before sinking the top row of his teeth into his lower lip – angry F. Anything can happen after that; smack, table flip, head shake before turning and walking off in disgust. But Baba's gone. I'm at the mercy of this old man.

"Well, I guess there's no point calling the cops," he says. "Let's have a look at that flat."

As I ride out on my patched tire into the stifling heat, National is alive with the afternoon melodies of car horns bouncing, bus brakes hissing, rumbling engines and zipping motorbikes. I pedal fast to cool my face as I head to Motor. Right or left? He warned me not to be like them, but I want to be like them, even though they left me there. Were we supposed to meet at the Arcade? Did I miss the signals? It was a daredevil feeling, getting tossed around in the back of his pickup, hot wind in my face, laughing with Worm and Speed. Right or left?

There's more of them, all gathered around the Mechanic's pickup, laughing and puffing smokers. I recognize some Pros and Olders from the playground. Lots of new faces.

"Brother Bean," shouts the Mechanic, blowing smoke rings. "Told ya he'd make it. Get over here, you little brown decoy. Look at everything we swiped! Come take your cut."

Speed and Worm hold smokers too, blowing short, quick puffs. Their gritty bucktoothed smirks and squinty eyes make it hard to tell if they're being cool or wincing.

"What's Beaner Boy gonna take," Worm chuckles between coughs. "He barely rides."

"Listen, shorty," the Mechanic sneers, setting Worm up, "you squealed like a girl when we took off," finishes him with "easy on the smokes, kid, they stunt your growth."

Laughs. Worm glances at the smoker in his hand, forces a smile. At the Arcade, Speed and Worm don't have the same air-conditioned cool they do at the playground. They sweat here.

"Take a tire pump, Beaner Boy," coughs Worm. "You need it the way you ride."

That wisecrack earns a soft shoulder punch from the Mechanic. I peer into the truck bed full of loot. The old man warned me to not be like them. But no Bugs, no Fertig or Pincus. Yes this is Sin. But a fun one.

"Take whatever, Brother Bean," the Mechanic blows another ring, "it's in your blood."

"My blood?"

"Mexikins steal, Beaner Boy," Speed explains, puffing, blowing, holding down a cough.

Fat Guy is Mexicki and taught me to steal lunches, but I stole from Sweet Lady on my own. Maman steals for fun. These guys just stole from the bike shop. My blood?

He's kidding with you; being friendly. Don't disappoint him.

"Your friend here is OK," the Mechanic pushes a final stream of smoke from his mouth, drops the butt, twists it into the gravel with his boot, "for a fucken beaner!" Winks at me.

Their laughter . . . is it mean? Or like the Olders in Tehran . . . I'm sure they have me.

"Choor, maing," I play along in funny Mexicki.

The laughter lights up their teeth in the purple air of the fading afternoon. I keep it up.

"Maybe I chuud change my name, esé," I suggest, sensing in the camaraderie that the time is right. "Call me Aztec or Cherokee, esé, Moto Mike--"

"—MJB," Worm chuckle-coughs, drops the butt, wipes his fingers on his jeans.

"Coffee?" asks the Mechanic, "like because of his brown skin?"

"Mexikin Jumping Bean!" Worm laughs, rolling into a full-blown cough he can't stop.

I laugh too. We're all cool for the joke; part of the game.

"How about Pinto," coughs Speed, dropping his smoker too. "Pinto Bean."

"Take one, Pinto," an Older holds out a pack. Camels, my Coat of Arms.

They've been lighting, puffing, tossing butts on the gravel all afternoon. When Maman lights up, it fills the air with an elegant, exciting aroma, fresh-lit tobacco. My turn.

"Chit, maing," I pull one and as soon as I put it to my lips a need to shit hits my stomach, moistens my ass. He flips a steel lighter and the flame makes me flinch. No elegant aroma as I puff, just bitter sting on my tongue. I push out, it escapes my mouth... I'm smoking...

"Take it in, Pinto," the Older says. "Inhale, then blow. This your first smoke?"

Deeper pull. Like a marauding cartoon ghost, the smoke rushes past my throat to my chest... cough! Can't keep it in. Cough. Laughter. Spit gathering; won't go down. Tongue thick. Need to shit. Straighten up... no, double over. No Bugs, no Fertig, no Baba. Cold sweat. Dizzy. Sky spinning. Might vomit. "I'm OK!" Cough. Spinning. No aroma no elegance...

...I open my eyes to heads silhouetted by a purple sky. Gravel digs into the back of my head and shoulder blades as I lie flat. The ground under me is hot, rumbling a familiar hum of engines and wheels as horns smear the air, busses roar, sirens careen on National Boulevard. Beyond the heads, frisky gonjeshk in synchronized packs dart to their trees for dusk, chirping innocent joy, satisfaction - another day of righteous living earning them peace. Above them all, an iridescent orange sun surrenders quietly behind the hills, slipping off to die alone. I roll over, it smells like asphalt and spit. I heave. From the deepest pit of my guts, eyes tearing, tongue out past my grimy teeth, ropes of clear thick liquid hanging from my lips, tasting like rancid oranges.

"Better get home to wash off, Pinto," says the Mechanic with an easy laugh. He has me.

I am Pinto.

Labor Day Weekend
September 1974

"Excuse me!" breaks the hum of chatter floating over the aisles of the Guild Drug. Sid and I are in Stationery picking out notebooks, folders and Bics. "Ma'am? I saw what you did."

"Vaat I did?" the accent is unmistakable; the tone, her "How dare you?"

I leave Sid by the candy bars, walk to the sound. Maman went to get candles. Tonight we're introducing Shideh and her parents to Amrika by having pizza and watching the Jerry Lewis Telethon. Maman, insisting on being a good host even with Baba gone, told us to say he's away for work. I find her leaning on the Revlon shelf in Cosmetics holding lipstick tubes, handbag hanging from her forearm, open. A brown-haired salesgirl is standing in front of her.

"Ma'am, you switched your old lipstick caps with our new ones. I saw."

"You are crazy? This is my lipstick," Maman pulls an old cap off of what looks like a new lipstick tube, twists, brings it up to her lip.

"Don't do it, Ma'am," the salesgirl warns. "It's stealing."

Maman defiantly dabs her lips, rubs them together and smiles. "See?"

"Ma'am! Please stay right there, I'm getting the manager."

"Is she crazy," Maman asks the air, looking around in pretend confusion. When her eyes land on me she gives a double-blink-lip-bite and whispers "let's go!" as she replaces the caps on her lipsticks, drops hers in her bag, then the caps on the store lipsticks, puts them on the shelf.

The manager and salesgirl return as Sid careens down the aisle, bumping into Maman.

"Can I help you, Ma'am," the manager asks.

"Good afternoon, ser," Maman in curvy Official Amrikayi. "I don't know vat its going here, ser," points to the salesgirl, "your byoodiful helper – such byoodiful hair! – she is make mistake. I use it my lipstick and she say I can' do dat? I can' use it my lipstick in your estore?"

The manager turns to the salesgirl. "Did this lady apply her lipstick or store lipstick?"

The salesgirl, sidetracked by Maman's words and dreamily stroking her flat brown hair, snaps out of it and pulls the lipstick Maman had used off the shelf. "She used this one. Burnt Sienna. Then tried to put her own cap on it. Look at her lips. Burnt Sienna."

"This is the sample, no?" Maman maintains her smooth, round Amrikayi.

A crowd gathers as Sid and I stand by Maman - me trying to disappear behind her, Sid wide-eyed and jittery. We know our roles: shut up and let Maman work.

"Please open your bag, Ma'am," the manager demands at the salesgirl's urging - she is sure Maman's bag holds new lipsticks masquerading as old ones. "Ma'am?"

"Shame on you," Maman shoots a fiery look; no more curvy Amrikayi. "You embarrass me because I am voman? You vant see my bag?" she opens her handbag. "See!"

She expects disappointed looks, knowing she put the lipsticks back. But the salesgirl looks surprised; the managers, confused. In Maman's purse: Milky Way, Snickers, two Chunky's.

She looks at us as Sid and I look at each other.

"What you did, bad boys?" she shouts for everyone to hear her sympathetic dilemma - a mom with naughty boys. She turns to the manager, "I don't know what these bad boys do," she shrugs. "Put it back, crazy boys," she screams at us, taking the candy out of her bag.

But she can't contain a secret grin, beaming at her Precious, her wicked little firecracker, her spinning top. She's not exactly proud that he almost got away with it - if not for that pesky salesgirl – but not mad either. Fairer-skinned, fairer-haired Precious gazes up at her with the devotion of a kitten that killed its first gonjeshk and dropped it at the feet of his goddess: naughty but innocent. He doesn't look at me to gloat; no need. I feel the breeze from the fluttering of his eyelashes.

"Ma'am, please wait here," the manager says. "We need information for the police."

"Police?" Maman's eyes go big. "But they put it back the shokolot."

"You took lipsticks and your handbag is full of stolen candy, we need the police."

After holding back floods of fear and waves of anger all summer, Maman finally let's go. "I fack your lipstick!" she screams, her hazel eyes blazing. "I fack your shokolot!"

"Ma'am, you're getting hysterical," the manager tries to calm her, "call your husband."

A rising swell quickly douses the fire in her eyes. "You vant I should call my husband?"

"I don't want to see you upset, Ma'am. So if you like, you can call your husband."

"He is not here; he is in the business. I can talk to you myself."

"Ma'am, are you divorced?"

The smoldering embers of hazel reignite. "You are ke-ray-zee? Ferst," pointing her finely manicured finger up as warning, "you don't say it to me *Mam*. Ya? In Amrika we say it *Miz*. Ya? And I am Irani from Persia, we not divorcing! Under-estand?"

"Yes, Ma'... Yes, Ms. Please relax; let's call your husband and sort this out."

She's been putting on the tough act since he left – singing, flirting, danger-shopping. "Wants to find himself," she'd mutter while doing dishes, "was he lost? So go! Seventy black years, go! Can't find yourself with us, go get lost. Think you can drop in with greasy chicken in a trashcan like a dehati. Koor khoondi! Manam Amrikayiyam. *I am voman hear me row!*" She's been seeking solid ground since we landed in Amrika, trying to find her footing on foreign streets as alien to her as the moon's surface was to the Apollo crew, a reluctant explorer hiding her terror while cooking dinners, answering questions, fixing problems – two 2's are 4; *why* is chera, *what* is chee - making it look easy, fun, mischievous. But she's finally out of answers.

The bell jangles with a pull on the door. He looks out of place at the Guild Drug. Gotten thin, moustache and combover gone, black hair ringing his dome grown out, makes him look soft. When he sees us, a nervous grin crinkles his eyes, adding an unfamiliar sweetness to his face. Not like he looked when he left. Baba has been through some things; and he's missed us.

Maman, standing arms folded beside the manager, gives him a narrow glance, looks away.

"Havar ya? I'm Manny Manoucherian," he announces like a guy from actual TV.

Sid and I step away. "Smooth move getting Maman busted, jackass."

"It got Baba back," he says with a smug smile. "Thanks to me. Too bad you're too chicken to steal. I made it happen. Afraid of getting caught, Beaner Boy?"

"They don't call me that anymore, idiot. I run with the Pros now; they call me Pinto."

"Like that shitty Ford car nobody likes? You sure they're not still making fun?"

"You wish! Got your mommy busted for holding your swiped candy, Oil Well?"

"Too chicken to even try, Beaner Boy?"

"Quit squawkin'! Swiping candy is kid stuff. You're not savvy enough to swipe big stuff. Me and my gang don't get busted when we swipe. Pros swipe big stuff, not candy."

"OK, Ford Pinto. Don't pretend you're tough with those words; they're not even yours."

I may take a ribbing from Pros, but not from Precious. I shove him into Revlon, tubes of lipstick fall on him. He lunges. I sidestep, watch him stumble into Maybelline. Up again, he turns, determination in his eyes. Almost feel bad cupping his head, straight-arming to hold him beyond reach of his punches, like the bully on *Sheriff Andy*. He swings wildly. Almost. He may be Maman's fairer-skinned, fairer-haired firecracker, but I'm still taller.

"Let! Me! Go!"

Baba looks up, brows starting to furrow like the old days. Maman rushes to her Precious.

I uncup his head and watch her spinning top roll back into Revlon with a beautiful clatter.

"Don't worry," I yell on my way out. "Your little Precious is fine!" jangling the bell.

Cars whiz by in the afternoon heat, their radios blaring songs I know by heart now. Soon I'll sing them on the playground, leaning on the beige stucco wall with the Pros, jeans and sneakers, talking about songs, sports, what a shitbrick sixth grade is, our divorced parents.

I cross National, turn up Pinnacle Palace, wondering if he's back, his explosions, heavy hands, harsh accent, dark brows, inspecting eyes – an outsider who didn't seem to care about being out. Was he pretending? Today a smile crinkled his eyes, a slump in his walk, offering his hand to the manager – new for Baba. Not for me - rejection, humiliation, surrender, outsider trying to get in. I know that look. Nons. Fertig,

Dudley, Pincus, Fat Guy, Rodrigo, a league of rejects, outsiders thrown together in that swamp of spit and venom. We are equals there, cozy. Now Baba is in with us…them. Not me. I've gotten used to Baba being gone. All summer it was near-emergency, something-off, Yom Kippur candles casting wild shadows as we felt our way in a new darkness. Not exactly buckteeth or freckles, but it'll do. I practiced my lines:

"Shit yeah, my perunts getting' divorced; what a shitbrick."

"My Mom'n'Dad split, rulee a drag."

"My Dad comes on weekends with a bucket of Kentucky Fried, dammit!"

"Pinto!" The Mechanic pulls over. Two Olders riding shotgun; Speed, Worm, two others in the back, elbows resting on the sides, taking in the afternoon sun. My stomach churns.

Why still churning? No need to be scared. They have you now, remember?

"We gotta game, wanna come?" the Mechanic asks. "More the merrier."

"Sure!" Relieved, ready to play any game they want. "Basketball? Baseball?"

They stare, like Maman's good-luck egg goo is on my shoes. Churning.

"Told you he won't get it," Speed says. "A fight, Beaner Boy. We're going to a fight."

Still Beaner boy? Fight? Stop trembling, chickenshit. Talk! Like them. Fearless.

"O'rite, cuzbloods! Fight? Shit yeah. Righton. Like, whose damn ass are we kickin'?"

"Gonna rumble with the Canfield Avenue gang," says Worm.

"Those total shitbrick fackin Canfield shits! What total ass shit did they pull now?"

Egg goo on the shoe look again. Speed shakes his head, "Jesus…"

You used 'shit' too much that time, idiot!

"For fun," Worm titters, "they didn't do anything. Us against them."

Dirty cowboys roping you in to get beat up, for fun. Or Jerry Lewis Telethon in an hour. Maman getting Pizza. Shideh. Pizza and TV, or pointless fight? Get out of it. Distract.

"Ooh chit, maing, I jus' rememburred, gat some erins to run, esé; can't figh' righ' now!"

One of the Olders cackles, "I hear ya, Cheech!"

They hear me! Easy going, fearless, cool as can be.

A jolt! *Not Late*. Maman's Mustang rolling up behind the Mechanic's pickup, Precious shotgun. Baba's Impala hisses up behind it. Churning starts again.

"Ooh chit, maing! Whass hapa-neeng?"

"Why are you talking like that," Precious sticks his head out the window.

Switch to Pro, loud for all to hear: "Cuzblood, you don't get it, so quit yer squawkin'."

"Chera eenjoori harf mizani," Maman out of her car, peering inside the pickup, at me, eyes lock. She sees my panic, nods. "Bereem khooneh; get away from these hamalls."

"Who's that," the Mechanic checks his back window, "why's she talking like that?"

"His mom," Worm titters. "Remember Open House? Careful, she's got a mean right!"

"Let's take her to the fight," laughs Speed, "she won't chicken out like Beaner Boy."

"Thought they call you Pinto," Precious snickers.

"Thought I taught you a lesson 'bout squawkin', cuzbro," I seethe. "Want more?"

"Basseh!" In his brown wide-collared shirt and flimsy black trousers held up by a thin belt that barely contains his belly, Baba swings the heavy door of the Impala and steps out. "I vanna catch Rickles and Hackett on the Telefon so shake de leg digeh!"

"That your dad?" Speed elbows Worm. "Didn't you say your parents are divorced?"

"You said that to them?" Precious sitting in Maman's car, shaking his head.

"Shut up you!"

Maman and Baba flash grim side glances; it's never good to tell family secrets.

The Mechanic adjusts his rearview. Rugged thief of bike parts; fearless fighter of the Canfield goons; wavy hair slow-dancing with the summer breeze, tickling the shoulders of his denim shirt, leather wristband, peace sign hanging from his neck. Air-conditioned cool, the Older all Pros want to be studies foreign, lumpy old Baba from his rearview.

Shiny-domed, slack-shouldered and limp from the summer heat, Baba eyes them with that new timid smile; eyes Maman. I pray he doesn't say another word.

"OK, bebee!" he grabs my shoulders and walks me past a smug Precious to the Impala. "Have a good von," Baba announces to the Pros, my gang, "we see you gators later!"

Don't turn around. Don't see them seeing you, seeing him, seeing us. Like that.

"Cool!" I shout. "Catch you tomorrow, cuzbloods! Kick damn asses!"

"Basseh," Baba nudges me in. Drives us to Albatross Lane.

He stands in the doorway like a shy visitor who doesn't know where to go. Sid heads to the living room to warm up the TV; Maman to the kitchen. She still has guests to get ready for, no matter how she feels about pizza, getting busted at the Guild Drug or needing Baba's help.

"Are you staying," Sid shouts the question we all want to ask, including Baba.

Maman clangs a bowl onto the counter, pulls dill, cucumbers and a tub of yoghurt from the fridge and grabs a knife from the drawer.

He leans in to catch her eye, but she's chopping dill, loud and hard. He steps in, practically on tiptoes, head humbled, pulls open a drawer to take out another knife.

She keeps chopping with focus and ferocity. He moves beside her, grabs a cucumber.

"Those are for guests," she says, eyes on the dill.

"Aren't you making mastokhiar," he asks. "I'll cut cucumbers."

"Do what you want," she shrugs. "The skin is thick and waxy on Amrikayi cucumbers," still looking down but checking him from the side, "watch you don't slice your hand."

He clutches the knife like it's a foreign object, starts peeling, slow.

"Don't cut too deep into the meat, and don't leave any of the skin either, it's bitter."

It's not like he'd flip a table over it - or even flash his furious "F"- but Maman's orders usually make Baba grumble; at least spit out a salty wisecrack. Aside from the odd Sunday when he waltzes in to make his famous parsley-scallion omelet, and the Bouillabaisse Incident, Baba isn't in the kitchen. The *Art of Pazirayee* is for wives. But he wants to come back; and she seems to be enjoying watching him try.

"It's starting," Sid yells from the living room. "Jerry is singing!"

Baba puts down the knife and rushes to the living room. He picks up the TV, carries it to the kitchen table and plugs it in. Then he takes the yoghurt, cucumbers, knives, bag of pita and, finally, Maman's hand – and brings them all to the table.

"I want to see this," he says to Maman as he starts dicing, "come sit." Then in English, "Jerry Lewis has the terrific comedy tempo."

She studies him like he's a new flavor of Corn Flakes she's not sure she'll buy, but it's her choice. From the minute he walked into the Guild Drug, he looked different: shabby but light, far from the King in his crisp suit crunching toast and slurping tea behind his morning paper. He looked beaten but less burdened because of it – like Amrikayi blue jeans or the Hamm's Beer Dads at Open House - dug in, taken root. Practically Amri-kayi. Invited to sit beside him, Maman gives him the once-over, a glint of power in her hazel eyes. Her choice. She sits. They mix dill and cucumbers into the yoghurt, toss in salt and pepper, cut pita into wedges, watching Jerry Lewis. He looks fresh in his tuxedo, bowtie not yet undone, hair slicked back, microphone in one hand, snapping fingers with the other. The Telethon has started; a long twenty-four hours ahead. Shideh and her parents will be here soon. Looks like Sid's question may have been answered.

I go to my room, slam the door.

She told us to put on nice clothes for them but I'm perfect in my t-shirt and jeans. In the mirror I dig my teeth into my lip, buck-style, part my hair down the middle like the Mechanic.

"What's this," she whisper-yells as the doorbell rings. "Like the hamalls."

Pros don't care what moms think. This ain't Beirut; this is how we dress in Amrika.

"I'll deal with you later," she says with a final tug on her blouse and touch of her hair before opening the door with her *Welcome In* smile.

Shideh's parents enter, showering Maman with an endless stream of Persian poetry, kissing both cheeks as Maman bows and sweeps her arms inward.

"Salaam o sadd salaam," Maman says, "our eyes alight at the sight of you."

As they step inside, fresh off the international jet that carried them from Tehran to Los Angeles, the exciting jet fuel, cologne and tobacco smells aren't enough to mask the permanence of Persian musk imbedded in their skin. Without the sharp piney smells of Amrikayi soaps, the mustiness of chicken-feather pillows, boiled meat, fried fenugreek and steamed saffron oozes from their pores like they just climbed out of one of Maman's pots.

Behind them, different than I remember, Shideh. Her hair isn't tied at the top like the crown of a tree anymore; no missing teeth signaling wisdom. Dark hair, like me. Olive skin, like me; bushy eyebrows almost connecting, like me. Unlike me, her mole is above her lip. Irani don't get freckles, we get moles: on our cheeks or jaws, above our lips. Our parents tell us they're a sign of elegance, royalty. They tell us about classic Persian beauty in paintings and magazines, all with moles. Even Europeans, we're told, have moles. Those not lucky enough, we're told, draw them on with black pencil, to be beautiful like us. Moles are nothing to be ashamed of, we're told. Still, Amrikayi get freckles, and seem happy with them.

"Mishel my bell, chetoree!" She hugs me so tight I worry her stink of boiled rice, soggy onions and sweat will stick to me. Way different from the coconut Coppertone and flowery Herbal Essence I have been smelling all summer. Still, deep within her funk is a trace of truth; and deep within that truth is a whiff of comfort that I am weak for, an aroma that makes me feel cozy, tucked-in, like sniffing an old pillow. I want to give in to it, bury my nose in it and inhale deep. But I don't.

"How'zit gow'en'," eyes half closed, in my best Amrikayi, curved and careless.

"Look how good your English has gotten, Mishel," she says in Farsi. "Better teach me."

"Um, yeah, fer-shur, wull givita try f'r sh'r."

"Chee shod, Mishel my bell, Farsi yadet raft?"

"Rullee, yeah."

She switches to English: "You not talking the Farsi wid' your mudder fudder?"

"W'l y'know, I don't rullee talk to my pairunts," thumb toward the adults, eye roll. "My dad's not even rullee stayin' w'thus anymore y'know. He left--"

"—Our dad is right there," interrupts Sid. "And he knows Farsi."

"Everybody," Baba jiggling ice cubes in his drink like he still lives here, like he never left. "Jerry Lewis on telev'zion. Twenny-four hour he sing with singer, dance with dancer, joke with comedian – de jack of de trades, so talented. Come! Shake de leg!"

Maman narrows her eyes at him. She had warned him not to bring up any nonsense about comedy, or his leaving. "Come to your senses," she had insisted as they prepared, like it was a condition to his coming back, "don't embarrass us with your clown dream. They are going to live here, be in our doreh, we will have come-and-go. You're a rug merchant, basseh!"

"I was a rug-merchant-son of a rug merchant," Baba had corrected her. "It was my fated path, my duty. But in Amrika, nothing is fated and there is no shame in trying to make your own destiny or chasing dreams. They're not tied down by history; you can try everything. That's why everybody comes here. Like the commercial says, '*Try it, you like it.*'"

"That was a commercial for heartburn!" Maman had reminded him. "That poor donkey got a sour stomach from over-indulging. Even he couldn't believe he ate the whole thing. Amrikayi excess got him sick. Learn from that poor idiot!" Maman had warned him.

"So, Manoucher Khan, tell us," Shideh's dad is bald like Baba but the hair around his dome is greased back. He is tall but loses a few inches because his big head is weighed down by meaty lips and a strawberry nose too heavy for his neck to hold up. His warm brown eyes are shaped like sad almonds, even when he's happy. "How are rug sales in Amrika? Do they buy?"

"Yahya jan, I am Manny now," Baba says. "Let's talk English so ve all learn bedder!"

"OK, Manny jan, ve vill trying," Shideh's mom is excited. Her wispy black curls bounce, her dark eyes sparkle against the glittery earrings hanging from her ears.

"Azizam, man Mannyam," then, like a light bulb went on, Baba does a rhythmic Persian beshkan, snapping his fingers and chanting, "Azizam, man Mannyam; Azizam, man Mannyam!"

Gitty Khanom's painted red lips get wide. "Mashala, Manny jan, I never knew you had such talent! Like Jerry Lewis! From where? Since when?"

Baba doesn't hear her, "I should include this in my routine," he says to himself.

"Your chee?"

He looks at Gitty Khanom, interrupted, and with a sheepish grin says, "My jokes."

"Manny, azizam," Maman picks up Baba's keys, "our guests are hungry. Get the pizza."

"Is OK, Honey, ve get delivery," says Baba, bold from the attention Shideh's parents showed. In Farsi he says, "gather 'round kids and I'll tell you the best thing about Amrika: you demand food by telephone, they bring it to your house. Hot! *Deli-very*! Amrikayi have a gift for inventions that accommodate their laziness." Another light bulb goes off and Baba switches to English. "Delivery is best Amrikan invenshen; dey are so lazy dey get esmart – no – they are so esmart dey get lazy. In Iran, ve are not esmart or lazy. Instead of delivering hot food custemmers order from telephone, ve valk on the estreet vid vatermelons and berries in sacks on the backs of donkeys, yelling 'I have de vatermelons, I have de berries, anybody vants?'"

"Basseh digeh," Maman flares, "go get the pizza. We're not calling strangers to bring food by our door," turning to Gitty Khanom with a nervous laugh, "are we royalty now?"

"Kidding aside, Manoucher," Yahya Khan gets serious, "what jokes?"

"Yahya Jan," Baba answers in earnest Farsi, "I'm looking into becoming...*komedeeyan*."

"Chee?"

Baba looks humbled again. There is no word for it in Farsi. "Joke teller," he offers with a timid chuckle, "like Jerry Lewis or Bob Hope, but," clearing his throat, "my own...jokes."

"As a vocation? You're not a rug-seller anymore? You're a joke-teller? From where?"

"Manoucher," fire in Maman's eyes lights up. "Stop bothering them. Go get the food."

"I still sell rugs," Baba is determined to be understood. "I open the shop each morning, close at night, a clerk handles customers while I write jokes. Then we go to nightclubs and I try the jokes in front of people."

"Please, Manoucher," Maman says. "Leave them be...with your silly ideas."

"You two still go to nightclubs? Every night? Mashala! Like old Tehran nights, eh?"

Maman and Baba look at each other for an awkwardly long time, so long that the smile on Yahya Khan's heavy lips freezes, like he realized he has hit on something sensitive.

"No," Baba admits. "We don't go together. I -"

"-Lashoon, Manoucher," Maman barks in Farsi. "Basseh digeh! Get the damned pizza."

Baba's eyes get round. He clenches his jaw - a look we haven't seen since before he left. Sid starts moving his hands up to cover his ears. I brace my shoulders. But Maman's stays fixed on Baba. Shideh's parents exchange glances as Baba inhales and exhales three times, then walks to the kitchen to lift the receiver off the wall and dial.

"Please for deliver, 'tree extra-large pies vid de mashroom aleev anyen and green pepper. Two-Eight-Seven-Seex Albatross. Charge to Manoucherian." Spells it. "Have a good von."

He returns to the living room looking stern. "I say in English because is easier. I lern new phalsapheh in Amrika. Called E.S.T. It challenge me to not play a role put on me by my heritage. It teach me

240

to see myself, free myself, be myself as I am, not who others say I must be. My pozeeshenality is my choice, in Amrika you can choose who to be. I choose komedeeyan."

Gitty Khanom looks to Yahya Khan, "What did he say, Yahya? You understood?"

Yahya Khan can only offer a blank stare, turns to Baba.

"I decided to leave Lily," Baba confesses. "With my neighbor. I write jokes, he gets me into nightclubs. Every venture has a price and, for me, it was leaving Lily and the boys until I figure this out. I go to nightclubs all the time, but not with Lily."

"Chee megee, Manoucher?" Maman tries keeping a festive smile but can't hide the panic in her eyes. "What dari-vari you tell our guests!" She turns to them with narrowed nostrils, trying to sound dignified in her Guweem voice. "He dragged us to this nation of cowboys and hamburgers, promising diamond-studded sidewalks. Tell them," she turns to Baba, "dragged us to live in this dehat. You leave, you drag us, you leave again – because the car salesman next door said you were funny? How dare you? Aren't you ashamed?" shaking her fists. "Basseh!"

"Well what's with you now," Baba in his familiar roar, jutting his hands at Maman like he's arguing with a driver in traffic. "Haven't I been taking care of you? Do you need to work? Have your spending or living arrangements changed?" He switches to English, "I vork dabbel to find my dream and keep my family, OK? You like breaking eggs, yes? Vell, you have to break eggs for omelet, OK? My turn to break eggs now, for me! Ve broke enough eggs for you, OK?"

The ringing silence when they stop is what makes them realize they've been yelling. Baba looks at his guests in a slight bow of apology. Maman covers her mouth in shock at her own behavior, but can't stop her lips from trembling, or a crazy giggle from spilling out, or a small "No" from escaping. She has failed at the Art of Pazirayee.

Baba goes to her, offers her his drink which she pushes away, turning her head. He puts the glass up to her mouth, tilts till it dabs her lips. She sips, swallows, coughs, resists giving in to his arms but crumples into them anyway, hiding her face in his chest, her shoulders shaking.

Doorbell. "Pizza!"

Maman lifts her head, wipes her cheek and runs to the kitchen; Baba goes to the door.

"Lily jan," Gitty Khanom runs after Maman, turns to Yahya Khan, "say something."

Yahya Khan chases after Baba, pulls out his wallet. "I have Amrikayi dollars, please."

Baba slaps Yahya's hand, "Crazy, you're my guest, put it away, I am your servant."

"I am the dirt under your feet, Professor. We've intruded on you, I insist," smiles Yahya.

"I am the mere froth atop your piss, Doctor, go sit," Baba says, a chuckle, watching Yahya Khan laugh, elbowing him, "See? These are the jokes I am trying to tell. These are--"

"Basseh!" Maman yells from the kitchen over the din of clanking plates and jangling forks. "Pay for the food and bring chairs!"

"Like gum!" Shideh taking her first-ever bite of pizza. "You sure we can swallow?"

We only get pizza on special occasions. Still, Shideh's excitement reminds me of the Non I was. I keep cool, roll eyes. "W'l yeah, f'r sh'r, it's, like, pizza y'know? Chewy?"

"You have torshi," Yahya Khan asks Maman, studying his steamy, wilting wedge of cheese and tomato sauce on flatbread like he's figuring out how to make it better. "This would go great with torshi," his sad almond eyes getting sharp, "or topped with khoreshteh gheimeh. Manny what do you think? Do they understand Persian food here?"

We're watching the Telethon. Jerry Lewis has loosened his bowtie, and already looks tired, microphone and smoker in one hand, pointing at the numbers on the big board with the other.

"Baaah! This Jerry Luwees does some good business," confirms Yahya Khan.

"You liking eschool?" asks Shideh, sticking with English and joyfully chewing her slice.

"School sucks," I sink my teeth in and pull a stringy mouthful of cheese – hot - chew fast.

"Chee?" She chews with care, swallows, dabs the sides of her mouth, focused on me.

"Stinks" chew hot, "like, it sucks" mouth roof burning, chewing "like, I hate it, Cuzbro."

She gives up and, with a smile, goes back to Farsi. "I'm coming to your school. Day after tomorrow. We'll be classmates again! You'll show me your Amrikayi friends?"

I remember my first day. Then I think about the day after tomorrow; Jodi S., Lisa W., the Pros. I'll be running with them ... if Shideh tags along ... "Tell them your name is Shirley."

Shideh in mid-chew, "Sherlee cheeyeh?"

"It's Shideh in Amrikayi," I take another bite. "Like Mishel in Amrikayi is Mykell."

"But my name isn't Amrikayi. Shideh. Shee-deh! It's easy."

"In Amrikayi 'Shid' sounds like a bad word. They'll use it on you."

"If they dare," Shideh warns; she knows bullies. "They can get lost."

"They call me Sid," Precious jumps in.

"Is that a bad word in Amrikayi too," Shideh asks.

"No, just easier than Saeed. I like it. We can be a team, Sid and Shid."

"Don't listen to him," I tear off another hot bite. "They make fun of him too."

"Too? Meaning what? They ridicule you?"

The gloater only half covers his mouth, pretend-hiding his glee at exposing me.

"No way," mouth full of dough, sauce, cheese that isn't going down. "Not anymore."

"You shared your lunches with them?" Shideh laughs gently.

"What are you talking about?" Precious asks.

"He used to give kids bites of his sandwich or sips of his soda so they'd be friends, remember, Mishel my Bell? You never had to with me or Ramin. We liked you from the start."

"He was always scared," Maman, back to her carefree Guweem and eager for a new topic. "His first day of school I had to lure him with the box of clay I got for the teacher because the class was full. Remember? You were so scared. I always have you. Don't be so scared."

"I wasn't scared," shifting unswallowed pizza with my tongue, packing it in my cheeks.

"He was scared of sheep too," Precious points his greasy pizza finger at me.

"Liar! You didn't even see it. You were so precious they took you inside!"

"I remember that song on the radio made you sad," Maman *lalaye-lye's* 'Those Were the Days.' "I tangoed with you whenever it played to calm you so you could finish your homework; I'd whisper in your ear to not be so scared, to be courageous and bold, you remember?"

She sees me, knows me best, my round eyes and flared nostrils. No matter what I say or how I say it, Maman knows the truth, catches me when I faint even if she knows I'm faking … stomach churns … dizzy … sauce, cheese, dough all expanding in my mouth … Jerry Lewis puffing smoker after smoker, numbers flipping on the big board for sick children sitting broken and helpless in wheelchairs but smiling for Jerry for cameras dizzy … that disorienting feeling when you realize the solid ground you've been standing on isn't solid, isn't even ground. Cold sweat beads my forehead, stings my armpits, chills; neck too weak to steady a wobbly head spit gathering nowhere to go throat shut seeps out no point keeping it in give up lay down let it take over gravity Earth's rotation spinning wild slanted unsolid nonground surrender if I have to vomit so be it in no condition to fight or stop it or even be afraid too late for any of that. I am nothing but a lump of flesh and bone the spirit has discarded abandoned left behind…

"Mishel my bell what happened to you? You're white as chalk!"

"…iss pizza sucks…" spinning…

"Maman, he's pretending to faint again!" Precious caterwaul echoing…

"Why? There's fish in the pizza?" Baba chuckling in ripples and skips…

"Manoucher, stop kidding, he's really fainting! Oh give me death, Adonai!" Maman normal panic tones returning… "bring water… Manoucher! Essagh!"

"Essagh? Mishel! Mishel my Bell…"

244

"…being scared is good…means you're alive…I was scared…left them to come here, alone…left them to find myself, alone…stood alone on stage in front of strangers telling Nixon jokes so I can be like the ones on Carson, too scared to be myself…Carson? Johnny…television middle of the night…Jamie, an Irani Jew who knows joke-tellers and club owners said 'just be you, not who you think they want'… like E.S.T. … kismet! … now I tell jokes about Irani life … compare it Amrikayi life … singular … more rare than rugs or a benz … only me. *I am Manny from Iran, in Farsi 'Manny' is 'Meaning' so I am Meaning…my friend Jamie give me advise 'don't be like everybody, be like you, be Manny' I should be Manny? In Farsi 'be Manny' is 'Vidout Meaning' so I should be Vidout Meaning?"*

"Jaleb," Gitty Khanom, cracks a sugar cube between her teeth and slurps her tea.

Eyeballs dry … blink. Mouth parched, sticky strings of sour tomato sauce on my tongue, bits of sweet dough on my back teeth. Involuntary baby spasms like after a tantrum. Sweaty armpits, damp shirt. My head on Maman's squirming lap; her stomach gurgling.

"And now you're finished with that nonsense, *tanks God*. Listen to your professor and just be Manoucher, who you are and have been. Save the jokes for home. For our friends."

"It humbles, trying for laughs getting silence going back to try again," Baba not giving in. "That's Amrika. In Tehran it was all preordained, duty, judgment. Here, there's no history. You can be anything; they don't care. Or you can fail and be nothing; they still don't care."

I'm keeping my eyes closed, too embarrassed to see them or have them see me. On the Telethon, Steve Lawrence has joined Jerry Lewis for a duet. I peek at Shideh and Precious on the floor in front of the TV, feet tucked snug under their butts, sipping hot tea with milk. I slide off Maman's lap and venture towards them, maybe to join them, wondering if they'll make fun.

"Bah Bah! Cheshmemoon Roshan!" Shideh announces with joy. "Zende baad! Have tea, Mishel my Bell," handing her warm cup over. Her smell, earthy and close but cozy, a mix of neck sweat, hot tea, warm milk and melted sugar. I take her cup, sip, like we used to. "Noosheh joon," she offers a firm smile. I tuck my feet under my butt beside her, sharing her tea, as we watch Steve Lawrence and Jerry now joined by Steve's wife and singing partner, Eydie Gormé.

"No head-or-foot, Manoucher?" Yahya Khan wonders, "or firm ground to stand on..."

"We've been raised like donkeys to carry histories handed down by ancestors; ancient burdens on our backs that we then burden our kids with and call it tradition. Amrika is light; they question tradition, create new ones, define themselves, dream new paths. It's the wild west and if they fail, they try again. After all, the Amrikayi Dream guarantees dreaming, not dreams."

"So you're not keeping Shabbat anymore?" Gitty Khanom in a tragic loud-whisper.

"We keep Shabbat!" Maman, defiant. "Manoucher, stop kidding. We are Irani Jews. We have Haft-Seen at Eyd, gondi and abgoosht on Shabbat. Despite what this kidder says."

Baba chuckles, "She's right, our heritage is the flavor we bring. The beauty of Amrika is everyone sprinkling their flavor, special herbs and spices they bring with them to help create a new, grand Amrikayi khoresht in the big Amrikayi pot. New flavors."

"We should put our tangy khoreshteh ghooreh on their pizzas!" shouts Yahya Khan, finger and eyebrows raised in excitement. "We'll make millions!"

"I have my own pots," Maman says, "I cook khoresht and tadeeg the way my mother taught me; I don't need Amrikayi French fries or pizza. Everything doesn't need cheese on it."

"Khoreshteh gheimeh on Ferench Ferye! We'll be printing cash!" Yahya Khan goes on.

"Azizam," Baba smiles at Maman, "they're all from somewhere else just like we are. What is Amrikayi food? Our food! What is Amrikayi? Us! Look at the TV. See that woman singing Amrikayi songs with Steve Lawrence and Jerry Lewis? That's Eydie Gormé. Torkeh!"

I turn to Shideh, we stare at them, at each other, smiling easy, passing the tea. Still warm.

Barely 8 and already hot. Standing by the lone palm in the back-yard, I look past the gold sunburnt shrubs on the dried-out hill, down to the empty street, and the playground across. The flipping trills of the gonjeshk and low buzz of lazy flies are louder on Labor Day; no cars on the street, people sleeping in. The TV was still on when I woke up, no-name celebrities begging us to call and donate before the next number flip. Jerry Lewis probably cheat-napping backstage. Baba stayed. And Shideh's parents. Precious and Shideh are still asleep on the couch. Tomorrow, summer is officially over, school starts and things go back to normal. Sort of.

Behind gonjeshk whistles and the whir of wings that keep the flies afloat in the morning heat, I hear echoes. Hands clapping, feet stomp-ing, voices singing. From the playground.

I run back in, tiptoe down the hall and sneak into our bedroom where Yahya Khan and Gitty Khanom are tucked into each other in my bed, their soggy cheeks pressed into my pillow, the musty air in the warm room hissing with nose whistles and snores. I pull on my jeans, a t-shirt and sneakers, tiptoe back out, up the hall and out the door.

Strong enough now to go down without holding vines, I cross the street, jump the fence and walk to the sound. Past the orange hoops of basketball, "*I like t' hear some fun'keh dik-silan...*" the tall brown walls of handball, "*priti mam' com' take me ba th' han'...*" the yellow boundaries of four-square, "*ba the han-han take me ba the han priti Mama...*"

Two lunch tables have been dragged to the back fence under the stomachache trees near room 7. Pros don't hang around the playground when it's summer school, but after summer school and before real school, the playground is No Man's Land. That's when they show up.

At one table, Speed and Worm sit with a dark-haired rockstar look-ing kid – short bangs in front, long in back (Baba was right). He's strumming an orange guitar as the others sing and clap.

"*I like t' hear some fun'keh dik-silan' priti mam' com' take me ba th' han'.*"

Jodi S., Lisa W. and Big Mouth Patricia are at the other table, snap-ping sour cherry gum.

I slip my hand in my back pocket, cool Pro style, and nod to their beat. "How's i'goin'."

"Beaner Boy!" Worm giggles.

Should I remind him I'm Pinto now? Don't want to break their groove.

"Chu'guys doin'?" Inching closer to their table, tapping my thigh to their rhythm.

"Havin' an end of summer hootenanny," the kid with the guitar says. "Wanna join?"

"He won't know the words, Johnny Watts," Speed dismisses it with a wave of his hand. "Let's keep going, Johnny Watts," his normally pursed angry-lips are wide, exposing his full row of corn yellow Sugar Pop teeth, not just buckteeth. There's a look of awe on his normally cool face. "Play that *Johnny Grove* song again, Johnny Watts. *Johnny Grove, o'ho, Johnny Grove!*"

"China Grove," Johnny Watts corrects Speed, twisting the knobs at the end of his guitar.

Worm giggles at Speed's flub.

"It's a joke," Speed glares, looks for a sharper comeback. "I know the song ... jackbutt!"

I jump in to save Speed, so he'll remember it tomorrow. "I thought it's *Go Johnny Go.*"

"That's *Johnny B. Good*, Beaner Boy," Worm shakes his head with a laugh. "Why don't you sing *Erés Tu* or *Feliz Navidad*? Those might be easier for you."

It lands - laughs all around ... they're slipping through my fingers. Gotta think – fast ...

"Chit, maing!" They love my joke Mexicki accent, "I nevurr luurned doz songs, esé!"

OK, they see me now, laughing the right way.

"Good one, Pinto," says Speed. "He does a good Cheech."

"I know *I Chot the Cheriff.* Can ju play dat, maing?"

"Still talking like that? Is that some sort of act?"

Behind me, Precious and his gloaty smile. Beside him, brown and musty Shideh, all the warm coziness from last night now baking and rancid under the harsh Amrikayi sun.

"Mishel my Bell, eena kiyan?"

"What are you doing here, you little shit," I hiss at Precious, "and why'd you bring her?"

"Dad's chopping greens for his famous omelet so I'm showing her around."

"Dey are your fe-rend?" Dark and shabby, pointing her jaw at them, expecting an answer, her stupid dark hair tied at the top again like the crown of a tree. Dumb mole over her dumb lip.

"Who's that," asks Speed.

I can't block their eyes or cover their ears. And I can't make either of us invisible.

"Just my jackbutt shitbrick little brother," avoiding their eyes.

"I know who he is," says Speed. "Who's she?"

Her? Who? Do I know her? Is she with me? Ignore? Talk Mex-icki to distract? She is in front of them today; she will be in front of everybody tomorrow. I keep quiet.

Shideh is fixed on the girls at the other table, all sun-bright and air-conditioned.

"It's *Vuku*," insists Lisa W. with her flowing golden hair and jade green eyes, now the most beautiful of them. Lisa W. looks like a giant star who stepped off an Amrikayi movie screen to sit with children. The morning sun glints off her gold hoops and shiny lips as she drops her gloss in her grownup lady bag. Her voice sounds important; a flirty pout, a heft in her throat. "*Vuku*, not *kuku*," she argues, "*Kuku* doesn't make sense. It's 'voulay *vuku* shaya vekmwa.'"

"It means *let's go to bed*!" Jodi S. scandal-whispers to Big Mouth Patricia, leaning in to grab her arm, pry her from Lisa. Jodi knows she's not top dog anymore and needs to make up for it with insight. "They are ladies of the night, you know. Prostitutes. Get it?"

"Nope. *Kuku*," Big Mouth Patricia, unconvinced, closes her eyes and shakes her head. She hasn't changed since second grade, skinny arms, pointy elbows, curly brown hair under her Rosie the Worker red scarf. "*Vuleh kuku shay a vek ma* is secret New Orleans voodoo. She sings it right at the start, *He met Mama Lawd down in old New Orleans*."

"It's French, you ninny, not voodoo," Lisa pulls her thick-bristled hair-brush with the wood handle out of her lady bag to work the feathers on her hair, moves her neck side to side like Cher so it falls gloriously around her shoulders. "Mama Lord is a French Madame - boss of prostitutes. She speaks French to the Johns – the customers. It sounds extra sexy. Get it?"

"You speak French?" Patricia asks Lisa, half not believing it, half impressed.

"I wiiish," flirty pout, like we should all feel bad about her unful-filled wishes. "You?" she asks Jodi.

"I wiiish," Jodi stretches it out too, trying to reach a pout as flirty as Lisa's.

Neither bother asking if Patricia speaks French; she's not glamorous enough.

"Je parl Faranceh."

They stop, look up at dark, shadowy Shideh, study her top to bottom - Mickey Mouse t-shirt, striped shapeless pants, black vinyl shoes. Shideh stares back with an easy, flat smile.

"Is this, like, your cousin or auntie?" Lisa turns her jade green eyes to me. "Who is she?"

"Beshoon begoo, Mishel my Bell."

Speed, Worm and Johnny are singing and clapping. I wanna sing too, their song, clap their rhythm. I ponder Chee or Chera.

"Na," I say, to all of them. A universal word. Same in every tongue. Final and cruel.

"Rast migi" Shideh in Farsi. "Let's use Farsi at school as our secret tongue. We'll only let the wise ones in. We'll show these guys who we are. You have me, Mishel my Bell?"

...ba the han-han take me ba the han, priti Mama...

Sixth Grade, September 1974

Mr. Siegel is a tall, gruff-voiced man with Brylcreemed black hair, eyes as stern as coal and sunken cheeks burnt pink from scrubbing. He wears a white short-sleeved shirt with a thin, dark tie – pens and pencils in the chest pocket. He pals around with the sporty boys, playful punches on the arms, smacks to the backs of heads. Every spring he takes his favorites camping at Idawild. Even Pros want to be on that list. Siegel has Room 22 across from the tall walls of basketball and some days after lunch he gets on the court to shoot with kids, his hard black shoes scuffing the blacktop – the same sound the Olders in Tehran used to make playing soccer on the concrete – makes my heart skip. It's coming together. Sixth grade is here.

I talk like them now, curves on my consonants, slanted twangs on my vowels. I stand like them, hips thrust, shoulders slightly slouched like I don't care, feet finally in the right shoes - Pro Keds. I found the denim shirt I'm wearing in the parking lot at Guild Drug. Just like the one the Mechanic wears. They'll call me Cherokee. Dynamite Mike. Pinto, at least.

Siegel is writing on the blackboard when the bell rings and the Pros start to stroll in. Hands not in back pockets anymore; front pockets now. I switch, lean on the wall by the door, orange vinyl notebook at my hip so they see the cool stuff I scrawled on the cover:

Property of Cherokee Dynamite Mike.
Anybody touching this notebook will get kung-fu-chopped by Yours Truly!
Rock RULES!
School SUCKS!

Look who's here! All dolled up and freshly creased like he just *Fell In To The Gap*: Red corduroy flares; matching red-and-gold-striped Rugby shirt; Puka shell necklace tight as a Keith Partridge choker. Collar up like a model in the Sunday ads, neck stiff, head tilted to make sure the collar doesn't slip. And permed his hair; brittle yellow curls. He leans on the wall at the other side of the door, trying for that "I could (couldn't?) care less" look: one hand jammed in his front pocket, the other tugging on his Puka shells so he can breathe.

I'll pretend I don't see him, or don't remember him: too busy all summer stealing, smoking, doing pop-a-wheelies with my Pros; his name, our connection, have slipped my cool, air-conditioned mind. But his pale blue eyes catch mine and lock. Shitbrick. He tilt-nods. I up-nod back. He gets off his wall and walks over. Got my curves and twangs ready.

"What'd you do t'yur hair, Cuzbro," smirk, shift eyes away, not waiting for an answer.

"Not a darn thing, my good Sir Dude," the words stumbling out of his big, stupid mouth. "This is like how my hair like is now. Spent like all summer at the beach with my new stepdad like shooting bitching curl tube waves, so like no time to comb it..." tugs his Puka at me with a side-glance and nod that seem to be insisting I accept this new version of him, his new story.

I got bigger fish to fry. Speed strolls in and I push off my wall, move past Fertig.

"I wanna lis'n t'that fun'ken dik-silan… hey 'sapnin'! Where's Johnny Watts today?"

"School. Duh!" A cool, empty stare, looking around the room, searching. Probably forgot I helped him out yesterday; probably too early to do my funny Mexicki for him.

Bigger fish to fry. She walks in with Moses and they approach Siegel at the blackboard. I get invisible, hide in the wave of milling kids, in the hum of *what-I-did-for-summer* and *how-my-hair-has-changed*. I shadow Speed, glance at Shantay, nod at Pincus, everyone hovering for seats because the seat you take on the first day could be your seat all year. I find one near the back, between Speed and Dudley, Worm next to Speed, Jodi in front, no empty chairs around it.

She's wearing a magenta turtleneck made for grownups, sleeveless, exposing her skinny brown arms. Her wiry black hair is parted on the side, held down by the same silver barrettes. The mole above her lip stretches towards her cheek from her wide smile, teeth white against her brown face. Standing between Moses and Siegel, she searches the room. I slide low in my chair.

When the bell rings Moses clip-clops out, leaving her alone up there with Siegel.

"Class," Siegel claps to get our attention. "Good morning. Up here, please."

She's beside him, back straight, neck locked, looking eager, not scared. She has wisdom.

"Even though this is the first day of sixth grade, many of you already know each other. This young lady is new to the school and our country, so let's welcome her. Her name is…" looking down in his book. "How do you pronounce that, dear? Shide?"

Is her ass getting as sweaty as mine did? And is again now? Heart pounding? Stomach churning? Will she remember to say "Shirley" and say it good? I slide down further.

"I am Shideh," she says with energy, "axaant-agu on e, tank you. Shi-*dé*. Hallo."

Can't hear any snickers or whispers.

"OK, Shideh. And how do you pronounce the last name? It's a humdinger. It's Khh-"

A smattering of titters. Throats scratch with exaggerated "Khh". My forehead gets hot, but Shideh smiles along with them, easy and excited like a contestant on a game show.

"Khodadaad," she says in crisp Farsi, looking at the entire class. "Shideh Khoda*daad*."

More chuckles, "khh-khh" throat scratching gets louder. Maybe she can't hear it.

"Class, Shideh is from the ancient land of Persia," Siegel says, "also known as Iran."

Fertig's brittle yellow perm turns to me. Shantay's clear brown eyes on me, smiling.

"We're practically cousins," Siegel goes on, "I'm Greek, you're Persian. Yes?"

Shideh looks confused, scans the room as I slide still lower in my seat, hide my face behind my hand, pretend to be scribbling something important on my notebook.

"OK," Siegel says abruptly when Shideh doesn't answer. "Take that seat and we'll get started," pointing to an empty chair at the table where Patricia and Shantay are sitting.

She tries catching my eye on her way, but I keep my head down, the heat from her disappointed glance hitting me as she takes her seat. Later. I'll atone later.

She pulls a red composition book from her black leather satchel - the kind Olders used to sling across their shoulders in Tehran. We were too young to have them but sometimes Olders would let us swing theirs after school; made us feel important. In Amrika, it looks out of place.

"Tell us about your country, Shideh" Siegel says.

"Vat?"

"What part of the world is it? What kind of government? They have a king, right?"

She question-stares, shoulders fall, eyebrows slant in the triangle of fear. *So many words*, she must be thinking. *What does he want?* she must be thinking. *Tink fast, rabbit*, she would be thinking if she had Bugs, weekdays at 3 Channel 11. They don't have Bugs on Irani TV.

I watch her eyes darting side to side. Maybe looking for help... but she doesn't have anybody...except me. She has me. Do I have her? I'm busy trying to be invisible.

"Vat?" she asks again, trying to catch her breath, her chest rising and falling quickly.

Why does she talk like that? She can't curve her consonants? Twang her vowels? Can't say "w"? That stupid magenta hand-me-down, what's wrong with her? Where's her wisdom?

"Shideh, you understand my question?"

"Yes...Iran is..." a tremble in her voice that she didn't have last night, has never had.

"I'm not sure you can be here if you don't understand me," Siegel keeps squeezing her. "Tell us what you're doing here. Or why you left."

They are quiet now, watching Shideh squirm as Siegel squeezes.

"We call this the Socratic method," Siegel explains to the class. "I ask, she answers, we have dialogue. She'll get the hang of it. Jump in, Shideh."

Her eyes dance around the room, searching. Bugs would concoct a plot. Maman would help her figure it out. Smiley would explain it to her. Fertig, even Fertig would at least correct her. Not me. Can't afford to. Been laughed at enough. Had my guts punched enough, shoved around enough. I just crawled out of that swamp. I learned their curves and twangs, their songs.

She's knocking on your door, looking for shelter, a place to hide. Open up!

Yom Kippur. I'll confess my sins, ask for forgiveness, on Yom Kippur. Not today.

"Let's try again, Shideh. What is the title of your leader?"

She finally finds my eyes. I see her lips quivering; she won't last much longer. Something needs to be done. Siegel should stop squeezing her head; take it easy on her.

"Cherah," she pleads from across the room for everybody to hear. "Cherah komakam nemeekonee?" In front of them? So they can all hear her? Us? Like that? All eyes on me.

"He's from Persia," Fertig points at me. "He speaks it. I've heard it. It's crazy. Do it!"

They called me Arab. They called me Beaner Boy. They called me Non. Because they see me. Sweaty, scared, stomach churning.

Think fast, rabbit... rabbit? No Bugs. No Smiley. No Shantay no Fertig no Pincus no Dud. Just Siegel squeezing Shideh until her eyes pop and mouth oozes. Maman said be brave, be bold. Fertig said do something big. To get them to see you; to get them to include you; to get them. Something heroic, at great personal risk. For someone else.

"Mr. Manoucherian, are you from Persia too?"

"W'll, yeah, sorta," I answer in the heaviest, most Amrikayi tone I can muster.

"Yes," says Shideh. "He Persian from Iran. We two from Iran. We play in Iran."

Her stupid accent! Don't want them to see me like they see her; or explain her.

"Mr. Manoucherian," Siegel asks, "if you can help Shideh, please translate."

Scared. Embarrassed. Tired of the humiliation.

"W'll, I, um, can't rullee cuz been here rullee long, forgotten a lot of it. Um, let's see..."

Pretend to think, to remember, maybe faint. Better to pray for invisibility, for goddamn *Adonai* to come down and save me for once. Gonjeshk songs outside; cars zooming freely.

"Or you can answer for her, since you can't translate. Tell us in English."

A voice, soft and easy. Smiley as Mr. Wizard, consoling Tooter Turtle, "*Be just what you is, not what you is not. Folks what do this has the happiest lot!*"

Baba jogging on Albatross Lane in his lumpy tracksuit. Maman singing with her windows down. Saeed the firecracker, fiercely defending them both. Nobody ever gets to be invisible. And what's the point? They always find you; the real you; dark and dirty. They laugh louder when they see you trying to hide it. On TV all summer: "The cover-up is worse than the crime." No spell or incantation, no shirts or shoes or haircuts can cover up who I am. No sweet dose of pity. My darkness, my nostrils, my mole, my smells, my tongue. Nowhere to hide.

"Khob ye-chizi begoo," Shideh tilts her head firmly, calmly.

Ye-chizi begam. Something big! Heroic, at great personal risk.

I surrender, shoulders squared. "Keshvareh Shahanshahiye Iran!"

I confess, neck locked. "Mohammad Reza Shah Pahlavi, Shahan-shahe Aryamehr!"

Fierce like a Captain, I bow to Shideh. "Khosh Amadeen!"

She bows back, claps her hands and smiles, her face lighting up, the mole above her lip highlighting her beauty.

"What was that," Speed surprised.

"That's not Mexikin," Worm confused.

"Is that Arabese," Lisa W. intrigued.

It is me.

I am Arab.

I am Beaner Boy.

I am Coward.

I am Devil.

I am Embarrassment.

I am Failure.

I am George, the saddest Beatle.

I am Humiliation.

I am Iranian.

I am Jerk.

I am Killer of salamanders.

I am Liar.

I am Mishel.

I am Non.

I am Outsider.

I am Pretender.

I am Quiet.

I am Rabbit.

I am Sinner.

I am Thief.

I am Ugly.

I am Victim.

I am Wisdom.

I am X of open scissors, bringing the bad luck.
I am Yogi.
I am Zero.
I am all that. That all is me.

ABOUT THE AUTHOR

Michael Isaac Shokrian is an Iranian-Jewish writer who was born in Hamburg, Germany and moved to Los Angeles from Tehran in 1971. He became a self-taught American via terrestrial radio and TV. In 2017, Michael launched the *Thieving Magpie* which began as a digital literary quarterly. He lives in Studio City, CA. *American Playground* is Michael's debut novel.